Scourge of Evil

In days when Evil grows,
And despair grips the land,
Then will come
The Scourge of Evil.
Three shall they be,
One to draw Evil out
And defeat it,
One to fight fire with fire,
And one to protect.
The weapons
That defeat the Evil
Shall be forged
From the Evil itself.
The Scourge of Evil will be
Of the Evil's own making.

The Prophetess Aria

Other works by Wendy Jensen:

The 8th House

ISBN 0-9709286-1-0

A novel of paranormal suspense

Be careful what you wish for...

Zoë Zignego thought she wanted to be psychic. Now she sees ghosts and dreams of murders. When she helps police solve a series of astrology-based killings in the Twin Cities, Zoë finds her psychic proximity to 'The Astrologer' too close for comfort.

Self-publishing on a Shoestring Budget

ISBN 0-9709286-0-2

Available Summer 2001

Detailed, step-by-step instructions on how to lay out books and design covers in Microsoft® Word 97 or 2000. Includes information on finding a commercial printer and an ISBN number for a reasonable cost, and how to make staple-bound pamphlets, comb-bound books, and perfect-bound paperbacks yourself.

Cataclysms 2003

ISBN 0-9709286-3-7

Available Fall 2001

Throughout history catastrophic changes have come in cycles. The cycle is coming again – sooner than you might think, and from a source that might surprise you. In southeastern Minnesota, a small town struggles to survive the coming cataclysm.

Sword Discarded
Sister

by Wendy Jensen

Limited Edition

12 of 100

Brave New Books
Red Wing, Minnesota

© Copyright 2000 Wendy Jensen
All rights reserved

Published by
Brave New Books
1114 West 4th Street
Red Wing, MN 55066
651-388-7914
BNB@wendyjensen.com

Cover art
By Wendy Jensen
Wendy@wendyjensen.com
http://www.wendyjensen.com

Interior Design and Layout
By Wendy Jensen
Wendy@wendyjensen.com
http://www.wendyjensen.com

Printed by
Wendy Jensen
Wendy@wendyjensen.com
http://www.wendyjensen.com

Printed in the United States of America

International Standard Book Number (ISBN)
Trade paperback: 0-9709286-4-5

This book is a work of fiction.

*To my mother,
who I wish I had known better
and to my stepmother
who sometimes knew me better
than I knew myself*

About the Author

Wendy Jensen was born in Oklahoma City, Oklahoma, on the planet Earth. Although some would dispute this fact, she has a birth certificate to prove it.

She grew up in various places, including Nicoma Park, Oklahoma; Miami, Florida; western North Carolina, and Costa Rica, Central America.

She currently lives in an imaginary world filled with fascinating characters and frightening events. Occasionally that world intersects with the real one in a 125 year-old house located in Red Wing, Minnesota. Her husband, four dogs and two cats keep her company there. Her teenaged son wanders through on occasion, and sometimes her grown children visit with some of her ten grandchildren.

Disillusioned with the traditional publishing industry, Wendy Jensen started her own publishing company and currently publishes her works under the imprint of Brave New Books.

http://www.wendyjensen.com

Wendy@wendyjensen.com

Chapter One

In days when Evil grows...
From "The Prophecies of Aria"

Year After Aria, 303

Inside Castle Darkfall flickering shadows chased each other across the wall of Balek's room. He hunched closer to the candelabra, squinting at his half-embroidered rune.

Balek's candles gave light, but no power. They were made of ordinary sheep tallow, not the tallow Necimus used for his candles. Necimus hadn't taught him how to make those — yet. After all these years of working for Necimus, Balek doubted he ever would.

Balek dipped the needle into the cloth of his robe and muttered a spell in the Old Tongue. "Varden mein, provekten mein — by the Unknowns!"

Unseen fingers gripped Balek's skull, unheard words called him towards the study down the hall. Balek flinched, and swore as the motion drove the needle into his thumb.

The Summons could only come from one person. Necimus.

Balek wiped his bleeding thumb on his dingy underclothes. His hands trembled as he tied off the thread. The rune would be left unfinished, its magic wasted. The Summons must be answered, and soon. Already his stomach clenched with anxiety, and the urge to obey his master overcame his desire to finish the rune.

Perhaps I should embroider a rune to Deflect Summons next, Balek thought. *Surely Necimus won't notice another black rune on a black robe in the dimness of Castle Darkfall.*

He pulled his robe on and slipped six medallions around his neck, cursing as the cords tangled in his scraggly hair. Balek cursed again as he stumbled into the gloomy hallway.

I should have brought the candelabra. The shutters had been closed for years, ever since Necimus and his night-loving Morgs took possession of the castle once known as Dawnfall. One sputtering torch illuminated the murky corridor stretching between Balek's quarters and Necimus' door. Balek scurried through the dimness, tripping on something that rolled away from his feet.

A skull? Balek shuddered and avoided looking back. He should speak to Necimus about the Morgs feeding up here. The nasty creatures should eat in their own quarters on the lower level. Balek would prefer that they were relegated to the dungeons — but Necimus had other uses for those.

In darkness similar to their native caves, Morg females gave birth to their young. In those dank cells Necimus' Morg and half-Morg soldiers were born.

Balek jumped back as one of those soldiers stepped from the shadows by Necimus' door. A full-blood Morg, with sharp canines protruding from its jutting jaws. The Morg's wide nostrils sniffed his scent, and its squinty eyes rolled towards Balek's bleeding thumb.

Balek wrapped the wounded digit in his robe. No need to give this carnivorous creature any ideas. He pulled himself up to the full extent of his puny height and glared up at the hulking Morg. "I'm here to see your master."

"Argh wugg grieg raarrk."

Why hadn't Necimus taught his minions to speak? Balek wondered. *Or at least, to understand human speech? One more way to ensure his undisputed power over the beasts, of course.*

Balek took a deep breath and tried again. "I - am - here - to - see - Necimus. Please - let - me — Ugh!"

Balek stumbled back as the Morg stretched, revealing hairy armpits that sent a malodorous wave in Balek's direction. Balek clenched his fingers over his nose and breathed through his mouth. *I should make a Medallion of Protection from Odor*, he thought, as the door to Necimus' quarters swung open.

Balek recognized the half-Morg who emerged as one of Necimus' favorites. Why Necimus should have favorites was beyond him; they all seemed equally stupid and ugly to Balek. The half-Morgs looked more human, but had inherited the worst from both races. They were still abysmally ugly, and taller than their full-blood kin.

At least they could talk. This one's name was... *Curds? No. Something more gravelly. Kurg, wasn't it?*

Balek still held his nose. Half-Morgs didn't smell much better than full-blood Morgs, either. "Imb here to thee Nethimuth, Kurg."

Kurg grinned, displaying canines more prominent that any human's. He jerked his head towards the door.

"Father will see you now." Kurg hit the Morg on the shoulder and they disappeared down the hall, conversing in grunts and snarls that sounded like a boar and a wolf engaged in mortal combat.

Balek shuddered. *Horrid creatures.* He hated dealing with them. But then, dealing with Necimus was worse. Balek shuddered again, and drew a calming breath before he pressed his palm to the door so the magical alarm could recognize and admit him.

Kurg hadn't closed the door. It moved slightly before his hand.

Balek eyed the candlelight coming through the crack of the door. He recognized the scent of these particular candles, and knew what they meant. Necimus had a spell in progress.

Perhaps it is the new spell, the one Necimus said would conquer better than his Morg armies. Perhaps he finally finished it and he will teach it to me, Balek thought.

Balek felt the old hunger for power rising in him. That hunger had brought him to Necimus years ago, when no one else wanted a mediocre magic-caster.

There were many words to describe Necimus, but mediocre wasn't one of them. Huge, evil, ugly — obviously. Intelligent — definitely. Powerful, unquestionably.

The promise of sharing that power had drawn Balek, captured him just like Necimus' Morg army took villages. Fear kept him captive after the promise had faded, when it became obvious that Necimus did not intend to share his power with Balek.

Fear sent him through the door. It wouldn't do to keep Necimus waiting.

"You called?" Balek asked.

Not really. 'Calling' would have been Necimus stopping at Balek's room and requesting his presence — unlikely — or sending one of his half-Morgs to relay his request in their guttural speech. No, a Summon spell was 'demanding', not 'calling.'

"Yes."

Necimus' voice reverberated as if echoing through caverns. *Probably the ones his eyes are set in,* Balek thought.

Necimus didn't rise from his seat behind the desk, and Balek was grateful. Bad enough that Balek had been born into a body whose height didn't even qualify as average. No need to emphasize his smallness by having Necimus tower over him.

His master didn't tell him to sit, so Balek stood. Necimus seemed preoccupied by bone fragments strewn across his desk, gleaming white against the polished blackwood surface.

Were they human bones? Balek wondered. Possibly. There were certainly enough of them left after the Morg's meals. *Of course, they might be sheep bones.* Balek avoided scrutinizing them. He concentrated on the candles instead.

The smell of magic hung in the air, wafting up from the squat purplish candles on each corner of the desk. Balek watched the melting wax ooze down the side like a ruptured pus wound.

The Morgs thought the candles were made with the blood of disobedient Morgs. Balek knew better. *The blood of such ignorant creatures wouldn't make good fertilizer, much less magic!* No, Balek knew the kind of blood used in the candles. He knew why Necimus always claimed human infants, especially unborn ones, for his experiments. That was the *only* ingredient that Balek knew.

Balek smelled powerful magic in the greasy smoke. It made his mouth water. More power than could be bound into words alone, for spells currently beyond his capabilities. With magic like that, he could be free of Necimus, free of this stinking castle full of Morgs. No doubt that was why Necimus never taught him how to make the candles.

"There is a problem." Necimus' deep voice sent vibrations through Balek's spine.

Balek gulped, and wrenched his gaze from the candles. "A problem, Necimus?"

Dark eyes bored into Balek from beneath overhanging brows, and Necimus' lips thinned to an almost invisible line.

Balek cringed, and lashed himself mentally — *don't forget his title, his self-proclaimed title!*

His ridiculous title. *Why did Necimus take such a perverse pleasure in flaunting his actions? Why couldn't he just settle for "Lord Necimus"?*

"I mean... I meant... a problem, Your Evilness?"

Necimus nodded, his lank black hair swaying with

the motion, a stark contrast to skin pale from lack of sun. A frown carved furrows across the wide expanse of his forehead. Balek's hand crawled to the medallions covering his chest. If Necimus was frowning, there was a problem indeed.

"Divination." Necimus' pitchfork-sized hand gestured at the bones.

Balek blinked. *Surely this isn't the spell he's been working on for so long?*

"Divination? But why do a spell for that, when a Sayer could..."

Wrong thing to say. *Never mention Sayers in His Evilness' presence, never!* The last time Balek had done that... but that was years ago. Years. Balek clutched his Medallion Against Magical Attack in one sweaty palm and waited.

"A Sayer wouldn't tell me what I want to know."

Stupid! Balek berated himself. *Of course a Sayer wouldn't tell Necimus what he wanted to know. Or anything else, for that matter. Not even if the Morgs were eating her alive.* Balek wiped his damp hand on his robe, hoping that Necimus didn't notice. "So... what do these bones tell you?"

"That I have an enemy."

Never laugh at His Evilness. Never! Not that Balek laughed often, but this was tempting. *An* enemy? Balek didn't need a Sayer to tell him that Necimus had many enemies.

"A new one. Deep in the mountains."

"But... no one lives deep in the mountains. There aren't even many villages in the foothills anymore." *Not since your Morgs destroyed them,* Balek added to himself.

"Someone lives there. Someone who is a threat to me. If the mountains are sparsely populated, well — that should make it easy for you to find this threat."

"Me?" Balek squeaked. He swallowed and tried again. "You want me to find it? Leave the castle, go... go to the mountains? Into the mountains?"

Irritation flickered across Necimus' broad features. "It shouldn't take long. You can ride the mounts. I'll send Kurg along, to... protect you."

Protect me? Or watch me? Balek wondered. At least Kurg was a half-breed. It could be worse. *But riding the mounts...* Balek's stomach quivered. Could he make a Medallion of Protection Against Nausea before they went?

Balek thought he saw amusement in his master's eyes, though the eyes were so deeply set into his face that it was difficult to be certain. Too late he noticed that the glass sphere at the end of the desk was alight, and saw his own thoughts showing in its transparent depths.

That wouldn't be happening if I had finished my Rune Against Thought Search, Balek thought, then cringed as he realized what he had done. *Don't think of that now, fool! He'll see the thought, he'll...* Balek's fingers crept towards his medallion-covered chest.

Necimus smiled, and his smile was more frightening than his frown. "Perhaps," he rumbled, "you should make a Medallion of Protection Against Wearing Too Many Medallions."

Balek's knees went wobbly with relief. Necimus was looking at him, not the globe. He hadn't see Balek's thoughts about the rune. *Think about something safe, you fool!* Balek focused his thoughts on the journey. "When... when do we leave?"

"At dawn."

"Very well, Your Evilness." Balek bowed his quaking self out of the study, and stumbled over his robes all the way back to his room.

At dawn, he thought, as he shut his door behind him. *Three hours away. Not enough time to make a Medallion of Protection Against Nausea.*

Balek wished he had made one already. His stomach told him he needed it now.

Wendy Jensen

Chapter Two

*"If we understood the Unknowns,
they would not be the Unknowns."*

Sayer Proverb

Year After Aria, 303

Dawn broke as dawn did in the mountains: a sudden purple chasm between the black of night and the snow-crusted peaks, a spreading violet rift, splitting the fabric of night and spilling lavender light into Valla i'Eyrs.

Only Erystra called it that. To the rest of the world it was an unknown, unnamed valley in an unexplored range of mountains. To Erystra and Skurgiil it was home, and a home should have a name.

Erystra named it in the Old Tongue, the language of scholars she had learned at Neston. In the Old Tongue Erystra could hide her peasant roots; no trace of dialect seeped through the lilting language which the prophetess Aria had used.

Erystra never taught Skurgiil the Old Tongue. In it the girl might discover things that were best left unknown. To Skurgiil it was simply Valley of Eagles.

The huge birds that inhabited the peaks when Erystra and Skurgiil arrived remained after the intrusion of the woman and child, and their numbers had increased. As Skurgiil grew the birds followed her on her mountain climbs, as if keeping watch over the infant that one of their kind had delivered to Erystra's arms so many years ago.

Erystra watched The Guardian's peak turn lavender, saw the lavender fade to white as the sun vaulted the towering mountain. Erystra saw it all through eyes of solid white, for Erystra was a Sayer, with sight beyond normal sight.

As easily as she watched the dawn, Erystra saw Skurgiil in the pool at the far end of the valley. The distance didn't hinder her Sight, nor did the boulders surrounding the pool impede her vision. Erystra watched the girl dive into the waterfall, saw her lips move with unheard laughter as the cascading water pummeled her naked body.

A hardy child, Erystra thought. The water fell a hundred feet from The Guardian's heart, chill even on a bright summer day. Only the knowledge of the Inner Heat kept Skurgiil's skin from turning blue. *A hardy child, indeed.*

/*No longer a child, Erystra.*/

"Aye." Erystra agreed with the inner voices, and sighed as the girl cut strokes to the pool's edge. *But yesterday, it seems, she was all ribs and elbows, and now...* Skurgiil stepped out of the pool, sloughing water off her bare body.

A child no more. The ribs were covered by womanly contours.

Ah, the horror that had been in the child's face, as those contours developed! *"Lumps, Good Mother, growing on my chest! See?"* Erystra chuckled at the memory. The child's tears of fright had been soothed with an explanation based on sheep, so she could comprehend the changes in her body.

The changes had continued. Her legs and arms lengthened and her shoulders broadened even as the dreaded lumps swelled, growing to a size that the function of a sheep's udder could not explain. Despite her towering height, Skurgiil would never be mistaken for a man.

But she would never be considered a beautiful woman, either. Her cheekbones were too broad, her chin was too stubborn, and her bulky nose was balanced only by the ample mouth and lofty forehead.

Erystra shrugged. In her opinion beauty was more a bane than a blessing. Skurgiil did not need it.

/She has grown tall and strong./

"Aye." *Strong from carrying wounded sheep and building rock walls, and tall from... well, things grow large in the mountains.* The pine trees were sturdier, the wolves huskier. Giants were even rumored to live beyond The Guardian. Skurgiil's height could be attributed to the mountains. Could be — but Erystra knew better.

/She must fulfill her purpose./

"She is young. Only seventeen on the last new moon."

At the pool, Skurgiil's hand paused as she reached for her rough tunic, then slid to a bone-handled knife. Her dark eyes scoured boulder-bordered crannies as she turned, searching.

"She improves."

/That she does./

Sighing, Erystra withdrew her Sight from the girl. Over the decades she had learned it was useless to argue with the voices. "When, then?"

/Soon./

"How soon?"

/It is not for you to know the hour, Erystra./

"I... I would go with her."

The voices inside were silent.

"She sensed my Sight at the pool, but there is much she does not know. She is very... innocent."

/The way is long, and hard. You are old, Erystra./

"I did not mean like this. I would be a Guardian. *Her* Guardian."

/You know the price./

"Aye. But I have no other work here." The corners of her cataract-covered eyes crinkled. "And, as ye said, I am old."

Internal silence followed. Erystra sensed a debate.

/What form, then?/

Erystra's withered lips smiled. Her request had been granted, her usefulness was not yet ended. "The necklace. Her mother's necklace."

/If she should lose it, or it is stolen..../

"I know."

/Then, Erystra, the hour is come. Thus shall it be done..../

Erystra listened, nodding. It was not such a bad fate. She had seen worse, in the course of her many years. "And so it begins," the old woman whispered.

/Soon it will end. It began long ago./

"Aye. So it did. I have not forgotten."

Chapter Three

By the grace and gifts of the Unknowns, it is given to us to See, and to Say what the future holds..."

Charter of the Sisters of the Sight, the "Sayers"

Year After Aria, 242
Peasant Year of the Falling Stars

Sixty-one years earlier...

Drogan's voice was gruff. "Ye'll be leaving after the festival."

The girl in the homespun tunic knew her father didn't mean to be harsh. That was just his way.

"There be a merchant train," her father mumbled around a chunk of bread, "going that way. The merchant says he'll see you to Neston. Costing me twenty fleeces, it is, the trip and your dowry."

The girl nodded, but kept her eyes on the table, on her own half-eaten dinner. If she raised them she would see her mother's sorrowful eyes, mourning that her only daughter's dowry was going to Neston instead of to a husband; she would see her father's discomfort radiating out from him like an aura.

He didn't like it when she looked at him. Said it "gave him the willies, it did", the way her eyes seemed to stare right through him.

Not just her father, either. All the villagers felt that way. They didn't avoid her, but conversations dwindled as she approached and whispers followed her as she moved away.

"Fey, be Brogan's daughter. That look in her eyes..."

"Talks to herself, too. Why, the other day at the well..."

"Comes of being born on the night of the colored moon, it does..."

At an age when other village girls were married, she hadn't had an offer. Not even any interest. The village boys eyed her like sheep watching a herd dog, and kept their distance. Her parents despaired of finding her a mate.

So her father had told her she was going to Neston. Of course, she already knew—the inner voices had told her. She merely nodded, and waited to be sent away.

He sopped the last of his stew with a chunk of bread, and cleared his throat. "Might as well go and enjoy the festival, lass. Be your last chance." He untied the strings of his pouch and pushed a few coppers across the table.

"Go on, take it. Go see the festival, Erystra."

⚜

Tall torches were thrust into the soft earth around the edges of the village green. Their tallow-soaked heads trailed greasy smoke and flames cast ruddy light on the crowds.

Erystra's bare feet wended through the makeshift stalls. She veered away from a burst of fire that spouted from a man's mouth. The open-mouthed peasants around him *oohed* and *aahed*, and coppers clinked into the hat at his feet. She passed merchants hawking their wares, and buyers from the lands below, looking for a good deal and haggling with the locals over the price of wool.

She paused at a gaggle of children, clapping and laughing before a tiny stage where dolls moved and spoke. Her Sight pierced the curtains surrounding the stage, where a sweating man crouched, his hands moving the dolls across the stage. Erystra smiled at the happy children, and wandered on.

She stopped at the center of the green. Two young men moved inside of a circle of silent onlookers in a graceful, lethal dance. Torchlight reddened the long steel blades in their hands.

Swordplay. Erystra watched with horrified fascination as the blades swept within inches of the men. She winced as the steel clashed in mid-air. So dangerous, so deadly.

But to one of the men, it seemed like a game.

He wore scarlet, the bright red of his clothing deepened to blood red in the torchlight. His dark hair swirled about his shoulders as he circled his opponent. He laughed as the other man's blade passed within inches of his ribs. Erystra heard his mocking words as he stepped back, gracefully deflecting the oncoming sword with his own.

It was over quickly. The scarlet-clad stranger suddenly advanced, beating back his opponent with blurred blows. Steel met steel with such force that Erystra covered her ears. The circle of spectators shuffled back, leaving her standing alone on the inner edge. There was one final *clang*, and a sword skittered across the trampled grass, stopping by Erystra's feet.

The crowd gasped and clapped. The scarlet-clad man bowed, sweeping his own sword out in a graceful arc while his opponent rubbed his wrist, muttering. They shook hands, and the winner's laughter echoed through Erystra's mind as he drove his sword into the grass and circled the crowd, hat outstretched.

Torchlight ran down the shining blade like reddened water — *or like blood?* The laughter — *or was it sobbing?* — and murmurs — *or were they distant battle cries?* around her blended, roaring in her ears. Erystra closed her eyes, blocking out the sword but not the Sight.

Something clinked in front of her. Erystra opened her eyes. He stood before her, hat in hand. She dropped in two of her precious coppers.

"Why, thank you." He shook the hat. "Enough for some more wine, don't you think?"

More? Erystra smelled it on his breath, saw the stains on his lips and teeth. *And yet he fought so well, just now.*

"Will you join me?"

Surely he is speaking to someone else? Erystra looked around. The other spectators were moving away towards the food stalls and the fire-eater.

Erystra stared at him. He didn't flinch from her gaze, and in his brown eyes Erystra Saw.

She Saw his home, a manor house on a distant farm. She Saw the tempestuous fights with his father, his hatred of the mundane existence in his father's house, his running away to live by his sword. She Saw his death, but a fortnight hence, in a drunken brawl. And she Saw herself, holding his child in her arms.

/Go with him, child. Do as he asks./

A star plummeted through the night sky as Erystra nodded and followed him to the tavern.

⁂

Five months later...

From her position behind her desk, the High Mistress of Neston stared at the Mistress of the Acolyte's Wing. "The girl is *what*?"

"With child, Mistress."

"This peasant family foisted their daughter on us when she got herself in trouble?"

"According to the girl, her parents didn't know."

"And the girl? Did she know?"

The Acolyte's Mistress nodded. "Oh, yes. She

knew."

"How did this escape our attention, when she came? We are Sayers, after all."

"Her Aura is powerful, Mistress."

"This isn't the one the School Mistress told me about? The one that shows so much promise?"

The Acolyte's Mistress nodded wearily. She had dreaded this moment since she first heard the other acolytes' whispers about the girl who had missed her bleeding. "None other. The girl who was born the night of the lunar eclipse, twenty-odd years ago."

"The Teaching Mistress tells me she goes through the exercises without effort, and can already cast a Healing Aura!"

"She had Sight, before the effects of pregnancy set in. It came frequently, though at random. And she says that... voices speak to her. Inside her head."

The High Mistress stared. "The last one to hear the voices of the Unknowns was Aria, three hundred years ago."

"I know. I think this one is special, Mistress."

The High Mistress considered this, then shook her head. "No matter. We can't have it said that Neston is the place to send your daughters to bear bastard children. She must go home. If she wishes to foster out the child and return later, she may do so."

"I think... you should see her first, Mistress."

꿈◉꿈

The girl who stood before the High Mistress was plain, from her brown hair to her knobby feet. Wide cheekbones in a broad face, sturdy neck, stout shoulders and rugged wrists—*peasant genes evident in every bone of her body*, the High Mistress thought. The simple gray robe did nothing to flatter her, but it helped conceal the growing bulge in her belly.

Four months pregnant? Five, perhaps? The High Mistress was sure the girl came to Neston less than six months ago, and equally certain she had not conceived within the gray walls of the Sayer stronghold, since no men were allowed to enter. How the life growing inside her had escaped the detection of so many Sayers thus far was amazing, but the High Mistress Saw it now.

She Saw something else, too. Something of vast importance, reaching through the years and into the future.

Words of dismissal died on her lips. The High Mistress realized that for the first time in history a Sayer would bear a child in Neston.

Twenty-two years later...

"She has no Sight? None?" The High Mistress sounded incredulous.

Erystra's nod confirmed the impossible. The woman whose power had earned her the name of Erystra True-Sight had borne a daughter with no Sight at all.

"And she wants to leave?"

Erystra nodded again. "Leave and be married, Mistress. A merchant's son from Surham is asking for her hand, and Sudain wishes to accept. She says," Erystra smiled wryly, "that she will bear no bastards."

The High Mistress gave her a sharp glance. "She is with child?"

"No. But she wishes to be, and she wishes to be married when she is."

The High Mistress pondered this. "She is your daughter still, Erystra. Raised by Neston, but your daughter by blood. Do as you think best, but a Sayer with no Sight is no Sayer at all."

Erystra nodded, and rose from her seat. "I will tell her to pack her things, Mistress."

As the door closed, the High Mistress of Neston leaned back in her seat. Years ago she Saw a promise in an unborn child; a promise that demanded to be realized. Now the child born of that promise would not become a Sayer.

The High Mistress flexed gnarled hands, wincing at the pain. These hands brought Erystra's daughter into the world, and they were wrinkled even then. No doubt Erystra would be High Mistress soon, for she was the most gifted of the Order. And her daughter will be a merchant's wife.

In an uncharacteristic moment of doubt, the High Mistress of Neston wondered if the Unknowns knew what they were doing.

Wendy Jensen

Chapter Four

Never was there a day without a night.
Never a joy without weal and woe.
    From the ballad "Champions of Light"
    attributed to Singer Sefrinel Lutesong

Year After Aria, 303

It is gone.

Whatever had been watching her was gone. Skurgiil didn't wonder how she knew this. She just knew, as she knew it was there before, as she knew she was now cold, because searching for the unseen presence took her concentration from the Inner Heat.

Skurgiil didn't question her innate knowledge as she pulled on her woolen tunic. Erystra always said she was a simple girl. While Skurgiil never understood the wonder in Erystra's voice when she said this, she accepted it as she accepted everything Erystra said.

Skurgiil lashed the lacings around her calves, over her wolf-skin foot coverings. She tightened the cinch of her knife belt, then used her blade to slash the side of her tunic where it covered her thighs.

It was a new tunic. Erystra had spun and woven the wool for it last winter, during the months when the snow piled up close to the cottage's thatched eaves.

The Good Mother will be a little cross with me, Skurgiil thought as her knife ripped through the tight threads of Erystra's weaving. Erystra would mend the rough edges tonight by the fire, muttering about Skurgiil showing a horse length of leg.

Skurgiil shrugged, and ripped the other side of the tunic.

How does the Good Mother expect me to run, with the tunic covering my thighs? And who will see the "horse length of leg?"

Trenton will. Trenton was coming to trade in a fortnight or so, and he would gawk at her. Why he stared at her legs and goggled at her chest was a mystery to Skurgiil, as strange as the Good Mother's insistence that he sleep outside the cottage. Erystra's cot was the only one in the cottage, but there was room on the floor for another bedroll even after Skurgiil spread hers out. Still, the Good Mother made Trenton sleep outside during his trading visits, and latched the cottage door every night.

Skurgiil ran one hand through damp hair, ignoring the tangles that snagged on her callused fingers. She scaled the boulders rimming the pool in two long-legged strides and paused at the top to look back at her pool.

My pool. One corner of her mouth twisted down as she grinned. *Of course it is my pool! Who else would claim it, in this valley? Erystra?*

The big girl in the woolen tunic laughed. *Good Mother would never brave the swirling waters.* She bathed from a kettle of water warmed by the fireplace.

No doubt there is a pot of stew bubbling on that fireplace now. Erystra had put it on to cook as Skurgiil left for the pool in the pre-dawn gloom. The sun had cleared the peaks now, and Skurgiil's stomach rumbled. Her thighs flashed through the new slits in her tunic as she ran the path to the cottage, scattering a flock of grazing sheep as she passed.

Erystra watched Skurgiil running, saw the muscles of her thighs and calves pumping with effortless ease beneath the ravaged tunic.

Such a big girl, and so strong, Erystra thought. *So different from the infant I carried into this valley — how many years ago?*

Seventeen. Seventeen years since the dappled gray mare picked her way down the trail, driving a dozen sheep before her and carrying Erystra on her back. Now the mare's bones were covered with grass and the descendants of the sheep dotted the valley. The infant Erystra had raised with sheep's milk pounded up the path to the cottage, dark hair flowing behind her.

Seventeen years. Seventeen years of casting a daily Aura of Protection, to foil the anticipated search for Skurgiil. Seventeen years of casting a daily Aura of Contentment, to prevent Skurgiil's inevitable questions about the outside world.

Seventeen peaceful years, which were over now.

Skurgiil sped up the path, and saw Erystra waiting at the cottage door. Skurgiil smiled as she slowed, approaching the cottage.

"Good Day, Good Mother. Is there food?"

Erystra's sightlessly seeing eyes squinted up at her. "Aye, there is food. Ye ripped your tunic, child."

"Aye." Skurgiil ducked through the cottage door before Erystra could comment on the visible stretch of legs.

Erystra followed, shaking her head. *So like Iskara!* Erystra thought. *In other ways, as well....*

Inside, Skurgiil had already scooped stew into a wooden bowl. "Plenty of garlic, Good Mother. As I like it."

"Lass, after ye eat, go and gather poultice plants."

Skurgiil arched one eyebrow. "Good Mother, the jar of poultice leaves is nearly full. I used some yesterday, on the old ram's hoof rot—"

"Do not argue, child! Go, and gather more."

Skurgiil shrugged one shoulder. "Aye. Eat, Good Mother. Ye have fasted since yesterday."

Erystra sighed. "No, child. I need no food today."

Skurgiil finished her second bowl of stew and reached for her harvesting bag. "I won't be long, Good Mother. A few plants will fill the jar."

"Go high, child. The lower slopes are over-harvested. Leave them to re-grow, and gather where none have yet been taken. Halfway up The Guardian, I should think."

Skurgiil paused before tucking her harvesting sack into her belt. "As ye wish, Good Mother. But then I won't be back until midday. Can ye wait that long for the poultice plants?" She grinned a familiar, lopsided grin.

Iskara had grinned thus.... Erystra brandished her cane.

"Impudent child! Aye, I can wait. Go, or ye'll not be back for the midday meal."

Skurgiil laughed, and loped off towards the mountain.

Erystra's Sight followed her, and she noted an eagle launched itself from a ledge and circled lazily above Skurgiil's route of ascent.

They follow her as they followed Iskara, Erystra mused. *Mayhap there is something to the legends that claim Sayers could once control animals with their Auras.*

But Iskara was no Sayer. Nor is Skurgiil, though the child has abilities. She learned the Inner Heat Aura, and she felt my Sight on her. But she has no Sight. Mayhap with time, and training — but there is no more time for training.

"'If we understood the Unknowns, they would not be the Unknowns'," Erystra muttered.

She sat in the warmth of the morning sun, and waited.

※◉※

Skurgiil's fingers gripped the rock, searching for a purchase. Satisfied with her hold, she straightened her legs against the stony face. Her arm muscles bulged as she pulled herself onto the ledge.

Thank the Unknowns, there are five poultice plants here. Surely enough to fill the jar, and high enough on the mountain to please Good Mother.

As she bent to pull them an eagle cried, gliding only yards away from the ledge.

"Rauk!" Skurgiil answered.

The eagle cried again, raucous and urgent.

Skurgiil's skin prickled, as it did when a wolf's howl shattered the night. She scanned the valley, searching for danger.

She saw it. Dropping out of the airy reaches, their leathery wings stretched in a wingspan that dwarfed the eagle, came two... *bats? Birds?* They seemed to be both, but neither; black furred bodies blended into feathered heads that housed massive mouths. Skurgiil saw the gleam of fangs, and the figures of the two riders.

Strangers. In this valley? No one but Trenton ever came here.

The eagle screamed as the creatures landed in front of the cottage. One ran forward, its gait an ungainly rocking motion; neither bird-like nor horse-like, not like any creature Skurgiil had ever seen. The rocks of Skurgiil's carefully constructed lambing pen tumbled as the beast crashed through it. A plump ewe rose in the creature's maw, bawling in pain and terror.

The first rider dismounted, tripping over a long black dress. Skurgiil caught the glint of metal as the other rider dropped to the ground. Together they started for the cottage.

"Good Mother!" Skurgiil breathed.

Before Skurgiil could move Erystra rushed the intruders, wielding her cane. Before Skurgiil could cry out the metal-clad stranger swung a sword, and Erystra collapsed before him.

"No! Nooooo!"

Skurgiil's scream was drowned in the eagle's shriek.

Kurg strode out of the cottage, his half-human features twisted into a snarl. "Curse your eyes, Balek! You said this looked like the place."

Balek fumbled for his Medallion of Protection from Blindness. "This is the only inhabited valley we have found. And it is deep in the mountains. This must be the place."

Kurg gestured at the old woman with his sword. "She's hardly a threat to His Evilness, and there's no one else here."

"Perhaps they are merely out for a while."

"No, fool. There is only one bed in there. A tiny one, at that. Suitable for her, or the likes of you."

"Perhaps she is a witch."

Kurg poked the crumpled body with his foot. "Not any more."

"Are you certain she is dead?"

"Magic-meddler! Of course I'm certain."

Balek groped for his Medallion of Protection From Violence as Kurg waved his sword.

"See the blood?" Kurg held the blade beneath Balek's nose.

Balek swallowed. *When I get back I'm going to make that Medallion of Protection From Nausea,* he promised himself.

There was a great deal of blood. It glistened on Kurg's sword, soaked the old woman's robes, and muddied the silver medallion around her neck.

Definitely a witch, then. Balek's hand shook as he

reached for the medallion. *Perhaps it is one I don't have*, he thought. *It could be useful. Ignore the blood. Just ignore it.* His fingers clutched the silver disk and turned it over.

It was old, worn thin with use. The emblem engraved on it was barely visible. The emblem of an eye.

Balek dropped the medallion as if it were hot. "A Sayer!"

"Let's get out of here. His Evilness will want to know about this," Kurg grunted.

Balek scrambled onto his mount, ignoring the sheep entrails dangling from between its fangs. He clutched his Medallion of Protection During Flight in trembling fingers, pulled the reins, and his mount leaped into the air behind Kurg's.

Skurgiil jumped from the ledge.

The impact of the twelve foot drop jarred through her ankles and knees and sent scree skittering down the grade before her; pebbles shifted beneath her feet, pitching her onto her back and starting a river of rubble cascading down the mountain. Rocks bounced around her, over her, on her; she banged into boulders as the torrent of stone hurtled her down the slope. She grasped at outcroppings, trying to slow her descent, but the rocky flow carried her adamantly on until it dumped her in a delta of debris at the base of The Guardian.

Skurgiil staggered from the dust, bruised and bleeding. She ignored the aches and abrasions as she sprinted across the valley floor. The creatures were disappearing over the mountains to the east and the eagle glided above her, but Skurgiil saw only Erystra.

"Mother! Good Mother!"

Skurgiil dropped to the ground beside Erystra, and saw the crimson stain spreading across the gray robes.

"Mother!" Skurgiil screamed, and the eagle above screamed with her.

"Lift... me up, child."

"Good Mother?"

Erystra's voice was faint. "Carry me... in."

Skurgiil cradled the withered body, and cried out when Erystra groaned. Gently, Skurgiil carried her into the cottage and laid her on the simple wooden cot. Carefully she cut the sticky cloth away from Erystra's stomach.

"Oh, Mother!" Skurgiil sobbed.

Blood pulsed from a gash the width of her hand, welling up like a bubbling mountain spring. Skurgiil pressed a fistful of the drenched robe into the wound until Erystra gasped in pain.

Poultice. The wound must be poulticed. Skurgiil fumbled for the poultice jar, groped for the mortar and pestle.

"Let it be, Skurgiil."

"But, Mother, ye are bleeding—"

"All things must end. 'Tis an end, and a beginning. Get me the necklace, and place it in my hand."

"But—"

"Obey me, child! There is... little... time."

Through tear-blurred vision Skurgiil searched beneath the cot. She drew out a wooden box and fumbled with the ornate latch.

Inside a chunk of uncut amethyst, wrapped in silver wire and suspended from heavy silver links, reclined on soft white wool. A dawnstone, Erystra had called it, when she took it out each winter to polish away the tarnish. Skurgiil lifted the necklace and laid it in Erystra's wizened hand.

"Listen...to me, child." Erystra's breath came in gasps. "Your...mother...was Iskara. She...gave ye life, and...this necklace. Carry it...near your heart...always. Never...part... with it."

The gasps became harsher, and her voice grew fainter. "Leave...this place, my child. Go...and fulfill...your destiny."

Erystra's voice faded. The rasping breath ceased. The hand clutching the necklace went limp.

Long moments passed as Skurgiil gazed at the empty face. Then cold realization sank in, and Skurgiil threw back her head and wailed.

Wendy Jensen

Chapter Five

"The Unknowns use those who least expect it."
Sayer Proverb

Year After Aria, 279
Peasant Year of the Morgs

Twenty-four years ago...

The kitchen was dark, but Iskara knew her way around by feel. Her fingers slid over the potato bin, and into the keg of apples. Her feet avoided the board that creaked as she snagged a piece of dried meat from the rafter.

It was three hours before dawn, and when it broke she would be sitting on a mountain watching the sky turn purple with the eagles wheeling overhead. *Much more fun than tending shop.*

No doubt I'll get a whipping for it when I return. Iskara shrugged one shoulder. An occasional whipping was worth escaping the tedium of stacking bolts of cloth and measuring out flour.

Perhaps I can climb up to the nest I found last week,

to see if the eggs have hatched, she thought. *If they have, I can feed the eagle chicks some dried meat. Should I take an extra piece, just in case?*

Poised on tiptoe, Iskara heard her mother stirring in the room above. In two deft steps, Iskara went out the door and into the darkness surrounding Surham.

The eggs had hatched. The mother bird rose squawking from the nest, revealing three globs of white fluff. Iskara squawked back, waving as the mother circled above.

She loved the great birds, and they must have liked her because they didn't dive on her as she approached their nest. Iskara could sit for hours watching them wheel across the sky in total freedom. Her mother said she was born in the Year of the Eagles, the year when the giant birds settled in droves in the peaks around Surham. Iskara was certain they had come to witness her birth.

Iskara threw her dried meat into the nest and watched three tiny beaks rend it apart in the dim pre-dawn light. Then she crunched into her apple, and sat down to watch the dawn.

Iskara loved the mountains, and the vast open places, empty of any people. She loved the freedom of being alone with no one telling her what to do, and the feel of the wind in her hair as the lands below spread out before her like a blanket for a giant's picnic. She loved the wildness of the peaks, rising rough and ragged before her, their rocky faces standing stark and black against the lessening black of the pre-dawn sky.

Sound carried in the mountains, traveled through the clear air and echoed in the ravines. At first she thought the shrieking came from the eagles returning to their nest. But as the sun rose, illuminating the sky with brilliant purple and outlining the column of smoke rising from below, Iskara realized the screams were coming from Surham.

There was nothing left when she returned. Three hours up the mountain was two hours down, and the village was smoldering rubble by then. No houses, no barns, no store. No living people. And no food.

Iskara didn't think of the food until dark was falling. She was done crying by then; done wandering through smoky streets. Done hoping she would find her mother or her father, or anyone else, alive. As the sun set, Iskara lay down on the soot-stained step of what had been her home, curled up around her empty stomach and went to sleep.

A clucking chicken woke her. A stupid hen, strutting around the green and proclaiming to a dead village that she had laid an egg.

Iskara found the egg. Found the whole nest, under the bushes at the edge of the green. A nest with six eggs, still warm from the silly hen. Iskara knocked the end off each egg and sucked it out.

Then she turned her back on Surham. With the raw eggs sloshing in her stomach, she set off down the road to the next village.

"Trouble again, I hear." Erystra's voice was stern.

Iskara shifted her weight to the other foot, and stared

at the floor. She didn't want to meet Erystra's eyes. There was something about them that made her nervous. As if they could see into her, through her, beyond her.

"Yes, Gran— Mistress." Iskara corrected herself sullenly.

The School Mistresses had made it plain she would get no special treatment because of her relationship to the High Mistress of Neston, and Iskara figured that meant she shouldn't give her a special title. If Erystra didn't treat her like a granddaughter, why should she give her the deference due a grandmother?

"A bucket of water on the school room door, Iskara? Just before the School Mistress entered?"

"If she were a real Sayer, she would have known it was there!"

Erystra sighed. After nearly a year at Neston, Iskara was as defiant as the day a Sword Sister dropped her on Neston's doorstep.

The Sword Sister's face had been grim. "Some farmers found her, on the road from Surham. Seems the village was overrun by Morgs. This one is the only survivor, and claims she's your granddaughter, Mistress." And Erystra Saw the destruction of Surham and the death of Sudain in Iskara's anguished eyes.

Defiant then, and defiant now. The smolder of her eyes only enhanced a rapidly developing beauty. Looking at the girl standing with sullen grace before the desk, Erystra could see none of herself, none of Sudain. *But there was something familiar, here, nonetheless....*

Erystra remembered dark eyes smiling into hers, offering of a cup of wine. *The stars falling across the night sky on the walk home, and the smell of the hay at the stack where we stopped to "rest"....*

But, like Sudain, this girl showed no gift for the

Sight, no desire to be a Sayer. No idea of what it meant to be a Sayer. "We use our Sight for the greater good, Iskara, not for unimportant things, like buckets of water on doors."

"Is that why you didn't See my mother's death? Because it wasn't important?"

Erystra closed her eyes, wishing she could close out her Sight. It was true. She had not Seen the death of Sudain, or the fall of Surham. She, who was called Erystra True-Sight. Why had the voices, which commanded her to lie with a young nobleman, failed to warn her of impending death for the product of that union?

"It is not always given that we See our own destinies. Or the destiny of those we love." Erystra opened tear-filled eyes and regarded her granddaughter. "For instance, I can not See yours."

Iskara squirmed. *I've gone too far this time,* she thought. *Gran— Erystra will have me whipped.* She raised her chin, and looked her grandmother in the eye.

"What are you going to do to me?"

"I think... I think I will send you to Castle Shield."

Wendy Jensen

Chapter Six

*...And they that would be Champions of the Light
Must bear scars of the Dark on their soul.*
From the ballad "Champions of Light"
attributed to Singer Sefrinel Lutesong

Year After Aria, 303

Loneliness crept in around Skurgiil's sobs, mingling with despair. The feelings lay like the yoke of the water buckets across her shoulders, weighed on her like a bale of sodden fleece. Erystra's hand grew chill in her grasp before Skurgiil wiped her nose on the sleeve of her tunic and sat back on her heels.

Alone, she thought. *I am alone.*

A fire still glowed in the hearth and the herb bundles still hung drying from the rafters, but the cottage, which had always been her home seemed empty and strange.

The spinning wheel in the corner would never turn again; the loom by the curving cottage wall would never hold another length of wool. The woman whose hands had spun, sewed, and cooked for Skurgiil all the girl's life now lay unmoving on the rough pine cot.

This cottage, with its stone walls that circled her like

the curve of Erystra's arms when she was still small enough to sit on the Good Mother's lap, was the only home Skurgiil had ever known. The length of the valley was her world, the mountains her boundaries.

It had always been enough. She had been content with the Good Mother. Tending the sheep and climbing the mountains, bathing in her pool and running through the valley with the wind in her hair and her body moving with powerful ease had been happiness enough.

The sense of contentment was gone, shattered by two strangers. Now the cottage seemed empty, the valley small and confining. For the first time in her life, Skurgiil felt alone.

An aloneness that was certain and absolute, vast in its implications. The sheep bleated outside the cottage, but not another human being lived in the valley, or for miles beyond it. Skurgiil knew nothing of what lay beyond those miles, except for the stories Trenton told when he came each spring to trade for fleece.

Trenton said there were people beyond the mountains, and a town called Fenfall. He had offered to take her there, last spring, but Erystra refused. "I am too old to make the trip," Erystra had said, "and too old to be left alone." So Skurgiil listened to Trenton's tales of the lands beyond the peaks, and waited for him to come again in the spring with new tales to tell.

I could leave with Trenton when he comes, she thought. *But that will be a fortnight yet.*

Skurgiil stared at Erystra's still face. The lips that had smiled at Skurgiil were bloodless, the mouth slightly agape. Emptied of the life that once filled it the corpse seemed unfamiliar. *The Good Mother is gone.*

The horrible aloneness overwhelmed Skurgiil again. *I can not wait a fortnight,* she thought. *A fortnight spent here alone, with only the sheep and Erystra's memory for company....*

No!

Another feeling rose up inside her. It was an unfamiliar emotion, dark and uncomfortable, churning her blood and driving other emotions before it.

Anger. Boiling anger at the two strangers who had taken Erystra's life, hot fury that solidified into cold resolve.

I will not wait for Trenton, Skurgiil thought. *I will leave the valley, leave it today, and go to the strange places across the mountains, where people live.*

Skurgiil crossed Erystra's thin arms across the bony chest and bent to place one last kiss on the old woman's forehead.

Silver links clinked a faint protest as they hit the floor. Skurgiil gazed at the necklace lying at her feet, then bent to retrieve it.

Iskara. Never before had Erystra named her mother.

Of course, Skurgiil had never asked. Skurgiil had never even asked what a mother was, until the spring that old trader Tragar appeared with a lanky young man who he introduced as his son.

Skurgiil's head came up to Erystra's shoulder that spring, and Trenton was still head and shoulders taller than Skurgiil. He looked astounded, then embarrassed, when she looked up at him and asked, "What is a son?"

A long conversation followed, involving things like sons and daughters, husbands and wives, and fathers and mothers. A look of sorrow had crossed Erystra's wrinkled face when Skurgiil asked, "Are ye my mother, Erystra?"

"Nay, child. Your mother is dead. She left ye in my care."

Tragar ruffled Skurgiil's hair. "Aye, and 'tis as good as a mother she's been to ye all these years, girl. A good mother, indeed. Now, come and see what I've brought for trade. Might even be some sweets for you!"

Then there were packs to open and bales of fleece to bring out from the shed, and friendly dickering between Erystra and Tragar over needles, shiny copper pots, sacks of flour, and a bag of the promised sweets. There was no more talk of mothers, but Tragar's phrase stuck in Skurgiil's mind, and she took to calling Erystra "Good Mother." Erystra never objected, and Skurgiil never asked about her mother again.

Now I know my mother's name. That was all she knew. *Her name, and that this necklace once belonged to her.* Skurgiil turned the gem in her hand. *From my mother, to me.*

Skurgiil slipped the chain over her head. As the stone nestled between her breasts it glowed faintly, but Skurgiil didn't notice. She set about her tasks, her grim resolve tempered by occasional sobs that seemed loud in the silent cottage.

She heated the iron poker in the coals of the fireplace, and pulled a tanned sheep hide down from the rafters. Tears dripped off her nose and sizzled on the poker as Skurgiil burned a message into the leather.

The Good Mother had insisted she learn to write, and patiently scrawled the letters in the dirt of the cottage floor until Skurgiil knew them all and knew what they meant. "No matter," Erystra had said, "that there are no books to read or parchment to write on in this valley. Ye must learn to read and write, for someday ye will need it."

Her first written missive would be her good-bye to Trenton. The lanky trader would be shocked to find he owned a whole flock of sheep, and still had all his trading supplies.

No doubt he would rather have me than the flock of sheep, Skurgiil thought.

It was no secret that Trenton liked her. He had paid her little notice in the first few years when he took over Tragar's trading route. But later, as Skurgiil reached his height, then surpassed it, and as her body grew shapes that showed under her tunic, he began to notice her. He turned sheep-eyed whenever he saw her, and tripped on his own feet while Skurgiil grinned at him. He even mentioned the thing called marriage, which made husbands and wives and sons and daughters.

Once Skurgiil asked Erystra to use the Sight and say whether she would marry Trenton, but Erystra had replied tartly that not even she could see that far ahead. Skurgiil had laughed, because she was young and marriage was not much on her mind anyway.

Leave the marrying thing to the sheep. They need to do it, to make lambs.

Skurgiil needed no people versions of lambs. "Babies," Trenton called them. When she asked him what they looked like, he had grinned and promised she would find out, if she married him.

"Go, and fulfill your destiny," Erystra had said.

Skurgiil stared at the body on the cot. "What destiny, Good Mother?" The only answer to her question came from inside herself.

Something beyond this valley. She knew that, just as she knew which ravine to search for a lost lamb.

Skurgiil threw the poker back in the coals. Whatever that destiny was, it was not to marry Trenton.

She nailed the message to the door of the sheep barn, propping it open with rocks. She propped the doors to the fodder sheds open, and unhinged the gates to all the pens.

She slashed holes in the grain bags for the flock to nibble through. She took her bedroll from beside the hearth, stuffed it with her extra tunic and some dried meat, and set it in the yard.

Then she filled the cottage with firewood.

Armload after armload she carried, covering the floor where she had slept, piling it under the loom, around the spinning wheel, over Erystra's body on the bed. The stool by the hearth where Erystra always sat on winter days, the shelves with their worn pots, the crocks of herbs and foodstuffs — all disappeared under pieces of split pine. And with them vanished Skurgiil's childhood.

The last rays of sunshine were retreating across the valley floor when Skurgiil struck a flint to a tallow-soaked torch. Her tears were gone, spent at Erystra's bedside. The only evidence of her grief was her red nose, swollen beyond its usual large dimensions.

She hesitated a moment, a lonely figure in an empty valley. Then she lifted her chin, and threw the flaming torch through the cottage door.

Skurgiil hoisted her bedroll and started up the trail, without even glancing at Erystra's tiny garden plot with its tender green shoots poking through the rocky soil. A yearling lamb she had nursed through sickness ran bleating after her, but Skurgiil strode on. Up the twisting, narrow road that was the valley's only exit she climbed. She did not look back until she crested the pass.

From her height she could still see the sun, but the valley below lay in shadow. The cottage flamed bright in the dusk. The sheep milled around outside the heat of the blaze, bleating in confusion.

The yearling twitched its tail halfway down the trail. It bawled up at her between glances toward the valley. An eagle drifted by, its bright yellow eye scanning the lamb. With a final protesting bleat the lamb bounced down the trail, heading for the flock and the security of numbers.

Skurgiil watched him, an unfamiliar weight forming in her chest. *I will miss him,* she thought. *I will miss all of them.*

She had tended the flock for years now, ever since Erystra's strength began to fade and Skurgiil's began to grow. She had raised every sheep in the flock up from a lamb.

And now I am abandoning them.

She hesitated just a moment, paused at the crest of the pass, between old and new, known and unknown.

They will be fine, she assured herself. *Trenton will be here before the next moon, and he will take them all away with him.*

I have other things I must do.

I must find my destiny.

And find the Good Mother's killers, Skurgiil added, as she turned her back to the valley where she grew up.

Beneath her sheepskin cloak the dawnstone glowed faintly with approval.

⁌◉⁍

The High Mistress of Neston paused in the door of the library. The acolyte who sat in the window seat was a slight girl, her fragility emphasized by exceptionally pale skin contrasting against extremely black hair. For a moment the High Mistress had the absurd notion that the sunlight entering the leaded panes passed through the girl rather than around her.

She was young, too. *Eighteen? And she came to Neston... two years ago.*

The High Mistress shook her head regretfully. No matter. She was still the best choice. There was natural talent in her beyond most acolytes, and the Sight that came to her murky blue-violet eyes was as strong as a full-fledged Sayer.

"Ilissa."

A dainty finger paused in its journey down an ancient page. "Yes, Mistress?"

"There has been a passing, child."

"I know, Mistress."

"You Saw it?"

"No, Mistress, but I sensed it. Great power passed on. It was important, was it not?"

"Yes. She was the oldest of our order. Yes, Ilissa — even older than I." The High Mistress smiled at the flush that rose on her pale cheeks, watched her dark lashes droop towards the yellowed pages on the girl's lap.

It does the young ones good, to think we still can attain the ancient powers, the High Mistress thought. *The power to command creatures, the power to See thoughts — none have attained it since Aria — but I believed it, at her age. It gave me hope.*

"There is little call for sorrow. She lived full term, and did her work. Besides," the High Mistresses voice dropped, "her work is not yet done. She has become a Guardian."

Ilissa blinked. Guardianship was a well-kept secret among the Sayers. Ilissa had heard rumors about it in the acolyte ranks, of course, but... *the High Mistress is openly discussing it? With an acolyte?*

"That is good, Mistress," Ilissa murmured.

"Yes, but not good enough. The one she guards needs

much help. We must protect her."

"Her?"

"Yes, her. You know, child, that the Sisters of the Sword and the Sayers have long shared strengths to protect these lands."

"Yes, Mistress. So she is a Sword Sister?"

The old Sayer tilted her head back, clear gray eyes staring into the invisible future.

"Not yet, child. Not yet."

Wendy Jensen

Chapter Seven

Year After Aria, 303

Snow clogged the high mountain passes, lingering drifts that resisted the wan sun of early spring. Skurgiil slogged her way through, pushing through gritty piles that rose to her knees, sometimes to her waist. She barely felt them, scarcely noticed the cold. She concentrated on the Inner Heat. It kept her body warm, and her mind off Erystra's death.

Somewhere, over the mountains, were two men. One in metal clothing, one in a long black dress, and both riding strange flying creatures. Two men, who had killed Erystra.

Days turned to nights and days came again. Skurgiil trudged the mountain trails, scaling the twisting paths on one side, slipping on loose shale down the other, sleeping between boulders until dreams of Erystra's death drove sleep from her and sent her plodding onward in the dim purple light of dawn.

The dried meat in her bedroll was gone when she crested the last pass. Below she saw the mountains falling away to the fells, and the fells giving way to a mottled carpet of brown and spring green squares. Stone cottages dotted the squares, and sprouting up like a clump of wild mushrooms were the thatch and slate roofs of taller buildings. The land flattened out to the fens, where the late afternoon sun reflected off the water and birds wheeled above the reeds. A massive building with colored cloth flying from its towers stood near the end of a neck of land that crossed the fens.

Fenfall, Skurgiil thought. *It must be Fenfall.* Trenton said it was the first town out of the mountains; said it was named for the fens that lay just beyond.

She would not reach it tonight. The mountains were casting long shadows, and the group of buildings below was several hours walk away.

Skurgiil stood at the pass staring at the town until night came and stars dotted the sky. Then she curled up in her bedroll and went to sleep over the protests of her empty stomach.

―◉―

Balek polished the face of his new medallion, wiping away soot and residual flecks of clay from the casting. The runes on it were well defined and the scent of fresh magic still clung to its brass surface.

Certainly his best work yet. He had spent days on the research, and had carefully calculated the materials, then calculated them again. Surely it would work.

Balek cast a rueful glance towards his scrap pot. Failed attempts of other medallions filled it.

He sighed. It was a shame he couldn't melt them down and re-use the metal, but once impregnated with magic — even failed magic — the metal was useless for other medallions. If the first attempt on this medallion didn't succeed there would not be another, for Balek had no more brass coins to melt down for metal.

He had plenty of copper coins, of course, but who would want a copper medallion? Not Balek. The baser the metal, the less magic it could absorb. Gold would be best, but there was no gold in Castle Darkfall. The Morgs' raids on peasant farms and villages yielded few brass coins, much less gold.

This one must work the first time, it must! Perhaps I should go down to the Morgs' quarters to test it, Balek thought. If anything could test a Medallion of Protection From Nausea, a stroll through the Morgs' living space could.

He slipped the medallion over his head and had taken one step towards the door when he felt it, like a huge hand around his skull, dragging him towards the door.

Curse Necimus anyway! Balek thought. *Why can't he just walk down the hall and knock on my door? Or even shout down the hall when he wants me?*

He knew the answer. It was Necimus' way of illustrating both his superior magical power and his control over Balek. Balek's only defense was to hide behind layers of medallions and to screen himself with camouflaged runes on his robe. *I'll definitely make a Rune of Summons Deflection next,* he thought.

He hurried towards the study. The faster he arrived, the sooner he would be free of the sensation that tugged at him. Outside his master's study, Balek fidgeted while the door's magic defenses accepted his palm, and nearly fell through when it opened to admit him.

"Yes, Your Evilness?" Balek recovered from his stumble and straightened his robe before looking up.

Oh, no. The bones covered the desk again, and His Evilness was looking — *well, evil.* Necimus was definitely displeased.

Necimus rose to his feet, and Balek shrank back.

In all the years he had served Necimus, Balek had never become accustomed to his size. Necimus was easily seven feet tall, and Balek suspected he might even be a few inches over seven feet.

"You failed me, Balek." Necimus' voice held the imminent threat of nearby thunder, and Balek's knees wobbled beneath his robe.

"F-F-Failed y-you, Your Evilness?

Necimus gestured at the bones. "The threat is still there. In the mountains."

"B-But, Your Evilness, the Sayer—"

"Are you certain she was dead?"

"There was blood. A lot of blood. On her, on Kurg's sword, Kurg stabbed her, he said she was dead, he....." Balek gulped. Necimus didn't accept excuses. "She looked dead, Your Evilness."

"Go again. Look again. Make certain she is dead. And search deeper into the mountains. Where there was one Sayer, there might be more. Or something else."

"Yes, Your Evilness. I'll tell Kurg to have the mounts saddled at dawn. As soon as it is light, we'll be on our way." Balek felt his robe sticking to his armpits as he backed to the door. Necimus' scorching stare followed him.

"Don't fail me again, Balek."

"No, Your Evilness, we won't. I mean, I won't. We'll—I'll find the threat this time, I promise."

Balek made it through the door. When it closed behind him he ran back to his room.

It wasn't until his heart stopped thumping against his medallion-covered chest that a thought occurred to him. He could take some of the copper coins with him, and get them changed into brass coins. Maybe in Fenfall.

It had been nearly twenty years since he set foot in Fenfall. Surely no one there would remember him.

Chapter Eight

...Then will come The Scourge of Evil...
From "The Prophecies of Aria"

Year After Aria, 303

The sparse stunted pines and scraggly bushes of the high mountains gave way to pine forests, then to great trees with odd shaped leaves. Skurgiil knelt beside a stream to drink, and stared at the forest around her.

Rough-barked trees twisted gnarled branches in a ceiling far above her head, where a furry creature with a fluffy tail chattered at her while eating something clutched in its paws. Deep purple flowers sprouted along the stream bank, and a bright red bird fluttered by.

Odd, Skurgiil thought. *Another world, this. Even the smells are different here.*

Skurgiil inhaled, testing the new odors. Not the sharp, clear scents of the mountains. The smells here were rich but muted, mingled until she couldn't separate or identify any of them. The air seemed thicker, heavier.

She moved on, following the contours of the land sloping down, always downwards, away from the familiarity of her mountains and into the unknown world below.

Outside of the forest she passed patches of trees

growing in straight rows, unlike any trees she had ever seen. Cottages appeared, thatched and circular, like her home in the valley. The cottages grew in size, and Skurgiil stared at ones that stood twice the height of Erystra's cottage, and covered more ground than the cottage and the sheep pens combined.

Perhaps they are pens for human lambs, Skurgiil thought. *Perhaps babies need more space than sheep.*

People began appearing along the road wearing clothes in colors no sheep ever grew, made of cloth so finely woven that Skurgiil could not see the weft. Men and women, many of them, of varying sizes, but none as tall as Skurgiil. They gaped as she passed with her bedroll slung on her back. She strode on, ignoring the stares, but a feeling clutched at her chest like the time so long ago when she got lost at the far end of the valley and had wandered, crying, until Erystra found her.

There was no Erystra to find her now, no aged hands to comfort her and lead her home. Skurgiil scowled to keep from crying. The crowd of people before her parted and Skurgiil hurried through them and into the town of Fenfall.

Skurgiil shivered. *Unknowns, what a place!* The cottages were all tall, standing shoulder to shoulder and glowering down at her from above. They hung out over the rocky path that wound between them, and Skurgiil edged forward warily.

If this were a mountain ravine, she would not have ventured in. The jumbled structures sent an itching feeling of unease down Skurgiil's back, making her think of possible rock slides.

The people seemed to think nothing of it. They walked up and down this man-made gully without fear or hesitation. They even ignored the miniature wolves of various colors that prowled the doorways, searching for food.

Food, Skurgiil thought. *I must find food. That means I must speak to these people, these strangers.*

Skurgiil stepped forward into the gorge, and broke out in a sweat as the buildings loomed over her. The people were thick here, bumping her, jostling her, moving by her with strange expressions on their faces, as if she were a wolf among their sheep. And talking, always talking, their voices blending until Skurgiil could only catch a word here and there, the overall effect worse than a full pen of sheep that had scented a wolf.

Skurgiil clutched at the corner of a building and let the people stream by. She gasped, fighting for breath as if she had just climbed to the Guardian's peak without resting, but there were no hills here, no slopes to account for the pounding of her heart. Skurgiil closed her eyes, shutting out the sights but not the maddening sounds.

Good Mother, what should I do? Where should I go? How do I find my destiny in this awful place?

There was no answer. She was alone, even in this flood of people. Skurgiil straightened, shouldering her loneliness like a weighty grain sack. She took a deep breath, and forced herself to face this world.

When she opened her eyes she saw a woman across the way, sitting on a stoop and combing out wool. Her gray hair fell to her hunched shoulders and her gnarled hands worked the wool brushes with such familiarity that she never looked down at them.

So like Erystra! Perhaps she will help me, Skurgiil thought.

She crossed the flow of people and stood before her, but the old woman didn't acknowledge her presence.

Finally Skurgiil gathered enough courage to address her. "Mistress? Where can I find food?"

"Eh?" Cataract-covered eyes looked up at Skurgiil. "Food, you want? Are you new in town?"

"Aye, Mistress, that I am."

The old woman cackled, and reached for more wool. "Peasants," she muttered, "always lost in town. Should stick to their fields, they should."

"Mistress—"

"Enough, girl! Dame Eldra I am, and mistress of

nothing save my wool brushes. Food, you want? Try the Lamb Chop Inn. Most travelers go there. Around the next corner to the left, about five houses down. I'd show you myself, if I could see, but since I can't you'll have to find it on your own. Has a sign in front of it that will tell you which building it is — if you can read."

"Aye, I can read." *The Good Mother was right about needing to know letters someday.* "I thank you, Mist— Dame Eldra, and a good day to you."

Skurgiil moved away, wondering why the old woman couldn't see. *Perhaps she was born blind.* There had once been a lamb born blind in the flock, and it had gone to the stew pot at an early age.

Around the corner and a few houses down stood a large building. A swinging sign proclaimed it to be The Lamb Chop Inn. Beneath the sign a plump woman was sweeping the stoop. Skurgiil approached her.

"Mistress, do ye have food here?"

The woman didn't look up as she answered, "Aye, for a price."

"What... what price, Mistress?"

"Five coppers."

"Five... coppers." Coppers were those round things with numbers and words on them that Trenton carried in a pouch.

"Aye, and for the best mutton roast in town, it's a bargain at twice the price. Why, for only five coppers you get...." The woman glanced up, and her voice faded as her eyes crawled from Skurgiil's chest to her face.

Melyssa stopped sweeping, and gaped. *Unknowns, I should have said ten coppers,* she thought. *Look at the size of this girl! Probably one of those mountain women, by the looks of her. Tall even so, and hungry, by the desperate cast of her eyes. No doubt she will eat twice the portion of a normal person, and the profits along with it. If she can even pay, that is.*

Skurgiil saw the woman's gaze take in her wrapped fur leggings and the frayed edges of her slit tunic. Maybe town people didn't like her showing a horse length of leg any more than Erystra did.

"Well?" the woman demanded. "Do you have five coppers?"

"Nay, I do not," Skurgiil stammered. Erystra always paid Trenton with fleece. Those fleece were still on the sheep, back in the valley.

"Begone, then!" Melyssa shook the broom at the young giantess, but not too vigorously, for this girl looked like she could strangle a body with one hand. "We'll have no beggars around here. Unless," she added, peering at Skurgiil's neck, "you want to trade that necklace for a meal?"

Or several meals, Melyssa thought. It was a fine looking necklace, made of heavy silver, with an excellent dawnstone. Melyssa scrutinized it, and gasped as the stone seemed to glow with a light of its own. Before she could be certain, the girl's massive hand closed around it.

Skurgiil clutched the dawnstone to her chest. Never part with it, Erystra had said. Skurgiil's stomach growled, but Erystra's word had always been her law. It still was. "I can not part with it."

Melyssa leaned on her broom, considering. She didn't want the necklace anyway. It was most likely enchanted or possessed, and she had an abiding suspicion of such things. But this was a big, strong girl. No doubt she could turn out a good day's work. There was plenty of work to do, ever since the lazy stableboy ran away with that floozy of a barmaid. "Would you work for a meal, then?"

"Aye, Mistress."

"My name is Melyssa. Save the 'Mistress' for those who deserve it. I'm just the cook. Doane is the proprietor, and it will be for him to say about you working. Go inside and speak to Doane."

The girl nodded and crossed the stoop in one stride. Melyssa clicked her tongue at the amount of leg showing under the girl's tunic, and gave the step another sweep before following the stranger inside.

Skurgiil took two steps into the dimness of the inn. As her vision adjusted she saw a robust man, paused in the act of polishing the bar.

The man stared at her, his eyes skipping her face on their downward journey to where the tattered edge of her tunic hung between her thighs. He dropped the polishing cloth, ran one hand through waves of only slightly graying hair, and stepped forward with his other hand outstretched.

"Well, well! The first customer of the day! What will it be? Some ale, or wine?" Doane gauged her size, calculating the amount of liquor needed to loosen moral standards. "Or is mead more to your liking?"

Skurgiil took the proprietor's proffered hand and gave it a friendly squeeze. "I would just like a meal."

"And she wants to work for it," Melyssa added, stepping from behind Skurgiil.

"A meal? Work for it?" Doane stammered, testing his hand for broken bones. "Well, Melyssa, we could use some help around here."

"So I've been telling you for the past fortnight."

"Not that you haven't managed quite well for the fortnight."

"Aye, doing the work of two people for the pay of one!"

"It's settled, then." Doane smiled broadly at Skurgiil. "Ten coppers a week, plus room and board." He turned to the disgruntled cook. "She can have the barmaid's room — ah, what was her name?"

"Ana," Melyssa supplied sourly. Melyssa did not suffer from night deafness. She knew that Doane knew the girl's name — and a few other things about her, as well.

"Ah, yes. Ana. Well, she's gone, so you can have her room. It is small, but comfortable." *And directly across the hall from mine,* Doane thought. His eyes gleamed, but Skurgiil didn't notice.

She considered his offer. *A place to sleep, those*

important things called coppers, and food. Above all, food. She could not fulfill her destiny on an empty stomach. "I will do it."

"Good, good." Doane rubbed his bruised fingers, and smiled, his thoughts moving on to the night ahead *Could this girl be as powerful in the bedchamber as her handshake implied?* he wondered

Doane caught Melyssa's suspicious stare and cleared his throat. "Ah, Melyssa, you can show our new help her duties now."

"I'll feed her first," Melyssa answered testily. "She'll need energy for her labors." With a final baleful glance at her employer, Melyssa ushered her new helper into the kitchen.

After dishing out a heaping plate of fried potatoes, Melyssa leaned against the cutting table and considered the girl and the situation. She knew what Doane wanted. What she did not yet know was if this girl would be as willing as Ana had been.

She is a strange one, Melyssa mused. *Not just her size, but her manner. Walking through town half dressed, and seeming to think nothing of it. She seems so... simple.*

Unknowns, but she can eat! Melyssa shook her head as the girl devoured potatoes. "Goodness, girl, how long has it been since you last ate? A week?"

"Yesterday," she mumbled around a mouthful.

"Where are you from?" Melyssa prodded.

Skurgiil gestured with her fork.

"The mountains? I thought so." Melyssa pursed her lips and nodded. "Mountain people are tall, usually. But you're tall even for a mountain woman. What is your name?"

"Skurgiil."

"Goodness, girl! What was your mother thinking, when she named you that?"

"I do not know. She is dead."

"How sad for you! And your father?"

Father? Skurgiil paused in her chewing. Tragar had been Trenton's father. Of course, she must have one, too.

"I .. do not know." Skurgiil frowned. Knowing about mothers and fathers had never seemed important, somehow. Not as important as building the lambing pens, or putting up fodder grasses for the winter. Now, when it was important, Erystra was gone and the answers were gone with her.

"I was raised by someone else," Skurgiil explained.

"Ah, a foundling!" Melyssa nodded knowingly. "Plenty of those, these days. Parents killed by Morgs, usually. Most are given to the Orders to raise."

Morgs, Orders, coppers—townspeople are strange, Skurgiil thought. *But what could you expect, living where the houses crowd each other like boulders in a rock slide?* Skurgiil shrugged off her unease. Somewhere out here were Erystra's killers, and Skurgiil's destiny. Perhaps that destiny included finding her father, since her mother was dead.

Skurgiil finished off her meal and rose to her feet. "What should I do?"

Melyssa looked at the head of dark hair brushing the strings of onions and herbs hanging from the ceiling beams, and decided the kitchen was no place for this one. "There's wood to chop," she instructed, ushering her new aide into the inn's back yard. "And water to carry, and horses to feed."

As afternoon came, Melyssa paused in the door of the kitchen to watch Skurgiil chopping firewood. The heavy double-bladed axe rose and fell, and chunks of split wood were piling up around the chopping block. Already the bin by the hearth was full, with extra split wood stacked conveniently outside the kitchen door. The water barrels in the kitchen were also full. As Melyssa watched, Skurgiil traded the axe for a pitchfork and headed towards the stable.

Aye, she is a worker, Melyssa thought. *Unlike that harlot, Ana.* Young, too, and from what Melyssa garnered while showing Skurgiil her tasks, too innocent for Doane's intentions. Melyssa knew innocence when she saw it, even if the lecherous proprietor did not. *Or maybe he does, and that is what appeals to him.*

It certainly wasn't the girl's prettiness, because she didn't have any. *A certain beauty, perhaps, if you liked the massive, unrelenting beauty of the mountains.* Melyssa raised her eyes to the horizon, where the peak known as The Guardian towered above the rest.

Skurgiil said she came from the base of that mountain, and had crossed the mountains between in six days time. Subsisting on dried meat, sleeping on the rocky ground in sheepskin cloak — Melyssa shook her head.

Poor girl. Big, homely, and endowed with the name Skurgiil. What kind of a name is that? But then, Rose or Daisy would fit her about as well as a silk dress would fit Doane.

Whatever her name, she deserved better than Doane's lewd attentions, and Melyssa intended to help her avoid them. Melyssa wiped her hands on her apron, smiling at the thought. She owed her employer a turn or two.

⇥◉⇤

Skurgiil brushed a bay gelding in the stable, breathing deeply of the moist air, heavy with the scent of animals. It had been years since she had tended a horse. The dappled gray mare had gone to her final rest before Skurgiil's head topped her broad back. Since then Skurgiil had tended only sheep. Skurgiil picked burrs out of the bay's mane, and wondered how those sheep were faring.

They are fine, she assured herself. *They will eat the grain and get fat, and Trenton will take them to a new home. And they will not be any more confused than I am, in this strange place.*

People. Everywhere she looked in this town, there were people. People in colored clothes, of finer weave than Erystra ever spun, people in the streets, talking and crowding and pushing until Skurgiil felt like a sheep in a shearing pen. And people like Melyssa, who asked where she was from and why she was named Skurgiil, asked about her mother and father. Everywhere she turned there were questions, but no answers.

Skurgiil sobbed and buried her face in the gelding's mane. *Good Mother, how am I supposed to fulfill my destiny when I do not know what it is? How I wish you were here!*

Pressed against the horse, the dawnstone glowed faintly, and the memory of Erystra's face rose up crisp and clear in Skurgiil's mind, along with her frequent advice.

/Patience, child. One cannot hurry the world./

Oddly comforted, Skurgiil threw down hay for the horses, and returned to the kitchen to see what Melyssa wanted her to do next.

"Again?" Kurg's shout was followed by a scowl, but Balek was already taking his mount down, circling towards the cottage's soot-stained walls as the sheep below raced towards the mountains.

"Why?" Kurg demanded, as he brought his mount down beside Balek's. "We've already searched here once today, and there was no one here."

"That's what you said last time," Balek snapped, "and I'm the one His Evilness is blaming for it."

"There isn't anyone here, you fool. Now or then."

Balek fumed inwardly, but not even his host of medallions could embolden him to antagonize Kurg. *Not here, not now.* Taking a half-Morg into Fenfall was risky enough, but an angry one? *No, best to be pleasant for now.*

Balek dredged up his best pleasant-to-half-Morgs tone."Then how did the cottage burn?"

Kurg stopped scowling, and wrinkled his narrow forehead in concentration. "Maybe the old woman

dragged herself in and started it."
How could this mutant inherit his father's size but not his intelligence? Balek wondered. *Pleasant, remember, be pleasant.* Balek gritted his teeth. "You said she was dead. Besides, someone let all the sheep loose. Go check the barns."

Kurg scowled again, but stomped off to the barns. Balek fingered the three scrolls in his belt pouch, and patted the sack of copper coins strapped behind his saddle.

Another hour. The shadows from the mountains were long; the valley was in dusk. If Kurg just spent a quarter hour or so poking around, then they would arrive in Fenfall after dark.

Which was what Balek wanted. The scrolls he had worked on all night would disguise and control the mounts once they landed, but they couldn't hide them coming out of the sky. The scroll for Kurg was the last one made, and a hasty job. It would barely disguise his half-Morg features, and Balek preferred it only be tested by lamplight.

If I can even get Kurg to agree to stop in Fenfall. Perhaps the promise of ale, Balek mused. There was no ale at Castle Darkfall anymore. *Yes, ale was the answer. Kurg would agree to go for ale.* Balek wiped his sweaty palms on his robe as the warrior returned.

"Nothing there, like I told you. If there's a threat to His Evilness, then it must be the big ones."

The big ones. Apparently the concept of giant doesn't fit in a half-Morg brain. But neither does anything else, Balek thought disgustedly.

In one thing, though, the mutant might be right. Maybe they were the threat to Necimus. They had sighted the giants several hours deeper into the mountains — certainly deep enough to qualify for the threat Necimus saw. At any rate, His Evilness would be interested in knowing that the fabled creatures were real.

Kurg was already climbing into his saddle. *Ale, remember to mention the ale,* Balek reminded himself, and took a deep breath.

"Ah... Kurg. It's early yet, perhaps we could stop at Fenfall? I can hide the mounts, and we could go to a tavern, have an ale together, maybe even two or three ales." Balek gulped. "What do you say, Kurg?"

The ugly warrior grinned, his lips peeling back from vicious teeth. "A tavern? Good idea. There will be women there."

Chapter Nine

And despair grips the land...
   From "The Prophecies of Aria"

Year After Aria, 303

The Lamb Chop Inn was well known in Fenfall for its excellent mutton roast and decent ale for a decent price. That the service had been slow in recent days could be overlooked, for the patrons were not above carrying an empty tankard to the bar for refills, or even standing at the kitchen door until Melyssa could heap their plates. Melyssa was a superb cook, Doane was a friendly barkeep, and if the former had a sharp tongue and the latter an eye for the ladies — well, everyone had few faults.

The Lamb Chop Inn was full, as it was most nights. Skurgiil peered through the kitchen door at the people in the main room. Every chair and bench was occupied, and still people trickled in, to lean against the bar or to sit cross-legged before the massive hearth.

Conversations in the room dwindled as Skurgiil stepped through the kitchen door with a roast leg of lamb. Scores of eyes stared at her, and Skurgiil paused, caught in their gaze like a rabbit cowering before the shadow of an eagle.

"Here, girl. Right here, where these good folk can come up and carve themselves some mutton," Doane called, patting the bar. "And where I can make sure they pay before they do," he muttered, as Skurgiil set the roasted haunch in front of him.

Skurgiil turned toward the kitchen, trying to avoid meeting the stares. But one table caught her eye.

Five women sat there, in identical attire. Not tunics, or skirts, but armor; gleaming chain over black leathers. A black shield leaned against their table, and on it Skurgiil saw the emblem of a silver sword fashioned in the form of a woman. Her head was the base of the blade and her outstretched arms formed the guard of the sword, while her body formed the hilt.

The women were looking at Skurgiil. Looking, not staring as if she were a two-headed sheep. One of them, a woman with three small braids in her blonde hair, smiled at her.

Skurgiil gaped, and didn't hear the call from the kitchen.

"Girl!" Melyssa appeared in the doorway, hands on her hips. "Skurgiil! What about the plates? Or do you expect these fine people to eat mutton roast in their hands?"

The patrons laughed and Skurgiil ducked back into the kitchen, her face hot and her stomach queasy. She reappeared with a huge stack of crockery plates. Her biceps bulged as she hoisted them onto the bar.

A drunken merchant next to her whistled. "Why, thatsh a big, shtrong girl," he told Doane solemnly. "Ish she that good at evershing?" The merchant gave the innkeeper a wink that seemed to overbalance him; he clutched the bar for support.

"Rom, my good man," Doane boomed. "Have another ale. On the house." He shoved a tankard into the man's grasping hands. "And stop interfering with my conquests before I make them," he added under his breath, as Skurgiil returned to the kitchen.

"Whatsh shdat you shay, Doane?" Rom inquired blearily, wiping foam from his mouth.

"Nothing, my good man, nothing," Doane snapped. "Drink your ale."

Balek sat in a corner of the inn so deeply shadowed that his black-on-black rune-embroidered robes seemed to dissolve in the darkness. He glanced at Kurg. The illusion he had cast on the half-Morg's face was holding up fine.

Balek took a sip of wine to hide his smile. Kurg had barely watched while Balek read the spell scrolls to bind and hide the mounts, and he hadn't noticed at all when Balek pulled the third scroll out. *What would Kurg say if he knew he now wore the face of a human?* Good thing the half-Morg wasn't prone to look in mirrors. Not that there were any mirrors in this room, and the illusion would have faded long before they returned to Castle Darkfall.

Which should be soon. Balek had already changed his copper coin in, despite the innkeeper's protests, so there was no need to linger. Balek sighed. Sitting in the company of humans was pleasant, but it was best to get Kurg home. The half-Morg was eyeing every female in the room, and had already suggested they grab the cook from the back door of the kitchen before they departed for home. Kurg watched the kitchen helper, too, but with less interest than he showed in the cook.

"A big girl," Balek murmured, staring after Skurgiil's retreating back.

Kurg glanced over the rim of his tankard and grunted. "Maybe she's half-Morg."

She's not ugly enough for that, Balek thought. "She's not a bad looking girl."

Kurg shrugged. He preferred to mate with human females who were smaller and daintier, despite the fact that they seldom survived his vigorous attentions.

Like the cook. Kurg watched her plump behind disappear into the kitchen, and growled. She had a sharp tongue, but those types were the most enjoyable. They struggled longer, past the point where more pleasant females had given up and died.

But that sniveling magic-caster refused to let him grab her on their way home, even though Kurg assured him they could be flying away before pursuit was launched.

Balek said he didn't want a ruckus, he didn't want the townspeople remembering them, His Evilness would not approve, that they weren't even supposed to be in Fenfall. Balek was a coward, and this time spent traveling with him had been worse than standing battlement guard duty in broad daylight.

Kurg glanced at the wizard, and found him staring at the kitchen door. "Change your mind?" Kurg asked hopefully.

"What?" Balek gave him a blank stare.

"Did you change your mind? About the cook? I'll let you go first." Kurg smiled.

Balek shuddered. *Leave it to that over-sexed mutant to be thinking of the cook!* Balek had been thinking about the girl. *There was something disturbing about her, something half-remembered....*

Kurg was looking at him, waiting. Balek shook his head.

Kurg slammed his tankard on the table. "Let's go home, then." Maybe the night wasn't totally lost yet. Perhaps near the borders of His Evilness' lands they would pass over a human village that hadn't been picked too clean. Kurg smiled at the thought of rolling some startled farmer out of bed and imposing himself on the farmer's shrieking wife. He stood up while Balek hastily drained the last of his wine.

On their way to the door they passed the table of armored women. The blonde one stared at him and wrinkled her nose. Kurg glanced at her without interest. He'd had some like those before, at Castle Darkfall. They were no fun. Once you freed them of the armor they endured in stoic silence until they died. They were tougher than most, though; some prisoners even survived a few months, as long as His Evilness didn't allow the guards to play with them too often.

Outside, Balek removed the Covering spell that kept their mounts unseen and the Binding spell that prevented them from gobbling up passersby, and scrambled for his saddle as the beast snapped at him.

"We'll have to let them feed soon," Kurg called to Balek, as they glided over the fens.

Balek nodded absently. He was still puzzling over the girl. It wasn't until they were wheeling over the flocks of some unwary farmer that Balek realized what had disturbed him.

It was the name that the cook used to summon the girl.

Skurgiil.

⁂

"A good evening, very good," Doane commented to no one in particular, as he counted copper coins. He had stacks of them across the bar already, and more yet to be tallied. That odd magic-caster had insisted on changing in copper for every brass coin in Doane's change box. Of course, Doane had charged him a fee for the exchange. Added to the usual night's take of copper coin, it was a daunting heap. Doane knew he wouldn't be seeing his bed for a while yet — or anyone else's bed, for that matter.

He glanced sideways at Skurgiil, who was swinging a mop across the floor with graceful ease.

"Don't wear yourself out, girl," he called.

Melyssa appeared in the kitchen doorway, wiping sudsy hands on her apron. "Dishes are washed," she said shortly.

Doane had no doubt that she had heard his comment to Skurgiil, and knew why he didn't want her tired. "Good, good," Doane answered, and resumed counting, but the cook didn't move.

"Ah, Melyssa, why don't you show Skurgiil to her room." He would like to do it himself, but there was always later tonight, after the suspicious cook fell asleep. "I'll be going to bed myself as soon as I'm finished here." He ignored Melyssa's glare as she led Skurgiil up the stairs.

Melyssa ushered Skurgiil into a room so tiny she couldn't even stretch her arms across the breadth of it. "It's small," Melyssa admitted, "but then, it's just for sleeping." *Or should be.* She rattled the latch on the door. "Best latch your door at night, girl. There's some rats that wander about at night," Melyssa's eyes flickered to a door across the hall, "and they can push your door open if it isn't latched."

"Rats? Where do they come from?"

"Oh, all over," Melyssa replied vaguely. "And they can give you a nasty bite while you're sleeping. Me, I latch my door every night."

Melyssa lit a stub of a candle off her own, and handed it to Skurgiil. "Good rest, girl. Latch the door."

"Aye. Good rest, Melyssa." Skurgiil dropped the latch bar in place and stretched out on the cot. *Too short by a head, like everything else in this place of people.*

Skurgiil sighed as she unlaced her leg wraps. *Good Mother, you should have warned me, prepared me somehow....*

How? What could she have said or done to prepare me for this strangeness? Skurgiil shook her head as she slid out of her tunic. *No doubt the Good Mother knew best.*

Skurgiil threw her bed furs on the floor next to the cot, as they had always lain next to Erystra's cot in the cottage. The big girl fell asleep, achingly aware that now the cot beside her was empty.

The next morning Skurgiil gave Melyssa a respectful look over her bowl of porridge. "I did hear some rattling at my door in the night. Ye must have some large rats."

Melyssa grinned merrily at Doane's red face. "Aye, we have some very large rats."

Roagen, Lord of Fenfall and the lands around it, looked down into his courtyard where an impatient stable boy held the reins of a saddled horse. He sighed and turned to the woman beside him. "Must you go?"

Her full lips smiled against skin that was nearly as dark as the black leathers beneath her chain mail. Combined with her black, slightly slanting eyes and domed forehead, the dark skin gave her an exotic beauty.

"Aye. If I require the other Sisters to take limited leaves of absence, I must do the same," she replied.

"It would be easier if I could visit you."

The dark-skinned woman laughed. "You know men are not allowed at Castle Shield, except for formal visits. Perhaps," she smiled, tilting her head of braided hair up at him, "you wish to limit your visits to formalities?"

Roagen groaned, the memory of her lithe body entwined with his still fresh from the night before.

"No, Tudae."

"I thought not." Her arms slipped up around his neck. Roagen hugged her, crushing her until he felt her chain mail biting through his shirt.

"Someday," he whispered fiercely, "someday. Someday we can leave the worrying and warring behind, and live like normal people."

Roagen knew it was a vain hope. Tudae knew it, too; he felt her sigh even though she didn't answer.

With a final hug, Tudae pulled away. Roagen watched her disappear down the stairs, watched her mount and ride through his gates. When her chain mail was just a silver spot crossing the land bridge, he sighed and turned away from the window.

Twenty years ago he had taken up his sword against a growing threat, dreaming of glory and keeping his lands and people safe. Now he was tired, and his dream was a wife and children to cheer his old age.

But the threat grew stronger. Slowly, insidiously, it grew. Necimus — demons eat his soul for lunch — always knew when to use magic and when to use brute force. His sorcery grew in strength while his over-sized mutant-spawn of an army grew in numbers.

As long as Necimus controlled the lands beyond, there would be no wife, no children for Roagen. There was only one woman he would take to wife, only one that would bear his children. And the dark-skinned girl who two Sword Sisters had found running away years ago was as trapped by Fate as Roagen himself.

Chapter Ten

❂

It is the dawn of evil things —
The Morgs have come out of the wilds!
From "Dawn of the Morgs"
by Wyflen Herdhummer

Year After Aria, 279

Peasant Year of the Morgs

Twenty-four years ago...

"Tudae!" Mammae's face thrust through the striped curtains of the cart.

Too late, for Tudae had already passed the oxen pulling the cart. Pappae smiled and winked at her and said nothing about the bonnet swinging in her hand.

Pappae understood. Pappae always understood — understood that she was tired of sitting in the rocking cart, tired of wearing her bonnet.

Mammae's voice followed her. "Put your bonnet back on, child. You are too old to—"

The wheels tilted over a rock, and Mammae clutched the side of the cart, one hand covering her swollen belly. Behind her a fretful wail announced that Tomo was awake, and Mammae slipped back into the curtains.

Perhaps little brothers were good for something, after all. Not that Tudae wanted another one. She hoped the new baby would be a girl.

She had told Pappae so, sitting on his knee the night he told her Mammae was expecting again, and that they were moving to a new land.

"But why, Tutu?" Pappae had asked.

"Because a sister won't wet her cloths and my dress when I hold her, or whine and cry and pull my hair."

Pappae laughed, and Tudae snuggled under his arm to feel the deep sound vibrating through his chest. She loved it when Pappae laughed.

Mammae threw down the comb, abandoning hope of unsnarling Tudae's wavy locks. "Child, if you kept your bonnet on, Tomo couldn't pull your hair."

Pappae smiled as he brushed the curls back from Tudae's face. "Ah, but she has such beautiful hair. Like yours, my Leja."

Tudae knew her hair was not beautiful like Mammae's. Nothing about her was beautiful like Mammae.

Mammae was slender and soft and graceful, while Tudae was skinny, hard bones poking through everywhere. Her hair was a mess of black waves, always tangling around combs, while Mammae's hair hung in many glossy braids. In two years, Mammae said, Tudae would be old enough for braids, but for now she must wear a bonnet. Tudae hated the hot, itchy bonnet almost as much as she hated Tomo. A sister would be much better.

"Make it be a sister, Mammae. Please?"

"We need a boy. Another boy, to herd the goats in the new land." Mammae sighed.

Tudae knew Mammae did not want to move to the new land. "Pappae, why must we go?"

"Because, Tutu, the rains come ever less, and the herd grows ever smaller. And we have ever more mouths to feed." Tudae felt the small sigh in Pappae's chest, and saw his eyes move from Tomo's basket to Mammae's still-flat belly. Pappae said the new baby—*a sister!*—would come from Mammae's belly, just as the kids came from the nanny goats when the rains came. It had been so with Tomo, Pappae said, but Tudae didn't believe that anything so noisy and smelly could come from beautiful Mammae, and Mammae had been very cross when Tudae asked if Mammae could put Tomo back inside her.

Pappae hugged Tudae close. "In the new land, Tutu, the grass grows because it rains all year. Sometimes the rain falls cold and white, covering the ground, and it is never, ever hot. You'll like that, won't you?"

Tudae nodded, *but how could rain be white?*

"And we'll find you a husband among the people of the new land. A good husband for my Tutu."

The people of the new land. Pappae said their eyes were like pieces of lapis lazuli, their hair like cactus flowers. Their skin was the color of washed wool. Perhaps it was the white rain that makes them so pale.

Tudae looked at Pappae's dark skin and curling black hair. No pale stranger could ever take the place of her Pappae. "I don't want a husband, Pappae. I only want you."

Pappae laughed and tickled her under her chin with his beard, but Mammae's voice was sharp.

"If you don't learn rug-making, child, you won't have a husband. What man would marry a woman who can't make rugs?"

"Then I shall never learn rug-making, and I shall stay with Pappae forever."

Mammae threw up her hands. "Darj, do something with her!"

Pappae's voice was stern. "Go to bed, Tutu. Tomorrow you will start a new rug. You will make it for me."

Tudae started the new rug the next day, sweating under the tent and scratching at her bonnet as she tied the strands of red and yellow wool. Red and yellow were Pappae's favorite colors, but Mammae said the red dye was too dear to use on a child's rug, and Tudae should start with the ugly brown and black wool that the long-haired goats made naturally. Tudae pouted, her full lower lip protruding from her thin face until Mammae said surely a hawk would roost there. But Mammae finally gave her the red yarn, and Tudae banged her comb against the threads and snipped the yarn until her fingertips were raw and a blister formed on the side of her thumb.

The rug was only half finished when they herded the goats north. Now the rug was rolled with Mammae's rugs under the folded tent that covered the wagon. There was no space for the loom in the cart, and Tudae was glad. She did not have to tie strands of wool to the lurching rhythm of the cart, or push Tomo away when he fell on her loom. It was bad enough making cat's cradles that he grew tired of, or pouring pretend coffee from the brass pot into little cups and telling him all the herdsmen were there to visit, while Mammae lay against the pillows and looked sick.

Mammae was always sick now. Her belly grew on the trip north, and she complained that the cart's movement made her queasy. But when they walked her ankles swelled and her back hurt, and Tomo could not keep up even with the slow pace of the oxen pulling the cart and wagon. So Tudae must carry him because Mammae could not, and she didn't know which was worse, the lurching of the cart around pretend coffee parties or Tomo's sagging weight in her arms as they plodded beside the wagon.

But sometimes, when Mammae and Tomo were both asleep, Tudae slipped out of the cart and ran ahead of the oxen, unburdened by her little brother or Mammae's watchful eye. She could shake her black curls loose from the bonnet, and feel the wind of this new land ruffling her hair.

Tudae was running ahead now, stretching her legs with freedom and watching the green trees flash by.

Sword Sister

There were so many trees in this new land. They rose taller than the biggest cactus, and the grass grew in such plenty that the goats were confused. Used to quarreling over each clump, the poor beasts followed each other in circles snatching at a morsel of grass another goat was eating, all the while trampling lush greenery under their cloven feet. Tudae and Pappae had laughed, and even Mammae had smiled.

Tudae was over the next hill now, the cart and wagon out of sight. The land opened up before her. Rolling hills and green forests, and ahead in the distance a few scattered houses.

Pappae said they were nearly there. Soon they would stop and sell Mammae's rugs, and use the money to purchase grazing rights for the goats. They would pitch the tents again, and make more rugs while they waited for her sister to come.

Tudae gave a little skip, and was about to race down the hill when she heard a scream.

Mammae!

Tudae whirled and charged back up the hill, her thin legs pumping under her skirts.

Great, ugly creatures came out of the woods. Their foreheads slanted back into their hair, their teeth protruded from their mouths, and they walked hunched over. Even hunched over they were taller than Pappae; two of them were closing in on him. Tudae saw Pappae's curved sword flash and turn red.

The oxen bellowed and went down, their throats chopped by a crude axe. The cart rocked and fell over, dragged down by the weight of the falling oxen. More ugly creatures were coming out of the woods, passing a man who stood at the edge of the trees.

A tall man, taller than any man Tudae had ever seen. Even the creatures looked short as they passed him. Tudae shivered, bumps breaking out on her arms.

"Run, Tudae!" Pappae yelled, then screamed as a spear pierced his back. Blood spurted out his mouth as he fell to his knees. "Run...."

Tudae ran. Back down the hill, back toward the open lands below. Tripping over her skirt, sobbing, eyes blurred with tears, she ran until she didn't think she could even breathe; ran until she collided with a horse.

"Ho, what's this?"

It was a woman's voice, and a woman's hand that lifted her up onto the horse.

"What goes, little one?"

Their accent was harsh, these strangers. Not like Mammae's soft words, or Pappae's lilting voice. But Tudae could understand them, and she hoped they could understand her.

"Aah... M-M-Mamm-ae," Tudae gasped. Her scrawny chest heaved and the air whistled chill into her mouth. "Pa-Pap-pae...." She pointed with one shaking hand, clutching the strange woman with the other.

"Let's go." There was another woman, also on a horse, and she spurred it forward, drawing a sword. It was a long, straight sword, not a curved one like Pappae's — *Pappae!* Tudae sobbed, and buried her face in the woman's shoulder as her horse followed the first.

What odd clothes, and what an odd smell. A metallic smell, like when Pappae sharpened his knives.

That's what this woman's clothes are made of, Tudae realized, as the bumping of the horse drove her cheek into the hard links. *Little pieces of metal, like the rings Mammae wore in her ears. But Mammae's rings were gold, and these were just steel, not at all pretty, and very hard. These women carried swords. What manner of women carried swords and wore steel clothes?*

And swore. Tudae heard the woman in front, and strange accent or no, Tudae understood. They were words that Mammae said a woman should never use; words that Pappae said, when the jackals took down a goat.

Goats. Tudae heard them bleating, and raised her wet face from the metal rings.

A few goats were left alive, standing between the cart

and the woods, bleating pathetically. They were the only things left alive.

Pappae lay face down on the ground, the spear sticking straight up from his back. His curved sword was gone, and a trail of blood led away into the trees. The cart lay on its side, its colorful covering ripped and rent, and as the woman with the drawn sword circled behind it she swore again.

Tudae felt the woman next to her sigh as she urged her horse towards the cart, picking her way around Pappae and the dead oxen.

Tomo lay there, his eyes staring up at Tudae, his mouth open in a cry she would never hear. And Mammae, beautiful Mammae, lay slumped against the wheel, her bulging belly bulging no longer, replaced by a bloody mass of shredded flesh and shiny intestines.

The ground jumped up at Tudae, kept out of reach only by the woman's powerful grip on her dress. Tudae hung off the side of the horse, retching, throwing up goat's cheese and Mammae's flat bread and the dried apples they had purchased in the last town.

"Morgs." Tudae heard the woman swear again, her voice moving away to the woods. "They were waiting in ambush. More than half a dozen of them. Strange. They don't usually attack in the daytime. And they aren't usually so organized."

"We can't follow them now." The other woman's hands hoisted Tudae upright and wiped her mouth with the hem of her dress. "Best clean up here and get back. Akrien will want to know about this."

The woman who liked to swear nodded grimly, sheathing her sword and dismounting. For the first time Tudae noticed the shield she carried; a black shield, with a woman shaped like a sword on it.

Tudae stared at the shield. It was better than staring at Mammae.

Tudae heard a grunt from the woman, and turned to see Mammae's body disappearing into the cart. Tomo's body followed, and Tudae watched this strange woman put her foot on Pappae's back and pull the spear out.

As she dragged Pappae's limp body to the cart, Tudae started crying. Hard, hurting sobs that wouldn't stop, no matter how tightly the woman on the horse hugged her. Sobs that didn't stop until after firewood was stuffed under the cart and lit.

She had run away. Away from Mammae, away from Tomo, away from the cart. Now the cart was burning, with all her family dead inside it.

Tudae laid her head on the hard, smelly steel shoulder and made a promise. A promise to Pappae, to Mammae, to Tomo, and to herself.

I will never run away again. Never.

Chapter Eleven

To Aragwen the vision came
In days of old, they say......
   From "Song of the Sword Sisters"

Year After Aria, 303

Ilissa walked the halls of Neston, two deferential steps behind the High Mistress. Other Sisters of the Sight smiled and nodded at her as they passed. Ilissa returned their greetings, but her smile was forced, and her gaze wandered wistfully over the pale gray walls.

She had known since coming that one day she would leave Neston. But she had thought that day would be far in the future, and she expected to be better prepared.

"Why me?" she asked, when told of the Mission.

"Because, child, this one needs our help. The one who seeks her hates our Order, so secrecy is crucial. The older Sayers are too well known, and the other acolytes do not yet have the Sight. You are our best choice."

The other acolytes were excited, yearning for the day when they, too, would be given Missions. But for Ilissa it meant leaving the peace that she came to Neston seeking. It meant returning to a world that she was not yet ready to face.

The High Mistress glanced back at her. "Never fear, Neston will still be here when your Mission is accomplished."

"Will I return, then?"

"Child," the Mistress chided, "it is not for us to See our own futures, but the futures of others."

Ilissa sighed and stepped out of Neston's peaceful confines. Already she felt like a stranger to these walls.

In the interest of secrecy she did not wear her gray robes. Instead she wore the clothes she had worn two years ago, when she presented herself at Neston's gate: a simple but flattering white frock and a cloak of deep blue to match her eyes, which her mother had stitched for her in hopes of a good marriage and many grandchildren.

Ilissa stared as a Sister led a horse from the stable. It was not the usual dappled gray of a Sayer's mount, but pure white, with pinkish eyes. The Mistress noticed her surprise.

"We purchased this one from a farmer. We did not want even your mount to betray your identity."

Ilissa nodded with the obedience she had learned over the past two years, and swung into the sidesaddle. She adjusted her lyre behind her. She was to proclaim to be a Singer, if any asked. Her lovely voice would lend credence to that explanation.

The High Mistress looked up at the dainty figure perched on the pink-eyed palfrey, and sighed. The white frock, cunningly gathered under Ilissa's breasts to give the illusion of fullness, was only a shade lighter than the skin above it. Waves of black hair tumbled out of the hood of the deep blue cloak and cascaded forward over her shoulders, contrasting vividly with the pale skin and murky blue eyes. The slight girl sat erect in the sidesaddle, with a grace that only the higher-born ever accomplished on a horse.

"You look like the lady of a castle, Ilissa. No doubt that is what your mother wished for you."

Ilissa nodded. "That is why I came here."

Sword Sister

"Was that your only reason for becoming a Sayer?"

"No, Mistress. There were also the dreams — dreams of sorrow and suffering. I wanted to prevent them from coming true."

Satisfied, the High Mistress nodded. Her voice took on the tone she used for conducting a schoolroom test as she asked, "Can you See where you are going?"

The head of black hair tilted back, and the blue-violet eyes searched through time and space. "Fenfall," she answered.

"Good. And the one you seek? Will you know her?"

Ilissa looked again. The image was clear, if strange, and she nodded. "I will know her."

"Good. Be on your way, then, and may the Unknowns go with you."

As Ilissa guided her palfrey down the wooded trail, the High Mistress nodded in satisfaction. *Aye, I chose well, with that one,* she thought. *She is definitely gifted.*

The High Mistress of Neston turned back to her duties, fervently hoping that being gifted would suffice for what Ilissa faced ahead.

※◉※

Tudae rode through gentle hills, dotted with farms and pastures, divided by streams and strips of forest. These were the Lordless Lands, occupied by farmers who owned their own fields and expected the Sisters of the Sword to protect them and keep the peace.

The farmers greeted her from their fields, waved at her from their barns. As she passed through a hamlet the village elder stopped her to discuss this year's taxation.

"Looks like a good year for apples," the old man said, squinting up at the Sword Mistress. "Should be able to send two cartloads this year. We'll be sending a yearling calf, soon as we do the spring slaughtering. Five new babes born over the winter." He stuck out his thin chest and gave Tudae a gap-toothed grin. "Two of them my grandchildren."

"Congratulations, Jarel. Your line always produces strong children — and many of them!"

"Seven children, nineteen grandchildren," Jarel agreed. "All of them healthy as oxen. Only lost two to Morg raids — if ye count the babe who weren't born yet." Jarel spat on the road, his watery eyes turning hard. "Curse yon sorcerer, anyway! Why would he take a woman with child?"

"I don't know, Jarel." Tudae shifted in her saddle. The subject brought up unpleasant memories, and more unpleasant unanswered questions. *Why, indeed? Why was Mammae...?* No need to think about that now. No need to give Jarel ideas about what might have befallen his daughter-in-law and his unborn grandchild.

"Merig remarried, anyhow," Jarel continued. "One of those babes born last snow was his. More children, more taxes." Jarel gave Tudae a wry smile. "We'll send that calf soon, Sword Mistress."

Tudae thanked him, and rode on.

More children. Since Sword Sisters were paid per head of the people they protected, that would mean more taxes. Of course, that meant they would need more Sword Sisters to protect those heads — Tudae sighed. There were few enough recruits these days, when joining the Sisters of the Sword meant almost certain violent death. Castle Shield's barracks stood half empty now, between the shortage of recruits and the battle losses of the past years.

The sun was high when she sighted Castle Shield. It rose up out of a large field, a construction of boulders so huge that they appeared to have been placed by the hands of a giant. Rumor held that the stones of the castle were actually placed by Sayers, herded across the field by gray-robed women in the long ago days when the Order could supposedly command the natural forces of the world as well as the natural forces inside of people.

Tudae didn't know how the castle was built, nor did she care. The squat, square structure had stood for centuries, an island of lawfulness in what was once a world of chaos. The bandits and armies of once-warring lords no longer ravaged the countryside, and the moat that had been the castle's first line of defense now sported rushes in its stagnant waters. The heavy drawbridge was always down, welcoming visitors rather than repelling intruders.

Never in the memory of the oldest grandmother had the castle been assaulted. According to the Sayers, the last assault on Castle Shield occurred in the Year Before Aria, 202. Castle Shield was safe, even if it wasn't pretty.

Castle Shield was definitely not pretty. It had no soaring turrets, no graceful archways like Castle Fenkeep. No gaily-colored banners flew above its battlements, bearing the insignia of a resident lord. Only the huge black shield above the gate bore any insignia at all, and that was the emblem of the Lady of the Sword.

History claimed that First Sword Mistress Aragwen received a visitation from the Lady, who instructed her to take up the sword to defend the land and its people and to encourage other women to do likewise. Aragwen used her dowry to have a sword forged, a sword fashioned with a woman in the hilt. With that sword Aragwen helped drive bandits and Morgs from the land, and she founded the Sisterhood of the Sword. That sword now hung in the great hall of Castle Shield, and was only used for swearing in new Sword Mistresses.

Sword Mistresses were always chosen from Sisters who excelled in swordplay. Such excellence was called being "blessed by the Lady of the Sword."

Tudae was so blessed, and her head proved it. Every hair was fashioned in tiny braids and every braid signified a victory in combat.

Because of the "blessing" she had been chosen to be Sword Mistress. Because of that, and Iskara.

Wendy Jensen

Chapter Twelve

That no children shall they bear...
From "Song of the Sword Sisters"

Year After Aria, 285

Peasant Year of Defeat

Eighteen years ago...

"It should be you, Tudae."

Tudae stared at her quartermate, her left hand massaging the dark skin of her right.

"Me? Why me?"

Iskara shrugged one shoulder, raised one eyebrow. "You're good. 'Blessed by the Lady of the Sword', as they say."

"So are you!"

"Yes, I know." Iskara's sword did a pirouette in the air, the spinning hilt landing in her palm with a faint smack.

Tudae winced. Her own sword hand was bruised from hours of battering against Morg bodies. She clenched and unclenched her fingers. The numbing ache that radiated up her arm seemed to encompass her soul.

"Better than you, actually." Iskara feinted and

parried, her sword weaving air patterns that Tudae knew by heart but her eye couldn't follow.

"You can't prove that! You've never—"

The point of the sword swished under her chin. Instinct threw Tudae against the rough stone wall and sent her aching right hand groping for her own sword. It lay out of reach on her bed next to the cleaning cloth.

"Never what? Beaten you? What do you call this?"

The full lower lip curled outward from Tudae's face, and her black eyes narrowed. "I call it unfair."

"Exactly." Iskara slid her sword, already cleaned and polished, into its sheath. "That's why it should be you. When have I ever cared what was fair?"

When indeed? Certainly not during practice, when Iskara was never above feigning a turned ankle, only to redouble her attack when Tudae gave her breathing space. Nor in the local taverns where Tudae's flagon mysteriously emptied twice as quickly as Iskara's, where Iskara would woo away any swain who smiled at Tudae, whispering in Tudae's ear that she, Iskara, had been pining for this man for a fortnight. Not that Tudae ever noticed Iskara pining. The longed-for man would always be forgotten in a week, and Iskara's gaze would shift to the next man who looked in Tudae's direction.

Which was why Tudae never mentioned Roagen, never looked at him when Iskara pulled leave in Fenfall with her. He might think her cold and fickle, but that was better than having Iskara warm his mattress.

"Besides," Iskara unbuckled her sword belt and threw it on a hook, "I might want to get married someday."

Tudae laughed — her first laugh since this day began. "You? Married?"

Her amused glance slid down Iskara's blood-stained mail. It was all Morg blood; neither of them had been wounded in today's battle. On the ride home Tudae had glanced back at the carts full of the severely injured, at the lines of still mounted Sisters sporting minor wounds.

"You and I were fortunate today, Iskara," Tudae had

said.

Iskara had laughed. "No, Tudae. We were skillful."

Fortunate or skillful, neither of them had taken wounds. Tudae's mind flickered to the hall below, where Erystra tended Sisters less fortunate or skillful.

Outside, on beds of firewood, lay the Sisters who were extremely unfortunate. On the largest bed lay the body of Akrien.

Sighing, Tudae picked up her cleaning cloth. It was best not to dwell on it.

"Oh, you never know." Iskara stretched on her bed. "After all, there is the Lord of Fenfall's son. Roagen, isn't that his name? Can't you see me as Lady of Fenfall? Mistress of my own castle?"

Tudae's nostrils flared as she glared at her quartermate. "The Sword Mistress is Mistress of her own castle — Castle Shield!"

"But the Sword Mistress may not marry." The bantering tone was gone. Iskara's face was grave, and her voice was somber.

Tudae chipped dried Morg blood off her sword hilt.

"Or bear children." Iskara grinned.

Tudae thanked the Lady that Morgs were more predictable than Iskara's moods. So was the wind, for that matter.

"Can't you see me with a little one in my arms, changing its cloths, singing it lullabies—"

"No. I can't."

"Come now, Tudae! I could bear Roagen a fine child! A son, I think. I could teach him swordplay, make him into a great warrior—"

"I can't see you as a mother, Iskara."

"I can. I do." Iskara's head tilted back, her brown eyes dreamy. "And I See you as Sword Mistress."

"That only works on the new Sisters, Iskara. I know better."

Iskara did an impressive Sayer imitation, but it was only an imitation. Granddaughter of Erystra, yes; taught at Neston, yes; gifted with Sight, no. Only because she was clever were her predictions so often right.

In one thing she was right again — the Sword Mistress could not marry. Sword Sisters could choose to leave, but the Sword Mistress was sworn for life. That thought left a cold feeling in Tudae's gut.

Tudae gauged the light seeping through the shutters, and sheathed her cleaned sword. "We should bathe. It's dusk already. The pyre-lighting will be soon."

Iskara uncoiled from the bed and slid her grimy chain mail over her head in one fluid motion. Tudae winced as she shed her own mail. Every muscle ached, including some she swore were new to her anatomy. From the lavender light of dawn to the slanting afternoon rays of the sun they had fought Morgs. Today's battle was the longest in Tudae's memory.

"And after the pyres burn will be the Choosing. Sword Mistress out, Sword Mistress in." Iskara's fingers flew over the lacings on her leathers.

No doubt she wants to dirty the water first, Tudae thought. "They will choose you, Iskara."

Everyone always chose Iskara. Iskara was served first in the taverns, Iskara was asked for the first dance. It was Iskara who the new girls quarreled to practice with, then took defeat at her hands with a flush of pride. It was Iskara, charming and beautiful in her chain mail, that the village children threw flowers at and the farmers and their wives bowed and curtsied to. It was even Iskara who earlier today rallied the scattered Sisters in a final charge to save the Sword Mistress.

Too late, to be sure, but who could have foreseen the deadly accuracy of the Morgs' spearhead attack straight to the Sword Mistress' position? *Who would have thought they could be so disciplined?*

"They aren't usually so organized." Words and scenes echoed from Tudae's memory: the cart overturned, Mammae's gutted corpse, Tomo's eyes forever staring. *At the edge of the woods, a tall man....*

"What a fate." The irony in Iskara's voice jolted

Tudae; her quartermate was stepping into the wooden tub. "Being Sword Mistress. Fated to worry, and plan, and — be fair!"

Iskara dumped the first bucket of water over her hair, gasping as it ran down her bare body. "You know I make my own fate, Tudae. I'll never be Fate's toy."

Tudae shivered as she slipped out of her leathers. Anticipation of her own cold bath, no doubt. But why did her empty stomach feel like she had swallowed stones, and why did that Sayer's phrase keep running through her mind?

How did Erystra word it?

"The Unknowns use those who least expect it."

⁊◉⁋

They chose Iskara. It was almost unanimous. When the wooden chips were tallied, only one did not say Iskara.

Mira, who had been second-in-command, raised her graying head from the counting to address the lines of Sisters standing at attention in the great hall.

She looks tired, Tudae thought. *Tired and beaten.*

She and the Sword Mistress had been close. The loss of her leader and best friend had taken its toll. Mira made it plain before the Choosing that she would not accept the position of Sword Mistress. *The Sisters need someone younger,* she said. *Someone with fire and enthusiasm to lead the Sisters against Necimus.*

Tudae thought it more likely that Mira did not intend to live much longer. She had seen that look in older Sisters' eyes before. A look that said they were tired of the fight and only wished to ride one last time into a battle — a battle from which they did not intend to return.

Whatever the reason, Mira's description of a young Sword Mistress, full of life and vigor, brought a murmur of approval from the ranks. As the Sisters bent to mark their chips, Tudae knew who they had in mind.

Who was more filled with fire and enthusiasm than Iskara? And Iskara could lead — lead the Sisters straight into the heart of Castle Darkfall if she wished. They would follow her, never questioning. Tudae marked her chip with Iskara's name, and dropped it into the bucket.

"It is done." Mira's weary voice carried through the hall. "The Sword Mistress has been chosen. Iskara, come forth and accept the sword."

The great hall filled with cheers as Iskara stepped out of the ranks and approached Mira. The cheering faltered and died as Iskara stood before Mira, making no move to take the outstretched sword with its woman-shaped hilt. Iskara looked at the sword, and shook her head.

"Sisters!" Iskara's voice silenced the murmurs. "This is a great honor, but I cannot accept it." Her hand raised as the murmurs started again. "Mira is right, we need a young Sword Mistress. But there is more to being Sword Mistress than just leading troops. A Sword Mistress needs more than just fire and enthusiasm. She must also be responsible." Iskara's mouth twisted, one corner lower than the other. "I ask you, am I responsible? By the way, who groomed my horse today?"

Laughter answered her, and even Tudae smiled. Who hadn't been left to groom Iskara's horse at one time or another? Or convinced to clean her mail for her, or to take her place on scrubbing detail? No, Iskara was not responsible, and all the Sisters knew it. Still, it was unlike Iskara to admit a fault, and Tudae had an uneasy feeling about her doing it now.

"So, I am not the best choice for Sword Mistress. But surely I was not the only choice. Mira, who else was chosen?"

Mira's hand went to the one chip lying to the side, and turned it over. "Tudae."

The heavy feeling in Tudae's stomach solidified into a knot.

"Tudae?" Iskara sounded faintly surprised, but Tudae saw her raised eyebrows, her pursed lips. Tudae had seen that look before. She had seen it over the last game of cards that Iskara played with the soldiers in Fenfall, the game she where she won the dawnstone necklace. Iskara was winning again, and she knew it.

"Tudae is a good choice. She has fire and determination, and she is responsible. And she is blessed by the Lady. I haven't even beaten her — yet."

More laughter. Iskara was playing the Sisters like she played a crowd in the tavern, like she played the men that fell over themselves for her. Iskara could play people like a Singer played a harp.

"I say we Choose Tudae to be Sword Mistress. I would be honored to be her second-in-command — if she will have me, that is."

The hall erupted in cheers. Tudae felt certain the cheers were more because Iskara would be second than because Tudae would be Sword Mistress. They could still follow Iskara into battle, and Iskara would have none of the tiresome duties of Sword Mistress. Iskara had taken the best for herself — again.

Mira raised the sword again. "Tudae, come forth and accept the sword."

The silence was suffocating. Every Sister's head turned in her direction. Every eye watched and waited. Tudae wanted to run — run out of Castle Shield and away to Fenfall, to throw herself in Roagen's arms.

Tudae closed her eyes and her nostrils filled with the familiar scent of oiled chain mail. Once that smell had been strange, as she had clenched her fingers in the front of a Sister's mail, and made a promise to herself.

"I will never run away again."

Her legs were moving, carrying her forward past rows of watching Sisters. There were no cheers now, only silence. Ahead of her Iskara waited, and Mira with the sword outstretched.

As her fingers closed around the Lady fashioned into the hilt, Tudae heard Mira saying the words, heard herself repeating them.

"...to lead the Sisterhood of the Sword, to protect and

keep safe the people of this land...."

The metal was cold beneath her hand. As cold as her heart, as cold as her reality.

"...married only to steel, to bear arms instead of children...."

Iskara stood beside her, dark eyes burning into Tudae's head, into her heart, into her soul.

"...for as long as I can wield a sword."

"Sword Mistress?" Lord Greoff's voice was a sputter, his expression incredulous. "You? You are replacing Akrien? Why — why, you're scarcely more than a child!"

"She is as old as I am, Father."

Tudae had avoided meeting Roagen's eyes since she entered Castle Fenfall and she avoided them still. It was easier to face the disbelief in Lord Greoff's face than the pain in that of his son.

"As I said, scarcely more than a child. Are the Sisters so short of choices that they must choose children to lead them?"

Iskara's voice was hard. "Tudae is very good, my lord."

Strange, that Iskara would defend her now. But then, everything Iskara had done recently was strange. Again, Tudae thanked the Lady that Morgs were more predictable than Iskara. If only Necimus was as predictable, they might have a chance against him.

"Humf!"

"She's *very* good." Iskara's voice grew harder. "She defeats me at swordplay, every time. I believe," Tudae heard a touch of humor, "she defeats your son as well. They frequently practice swordplay, among other things."

Lady, silence her! Tudae glanced sideways at her Sword Sister. Iskara was grinning, her hands resting lightly on her sword hilt. Tudae straightened her back a little more, a dull ache creeping from her neck to her shoulders.

"It is true, Father. Tudae is exceptional."

For the first time Tudae risked a glance at Roagen. He was regarding Iskara gravely. His expression was sad rather than angry. Tudae ignored the sudden thump in her chest and returned her attention to Lord Greoff.

The old man stared at her quizzically, his gray eyebrows scrunching above piercing eyes.

"Well." The old lord's voice turned thoughtful. "A compliment from my son is a compliment indeed."

Lord Greoff motioned, and a servant came forward with goblets. "We must drink to the new Sword Mistress, of course." He hoisted the first goblet, and waited until his guests had been served.

"To the Sword Mistress, then. Long life, good health, and victory in battle!"

Voices around her repeated the toast, but Tudae heard only one voice, felt only one pair of eyes on her above the rim of the chalice. The future lord of Fenfall's eyes finally met hers.

"To the Sword Mistress."

⊰◉⊱

"We should have sent the troops she asked for, Father."

"Eh?" Lord Greoff squinted at his son. "We? Who is we?"

Roagen flushed. *Leave it to Father to make me feel like a child,* he thought. *Right on the heels of treating Tudae like a child as well.*

"You don't rule Fenfall yet, boy."

"Nor shall I for many years, the Unknowns willing."

"Humpf! Unknowns, is it now? You sound more like a Sayer than a soldier, son. But then," Lord Greoff scowled, "what can I expect from a boy who lets a girl best him at swordplay?"

"Tudae is very good with a sword, Father. And I'm not a boy anymore. Nor is she a girl."

"Humpf. Bedding that dark beauty doesn't make you a man, son, nor does it make her a woman. Akrien — now there was a woman! Damn fine Sword Mistress, too." Lord Greoff leaned back in his chair, emptied his goblet, and motioned a servant to refill it. "I'm going to miss her."

"Of course you are, Father." Roagen's mouth twisted. Lord Greoff's dalliance with the former Sword Mistress was well known. Roagen knew that a dalliance was all it was. Perhaps it was the shock of losing his own love in such an unexpected fashion that made him add, "There are still tavern maids aplenty in Fenfall."

"Tavern maids, humpf." If Lord Greoff noticed the bitterness in his son's voice he did not mention it. "Empty headed lot, those. I'd stay away from them, if I were you. Next thing you know, they'll be claiming a bastard on you and it like as not sired by the guardsman who was there before you. Only an hour before you, at that." The coarse joke made Roagen wince, but his father was serious. "No, tavern maids are good enough for the men-at-arms, but the Lord of Fenfall has to watch himself. Can't be spreading bastards around, real or imagined."

"Which is why you bedded Akrien."

"Well, she did take the oath not to marry, or bear children. Good choice for a widower like me. Never whined about needing a ring and a title, and wasn't going to be bringing me a bastard. Of course, she was a mite old to be having children. As am I." Lord Greoff sighed, and motioned a servant to fill his goblet.

Leave it to Father to be practical, Roagen thought bitterly. *Had he ever known the grip of love?* Not that Roagen could tell. No mention of loving Akrien, or desiring her companionship. Just the practical considerations of no marriage and no bastards. The subject of marriage and Sword Mistresses was a sore one with him right now, so Roagen switched the conversation back to military matters.

"We— You should have sent the troops."

"Eh? Still thinking on that, are you?" The shaggy gray head shook slowly. "No, son. My troops are to guard my land, and they are paid with my taxes. The Sisters guard the Lordless Lands, and collect their own taxes to do it. How would my townsfolk feel, knowing their tax moneys were paying my men to do the Sisters' job?"

"They won't object if it saves them from the fate of Dawnfall."

"Dawnfall's fate is sealed, son. Nothing we can do about it now."

"We could help the Sisters take it back."

"And do what with it? Lord Langtry is dead by now, and his sons with him. Who would rule Dawnfall now? If I had a second son, it might be different Roagen, but I have only you. And Fenfall is plenty enough for you to rule, trust me. I've been doing it for two dozen years."

"And you will do it for many years more, the Unknowns—"

"Yes, I know, the Unknowns willing!" Lord Greoff slammed his goblet on his chair. Wine sloshed across his lap. "Damn it, son, you remind me of your mother sometimes!"

According to the servants, he could do worse, but now wasn't the time to mention that to his father. Doggedly, Roagen steered the conversation back to Tudae's — *no, the Sword Mistress'* — how that thought irked him! — request.

"What if this new wizard," — *what was his name?* The scouts had brought word from peasants who survived the attack — "Necimus."

The name had a vile taste in Roagen's mouth; the scouts also brought descriptions of the atrocities committed on those peasants, and an estimate of how many infants would be slaughtered nine months from now. Peasants never allowed half-Morgs to live.

"What if Necimus isn't content with just taking Dawnfall? What if he tries to take Fenfall as well?"

"Then we'll deal with him then. He'll have to come through the Sword Sisters first, then through the fens or across the land bridge. You forget, Roagen, Fenfall has excellent natural defenses."

"And you forget, Father, that Dawnfall also had excellent natural defenses."

"Hmm... yes. Still does, too. That is part of the problem. The Sisters will never take back that rock Castle Dawnfall sits on, with or without my troops. Why waste the lives of my men on a lost cause?"

Because if we don't stop Necimus now, we may never stop him, Roagen thought, but his father was still talking.

"...and he uses magic. The soldiers don't mind fighting Morgs — well, normal Morgs. But these Morgs are different. Never heard of a Morg fighting in formation before, and there's magic behind that, mark my words. My men don't like going up against magic."

"Then perhaps it is time we used magic, too, Father."

"Heh? Hire a magician? Different thought, that. We Fenkeeps have never had a magician in our ranks since..." Lord Greoff thought a minute. "Well, since never. Townsfolk wouldn't like it; taxes would go up. Magicians are expensive, son. Aren't any magicians to be had in these parts, anyway."

"There was one last fortnight, Father. Looking for work. His name was Balek."

"What, that weasely faced man? You must be joking. I wouldn't trust that one to magic my chamber pot to keep it from stinking. He left, anyway. Went north, I heard."

"I'll ride north. Maybe I can find him. Who knows, maybe the Sisters would hire him, since you won't."

"The Sisters have no dealings with magic either, Roagen."

"They deal with Sayers!"

"Sayers aren't magicians and Sayers are all women.

Balek is a man — of sorts — and the Sisters don't allow men to sleep inside the walls of Castle Shield."

"Then I'll camp outside the walls." The last phrase was muttered, but Lord Greoff heard it. Roagen cursed his luck as the gray eyebrows shot up.

"So that's it, is it? More interested in seeing that dark-skinned little Sword Mistress again than you are in finding the magician?"

"No reason I can't kill two quail with one arrow."

His father laughed. "Only if they are lined up properly, son. And speaking of proper — I'd leave the Sword Mistress alone, if I was you."

"You should have taken your own advice years ago, Father."

"Akrien was different! I am an old man now, with no need of wife or children. A Sword Mistress will neither be your wife nor bear your children. I would have married you to one of Langtry's daughters, when they were old enough, but now..." Lord Greoff shook his head sadly. "Leave the Sword Mistress alone, and look for a wife. The Lord of Fenfall will need a wife and children to continue the line of Fenkeeps."

Roagen swung his cloak around his shoulders, and turned to face the older man.

"But as you have said, Father, I am not Lord of Fenfall yet."

⁃⃝⃪

Tudae and Iskara were sitting in the study when a Sword Sister poked her head in the door. "Roagen Fenkeep, of Fenfall."

Tudae's stomach knotted at the Sister's announcement. Iskara arched one dark eyebrow, and muttered "So soon?" but she didn't move from her seat.

As Roagen stepped through the door of the study, Tudae rose to her feet. Her back was straight, her head high, but there was a suspicious wobbling around her knees that she hoped neither her second-in-command or her former lover would notice.

"Sword Mistress." Roagen bowed formally.

Tudae closed her eyes momentarily to shut out the sight. *Was this all it would be now? Was this the end to the long afternoons spent "patrolling" the edges of the fens?*

Tudae stifled a sigh, then opened her eyes to find Roagen regarding her gravely. Iskara seemed to have a hangnail. The tip of one finger was absorbing all her attention.

"Castle Shield welcomes the Lord of Fenfall's son." The formal greeting nearly choked Tudae, but she continued resolutely. "Your father has reconsidered my request for troops?"

"No."

The answer was blunt. Tudae noticed the tightening of Roagen's lips. He didn't approve of his father's decision, but Tudae could have guessed that.

What had he promised her, as they lay in the long grass together, their horses cropping the shorter grass nearby? Anything she wanted. *A wedding ring, his future title, fine horses, silk dresses....*

Tudae had laughed. Fighting leathers and the once-strange chain mail were like a second skin to her now, and she could no more see herself in a silk dress than she could see Roagen in one.

And his undying love. He had promised her that, too, as the day waned and The Guardian's distant peak turned lavender. All she had to do was leave the Sisterhood of the Sword, and become his wife. Tudae had whispered that they were both young yet, but she would consider it.

No doubt Roagen thought that this was the result of her consideration; that his offer of love could not compare with the prestige and power of being Sword Mistress.

Prestige and power! Tudae thought bitterly. Problems and perils were more like it. Already they beset her on every side: how to win recruits in a Morg-ravaged land, how to glean tribute to equip the Sisterhood from that same land as word of the Sister's defeat at the hands of Necimus spread ripples of dissent through the peasantry, and above all, how to win back Castle Dawnfall and the Sisterhood's honor.

Those were her problems now, not Roagen's. His problem was to forget her and find some one else to call his wife. Against her heart, Tudae hoped his problem would be more easily solved than hers.

"Tu— Sword Mistress, I come seeking a man called Balek, a magician who possibly passed this way. Have you seen him?"

Tudae shook her head, disappointed and relieved that Roagen hadn't come to see her. "No. He didn't stop here."

"Would any of your patrols have seen him, do you think?"

"I can ask." Iskara unhooked her leg from the arm of her chair, and grinned at Tudae. "I'm sure the Sword Mistress doesn't need me here to... ah... entertain Lord Greoff's son."

Tudae felt heat slide up her face. She stared at the floor, cursing Iskara's tongue and thanking the Lady for her own dark skin that would hide her blush.

When the door closed behind Iskara, Tudae raised her eyes to Roagen's and immediately wished she hadn't. The sorrow she saw there mirrored her own.

"Wine?" Tudae didn't wait for Roagen's nod. The wine was a good excuse, a chance to turn her back and avoid those hurting eyes.

How could she battle Morgs undaunted and yet her hand shook while pouring wine? The bottle clattered against the goblet's lip even as Tudae tried to steady it with both hands.

Roagen's hands covered hers, his arms coming around her from behind. Tudae felt his breath on her neck, his body behind her. Her entire body shook. Roagen gently guided the wine bottle down to the table and pulled her around.

His lips were on hers, a soft and surprising contrast to the hard muscles of his arms, pulling her tighter to his chest until their bodies must surely be one. There was no study around them, no Sisters, no Morgs, no Necimus. Only Roagen's closeness held any meaning.

The study door opened, and shut immediately. As Roagen pulled away from her, Tudae heard Iskara's voice in the hall.

"Been her quartermate so long, I forget I'm supposed to knock now! Guess I'd better observe proprieties, huh?" There was a murmured assent outside, then a knock.

"Enter." Tudae seized the goblets, and handed one to Roagen as Iskara and another Sister stepped through the door.

"You asked about a wizard named Balek." Iskara's voice was smooth. Nothing indicated that she had just caught the Sword Mistress in a lovers' embrace. "Orien, here, thinks she saw him."

The other Sister nodded. "Black-robed little man, with a weasely face?"

Roagen smiled wryly. *Father's description, too.* "That would be Balek."

"Seen him almost a fortnight ago, while evacuating peasants. He was on the road to Castle Dawnfall. Told him about the problems up there, told him he shouldn't go north."

A fortnight ago. He could be anywhere by now, Roagen realized. "Which way did he go?"

Orien frowned, thinking. "Why, I believe he went north."

Chapter Thirteen

That they shall be married only to steel....
From "Song of the Sword Sisters"

Year After Aria, 303

The hooves of Tudae's horse echoed on the drawbridge as she passed into the castle that housed those duties and had been her home for twenty-four years. A burly trainee grasped the horse's reins. "G'day, Sword Mistress. Daena would speak with you."

As she dismounted Tudae glanced at the familiar head of blonde hair on the exercise ground. "Tell her I will be in my study."

A few minutes later a sturdy girl with three small blonde braids sat across from the Sword Mistress's desk. Tudae glanced with approval at the girl's sweat-stained leathers.

"We should have a bout ourselves, Daena. It has been a while."

Daena grinned. "Certainly, Sword Mistress. I can always use another lesson in defeat."

Tudae dropped the meat requisition forms she had been perusing. "You returned from patrol last night."

"Aye."

"And the borders? Are they safe?"

"As safe as can be expected, with His Ugliness controlling the lands beyond."

Daena was a good scout, too good to request an audience just to report that the borders were reasonably safe. "And?"

"Last night we supped at the Lamb Chop Inn. There was a black-robed magic-caster there, with a big warrior. When they left I got a whiff of something as the warrior passed by. Smelled like a Morg."

"Half-Morg?"

Daena shrugged. "He was about the size for one, but he looked human."

"Appearances can be changed with magic. I've seen it done." Tudae frowned. *Of course, that had been with the gates, inanimate objects. Could it be done with a living creature?* Tudae didn't know, but she wouldn't put anything past Necimus. And Daena had said there was a magic-caster, too.

"The magic-caster. Was it Balek?"

Daena shrugged again. "I've never seen him, Mistress. That was before my time."

True. Balek had joined Necimus shortly after the fall of Castle Dawnfall, and hadn't been seen in Fenfall since. And that was well before Daena joined the Sisters; she would have been scarcely out of cloths when it happened.

"Was he small, scraggly-haired, with a clever, cowardly face?"

Daena nodded. "Aye."

Tudae scowled at her desk. It was Balek. And who else would Balek keep company with, if not a half-Morg? *How did they get across the land bridge and past Roagen's guards? Magic, again?* The two of them, walking the streets of Fenfall like common folk. The possible consequences made Tudae shudder. "I'll speak to Roagen about this."

Daena was waiting.

Tudae looked up. "There's more?"

Sword Sister

"Aye. There was girl at the inn, working there. Someone new. A big girl, full head and shoulders taller than I. With a build like that, she might make a good Sister."

"Who is she?"

Daena shrugged. "I don't know, but they called her by a very strange name. Skurgiil. I've never heard that name before."

Skurgiil. Tudae let out her breath slowly, one hand crawling up to rub her neck.

"I have heard it." *Years ago. How many, now? Sixteen? Seventeen?*

Tudae had first seen that name scrawled in birth blood across the belly of wailing infant girl. Since that time, Tudae had steadfastly put the name from her mind, lest an unwary thought or an unfettered dream fall in the path of Necimus' angry search. For seventeen years, Tudae had buried sorrow and hope together, waiting for the help they so desperately needed.

Daena's voice cut through the memories. "Who is she?"

"She is Iskara's daughter."

Daena frowned, trying to remember the history of the Sword Sisters. "But — Iskara died at Castle Darkfall!"

"Yes. Died giving birth to a girl baby, who she named Skurgiil."

Comprehension and horror dawned on Daena's face. "But that means that her father is...."

"Yes." Tudae frowned. And two of Necimus' minions were at the same inn as the girl. Even if Erystra's presence still guarded her from search by magic, it would not protect her from simple eye contact.

"What shall we do, Mistress?"

"We shall bring her in."

⊰◉⊱

As the four sword sisters dismounted in front of the Lamb Chop Inn, Tudae's dark eyes scanned the building with practiced care. Nothing seemed amiss, but there was no sense in taking chances. If magic had gotten Balek and a half-Morg into Fenfall once, it could do it again.

"Go through the back," she instructed the others. Daena nodded, and she and the other two slipped around the side of the building.

Tudae breathed a prayer asking the Lady of the Sword to protect her own and stepped into the inn.

"Sword Mistress!" Doane stepped out from behind the bar, smiling broadly. "It has been long since you graced my establishment with your presence. What would you like today? A cup of wine? A meal?"

Tudae shook her head, ignoring the proprietor's appraising eyes sliding over the curves of her chain mail. The inn was empty, quiet.

"No, Doane. I'm here on business."

"Business, Mistress? All has been peaceful here. We haven't even had a brawl for..." Doane thought a minute, "Three nights now."

"I'm not here about brawls, Doane. I'm here about the new girl you hired."

"Skurgiil? Why, Mistress, I just gave her a job because she was hungry, I had no idea..."

"Enough, Doane. I'm sure your motives were... ah... commendable. I just want to talk to her."

"Certainly, Mistress, certainly. She's out back." Doane gestured towards the kitchen.

Tudae was halfway to the kitchen door when Melyssa screamed.

⚜👁⚜

Skurgiil had been chopping wood for half the morning, and showed no signs of tiring when Melyssa last glanced out of the kitchen. Melyssa shook her head admiringly at the split wood that was piling up around Skurgiil, and returned to her cooking.

Daena's thoughts were not so flattering. She saw a very large, muscular girl wielding a heavy axe. The memory of Skurgiil's parentage fresh in her mind, Daena drew her sword. The other two Sword Sisters did the same.

Skurgiil glanced up from chopping a tree limb to see three armored women advancing on her. The first one she recognized as the blonde girl who had smiled at her the night before.

She was not smiling now. Her blue eyes were as cold as the yard of sharpened steel she held in her hand.

Skurgiil shifted in mid-swing, her axe crashing into the blonde woman's shield instead of the tree limb. It was a move that felled a mountain wolf, one hard winter when the starving animals came into the valley looking for food.

Daena staggered under the blow. Skurgiil swung the branch she had been chopping, sending the sword of one woman flying through the air and leaving the other one clutching her wrist.

At the first clash of metal Tudae drew her sword and ran through the kitchen. As she passed the screaming cook, Tudae saw Skurgiil leap over a heap of firewood and turn to face her attackers.

Definitely Iskara's daughter. Even within the overgrown form she inherited from her father, Tudae could see the familiar grace of her former sword sister. Muscles rippled down Skurgiil's arm as she raised the axe for another swing. From the kitchen door Tudae called out, "Halt!"

The three sword sisters stopped their advance and Skurgiil paused, the axe held effortlessly in mid-air.

"What is the meaning of this?" Tudae demanded.

"She was armed, Mistress." Daena's face was sullen.

"Do you attack every woodcutter you come across, just because they carry an axe?"

"But, Mistress, you said—"

"I said to bring her in, not kill her." Tudae looked at Skurgiil. "Put the axe down, girl."

Skurgiil stared at the woman with skin the color of overbaked bread. "Who — what are you?"

"Ignorant girl!" Doane stepped out of the kitched. "She's the Sword Mistress! Do as she says!" Behind him Melyssa's head bobbed rapidly, her eyes wide with terror.

Tudae stepped into the yard and stood before Skurgiil. "I was also your mother's friend."

The axe dropped. The blade sank into the log, but Skurgiil kept her hand on the quivering handle. "You knew my mother?"

"Yes, very well. We were Sword Sisters. That is her necklace you are wearing."

The dawnstone glowed briefly. Daena gasped. The other two Sword Sisters exchanged glances.

Best to get her out of public view, Tudae decided. "Skurgiil, why don't you come with us to Castle Shield?"

Skurgiil considered this. *'Go, and fulfill your destiny,'* Erystra had said. Surely discovering her mother's past would be a step in the right direction. This woman said they were friends. Surely the Good Mother would approve.

"I'll get my bedroll." Skurgiil ducked through the kitchen door.

As she came back down the stairs Doane cleared his throat. In his outstretched hand were three copper pieces. "You didn't work the full week," he muttered gruffly.

Skurgiil fingered her first wages while Melyssa hugged her around the waist.

"Take care, girl," she whispered.

As Skurgiil fell in step beside the Sword Sister's horses, Doane gave Melyssa's shoulder a comforting pat.

"She was a good worker," he commented thoughtfully. "Perhaps she will be good at other things, too."

Melyssa knew that for once he was not speaking about things in the bedchamber.

⇥◉⇤

Balek stood in the hallway, fiddling with his

Medallion of Protection Against Magical Attack and trying to compose his thoughts before he entered his lord's presence.

The time spent trying to find a real or imagined threat to His Evilness while also trying to control that idiot half-breed Kurg had taken their toll on the wizard. Last night had been particularly harrowing.

With his mind preoccupied with the girl, Balek had left Kurg to do as he pleased at the border farm. Balek had waited outside, concentrating on the sound of his mount crunching sheep bones rather than listen to the sounds coming from inside the cottage. When Kurg finally came out, Balek didn't even ask what he had done.

Balek spent the better part of the day recuperating in his quarters, and searching through some old tomes to verify what he already suspected. He would have to face Necimus sooner or later, and it was better to come voluntarily than to wait for a Summons.

Balek raised his hand, pressing it against the door's polished blackwood surface. As he waited for the door's magic to recognize and admit him, he went over the things he was going to tell His Evilness. The door swung open before his mental list was completed, and Balek stepped into his lord's presence ill prepared and slightly flustered.

The massive head behind the desk inclined once, and Balek sat on a black chair carved in the semblance of a mutilated human. Dark eyes bored into Balek as he rapidly recounted the events of the past few days, saving the worst for last.

"There was a girl, a big girl, very big," Balek stammered. "At an inn. They called her Skurgiil."

When his master did not answer, Balek added diffidently, "In the Old Tongue, that means...."

"I know."

"You do? I mean, of course you do...."

"Skurgiil." Necimus' voice rolled through the room like an invading army. "Skurg i'Il. The Scourge of Evil."

Balek nodded. He had read that translation in a dictionary of the old tongue this morning, and followed it with some painstaking translations of prophecies by an ancient Sayer.

Balek wondered if Necimus was familiar with those, too, but decided this was not the time to ask. His Evilness appeared to be in an ill temper.

"You may go." Balek bowed himself out, and Necimus sank back in his chair, to ponder this new turn of events with the cold detachment he had developed as a child.

Once, in a past so distant he hardly remembered it, Necimus had been sensitive. The taunting cries of *"Bastard!"* from the other children hurt, and he had buried his emotions to escape the pain. That strategy worked so well that Necimus never stopped using it, even after fear of his increasing size silenced the taunts.

Some of the villagers whispered that his sire must have been a true mountain giant. In view of Balek's information, it was a possibility.

Necimus did not know who his father was. His mother, the old witch, had refused to tell him, even when he strangled her to death. What she said as his huge hand tightened around her throat, was that his undoing would be of his own making. Or perhaps she said of his own mating. Necimus couldn't be sure, because her tongue was already swollen and protruding from her ugly mouth.

After she died, Necimus used her magics to bring an unnatural sleep upon the village. Then he visited a certain village girl, waking her so she could feel her punishment for calling him a bastard. And he left her tied to her bed when he set fire to the village, so that none would live who knew he was a bastard.

Mindful of his mother's dying words, Necimus made certain that every creature born of his seed was magic-bound to him at birth, and would obey him throughout its life.

Perhaps because of the early jibes of *"Bastard!"* Necimus took a perverse pleasure in creating bastards of

Sword Sister

his own. Half-Morgs, all, for the human female prisoners he gathered rarely survived the full term of their pregnancies. The few that were brought to the labor bed were incapable of birthing his overgrown offspring; mother and child both died in the attempt.

Except for Iskara. The Dark Lord's deep-set eyes burned with a passion that her memory rekindled.

Beautiful, defiant Iskara, who foolishly thought she could take him with the might of her sword alone. Necimus had defeated her in battle, and again through the long nights she spent chained to his bedpost.

When her belly began to grow Necimus took special care of her, allowing no one else to violate her and satisfying his own desires elsewhere. He wanted that child to survive, hoping for an heir less stupid, less ugly than his Morglings. He would have bound the child to his will with magic, and trained it to follow in his footsteps. He might even have married its stubborn mother, so that no one could cry *"Bastard!"* at his heir.

But she had escaped, the bitch.

Two months before her time she climbed to the tower battlement and gave birth. When Necimus found her she was dead, and the child was nowhere in the castle, though a Morg guard reported an eagle flying away with something the size of a large rabbit in its claws.

Necimus searched for that child. By every means, magic and otherwise, he searched, but in vain. Either the child did not survive, or some power hid it from him.

Was it coincidence that the bones recently indicated an enemy of evil somewhere in the mountains, and the minions sent to find it returned only with a report of an oversized girl named Skurgiil? Necimus doubted it. He, too, was familiar with the ancient prophecies, and it did not sound like coincidence.

A miniature bolt of purple lightning crackled from Necimus' fingertip, striking the globe at the far end of his desk. The globe paled, and in its transparent heart Necimus saw the town of Fenfall.

Rapidly he searched, sorting through the physical

shapes and the gaseous forms of thoughts and dreams. He passed the Lamb Chop Inn, but there was no girl that matched Balek's description, and the proprietor and his cook were so busy with their work that their thoughts held nothing else. When the town yielded nothing he sent his search out in widening circles, paying special heed to the mountains.

The sorcerer was about to abandon the search when he found them.

Four Sisters of the Sword, that hated Order to which Iskara had belonged. Of the four, one was the Sword Mistress herself, and her thoughts were typically controlled and stoic.

But the other three were young and not so disciplined. The blonde one's thoughts were of Skurgiil.

Necimus' eyes glowed. Yes, she was Iskara's daughter. Iskara's, and his.

Necimus chuckled at the anger that thought generated in the blonde Sister's mind. Then his huge forehead creased in a frown, for apparently these Sisters were taking Skurgiil to Castle Shield, yet he could not see her. Puzzled and frustrated by this, Necimus leaned back in his chair, allowing the globe to darken.

His study door opened, and a female half-Morg entered, carrying his supper.

Necimus spared it a glance. Lamb's eye stew. Necimus motioned for her to set it down, but she still lingered. A young one, and apparently in her first heat.

The shorter life spans of Morgs lent themselves well to his genetic experiments. Already he had bred an entire army of half-breeds.

An army that was still an infantry, for horses loathed Morgs. Just the scent of Morg spoor was enough to send an untrained horse into a rearing, snorting panic, and even caused horses trained for war to stomp and sidle unpredictably. Since his Morgs could not ride horses Necimus had trained his soldiers to take out the horses first in any conflict, thereby removing the enemy's advantage of cavalry.

Sword Sister

His experiments with creating mounts of his own were less than successful. Only two of the beasts survived and functioned, and their functioning was incomplete. After years of trying to breed the pair, Necimus realized that his prized hybrids were sterile.

A Sayer could cure that. Those damnable Sayers, with their control of living functions and their prophetic dreams of the future. He hadn't realized how those dreams could destroy his plans, until the day he faced one in Asklain.

It was a small town, isolated in the mountains, calling no one lord. A perfect town for his taking, filled with imbecile peasants, fodder for his Morgs and his magic experiments. A raid at dawn would take it; would fill his larders and cages with specimens. It would be unexpected, and so easy.

But the villagers were prepared. Behind every corner they waited with pitchforks and dogs and burning brands that sent his Morg attackers howling away in pain. In the flaring torchlight, Necimus saw the woman in gray robes, raising her hands and chanting.

Erystra. Necimus learned the name from a captured shepherd, a boy so foolish he slept alone in the hills with his flock. Necimus let the Morgs eat the sheep first, while he questioned the boy.

Erystra was a Sayer, and used a magic that Necimus could not comprehend. Sayers healed, foresaw the future, cured or promoted infertility as needed, brought the babies into and ushered the dead out of life.

Erystra's powers hadn't healed the boy, nor ushered him out of life. Necimus let the Morgs usher the boy out, in pieces, while Necimus pondered the power of Sayers in the midst of the lad's screams.

Erystra's powers hadn't helped Iskara, either, for the spell of infertility that she cast on all the Sword Sisters wore off, and Iskara swelled with his child, just as so many Morgs had before her.

The female half-Morg still hovered by his desk. Necimus sighed.

He was tired of female Morgs, and the half-breeds were only slightly more attractive. That they were his children did not bother Necimus, it was their appearance and stupidity that displeased him. His search into Fenfall reminded him of how exciting human females could be. Of course, he could create a magical form of a human around this Morg.

Necimus gestured for her to stay, as a thought occurred to him. For old times sake, he would give her the form of Iskara.

His Evilness smiled in anticipation.

Chapter Fourteen

Castle Dawnfall lies to the north -
That is not the sun, my child!
  From "Dawn of the Morgs"
  by Wyflen Herdhummer

Year After Aria, 285
Peasant Year of Defeat

Eighteen years earlier...

"We'll take it this time." The voice of the second-in-command of Castle Shield was confident.

But then, Iskara was always confident. Tudae wished she felt as confident; wished even more that the column of Sword Sisters riding behind her felt that confidence. The column rode silently, save for the scuffle of the horses' hooves through brown leaves, and the faces of the women on the horses were as bleak as the autumn sky.

Small wonder. The loss of Akrien brought home to all of them just how mortal they were, and just how difficult the task ahead was.

Castle Dawnfall had been built for defense. Its location alone was a masterpiece of strategy. Rising up on a hill of solid rock, it had no need of a moat. The only attack route was straight through the main gates, and those gates had proven impregnable in the past.

Except for Necimus' troops.

Tudae wondered, again, how this strange wizard, with an army of stupid Morgs, managed to breach the defenses of Castle Dawnfall. That same question was on the lips of every patron of every tavern for miles around. No one knew the answer.

Actually, everyone knew the answer. It was magic, it had to be. The question was: what kind of magic? What kind of magic let a Morg army into an impregnable stronghold?

No one knew. No one except Necimus. As the questions flew, the already suspicious populace developed an even deeper hatred of magic.

"Well, would you look at that!" A low whistle from Iskara drew Tudae up short, and she raised her eyes to Castle Dawnfall.

It towered on the rocky hill, the first wall of defenses followed by another, inner wall, and the central tower jutting like a spearhead from the center. Nothing was different, except the gates.

The gates hung askew. One of them was wrenched nearly off, and two Morgs guarded the gap. A few more patrolled the walls above, but the castle looked very quiet.

Almost deserted.

"Looks like our sorcerer friend has other enemies! Either that, or he had one hell of a housewarming party!"

Iskara's comment brought chuckles from the column behind them, but Tudae shook her head.

It didn't seem right, somehow. Those gates were solid oak, and a foot thick. Tudae had seen them when she covered the backs of the retreating Sisters who carried Akrien's body.

"Nothing could do that to those gates! Nothing short

Sword Sister

of giants."

Iskara arched one eyebrow. "So, perhaps he invited giants to his housewarming party!" Laughter coursed the column again. "Or perhaps his cursed magic finally exploded in his face. Not that it would damage his looks much," Iskara paused for the inevitable chorus of laughter, "but it did a good job on those doors."

"I don't like it, Iskara."

"What is there to not like? Why, he's practically inviting us in. I, for one, am happy to oblige. We can throw him a party, too." Iskara twisted in her saddle. "What do you say, Sisters? Shall we give this wizardly stranger a Sword Sisters' welcome?"

The rousing cheer must have been audible on the castle walls, and the sun glinted off rows of chain mail, but the Morgs on the walls barely moved. No alarm sounded, no troops poured out to man the defenses. Tudae felt her throat constrict, felt the muscles in her neck tighten.

"No!"

The cheers died, and the faces in the column varied from confused to sullen. Iskara's charm had worked its usual magic. The Sword Sisters were ready to follow her.

"Come, now, Tudae! You're not going to let a chance like this get away, are you? If we wait, he could repair the gates gates and we'd be right back where we started."

"We need more information."

Iskara sighed, an exaggerated sigh of exasperation. "If it will make you feel better, Sword Mistress, I'll lead a scouting party to inspect the gates. Who will go with me?"

The answer was deafening. *The Morgs on the walls must have heard it!* But they just ambled along the parapet, stopping to scratch or yawn occasionally. Tudae shifted in her saddle, as Iskara picked twenty Sisters to ride with her.

"Be careful."

Iskara turned, grinning, and raised her sword in a salute. "But of course, Sword Mistress."

And then she was gone, chain gleaming in the morning light, dark hair flowing out behind her as she rode, with twenty Sword Sisters thundering at her heels.

Tudae turned to the others. "Get ready for a charge, if she gives the signal." Swords cleared their sheaths all down the column, and Tudae turned back to watch Iskara. She was riding into the very shadow of the walls, and not a shot fired. *Something was wrong, definitely wrong. Iskara should come back, come back now....*

Tudae watched as Iskara took down the first Morg by the gate; saw her duck her head and ride her horse through the gap in the gates; saw the others follow.

Tudae watched in disbelieving horror as the illusion of the damaged gates shattered and two perfectly sound gates boomed shut behind them.

<hr />

The gates closed behind them with an ominous clang — gates that hadn't been there a minute ago. The empty courtyard was full of snarling Morgs — Morgs that hadn't been there a minute ago, either.

Iskara turned in time to see the gates close. She saw the Sisters' expressions change from jubilation to fear, then to resignation. They would die and they knew it.

Then there were only snarling Morgs, slashing swords, and screaming horses, as her comrades went down, one by one.

Iskara's horse was the first to fall. *Clever, these Morgs, to always go for the horses first.* Once the Sisters were dismounted the ugly creatures could use their massive size and strength to their best advantage.

Ugly, stupid creatures, Iskara thought, as a vicious flurry of her sword took two down. *Where did they learn such strategy, these monsters who spoke in grunts?*

The answer lay inside the castle. Iskara jumped over the Morg bodies and raced for the door.

I will die this day, but by the Lady, I will take Necimus with me!

Necimus stood on the tower, watching the Sisters ride into the castle. Balek stood beside him, controlling the illusion of the damaged gate and the illusion that masked the presence of the waiting Morgs.

Necimus chuckled as Balek let the illusion dissipate, and laughed outright as he himself cast the spell to close the gates. *We work well together, this little wizard and I. The trap was flawless.*

Necimus regarded the lead figure below with interest. Oh, she was a proud one, this Sister. She rode into the trap with head held high, sword at the ready. Necimus grinned as she vanished into the castle door.

"Well, Balek," Necimus turned to his underling, "shall we give our guest a proper welcome?"

The halls of Castle Dawnfall stank of dried blood and Morg excrement. Here and there Iskara glimpsed the remains of a partially eaten corpse, well on its way in decomposition. Apparently Necimus was not fond of housekeeping, at least on the lower levels. *But he probably doesn't live on the lower levels,* Iskara reasoned.

At Castle Shield, the Sword Mistress' quarters were the largest rooms in the upper stories. No doubt Castle Dawnfall was constructed in a similar fashion.

Iskara took the largest staircase going up, beheading a Morg that was coming down. He didn't snarl, or cry out; there were just the two thumps of his body and head hitting the steps. Good. Surprise was still on her side. With practiced silence, Iskara eased up the stairs.

The long hallway posed a dilemma. Too many doors, all closed. Which one hid Necimus? Perhaps if she listened at each one—

Then he was there, turning the corner at the far end of the hall.

The few refugees who had actually seen him hadn't lied. He was as tall as they said, taller than the Morgs, and just as ugly. He stood there, purple robes billowing around him, thin lips stretched in a smile. He just stood there, smiling.

"The bigger they are, the farther they fall," Iskara muttered, and charged down the hall.

She couldn't move. Not a muscle would answer her command. Her eyes wouldn't even close, but her breath still came in gasps, and her heart was still beating.

She wished it wasn't. She wished she could die now, before they reached her.

They were walking down the hall towards her — Necimus, and the little man in black. The man Iskara didn't see when she started her charge. The man who had been waving his hands and chanting.

"Nice work, Balek. I'm glad I taught you that spell." The tall wizard's voice was deep and harsh. It would have sent shivers through Iskara, had she been able to shiver.

"Well, you are a beauty, aren't you?" Necimus leaned down, to stare into her unblinking eyes.

As his huge hand caressed her hair, Iskara knew there would be no warrior's death for her.

The barrage of arrows drove them back. Hundreds of crossbow bolts raining down upon them, hundreds of Morgs, appearing on the empty battlements. Two horses down, riddled with arrows, and Nina, a crossbow bolt through her eye, now riding face down over another Sister's saddlehorn.

All up and down the column, Sisters sprouted crossbow bolts. Tudae turned to look, to make sure they were still all upright in their saddles, that they would make it back to Castle Shield. Cerrain drooped over her

Sword Sister

saddlehorn, two bolts protruding through her shoulder, and another in her thigh. The Sister riding beside her reached out a steadying hand.

Tudae urged them on. "Come on, Sisters! Just a few more miles!"

A few more miles, and Erystra would be very busy tending the wounded. And Tudae would be very busy explaining what happened to her granddaughter.

That the Head of the Order of Sayers had given up her place as High Mistress of Neston and taken up residence at Castle Shield after the fall of Castle Dawnfall was an indication of the severity of the situation. Erystra had said merely that she felt she was more needed here, and that another could be High Mistress at Neston as well as she. But seeing the old woman walk the halls of Castle Shield had left a cold feeling in Tudae's gut. A feeling that Necimus might be more than the Sisters could handle.

So far that feeling was proving true. They had lost Akrien, and now Iskara, and still Castle Dawnfall stood unscathed. Tudae tried to forget the snarls of Morgs, the screams of horses, and the rapidly diminishing battle cries of Sisters that came from inside those walls.

Tudae brushed tears away, but they weren't just tears. Snowflakes dotted her face, her horse's mane. An early snow, to add to her troubles.

There had been nothing they could do. The gates were closed, closed solid, by the time the charge reached them. There were no Sisters to defend, no Morgs to battle outside the walls; only a barrage of crossbow fire from above. How did the Morgs go from throwing stones to firing crossbows in just five years?

The Sisters couldn't take the castle like this. The Sisterhood had been taught to patrol and defend the Lordless Lands, not to lay siege to a dead lord's castle. They needed more troops, and siege machines.

Damn Lord Greoff! Can't he see what's at stake here?

Tudae spurred her lagging horse forward. If Lord

119

Greoff wouldn't give her troops, perhaps he would lend her some siege equipment.

Tudae stared at the complex designs in the rug covering the floor in the Sword Mistress' study. Tudae knew the designs by heart. She had watched Mammae make this rug in the long ago days when Tudae was still a child, with no greater worries than whether she would have to keep Tomo happy. The rugs had come to Castle Shield as her dowry, delivered by a man who retrieved them from the destroyed wagon at the place of her family's deaths. Now Tudae's worries were many, and as complex as the patterns woven by her dead Mammae.

Tudae sat in the big chair before the fireplace. It was a comfortable chair, leather stuffed with wool, but Tudae felt no comfort. It was the Sword Mistress' chair, and right now Tudae wished Iskara were sitting in it.

"I can't try again. We can't get through the gates, and... I can't risk any more losses." Tudae stared into the fire, trying not to remember those losses, those last two assaults.

Mira, fighting like a madwoman, finally taken down by seven Morgs. Loranda, the quiet peasant girl who became a Sister to escape the drudgery of farm life. Frodica, the merchant's daughter, who came to Castle Shield the same day Tudae did. Ertha, Darean, Spirith.... the list went on and on. Good Sisters, all, who died on the rocky slopes of Castle Dawnfall.

"Aye, I know ye can't."

All those years at Neston, and still Erystra spoke the peasant dialect. They said you couldn't make a silk purse out of a sheepskin. You could make a damn fine Sayer out of a peasant, though; Erystra proved it.

I wish she hadn't agreed with me, Tudae thought. *At the advice of a Sayer like Erystra, I might risk it again.*

That was the problem. No Sayer could see truer than Erystra, and if she agreed with Tudae then it must be a lost cause, especially since it was her own granddaughter being held prisoner.

Her granddaughter, and my friend, Tudae thought. *How can she bear it? How can I bear it? How will I bear it, if Iskara dies?*

"She lives, still?"

"Aye."

So she could See her still. Tudae glanced at the gray-robed woman stretching gnarled hands to the fire. Erystra's hair was as silver as the eye-embossed medallion she wore, and cataracts were clouding her. Tudae wondered how much longer Erystra would have sight of any kind.

For now, she could still See. See better than any other Sayer, which had earned her the name of Erystra True-Sight. And right now, she was the only Sayer who could still See Iskara.

It was the blood-link, Erystra claimed, that let her See past the magical wards against the Sight that Necimus had erected around Castle Dawnfall. Ever since they went up, no Sayer had been able to Say what lay beyond them.

Except Erystra. Even so, it was only Iskara that Erystra Saw — Iskara and her immediate surroundings. The old Sayer had tried, but couldn't tell Tudae how many Morgs were garrisoned there, or what magical traps awaited the attacking Sisters. She couldn't even tell her if any of the other captured Sisters still lived.

I can't risk any more losses for the sake of one live prisoner, even if the prisoner is Iskara, Tudae thought.

She had tried twice already, and the fervor the Sisters showed for rescuing their favored second-in-command waned as they carted their dead away from Castle Darkfall.

I can't ask them to try again. The snow lay deep now. It would take all her resources to protect the countryside from Morgs who ventured out of their new stronghold on raids.

"Perhaps in the spring." Tudae sighed.

Perhaps. Perhaps there would be more recruits over the winter; perhaps Lord Greoff would lend her siege equipment, if not troops; perhaps Necimus would be devoured by demons.

"Perhaps," Tudae whispered.

She realized with a chill that there was no answering "Aye," from Erystra.

Chapter Fifteen

...And one to protect...
From "The Prophecies of Aria"

Year After Aria, 303

The pink-eyed palfrey plodded through the sequestering forests surrounding Neston and into the cultivated lands beyond. Ilissa breathed deeply as she passed an apple orchard exploding into bloom, and smiled.

Nearly two years ago Ulric had left her at Neston's gates; nearly two years she had spent in the cloistered gray walls of Neston. Months spent in silent meditations, memorizing chants, and poring over vellum pages that were old when Ilissa's grandmother was born.

I had forgotten, Ilissa mused. *Forgotten what spring is like at home. Forgotten what home is like,* she added, as the stone walls of a manor house came into view, so like her father's house that Ilissa felt an unfamiliar throb of homesickness.

The palfrey twitched a white ear towards the house as three children ran across the lawn, shrieking with the thrill of a game of tag. Ilissa smiled at the children, remembering a child with eyes the color of wood violets who had played the same games a few years gone. It was a peaceful country, well suited for peaceful, happy childhoods.

Ilissa's childhood was neither. The days had been lovely, but Ilissa's nights were haunted by dreams.

They started before she reached her tenth birthday. Vague nightmares at first, of large, ugly but strangely human-like creatures. Visions of villages raided, women and children dying, and unspeakable acts of violence that the child Ilissa could scarcely comprehend. The settings were unfamiliar at first, semi-barren lands to the north that Ilissa had never seen. But gradually the terrain became more familiar, until one night Ilissa dreamed of a village where her father purchased horses the year before. A fortnight later when the village was destroyed, Ilissa watched disbelieving horror spread across her parent's faces as she told them she dreamed it would be so.

Such was their reaction that Ilissa spoke no more of her dreams, especially when she saw, in a sleep-filled mind, the image of her own home gutted. Already she was beginning to judge time by the clarity of the images and knew that it would be years before it happened. But Ilissa knew with equal certainty that it would indeed come to pass.

And so at her coming of age party on her sixteenth birthday, when her mother was hoping she would turn her dark blue eyes on the local swains, Ilissa announced that she would be giving her dowry to the Order of Sayers. They were reputed to have visions of future events, and also to use their knowledge to protect people from catastrophes. Ilissa hoped they would show her how to save her family from the future.

None of this made any sense to her weeping mother. The woman had hoped that her only daughter, with her night-sky hair and skin the color of new cream, would snare a good husband. A lord's son, perhaps, so the proud grandmother could visit the castle often and give copious advice on breastfeeding and how to deal with

Sword Sister

teething babies.

    The only person in her family who did not go against her decision was her eldest brother. Ulric was already wed, with his first child on the way, and Ilissa suspected he was concerned for the future, too. Not once during the journey to Neston did he ask her to turn back.

    When they stood beneath Neston's gray walls, Ilissa had turned to him. "It will be a boy, Ulric." Her brother flashed one of his rare smiles at her before he rode away.

    It was a boy. Ilissa's family sent no word, for the Order of Sayers did not allow acolytes to receive missives from their families. The Order hoped to encourage the development of the Sight in this manner and apparently it was successful, for Ilissa dreamed often of her family.

    The other dreams diminished. Through the Sayer's teachings Ilissa learned to channel her gift, rather than have it bring her dreams at random.

    For practice, Ilissa swept her Sight ahead over the terrain remaining between her and Fenfall. It looked peaceful enough; a glorious spring hodgepodge of cow-cropped meadows and fields turning to brown velvet under farmers' plows, all criss-crossed with stone walls pocked with simple wooden gates.

    Illissa judged the distance to Fenfall. She wouldn't reach the town before dark.

    There was a castle, though, this side of Fenfall. Ilissa tilted her head back, scrutinizing the building that was still miles away. A huge black shield hung over the gate.

    It must be Castle Shield, the fortress of the Sisters of the Sword. Perhaps she could spend the night there, and go on to Fenfall in the morning. The High Mistress said that the two Orders often combined strengths, and besides, almost every castle welcomed the stay of a Singer.

    With this in mind, Ilissa brought her lyre out from beneath her cloak and practiced singing "The Song of the Sword Sisters."

    The High Mistress of Neston chose that moment to

use her Sight to check on her young charge, and smiled.

"Needs garlic." Skurgiil shoveled food into her mouth.

Disturbed from her thoughts, Tudae frowned. "What?"

Skurgiil motioned to her plate while she swallowed a mouthful of potatoes. "The food. It needs more garlic."

That didn't prevent her from devouring three plates of it, Tudae thought. *Can this girl be growing still? Lady, I hope not!*

It would be difficult to fit her with armor, as it was. No doubt a coat of chain mail would have to be specially made, and a sword, as well. A sword long enough to fit her height, and weighted to match her strength.

Tudae's eyes dropped to the dawnstone. She remembered that necklace well. Iskara called it her good luck stone.

Tudae's lean brown fingers slid under her tiny black braids, kneading stiff neck muscles as she recalled the stone's pulsing glow at the Lamb Chop Inn. Tudae knew the meaning of the glow even if the younger Sword Sisters did not.

Erystra was no more, at least not in flesh. That the Unknowns of the Order saw fit to give Skurgiil a Guardian was significant. That the Guardian should be Erystra, not only Skurgiil's protector in life but also linked to her through blood, was practically an omen. An omen that perhaps this girl truly was the weapon they needed to defeat Necimus.

Across the table Skurgiil finished her meal and regarded the Sword Mistress with serious eyes. "Tudae?"

"Yes, Skurgiil."

"Tell me about my mother."

What to say? Tudae wondered. *Tell her too little, and I'll lose her. Tell her too much, and... I can't think about that.*

Sword Sister

Tudae sighed. "Your mother was beautiful and brave, and a warrior born. She was my Sword Sister, and we fought many battles together."

"And my father?"

Lady, help me! Tudae prayed, and drew a deep breath.

"Your mother never married, Skurgiil. And she never told me who your father was." *True. Iskara never told her that, or anything else about Skurgiil. The last time Iskara spoke to her was the day Iskara rode towards Castle Dawnfall, never to return — and that was eight months before Skurgiil's birth.*

Behind Skurgiil Tudae saw Daena's eyes widen in questioning surprise. Tudae met the look steadily and sternly, and the younger Sword Sister lowered her eyes without comment.

Skurgiil frowned. *Never married? How could that be?* The Good Mother said that for people, breeding was called marriage.

"But I had a father." She had to have a father; the ewes bore no lambs after a wolf took the old ram. Not until the young ram was old enough to do the marrying thing had there been any new lambs.

Skurgiil smiled as a thought occurred to her. "Perhaps he is alive still. Perhaps I can find him. Perhaps he knows what my destiny is."

Lady, preserve us! Tudae groped through her mind, searching for something else to talk about, something to distract the girl.

"Your mother died at Castle Darkfall, not long after you were born. That castle is held by Necimus, an evil sorcerer known as His Evilness to his doting Morg army. Necimus is directly responsible for your mother's death." *And your birth,* Tudae added mournfully to herself.

Skurgiil fingered the dawnstone, her thick eyebrows lowering over deep-set eyes. *My mother killed by someone called Necimus, and the Good Mother killed by two strangers. A past full of death, and a future full of... what?*

Tudae waited. The other women watched her. The whole world seemed to be watching her, waiting for her to do... what? *"Go, and fulfill your destiny."*

Skurgiil leaned back, closing her eyes against the stares of these strangers. *Good Mother, what should I do?*

The image of Erystra sprang up in her memory, the withered lips smiling in infinite compassion.

/Follow in your mother's steps, child. Become a Sister of the Sword./ The dawnstone pulsed once.

"Aye. I'll do it."

Unknowns, but she looks like Iskara! That jut of the chin, that fire in the eyes.... Tudae shook herself. "Do what, Skurgiil?"

"Become a — what ye are. What my mother was."

Well done, Sayer! Tudae thought. *Guide her, as neither you nor I could ever guide Iskara....* Tudae sighed. The past was gone. Now there was only the present, and the future. And perhaps, finally, some hope.

"Welcome to the Sisterhood of the Sword, Skurgiil. Lia!" The Sword Mistress called to one of the younger Sword Sisters. "Take Skurgiil to Storna. Her lessons will start immediately."

As Skurgiil left the room, Tudae met Daena's questioning stare. "Yes?"

"Why didn't you tell her the truth, Sword Mistress?"

"I didn't precisely lie to her, did I?"

The blonde girl shook her head.

"Think about it — would you want to find out that *he* was *your* father?"

⊰◉⊱

The Training Mistress of Castle Shield was a big woman, large of limb and stocky in the torso. Her mouth dropped open slightly as she stared up at Skurgiil. "What are ye, a mountain giant?"

"I am from the mountains," Skurgiil admitted.

"You're supposed to train her," Lia offered.

Sword Sister

"Very well," Storna grumbled. She had worked with big girls before, though never as big as this. They were strong but slow, both in movements and in wits. She tossed Skurgiil a hardwood staff. "This is a quarterstaff. Have ye ever used one?"

Skurgiil shook her head. Storna threw another staff to Lia. "Ye will be her partner."

Lia, who had seen Skurgiil wield an axe, stepped forward reluctantly.

"Ye hold it so — no, hands farther apart!" Storna shouted at Skurgiil. "And place your feet so. Watch your opponent, always. Now swing the staff so...."

⁂

The sun was sinking when a white horse bearing a cloaked figure approached the gate of Castle Shield.

The guard looked the figure over critically. *A slight woman.* Unless she was a magic-caster, there was no danger in her.

"Who goes there?" the guard called, dropping her halberd out of habit.

The hood fell back, revealing a pale face framed by black hair. "I am Ilissa," a musical voice answered. "I am a Singer, and I request a night's lodgings."

The guard smiled. *There would be music tonight!* Her shift would be over in two hours, so perhaps she could catch a few ballads.

"Greetings, Ilissa. Singing is welcome, but you will still have to be cleared by the Sword Mistress. And I must search you first," the guard added apologetically. "Rules, you know."

Ilissa nodded, and the guard raised the blue cloak. "A fine instrument," the guard murmured, running an appreciative finger over the strings of the lyre.

"Pass in," the guard waved toward the castle. "Someone will tend your horse and take you to the Sword Mistress."

129

Tudae glanced up as a Sister ushered a cloaked figure through her study door. "Yes?"

"A Singer, Mistress, asking a night's lodging."

Tudae's gaze scanned the cloaked girl, lingering on the deep blue eyes. "You came alone?"

When the girl nodded, Tudae turned to the Sword Sister. "She stays. Prepare her a quarter." After the Sister nodded and left, Tudae returned her attention to the girl.

"Your name?"

"Ilissa, Mistress."

Tudae smiled. The idea of one so young, lovely and frail traveling unguarded from town to town and singing for a living was preposterous. She wouldn't last a week. A lovely voice, but this girl was no Singer.

Tudae had known enough Sayers in her time to recognize one. There was something about the way they held their heads, and the eyes, as if they always saw more than was actually there. This girl's eyes, the color of the sky in the moments before the purple dawn, seemed to be made for the Sight. "You're from Neston."

It wasn't a question. Ilissa stared at the Sword Mistress with surprise. "My Mistress informed you of my coming?"

"No, girl. Ilissa, you said your name was?" The ersatz Singer nodded. "Well, Ilissa, I have seen many Sayers in my day, and you are definitely a Sayer. Besides," Tudae added, "enough strange things have happened today that a Sayer arriving in disguise doesn't really surprise me. What brings you?"

"A Mission, Mistress. I go to Fenfall, to find someone."

"Would this someone happen to be a very large girl?"

The blue-violet eyes widened. "Why, yes, Mistress."

"I don't think you have to go to Fenfall." Tudae gestured to the wall behind her.

Ilissa tilted her head, allowing her Sight to pass

Sword Sister

through granite walls. In the training ground beyond, Ilissa saw the person she sought, engaged in mock combat with a Sword Sister.

As Ilissa stared the girl turned, her eyes searching in Ilissa's direction. Her opponent took the opportunity to drive her quarterstaff into the big girl's ribs.

Puzzled, Ilissa withdrew her Sight.

"Is that the one you seek?"

Ilissa nodded. "Yes. And," she paused, frowning, "I think she Saw me. Or sensed my Sight on her."

Tudae raised her dark brows. "It wouldn't surprise me. I don't think anything about that girl would surprise me. She is descended from a Sayer, among others. She is very special, that one."

"Who is she?"

Tudae sighed and gestured for Ilissa to be seated. "It's a long story. She is Skurgiil, great-granddaughter of the Sayer, Erystra, and daughter of my former sword sister, Iskara...."

Wendy Jensen

Chapter Sixteen

*...The Scourge of Evil shall be
Of the Evil's own making.*
    From "The Prophecies of Aria"

Year After Aria, 286
Peasant Year of Despair

Seventeen years earlier...

"Siege machines?" Lord Greoff raised one shaggy eyebrow. "I have a few. A couple of catapults, two or three battering rams. Haven't had much use for them of late, these being peaceful times and all. Meaning," the Lord of Fenfall added, as Tudae's dark eyes flashed fury, "that we Fenkeeps haven't gone around attacking anyone recently. Haven't needed to."

My, but she is a beautiful young woman when she's angry! Lord Greoff's admiring glance ran from the flashing eyes and heaving breast to the slender brown fingers clenched on her sword pommel. *Reminds me of a high-strung mare, she does. Can almost understand what the boy sees in her. Almost.*

Speaking of the boy — what was he saying?

"...you'll lend them to her then, Father. Since you don't use them."

Lord Greoff scowled. *Damn the boy's impudence! Dead set on helping these women, he was.*

"You did say you didn't need them yourself, Lord Greoff."

Amazing, that this young Sword Mistress could speak so calmly, when she obviously was not calm. Maybe the Sword Sisters knew what they were doing in choosing her, after all.

"Hmph. I suppose there's no harm in it. Of course," Lord Greoff leaned back in his chair, "you'll be needing men to handle them. Unless you women know how to load and aim catapults?"

Lord Greoff watched the look of dismay flicker across Tudae's dark features. So there were some chinks in the Sword Mistress' armor, after all. The Lord of Fenfall chuckled.

"Thought not. Well, I suppose I could spare a few men with the siege equipment. But only to handle it, mind you! They're not to fight your battles for you."

Tudae gave him a slight bow. "You are generous, Lord Greoff."

"Hmph." The Lord of Fenfall watched her move to the door, watched as Roagen followed her out.

"I'd say you owed me one, Missy," Lord Greoff muttered into his goblet, "but I think my son will be the one collecting it."

⊰◉⊱

Roagen sat at the meeting place, watching the gleaming column of riders pour over the hill.

Tudae must have turned out the whole garrison. Sister after Sister crested the hill, side by side, black shields contrasting against shining chain mail. Roagen turned to look at his own tiny band of soldiers, and cursed.

Twenty men, two catapults, and one battering ram. This is Father's notion of "helping the women."

"If you wanted to prove your superiority, Father, you should have sent enough to prove what your troops can do," Roagen muttered.

"Sir?"

"Nothing, Ralf, nothing." Roagen turned to the wagoner. "Turn the horses. We'll march in the fore."

"Ho, right face!" As the draft horses turned to Ralf's clucking and rein-slapping, Roagen spurred his horse forward to meet Tudae's. The gleaming column came to a halt. Roagen's eyes widened at the sight of one figure that did not wear chain mail.

"Greetings, Sword Mistress. Greetings, Sayer." Roagen bowed over his saddle horn at the wizened woman in gray robes. "You accompany us to Dawnfall?"

"Aye," Erystra nodded. "That I do, young Fenkeep."

"She will heal the wounded. Besides," Tudae's expression darkened, "Iskara is her granddaughter, and she wishes to be there when we rescue her."

"Rescue...." Roagen's voice faltered. Iskara had been a prisoner in Castle Dawnfall since last autumn! Roagen glanced from Tudae to Erystra. "But, she may not still be alive."

"Erystra says she is, even now." Tudae looked to the Sayer, who tilted her head, then nodded.

"Aye. She lives."

"Amazing," Roagen muttered. *And perhaps unfortunate.* His eyes strayed to the wagon straining through the snow-melt mud ahead — the wagon filled with kegs of oil.

Just because she was alive now didn't mean she would be when the siege was done. But how could he explain that to Iskara's grandmother and best friend?

Tudae's eyes caught his, and he saw sorrow in their dark depths. Roagen sighed as he turned his horse alongside hers.

The best friend, at least, knew.

"No guards? None?" Roagen squinted at the castle. It loomed ahead on its rocky pinnacle, just as he remembered it from his last visit... *when?*

Over a year ago now, since he and Father attended the coming of age feast for Lord Langtry's eldest daughter. Roagen had known then what his father and Lord Langtry discussed in low voices at the head of the table. He had ignored them, just as he ignored the provocative stares from the girl across the table.

Sara had been a comely girl, and pleasant enough, Roagen supposed. But his mind had been on Tudae. He had no intention of marrying anyone else, no matter what his father schemed with Lord Langtry. He had been polite to Sara, but nothing more, and had avoided discussing marriage with his father on the ride home.

He wouldn't have to marry Sara now. Iskara might still live behind those walls, but Roagen doubted Sara had survived, or any other member of Lord Langtry's family, even though ragged remnants of the Langtry standard still drooped above the battlements. Above battlements that were suspiciously empty.

"Does Necimus think he's invulnerable, that he posts no guards?" Roagen frowned.

It didn't seem right, somehow. No commander with any sense failed to post guards in hostile territory. If Necimus didn't think this land was hostile to him... well, he'd soon think differently. Roagen motioned the catapult handlers forward.

"Aim above the gates. You will provide cover for the battering ram."

"Cover from what, Sir? There's no one on the walls."

"There will be soon, I'm sure."

"Aye, Sir. Oil?"

"Ah... no." Roagen glanced back to where Erystra sat on her dappled gray horse. "Rocks first, to... get your aim right."

Sword Sister

The soldiers nodded, and loosed the catapult from the horses. As they pushed it towards the gates, Sisters dismounted and selected boulders from alongside the road, rolling them uphill after the catapult.

Roagen turned to the other men. "Ready the ram." Eight men grasped the handles and heaved the steel-shod log off the wagon. Four on each side, they trudged up the hill.

The men with the battering ram positioned themselves between the catapult and the gate. Tudae rode down the ranks of Sisters, issuing orders and positioning them for the charge. A boulder was maneuvered into place on the catapult arm, and the handlers crouched behind it, squinting at the gate and discussing the angle. After a few adjustments, one nodded at Roagen, who nodded at Tudae.

"Get ready, men." The soldiers with the battering ram tensed, preparing for their run. All down the lines Sisters drew their swords, holding in their mounts as the horses fidgeted, sensing the forthcoming action. Nerves stretched to breaking as they waited for the siege to begin.

The soldier pulled the lever on the catapult. The first stone was away, arcing toward the wall above the gate, slicing through the air, aiming true, and the battering ram was in motion, hurtling over the ground between the eight men, charging straight for the wooden gates.

Horses reared and neighed as the boulder crashed back, bouncing down the road among the assembled Sisters, rolling down the slope from Castle Darkfall. The battering ram rebounded, sending its bearers stumbling backwards, slipping on the shale roadway and cursing.

"What?" Roagen forced his horse up the road, up to the catapult. "What happened?"

The catapult handler shook his head. "Don't know, Sir. It was flying true, and then it... hit something."

"The wall?"

"No, Sir. Not the wall. It was ten feet from the wall, and well above it when it bounced."

"Same here." One of the soldiers came down the road from the battering ram, helping another soldier who limped. "The ram fell on his leg when we hit, Sir. We didn't hit the gates. Weren't even close to them yet."

Magic, again! Roagen scowled up at the castle. On the second line of battlements stood a tall figure, black hair and purple robes billowing in the breeze.

"Burn it."

He couldn't worry about Erystra's feelings anymore. They wouldn't get Iskara out alive, and no doubt the Sayer knew it. She slumped over her saddlehorn, shoulders shaking. Roagen looked away from her and watched the soldiers roll the first keg of oil up the hill.

It fell back, splintering on the rocks by the roadway, splattering oil on the catapult, on the handlers, on Roagen. The future Lord of Fenfall swore and wiped oil from his face, waving the torch bearers away.

"Fall back, and regroup." As the Sisters backed down the road, Roagen surveyed the land. Hilly, and the largest hill the one where Castle Dawnfall stood. Still, a long shot from a catapult was better than no shot at all.

"Take the catapults around to the sides," he instructed the handlers. "One on the left, one on the right. Split the oil kegs between them." Roagen cast a baleful glance upwards as he spurred his horse down the road. "He can't defend all sides, at once."

The sun was low in the sky when Roagen finally admitted he was wrong. They had spent hours trundling the catapults over rocky terrain, Sisters shoulder to shoulder, pushing the machine up and down gullies, with other Sisters following behind, carrying the kegs of oil over ground that the wagon couldn't traverse. When the catapults were finally in position the results were the same. The kegs hurtled through the air, only to crash and burst on the ground after colliding with an unseen barrier.

Roagen rode his horse into a lather, racing back and forth between machines, coordinating them until the launches were simultaneous, but on both sides the same

Sword Sister

thing happened. In desperation he told his archers to send in the flaming arrows, but they too fell before the barrier, falling and igniting the splattered oil outside the castle walls. Roagen even sent the battering ram back to the front gate, but the barrier was still there, too, and the steel head on the end of the log rebounded as if striking stone.

Necimus could defend all sides at once. Roagen glowered up at the castle.

The barrier that foiled their siege attempts didn't block the sight of him on the castle parapet, or prevent the deep sound of his laughter from drifting down from above.

※◉※

Necimus chuckled as he watched them leave, dragging their pitiful siege machines home behind their beaten backs.

It was well worth the winter months he and Balek had spent, crafting the barrier, expanding a simple spell until it encompassed the entire castle, centering it on a sphere housing seven of his magic candles. The barrier would never go down, save when Necimus desired it to, to let his Morglings out to rampage the countryside. He could snuff the candles himself, and relight them in seconds, seconds enough for the Morgs to exit or enter but not long enough to ruin the spell. Those candles would power the spell forever, as long as the old ones were replaced with new as needed.

He was safe in this castle — unreachable, indestructible.

※◉※

Forty-two. Forty-three. Or was it forty-four?

Iskara's fingers clenched the stone as she tried to remember. Not that it mattered; she had no idea how many stairs were in this tower, no idea how many were left before she reached the top. No idea, even, what she would do when she reached the top. For now, the cold stone steps beneath her were her only reality besides the pain. Iskara counted the steps to avoid thinking about the pain.

It came again. Wrenching, blotting out the world in its intensity. Iskara rolled to her side, pressing her back against the curving stone wall. The edge of the step cut into her ribs, but it was nothing compared to the pain inside her.

Inside her. In all her life, Iskara had never had an enemy she couldn't fight if given the chance. Now she was alone, fighting a battle with an enemy within.

The pain passed finally, as all the others had passed before. But they grew worse each time, and closer together. The last one had been only ten steps ago, the one before that less than fifteen. This was the third pain since she had started up the stairs. How many more before she reached the battlement? How long before her reality became one constant pain with no end?

Too soon, no doubt. Iskara pulled her trembling knees up and reached for the next step.

Forty-eight. Forty-nine. Fif... Her fingers slipped off the edge of the step as the internal assault began again.

"Fight fire with fire." The Training Mistress' words echoed from the past, and with her warrior instinct Iskara clamped her teeth into the flesh of her hand.

A new pain, to fight the old pain. Not that it was much competition, but it gave her something to concentrate on. And it kept her from screaming.

If only she could cry out! If only she could shriek her defiance at this enemy that couldn't be fought, much less defeated!

But she knew better. The Protective Aura she had cast prevented the Morgs from seeing her, but it wouldn't prevent them from hearing her.

Odd, that she was able to do that. Odd that she even remembered how, especially since the pain was already clouding her mind by then, giving the world around her a slightly unreal quality. But remember she did, more clearly than when Erystra quizzed her in those long ago days at Neston. And it worked, for she stepped out of her cell and stumbled through the hallways of Castle Dawnfall like a ghost that the Morgs couldn't see.

Too bad she couldn't remember a Healing Aura as well. But Healing had never interested her — her purpose was to make others need healing. And she didn't have the strength to cast a Healing Aura now, anyway. Iskara wasn't even certain she had enough strength to reach the top of the stairs.

The pain inside passed again, leaving only the pain in her hand. As Iskara unclenched her teeth from her own flesh she tasted blood.

More blood to leave a trail, guiding the Morgs to her like a dinner bell. Not that there wasn't a big enough blood trail already. The trickle down her thighs had started before she left her cell, and her tunic was soaked with blood now.

Oh, there was enough blood along her trail. Enough for the Morgs, with their primeval sense of smell, to follow, even in the dark. In fact, the light was her only hope now — the light of dawn. Through the arrow slits in the tower Iskara saw pale stars set against deep purple. Morgs were nocturnal creatures. The few she passed in the hall had looked tired. Dawn must be near, and all but the guards would be sleeping soon. Her blood trail might escape notice long enough for her to reach the battlement.

If the pain didn't kill her first.

She had tarried too long on this step. The pain caught her again. Iskara braced her legs against the wall and fought the scream inside her.

When the internal fist released its grip her face was damp with sweat, turning clammy in the chill air; an odd contrast to the sticky warmth between her thighs. For the first time, Iskara realized she might bleed to death before she could throw herself off the tower.

So that is my plan, Iskara thought dully. *After all, what other plan could there be?*

The gates were locked and guarded, and the Protective Aura that took her past Morgs unseen would not get her through barred gates without a fight.

She was too weak to fight. Muscles once hard and strong had grown weak from months spent in chains, and her bulging belly made wielding a sword almost impossible. So she had headed for the highest point of the castle. Driven by the same force that sent her climbing the mountains around Surham during her childhood, Iskara went to the tower.

Once there, jumping off was the only choice, the only way to cheat Necimus of his prize. Death would end her pain. And end the life of the monster Necimus created inside her.

It would be easier than starvation. Iskara had tried that, when she first realized she was pregnant. But she couldn't do it. She couldn't ignore the food the Morg servants laid before her, steaming and delicious, couldn't ignore the hunger inside. It drove her to the platters, forcing her to eat.

And eat. And eat. Iskara had never known hunger like this, not even when she returned that day from the mountains to find Surham a smoldering ruin. Then she had eaten raw eggs, warm from the hen who had clucked indignantly at the child raiding her nest. But that was just hunger and the need to survive, not an irresistible urge to eat when survival was neither desirable nor desired.

As the pain engulfed her again, Iskara cursed her own weakness. If she had just starved herself then, she wouldn't be here now, dragging her belly up cold stone steps, bleeding, hurting, alone.

Alone. I am going to die alone.

That thought was as cold as the air coming through the arrow slits; air that smelled like spring. Odd, because Iskara was sure she wasn't due until summer. Time had no meaning in her windowless cell. Iskara never knew if it was day or night. But the leaves were brown and gold on the day of that fateful assault, so she had to be due in summer.

Sword Sister

It was too soon. That was why she was bleeding, why she wasn't watched more closely, why Necimus wasn't prepared. There were supposed to be preparations. She heard Necimus and that weasel of a wizard discussing it in the hall outside her cell.

"We'll move her after the next full moon." The deep, vibrating voice still sent shivers down Iskara's back, even though he hadn't touched her recently. He hadn't touched her in months, actually. Not after the first month, when he told her she had missed her bleeding. Without the bleeding for a monthly timekeeper, Iskara had no idea how many months had passed, but they must have been many, for her belly had grown enormous since the last time Necimus touched her.

"Then I should prepare the room?" Balek's voice was a squeak compared to Necimus'.

"Yes. I want this child bound to my will at birth."

"The candles, Your Evilness...."

"I will provide the candles when it is time, Balek!"

"As you wish, my lord." The squeak escalated to a new nervous pitch.

There was an uncomfortable silence. Iskara could imagine those deep-set eyes boring holes through the quaking wizard.

"M-my lord, about the woman... and the child...."

"Yes?"

"All the others died, my lord. Your Morgs can birth their own, but these women.... Perhaps if we had a Sayer, Your Evilness...."

"No!" The word cracked like a whip, and even Iskara cringed.

"B-B-But, my lord, perhaps a Sayer could...."

"No, Balek." There was a rustle of robes and the deep voice receded down the hall. "No Sayers!"

Why would that sniveling wizard brave the wrath of Necimus, asking for a Sayer to ease her through childbirth?

Perhaps it had something to do with the way he had looked at her, when he came to Necimus' quarters while

143

she was chained, naked, to his bed. Through the haze of hate and fear Iskara had felt Balek's eyes on her, but she was used to that. Men always looked at her, ever since she was sixteen and the fullness of her womanhood developed. She had played them like instruments ever since, using their own desire against them like she used a sword in battle. She had even considered trying to use Balek against Necimus, until she realized the wizard's fear would never allow him to confront his master.

But now, when her body was bloated and ugly, he tried to get a Sayer to help her. Perhaps there was more to the whining wizard than Iskara imagined. Too late to realize it now — his scrawny face at the door of her cell was regretful, but still not strong.

There were preparations to be made, preparations that Iskara did not even want to think about. Balek had turned away with a sigh, no doubt to begin those preparations— preparations that would end her life and begin a nightmare.

But she had been warned. Warned of her approaching death, and of Necimus' evil plans. So, when the pains began two meals ago, Iskara had laid plans of her own.

She thought it was indigestion at first. Perhaps the food the Morgs brought wasn't well cooked, though Necimus made certain she was always offered the best. Her stomach cramped through her restless sleep, plagued by dreams of the eagles that nested in the crags surrounding Surham. In her dream she was an eagle, flying over the world without care for the beings crawling earthbound across the surface below.

The pains woke her, gasping, in the dark of her cell. Perhaps she had taken ill, and would die of sickness before Necimus' plans ever came to fruition. But when wetness spread down her tunic and splattered in the straw below, she knew the truth.

Then she threw up her meal into the chamber pot and ordered the Morg guard to remove it. He was a stupid guard, typical of his race. He entered her cell unarmed save for a dagger, and carrying the keys on his belt.

Sword Sister

Perhaps he thought she was helpless, cowering in the straw. When his back was turned Iskara wrapped her chain around his neck, strangling his snarls in links of cold steel. Desperation gave strength to her hands, and she had gritted her teeth against the pain in her middle as the Morg's bucking back rammed into her swollen belly again and again. Iskara's fingers found the Morg's dagger and brought it across his throat with satisfying finality.

Her bleeding started then, though Iskara barely noticed. The keys opened her collar, and the cell door stood ajar. With the bloody dagger in hand, Iskara cast the Protective Aura and stepped into the hallway.

The Morgs she passed didn't notice her, save for a wrinkling of their ugly noses. At first Iskara thought it was her bloody dagger, and cleaned it on a ragged tapestry. But when the next Morg sniffed the air she realized she was leaving drops of blood behind.

Fifty-two. Fifty-three. Fifty-four, and the pain took her again. No matter, for ahead Iskara saw a purple rectangle of light.

The battlement, and the sky. How long since she had seen the sky? *Months.*

She would not die a warrior's death, despite the braids in her hair, and she would die alone, but at least she would die with the sky above her.

If the pain allows me to reach the battlement. They had trained her for pain, the Sisters of the Sword. Pain from hunger, cold, fire, and sword. But never had they trained her for a pain that came from within.

Did the trainers even know the true meaning of torture? Iskara doubted it. None of the training mistresses had borne children, or expected her to bear any. The slash of a sword and the kiss of a torch were fleeting and bearable compared to this. As the pain racked her body Iskara thought of the only woman who had ever trained her who knew what she was going through.

"Grandmother!"

More a gasp than a cry, Iskara's voice conjured up a vision. A vision of Erystra, sorrowful and sad, beckoning her from the doorway to the battlement. Iskara reached for the next step.

Fifty-five. Fifty-six. Fifty-seven, and only three more to go. The pain washed over her, and Iskara's grip on the step slipped.

The tower. The battlement and the edge. Down the steep walls of Castle Darkfall lay peace, an end to pain. An end to the evil plans of Necimus. Iskara inched up the last steps, gritting her teeth.

Iskara lay on the battlement, the lavender sky above her. The count was gone, lost in the miasma of pain that gripped her body.

It didn't matter now. Nothing mattered. She had made it, made the battlement. If only the pain would go away long enough to throw herself over the arrow guards, all would be well.

But there was no pause between the pains now, no break in which she could hurl her mortal remains and those of her unborn child to an instant death. They racked her body, pains worse than a sword slash, cutting swaths through her middle. Swaths without scars, for there was no blade behind them. Iskara bit her lip to stifle the scream, and let the pain take her entirely, blotting out the world.

A thin wail that roused her from the painless warmth that engulfed her body, radiating up from her belly. The wail seemed to originate from between her legs, and Iskara pulled herself to a sitting position to look.

It wasn't a monster. It was a girl, tiny and red, shivering in the cold spring air. Dreamily, Iskara pulled her tunic over her head and bent to wrap the infant in it.

The child waved her arms and legs, squalling against the cold air and the light of dawn. A tiny fist caught in the silver links of Iskara's necklace.

Her luckstone, the color of the lavender dawn above her head. This child would need luck. Iskara lifted the heavy silver chain off her neck and laid it over the child's head. The purple dawnstone hung past the girl's belly, laying against the rope that twisted between Iskara's legs.

The child could not escape, not tied to Iskara by that cord. The Morg's dagger flashed in her left hand, and blood sprayed her naked breast.

Iskara didn't know how to birth babies, but staunching blood was basic training for a Sister. The dagger slashed a strip of cloth from the tunic, and her fingers fumbled it into a knot. The blood flow stopped. The child would not bleed to death.

There were other ways to die, however. Unpleasant ways, if they involved Necimus. The step off the tower was quick and easy, but Iskara could no more do that now than she could starve herself over the months of her pregnancy.

She needed an escape. If not for her, at least for the child. The child deserved to live, tiny and wrinkled as she was, screaming against Fate as Iskara only wished that she could scream. Iskara's eyes scanned the paling sky, searching for an escape.

There. That dot in the sky — could it be?

Iskara threw back her head and called, as she had in those long ago days when she climbed the mountains above Surham.

It came. Dropping out of the airy reaches of the gray clouds, Iskara saw the form of an eagle. No ordinary eagle, but one of the giant varieties that flourished among the mountain peaks. Far from home, it coasted down the air currents, its circle narrowing until it perched on the battlements.

The twenty-foot wing span fanned air against Iskara's face as it landed. Crouched over the child, Iskara realized that here was the child's salvation. The eagle was large, and strong. It could carry the wailing bundle out of Necimus' reach. It could carry her to Erystra.

A name. Every child needed a name, and it was likely to be Iskara's last gift to the child. The blood pooled between her legs, beneath the tunic encompassing the infant. Iskara dipped her finger in the red liquid.

Skurgiil? Where did that name come from? It was no name that Iskara had ever heard, no name that she had ever considered. Not that she had spent time thinking of names. Her thoughts during captivity were on escape and revenge, not on names for infants. But there it was, written across the infant's belly in blood, and her hands were already knotting the tunic, forming a sling that the eagle could carry. A yellow eye regarded her endeavors, while the ever paling lavender sky reminded her of the passage of time.

"Carry."

Iskara's hand held up the knot, and the eagle beat its wings. In a moment, the eagle and its suspended bundle were specks against the sky, wheeling away to the south.

Iskara lay back and watched it go, watched until it disappeared from sight. *The battlements,* she thought dreamily. *Have to jump off the battlements.* But it was comfortable lying here, the pain finally gone, and she was tired, so tired. Tired and weak. Iskara tried to sit up, tried to reach for the arrow slits in the battlement wall, but she slipped in the blood that spread out around her body in an impossibly large circle.

So much blood, Iskara thought as she collapsed into the puddle. *Haven't seen this much blood since the battle where Akrien died.*

The battlement was circling around her, moving slowly to the rhythm of her heartbeats. *Jump,* Iskara chided herself, *have to jump. But I'm so tired. Need to rest, to get my strength up to jump. I'll just rest here a minute and watch the dawn.*

Dawn broke, and the sun found her staring unseeing at the lavender sky.

Chapter Seventeen

It is said that in days of old our Order could control the animals.
From "The Teachings of Aria"

Year After Aria, 303

The strains of a lyre drifted through the great hall at Castle Shield, accented by Ilissa's musical voice.

To Aragwen the vision came
In days of old, they say.
Of the Lady of the Sword, who taught her how
To live the Sword Sister's way.

The faces that were turned toward Ilissa were mostly young, for few Sword Sisters lived to old age. Their expression varied from rapture to wistfulness, as each translated the music into her own hopes and dreams.

"I give you skill," the Lady said,
"To wield a sword fair well,
This blessing shall you use for good
And to future Sword Mistresses shall you tell:

Tudae leaned back, as relaxed as she ever was, and surveyed what amounted to half of her garrison. She noticed the expressions on the women's faces and sighed.

She knew what they were feeling. Even those who chose this profession, either out of a desire for adventure or a sense of duty, gradually tired of the constant slaughter, the ongoing struggles, the misery, the hardships they always faced. Even in Sword Sisters the nesting instinct surfaced eventually, and they longed for a peace that was broken only by a baby's cry.

That no children shall they bear,
That they shall be married only to steel,
And they shall lead the Sisters of the Sword
For as long as a sword they can wield...

It was one of Fate's ironies that Iskara, who had made certain that Tudae would be Sword Mistress, purportedly to leave Iskara free to bear children, should die in childbirth. Tudae remembered that day all too well.

From the battlements of Castle Shield Erystra had Seen her great-granddaughter's birth, and Iskara wrapping the child in the remains of her tunic and summoning the eagle. Erystra told Tudae to look for the bird while Erystra watched her granddaughter die.

Tudae had never understood Iskara's ability to command the proud birds. She had first seen this ability on a patrol of the foothills, when she and Iskara were both wearing their first braid. The giant eagles had come circling down out of the sky, wheeling ever closer as Iskara called to them in sounds that matched their own cries perfectly. Tudae had gaped in amazement.

"I'm a daughter of the mountains." Iskara shrugged. "They like me."

Daughter of the mountains, and granddaughter of a Sayer. Not just any Sayer, either — Erystra was High Mistress of Neston, and the most skilled Sayer alive. Tudae knew the story, amazing in itself, of how a Sayer had born a child in Neston. Born a child with no Sight, who left to become a merchant's wife. And the merchant's wife had born a daughter who also had no Sight.

Iskara might have no Sight, but Tudae suspected the Sayer blood showed in other ways. Could just her beauty account for the way she controlled people? Tudae doubted it. Tudae had seen other beautiful women, and she herself was not considered uncomely. Tudae's slender form caught men's eyes, and her slanting black eyes, set in skin almost as dark as her hair, had bewitched more men than just Roagen. But only Roagen ever stayed by her side when Iskara was with her; other men flocked to Iskara. Iskara was always the center of attention, wherever she went.

No, Tudae didn't think it was just Iskara's beauty. She had a power about her; a power to charm people to her way of thinking that was suspiciously like a Sayer's Aura. There was one major difference, though — Sayers used their Auras for the good of the people, and Iskara used her charms for her own good.

Iskara could also calm a skittish horse with an ease unequaled even by the horse trainers. *If that amazed the other Sisters, what would they say if they could see Iskara now?* Tudae had wondered. The eagles followed Iskara as she and Tudae rode across the foothills. When they camped for the night, one lordly bird perched on a dead tree nearby.

Iskara made raucous sounds at the eagle, and it dipped its head at her and preened. Iskara had laughed as Tudae stared at her.

It was said that Sayers of old could influence animals as well as people. Tudae had seen Iskara do it then, and apparently she had done it now. From her post on the battlements Tudae saw a speck in the northern sky. It came closer, resolving into a great eagle with something dangling in its claws.

Tudae crouched behind the arrow guard as the giant bird swooped down, its wings beating air against her face as it slowed. In another moment it was gone, its claws empty.

The bundle the great bird deposited at Castle Shield contained a baby girl, large for pre-term. Around the baby's neck was a dawnstone, and across her belly, scrawled in birth-blood, was the word "Skurgiil." Tudae held the girl, trying to quiet her cries, as Erystra prepared to flee into the mountains.

"My presence will shield her from search by magic," Erystra told her, as she mounted. "But have care for your thoughts, because his magic can see those, too. Do not think of Skurgiil, and he will not be able to find her. When the time is right, she will return."

"But, Erystra, I don't understand;" Tudae replied as she handed the child up to the old Sayer.

"Read the prophecies of Aria and you will." Erystra regarded the wailing bundle mournfully. "I always knew this would come to pass," she murmured, "but I never thought it would come of my bloodline."

And Erystra, bearing the baby Skurgiil, had ridden into the mountains.

The girl the baby had become sat beside Tudae, a massive form on the simple chair. Erystra was gone, and now another Sayer had come to Castle Shield to continue her work. The care of Iskara's daughter had been left in Tudae's hands.

Chain mail left to clean, a horse left to groom, the position of Sword Mistress, an overgrown daughter—what hadn't Iskara left her? Tudae sighed. It was an unlikely friendship they had forged, that her sense of responsibility to a deceased Sister should span so many years. Now there were new friendships to be made and nurtured. Tudae beckoned to a Sword Sister, and whispered in her ear. Nodding, the Sword Sister left the room.

When the water clock struck the eleventh hour, Tudae rose from her chair. "Dawn comes all too soon, Sisters," she said, "and our enemies will not cease their attacks merely because we are tired. I am sure," Tudae's eyes sought Ilissa, "that the Singer will be willing to stay a few more nights." Ilissa inclined her head, and the Sisters gave a cheer. "More singing tomorrow night, then. For now, rest."

As the Sisters departed, Tudae turned to her guests. "Since the two of you are new here, you will be sharing a room. I trust that is acceptable?" Ilissa nodded, while Skurgiil shrugged. "Very good. I will show you to your room."

The two girls followed. *A strange looking pair*, Tudae thought. Ilissa didn't even come up to Skurgiil's shoulder. Tudae hoped the Mistress of Neston knows what she was doing, sending this one to be Skurgiil's companion. The girls' survival, and the survival of many others, would depend on their ability to get along with each other. That was the reason Tudae had roomed them together, hoping that the close quarters would speed their acquaintance.

It sped the acquaintance of a more unlikely pair, Tudae recalled.

Wendy Jensen

Chapter Eighteen

*Of the Lady of the Sword, who taught her how
To live the Sword Sisters' way....*
From "Song of the Sword Sisters"

Year After Aria, 279
Peasant Year of the Morgs

Twenty-four years earlier...

The sun was near setting when they entered a huge castle. Tudae hadn't noticed the country they rode through, had scarcely seen the town they paused in briefly, while the swearing woman spoke softly to a man with a wagon. She sat unmoving and unspeaking in the crook of the other woman's arm, not even answering the questions about where she was from. The sound of hooves clattering on the wooden bridge and the sentry's hail were the first sounds to rouse Tudae.

"Ho, Ulla, what goes?" The voice was friendly, Tudae noticed. "What have you got there, Ulla? A new recruit?"

Tudae felt the steel covered chest rise in a sigh. "I

suppose so. Courtesy of the Morgs. Took her family out just beyond Hilfer."

"That close?" The voice wasn't friendly anymore, and Tudae raised her head and faced the speaker. A freckled face under hair the color of glowing coals regarded her with amazement.

"Dark one, isn't she? Where's she hail from?"

"Hasn't said. Hasn't said anything since she stopped crying. Must be from the south, though. Far south."

The red-haired woman pursed her lips and nodded, then pointed into the castle. "There's a group of new ones over there, just arrived. Akrien is coming to welcome them. She'll want to hear your news."

Ulla nodded wearily and urged her horse forward. Not that it seemed to need much urging — it whickered eagerly, and tried to make straight for a building to the right.

"Whoa, Greedy. There'll be oats and a stall for you in a moment." Ulla pulled the impatient animal up by a group of five girls, standing in the courtyard with bundles at their feet.

The woman swung Tudae to the ground. "Wait here, child. Wait for the Sword Mistress." Ulla rode away, leaving Tudae standing with the girls.

They stared at her. They were all pale-skinned, though their hair color ranged from almost as black as Tudae's to a dull brown. They were older than Tudae, and bigger. None of them said a word. They just stared. Tudae stared at the ground, and wished desperately for Mammae.

"Recruits!" A forceful voice rang across the courtyard and Tudae risked a glance. A stern-looking woman beckoned. As the girls picked up their bundles and approached her, Tudae followed them.

Ulla said she was a recruit, too. Perhaps that was these strangers' word for girl.

Tudae couldn't see the woman anymore. The other girls were standing in front of her, blocking her view, but she could hear the woman talking. Something about duty

Sword Sister

and honor, trials and tribulations, working hard, and training starting at dawn.

Nothing about goat herding or rug-making at all. And when the woman said, "Dismissed!" Tudae wondered if that meant she was dismissing everything she had just said. *Odd people, these strangers.*

"Hey, you!"

The other girls bent to pick up their bundles. Except for one, who stood with her hands on her hips looking at Tudae.

"Yes, you." The girl grinned, her dark hair blowing across her face in the evening breeze. "Since you don't have a kit, you can carry mine." The girl pointed at the bundle at her feet.

The other girls were moving off toward a large building and the stern looking woman was strolling away, talking to Ulla. There was no one nearby.

"Hey, are you deaf? I said, carry my kit!"

The dark-haired girl shook Tudae by the shoulder, looming over her like the ugly creature had loomed over Pappae. With a strangled shriek, Tudae jumped at her.

The girl was taller than Tudae, slender but not skinny. Still, the force of Tudae's attack bore her down. Tudae glimpsed surprise on the girl's face as they hit the ground.

Tudae's bony little fists were a blur, battering against the girl's face. The girl raised her hands to ward off the blows, and her knee came up, knocking Tudae off her.

Tudae scrambled to her feet, tripping over her skirt. The girl wore those funny leggings the men wore around here, and she was weaving gracefully back and forth, her hands ready.

Tudae shrieked again and rushed her. The girl whirled to the side, one booted foot extended. Tudae sprawled face first in mud and straw.

Tudae heard the girl behind her gasp in pain, and Tudae rose up into the air, suspended by an iron grip around her neck. The world rotated, leaving Tudae with her feet a foot off the ground, facing her enemy.

The girl had problems of her own. Her right arm was twisted behind her back, held fast by the stern-faced woman who had addressed them earlier.

"What goes here?" The woman's voice was as stern as her face.

"She attacked me, Mistress." The girl's face was sullen, but her tone was respectful.

"Why?"

"No reason, Mistress." The girl stared defiantly at Tudae, who snarled and lashed the air with her fists.

"Here now, stop that!" The voice was Ulla's and the hand around her neck shook Tudae until her eyeballs sloshed in her head.

"Set her down."

The ground met Tudae's feet and she staggered. The other girl rubbed her right arm. The one she called Mistress looked at the other girl, arms folded across her chest.

"Your name, girl?"

"Iskara."

"From Neston."

Iskara nodded, and the stern-faced woman frowned. "Your grandmother spoke to me about you. Said you were causing trouble at Neston." Iskara shifted her weight to the other foot, eyes on the ground. "Seems you're causing trouble at Castle Shield, as well. Shall I send you back to Neston?"

Iskara's voice was low. "No, Mistress."

"Then we'll have no more trouble." The sharp eyes turned in Tudae's direction. "And who is this one?"

"I was just telling you about her, Sword Mistress. The girl we found, her family slaughtered by the Morgs."

Tudae scowled at Iskara, who scowled back, but at Ulla's words a strange look crossed the older girl's face.

Was it pity? Tudae raised her chin. She didn't want this stranger's pity.

"Oh, yes." The Sword Mistress' hand came out, touched Tudae's cheek. "She is dark, indeed. Are you from the south, child? What is your name?"

Tudae's lower lip trembled, but no words came out.

After a moment the Sword Mistress turned to Ulla. "Can she talk?"

"Hasn't yet. Made some funny sounds, when we first found her, but no words. She may be mute."

The Sword Mistress shook her head regretfully. "Mute orphan or not, I can't let this behavior go unpunished. Take them both to the main hall, Ulla, and give them each half of it to scrub. Whoever finishes first will eat supper."

Tudae curled into a ball under her blankets, hoping to ease the cramping in her stomach. She hadn't eaten since morning and that meal had been left in half-digested puddles by the burning cart.

Mammae always exclaimed at the amount of food Tudae could put into her skinny body and at how frequently she wanted to eat. Mammae refused Tudae's pleas for mid-morning and mid-afternoon snacks, so Tudae had learned to gorge herself when mealtimes came around to ward off the inevitable pangs of hunger. Now she had been without food in her stomach — that stayed in her stomach — for a full day, and her body screamed at the lack.

It was all that girl's fault.

That horrible, grinning, dark-haired girl who ordered Tudae to carry her bundle for her. The girl bigger and stronger than Tudae, who scrubbed her half of the floor in a quarter of the time it had taken Tudae to do hers. The girl who dumped her bucket of dirty water on Tudae's side of the floor, soaking Tudae's skirts and doubling her mop up time.

The arrogant, selfish girl that Tudae hated. The girl who cheated. The girl with a full belly, who lay not six feet away from her in the dark.

Tudae remembered the words of the one they called Sword Mistress, standing in the hall after the strangers had finished their meals.

"Quarter them together," she said. "Either they will learn to get along, or they will kill each other."

A woman in smelly metal clothes had nodded, taking them to a small room with two beds and sliding a bar across the door on the outside.

Get along with her or kill her. Tudae much preferred the second option, but right now she was too weak from hunger to try. Perhaps tomorrow the hunger pangs would ease up. Tudae wasn't sure, because Mammae never sent her to bed supperless. But if they did, Tudae would wake up before the nasty, cheating girl and claw her mocking eyes out before she awoke.

"Psst!" The voice from the other bed was a whisper.

Tudae ignored it.

"I know you're awake. I heard your stomach growl, and I know you can't sleep through that."

How would she know? Tudae wondered. *She got her supper.*

There was a rustle from the other bed, and the sound of metal hitting stone. Tudae tensed for an attack, but the only assault was on her eyes. There was light.

Tudae squinted, and saw a stub of a candle in the other girl's hand. It illuminated her face, and her eyes were not mocking Tudae. They were serious, and... concerned.

"Hungry?" the girl queried.

Stupid stranger. Tears stung Tudae's, and she turned her face to the rough stone wall. *She is mocking me, after all.*

Tudae flinched away from the girl's touch on her shoulder, but the stranger wouldn't go away. Instead, she shoved something under Tudae's nose. Something that smelled good.

Tudae opened her eyes. Before her was the most luscious-looking apple she had ever seen. Not that she had seen many; they didn't grow in the desert, and in the towns they passed Mammae always purchased dried ones. They were cheaper, Mammae said, and kept longer.

Sword Sister

But this one wasn't dried. It was full and round and plump, and smelled incredibly good. Her stomach rumbled again. Tudae snatched the apple and sank her teeth into it.

"I have bread and cheese here, too." Tudae heard a crunch behind her, and rolled over to see the obnoxious girl biting into an apple of her own.

Two apples? Was this nasty girl wealthy, that she could afford such luxuries?

On the girl's bed were a piece of bread and a chunk of cheese. Tudae eyed them greedily.

The girl tossed them to her. Tudae caught the cheese, took a bite, and retrieved the bread from the floor. Honest dirt never killed anyone, Pappae always said, so Tudae bit into the bread as well. She chewed, cheeks bulging, and eyed the strange girl across from her.

"Whar ded yu git thees?" Tudae's mouth wasn't empty yet, but curiosity was eating her faster than she was eating the apple. And Mammae wasn't here to say *"Are you a goat or a girl?"*

The other girl's dark eyebrows shot up. "Oh, so you *can* talk? And the Sisters thought you were mute!" The other girl shrugged. "I'm Iskara. I took them from the kitchen, when I brought my dish in for washing."

"Yu stold thim?" Tudae shoved the mass of apple-cheese-bread to one cheek and stared at Iskara.

"Not 'stole.' Took." Iskara grinned. "It was for a good cause. Can't have a future Sword Sister dying of hunger, can we?"

Tudae didn't know what a Sword Sister was, but the only one dying of hunger here had been her. Tudae stared at Iskara in amazement as she realized, *she stole them for me!*

Tudae remembered Mammae's teaching on manners, swallowed her mouthful of food, and bowed from the waist. "Thank you. My tent is your tent."

Iskara laughed. "You don't have a tent, and I wouldn't want it if you did. How about we just be friends?"

When Tudae nodded and smiled, Iskara added, "And you don't have to thank me. I'm the one who made you miss supper in the first place."

Chapter Nineteen

The Power of a Sayer is her Aura, with which she can work good....
Teachings of the Sayers

Year After Aria, 303

In their room, Skurgiil regarded Ilissa by the light of a single candle.

She is so tiny, this girl! Skurgiil thought. *Tiny and fragile looking, like a newborn lamb. A lamb with big, beautiful eyes that seem to see right through me.*

Then Ilissa smiled, and it was as if dawn broke in her eyes. Her voice was sweet, melodic, as she said, "I hope we can be friends, Skurgiil."

Friends. The eagles in the mountains were her friends, following her as she climbed the peaks, answering her calls as if she were one of their own. Trenton was a friend, she supposed; a friend she saw each spring. But a friend who was a girl, about her age, and in the same room? A girl whose waist was the size of her thigh? A tiny, frail girl, like a newborn lamb, needing help and protection?

Skurgiil's feelings of awkwardness dissolved. Instead of feeling big and ugly next to this girl, she suddenly felt strong and powerful. Which was precisely what Ilissa intended she feel, when she sent out an Aura of Ease.

"I...I think we can be... what is your name?"

"Ilissa." The Sayer extended her hand.

Skurgiil took the hand carefully, giving it a very gentle squeeze. "I think we can be friends, Ilissa. I... I do not know much about friends. I grew up in the mountains."

"How fascinating! You must tell me all about it." Ilissa sat on her bed.

"It was beautiful there." Skurgiil lowered herself onto her own bed, which creaked a protest at her weight. "The mountains were steep, and there was a waterfall where I bathed...."

Ilissa wasn't listening. Her body had gone stiff and her eyes were wide. She stared over Skurgiil's shoulder, and her expression spoke horror.

"Ilissa, what...."

Purple light suddenly suffused the room. Skurgiil stared at her chest. The light came from her necklace.

Skurgiil felt a tingling on the back of her neck, like when a wolf was staring at the flock. She seized her knife and scanned the room. "Ilissa! What is happening?"

Ilissa didn't respond. Her eyes closed and her tiny frame trembled. Abruptly the purple light faded. Ilissa drew a shuddering breath and opened her eyes.

Skurgiil's hand grasped her dawnstone, but it was cool as always to her touch. No evidence of the strange occurrence remained, except for the horror on Ilissa's face.

"I wasn't ready for him," the slight girl murmured, as if to herself. "I must be more vigilant."

"Ilissa! What happened?"

The deep blue eyes regarded Skurgiil with sorrow and pity. "We were scanned by magic. He is looking for you."

"Who? Who is looking for me?"

"Necimus." Ilissa shivered. Just for a moment, she had Seen him. Her Sight and his search met and she looked into the deep-set glowing eyes.

Sword Sister

"Necimus is the evil sorcerer the Sword Sisters fight against, right?" When Ilissa nodded, Skurgiil continued, "So why is he searching for me? I'm not even a Sword Sister yet."

Ilissa sighed. She didn't want to explain yet, not until she knew Skurgiil better. From her conversation with Tudae, Ilissa knew that the explanations would have to be worded carefully, that half-truths were necessary for now. "It goes back to a Sayer prophetess, Aria...."

"Sayer? Erystra was a Sayer."

"So am I, Skurgiil."

"But ye said ye were a Singer!"

"I had a good reason for saying that. The prophetess Aria foretold, three hundred years ago, the rising of great evil in this land. She also foretold that his demise would be caused by one known as *The Scourge of Evil*. Aria wrote in the Old Tongue, and in that language Scourge of Evil is written Skurg i'Il — Skurgiil."

"But... that is my name!"

"Yes. Necimus has been searching for one by that name for years. Erystra's presence protected you from his search these years past. And protects you still," Ilissa added. "I could not have held off his search by myself."

"What do ye mean, protects me still?"

"The dawnstone, Skurgiil. You saw how it glowed? Erystra's spirit has passed into it. She has become a Guardian, an honor only the best Sayers can ever hope for. She will be with you, watching over you, as long as you wear the stone."

Skurgiil's mind went back to Erystra's dying moments. "So that was why..." Skurgiil regarded Ilissa wistfully. "If she is still with me... Can I talk to her?"

/Yes, child./

By the faint pulsing of the stone and the surprise on Skurgiil's face, Ilissa gathered she had received her answer.

"Good Mother!" Skurgiil's voice was soft, choked with tears. "I...I miss you."

/Yes, Skurgiil. The way is long and hard for you, but I

will be with you. Rest now, for there be much to do on the morrow./

Obediently, Skurgiil lay back on her bed. Ilissa took this opportunity to close her eyes and meditate on creating an Aura of Peace. When she opened her eyes again, Skurgiil was asleep.

Ilissa reached into her saddlebags and pulled out two books with worn covers. The High Mistress had instructed her to bring them, and to study them faithfully. One was the book of mental exercises Ilissa had been learning for the past year. The other volume was titled "The Prophecies of Aria."

Ilissa opened this book, flipping through the pages in search of one particular prophecy. She found it, and translating from the old tongue, she read:

In days when Evil grows,
And despair grips the land,
Then will come The Scourge of Evil.
Three shall they be,
One to draw Evil out and defeat it,
One to fight fire with fire,
And one to protect.
And the weapons that defeat the Evil
Shall be forged from the Evil itself.
The Scourge of Evil will be
Of the Evil's own making.

Ilissa read it and re-read it, pondering its meaning. Then she opened her book of exercises, and practiced strengthening her Protective Aura until the candle guttered out.

⌐◉⌐

Necimus sat behind his desk, unclothed, staring at his globe in frustrated rage. He had sent his search through Castle Shield looking for the one called Skurgiil. All it had shown him was one young Sayer in a room bathed

Sword Sister

with purple light. He knew she was a Sayer, even though she did not wear the robes of one, because in the instant her eyes met his he knew she Saw him. Then she had closed her eyes and a Protective Aura repelled his search, causing his globe to flicker and darken.

Necimus shot another bolt of purple lightning at the globe, directing the search to return. The globe paled for a minute, then faded to darkness again.

With practice born of power, Necimus controlled his anger. He leaned back in his chair and considered the situation.

There was a Sayer at Castle Shield whose Aura impaired his search. That she did so successfully surprised him, for she was young, and it took a Sayer of great strength to impede his magic. Erystra had been such a one, which was part of the reason he had taken such delight in holding her granddaughter prisoner and creating a child in her.

Erystra! Necimus' huge fist crashed down on the blackwood desk, causing the globe to jump and the figure on the bed behind him to tremble. Of course! Why didn't he think of it before?

In his rage at losing Iskara's child, he had forgotten the child was also Erystra's great-grandchild. No doubt Iskara, the witch, sent the eagle to Erystra, and the old hag had guarded the child all these years. No wonder his magical searches yielded nothing. Her Aura was powerful.

Necimus frowned. Balek had found an old Sayer living alone in the mountains. Necimus considered questioning Balek again, but decided against it. Kurg would be easier to question. He wore no medallion of Protection Against Magical Search.

That was something about Balek that irritated Necimus. The frail wizard wore so many medallions of protection against one thing or another that it was a wonder he could walk. The wizard had also begun embroidering runes on his black robes, using black thread. Necimus had laughed. As if black on black would prevent him from seeing them!

Balek obviously did not trust him. For that reason, if no other, Necimus did not trust Balek. He regretted the necessity of keeping the wizard at Castle Darkfall, but had long ago decided it was a price he must pay for keeping himself within the safety of his castle walls.

Balek was a useful servant. He brought back word of the girl Skurgiil, which Kurg missed. However, for information on the old Sayer, Kurg was a better choice. After all, according to Balek, Kurg had killed her. With a movement of his fingers and a murmured word, Necimus sent forth a Summons and waited.

The door opened, admitting a disheveled Kurg. Necimus motioned for him to be seated.

The half-Morg gaped as he sat, for Necimus was even more impressive undressed than he was clothed. Even his half-Morg son did not have the massive proportions of Necimus himself.

Irritated, Necimus donned his robe before igniting his globe with purple lightning. Couldn't have the dolt's mind wandering while Necimus was trying to question him.

"Tell me about your first excursion into the mountains," the sorcerer commanded.

Haltingly, Kurg recounted the events of the flight. Necimus did not look at him, and scarcely listened to his words. Instead he watched the globe, as the vague forms of Kurg's thoughts materialized there.

He saw a cottage, in a small valley at the foot of The Guardian. He saw a tiny old woman run out of the cottage, waving a stick.

It was Erystra. Many years older than when he had last seen her, but Erystra nonetheless. He saw Kurg's sword slide into her body. Erystra was dead.

As images in the globe changed to pictures of lust, Necimus glanced sharply at Kurg. His half-Morg son stared open-mouthed at the figure chained to Necimus' bed.

Necimus had forgotten about her. By the images in

the globe he could tell that Kurg saw a beautiful, dark haired human female struggling weakly against her bonds.

He had crafted the illusion carefully, searching his memory for all the details of Iskara he learned in the months she was his prisoner. For his own amusement, he enchanted the female half-Morg to respond as Iskara did, so many years ago.

It was an excellent illusion. A wizard such as Balek might notice the slightly fuzzy lines, but no one without magical powers would know the difference.

Necimus glanced back at his son. Kurg was a good guard. A bit dense, but what could you expect from a Morg mother? *A bit too interested in human females, too,* Necimus thought wryly, noting the throbbing pictures in the globe.

Kurg had served him well. Erystra was dead because of Kurg, though it puzzled Necimus that she died so easily. A Sayer of her power should have been able to influence a half-Morg with her Aura. Perhaps her power had waned as she grew old. *Older,* Necimus corrected himself. *That hag had been old forever.*

Kurg deserved some kind of reward, and Necimus knew the kind of reward Kurg wanted.

"Help yourself," Necimus growled, gesturing towards the bed. It wouldn't matter now. He had seeded the female. In a few months she would give birth to a child that was one-fourth Morg and three-fourths Necimus. All that remained was to record the breeding in his genetics log, and hope that the child turned out more intelligent than its predecessors.

More intelligent and with some aptitude for sorcery, Necimus thought, as he cast a zone of silence around himself, drowning out the noises from the bed. So far not one of his half-breeds had been able to cast even the simplest of spells.

It comes of being half-Morg, Necimus thought disgustedly, sending a bolt of purple lightning to erase the pictures in the globe. Morgs were too fond of satisfying their lusts to concentrate on sorcery. Perhaps a human child would have an aptitude for the art.

As Necimus pondered this, watching the purple glow fade from the globe, a thought struck him. The thought was stunning in its simplicity, staggering in its import.

Perhaps he did have a child with an aptitude for sorcery! The room where the young Sayer sat had been bathed with a purple glow. Perhaps it wasn't just the Sayer's Aura that impeded his search. Perhaps this Skurgiil was a sorceress in her own right. Necimus leaned back in his chair to consider the implications of this.

A girl — *no, woman, it had been what? Seventeen years?* — who was half Iskara, half Necimus. She had apparently inherited his size, his ability to perform magic and surely she would have inherited some of her mother's beauty. She would be a woman to be reckoned with, a woman to be proud of. A woman who could be a fitting consort for Necimus; a woman who could bear his offspring without dying. Offspring who would be three-quarters Necimus, and one-quarter Iskara.

For years Necimus had dreamed of populating the world with his own race. Here, at last, was his answer.

Chapter Twenty

We must flee, my darling child...
*From "Dawn of the Morgs"
by Wyflen Herdbummer*

Year After Aria, 275
Peasant Year of the Raids

Twenty-eight years earlier...

"Sir, the... lass... will die. And the child with her."

Algnor ceased clawing his gray beard and focused on the midwife's apprentice. Breena was thirtyish, plump and plain, and a good woman, Algnor supposed, judging by her kindly face. But he heard the pause before the word "lass," saw the horror lurking in this woman's eyes, and he knew why.

The illusion spell he cast yestermorn had worn off shortly after this day's dawning. In the confusion and worry of the preceding night, Algnor had forgotten to renew it.

The screams warned him of his mistake. There had been screams aplenty through the long night and into the morning, but these screams were different. They weren't Glenda's.

Algnor had rushed through the curtained door of the bedroom. Perhaps the mice and snakes he kept for experiments had escaped the laboratory. Women were fussy about such things.

There were no mice or snakes in his bedroom. Only Midwife Triil, making warding signs with her withered hands, and Breena, her back pressed to the wardrobe door, muffling her screams in the cooling cloth that dripped in her hand.

And, of course, Glenda.

Algnor gaped at the huge mound of belly that rose above the bed. It moved, writhing beneath the scarred skin like a giant flesh worm straining for release. Glenda added her screams to Breena's, staring at him with beseeching eyes from the remnants of her face.

"Silence!" Algnor was a mild man, a meek man, but he was a man still, and a wizard besides. The screams stopped.

Glenda fainted. Breena whimpered. Midwife Triil watched him with wary eyes.

"Tend her." Algnor's tone was gruff, but his chest ached with pity; the same pity that caused him to shelter Glenda nine months ago and to cast an illusion spell around her ruined form.

Breena's fingers trembled as she laid the cooling cloth across a forehead devoid of hair, across skin taut and gleaming with scars. Seconds ago the she had been tending an average girl in her first childbirth, and now... Breena shuddered. The creatures of her childhood nightmares were more appealing.

Algnor saw the shudder. He rubbed trembling fingers across his aching temples and tried to think. The illusion was gone, and he hadn't studied the spell this morning.

He hadn't studied any spells this morning. Glenda's pains had started yesterday afternoon, and through the night her moans changed to screams.

Algnor couldn't sleep, couldn't study, couldn't think.

Couldn't do anything but pull his straggly beard and pace the sitting room, like the expectant father the townsfolk believed him to be.

⇥◉⇤

Glenda writhed on the bed. *Her hands clutched at the ropes that bound her wrists. Her fingers searched for the knots. But her hands were going numb from the rope, and the pain inside her was nearly unbearable. It was the fire, the flames, licking up around the bed, and the knots wouldn't untie, the ropes wouldn't give. She was going to die, here in this bed, and it was all his fault.*

Breena watched the girl's hands groping at the headboard. At least, they had once been hands. Now they were claws, with pale bone showing through scars where there should have been flesh. Breena shuddered again, and averted her eyes as she changed the cooling cloth.

⇥◉⇤

Glenda had once been pretty. Not just pretty, but the prettiest girl in the village, or so her mother said, and Glenda quite agreed. No other girl had such thick blonde hair, or such brilliant blue eyes, or such full pink lips and cheeks. If it surprised her mother that at eighteen Glenda was not yet wed, it was only because there were things about Glenda that her mother did not know.

Glenda was vain. She polished her little tin mirror with loving care, and made frequent trips to the well. Glenda's mother thought her a very dutiful daughter, to always fetch the water.

Glenda wasn't dutiful. She was vain, and she was ambitious. There were men enough in the village of Sekrun willing to marry her, but Glenda had heard that in the large towns outside the mountains there were mirrors of silvered glass, that showed reflections even better than the water of the well on a still day. Glenda wanted such a mirror more than a new frock, or ribbons for her hair, or even a husband. More than anything, Glenda desired a silvered glass mirror.

So Glenda carried water from the well and flirted with the swains and hoarded the coppers from selling eggs, and dreamed of the day she would leave the village and go to a town that had silvered glass mirrors and men to marry who were rich enough to buy her one of her very own.

Glenda had once been pretty, but only Glenda knew that now. Breena did not know that. Nor did Algnor. The creature he found one night last summer was not pretty.

Algnor would not have found her at all if it hadn't been for Spell.

Algnor had fallen asleep that night, nodding in his chair by his fire, and smiling at his dream. It was a pleasant dream of children, laughing and climbing on his knee. Algnor liked children, loved to delight them with his colorful illusions. In the dream he created an especially fine illusion and the children all laughed and clapped. One dark haired boy climbed onto Algnor's lap and kissed him.

A cold, wet kiss. Not like a child at all. More like a dog.

"Spell? Down, boy." Algnor fumbled for his pet's muzzle and groaned as one paw pressed into his bladder. Algnor was an old man, and he couldn't hold it like he used to. Spell was an old dog. Algnor guessed he couldn't hold it like he used to, either, because he was scratching at the door, whining.

"Coming, Spell, coming," Algnor muttered. Might as well relieve himself too, since he had to let Spell out. Algnor just hoped they didn't choose the same bush.

Algnor got the bush all to himself. Spell whined and sniffed the air. Algnor regarded the yellow puddle forming at his feet.

"It's not that bad, Spell. You've done worse yourself." The old wizard cast a reproachful glance at his pet, but Spell was gone. Algnor heard him whining in the woods behind the cottage.

Algnor swore, but not too strongly. He was a mild

man, not given to strong language, or strong drink, or even strong opinions. But tonight he was tired, and he wanted to go to bed and sleep without being disturbed at all hours of the night by a wayward Spell who finally wanted in after a night of chasing rabbits, like he had that one night, years ago, and.... *Years ago.*

Spell hadn't chased rabbits in years and he wasn't chasing one now. Algnor could still hear him whining, and the whining wasn't moving.

"Spell? You find something, boy?"

That yip must mean "yes." Algnor would have to go see, or he'd never get to bed. But he wouldn't go in the dark!

"Light," Algnor muttered, and a ball of white light appeared in his left hand. Algnor squinted, and stepped into the woods.

The smell was bad. He noticed it when he entered the trees. A sickly, sweetish, burned odor that grew worse as he got closer to Spell's yips.

The smell was bad, but it was nothing compared to the sight.

Algnor held the globe of light aloft, illuminating the ground below. Spell cringed to one side, whining. In the circle of light lay a girl.

Algnor could tell she was a girl, because whatever clothes she once wore had burned away, as had her hair, and most of her skin. The burns were a furious red, splotched with festering white, and dotted with bits of flesh burned black. Out of the mess that had once been her face, Glenda gazed at Algnor with brilliant blue eyes and whimpered.

The light shook in Algnor's hand. With great care he set it on a fallen tree trunk and with equal care he leaned over the tree trunk and lost his supper.

⁂

The Mission to serve the people of Troghaven was not a very good Mission, but Sora was not a very good

Sayer. Unlike many who came to the Order, she had no innate gift of Sight. She came because people respected Sayers and as the eighth of ten children, Sora craved respect.

Sora did not complain about her Mission. Troghaven was a remote mountain village, but Sora was the only Sayer there. For the first time in her life there was no competition. No older or younger siblings to compete for the scant food or meager attention from her mother, no other acolytes who were smarter and more gifted, no other Sayers who were more powerful. There was only Sora in the village of Troghaven and the people there respected her.

The Sayer's training gave Sora some Sight. She could find a lamb lost in the mountains, warn the shepherds to bring in the flocks before a bad storm, and predict a drought so the farmers would be prepared to water and prevent crop failure. She knew the ceremonies for weddings and deaths, and she could heal. Healing was the one thing Sora could do exceptionally well.

So Sora wed the couples, blessed the children and the crops, performed the funerals, and healed the sick and injured of Troghaven. She never worried about the problems of the more civilized world she had left behind, or the greater scheme of things beyond her small village. Never, until the night that Algnor knocked on her door.

He couldn't touch her. She was a girl — a naked girl.

Algnor was not accustomed to touching naked girls. And she was hurt, so dreadfully hurt, that he was sure he couldn't touch her without hurting her more.

She needed help. Those bright blue eyes, contrasting so awfully with the burned flesh of her face, cut into his heart, and her pitiful moans grabbed at his soul. Algnor wiped vomit from his beard and tried to think.

His mind darted through his little cottage, scanning his kitchen, his laboratory, his bedroom for something,

Sword Sister

anything that would help. He saw only an old wizard's cottage, clean and neat, to be sure, but... *of course!*

Algnor hated housecleaning. He could have hired a woman from the village to clean his cottage, but they made him nervous, so he developed a spell. He called it his Servant Spell. His cottage grew very dirty over the weeks it took to develop the spell, but in the end he had a spell that could sweep, wash, turn his bed down, and carry water and firewood.

Carry! That was it! The spell could carry the burned girl to his cottage, and never hurt her. Then he could get someone to help her, someone who could heal her hideous wounds.

※◉※

Sora applied the poultices she brought with ease born of practice. She had never seen such severe burns before, even though she had treated Dowren's son the day his mother's washing pot turned over on him, and the blacksmith frequently came in for a poultice for burns from his furnace. The girl had cried piteously when the poultices went on, until the old wizard cast a Sleeping spell on her.

Sora glanced at Algnor as she finished applying the wrappings. She didn't ask how the girl came to be so terribly burned. Sora was not a powerful Sayer, but she could See that the kindly old man was not to blame. She had no doubt that the poor girl owed Algnor her life.

But Sora doubted the girl would be grateful when the wrappings came off and she saw her face. Or what was left of it.

The girl would live, but Sora could not replace burned flesh, or turn scar to skin. Sora asked no questions, but cast her Healing Aura on the girl until it was gone.

It was not until she was ready to leave that the Sight came to her.

Algnor winced at the girl's cries as the poultices went on. He could not even bear to see a mouse suffer in a trap, so he had developed a sweet tasting potion that he when poured on bread, which sent the mice to a sleep from which they never awoke. Algnor had no cat, so he kept a good supply of potion on hand at all times, lest the field mice take over his cottage.

Algnor wished he could give this poor girl a dose of it. She needed it more than the mice.

Algnor reproached himself for the thought immediately. He didn't bring her into his cottage, lay her in his bed — a bed that had never had a girl in it, burned or otherwise — just to ease her out of life now. But — she had suffered so much already! Then Algnor remembered the scroll. The one with the Sleeping spell on it. The spell he used to cure a villager's occasional bout of insomnia.

The Sayer glanced at him as he brought in the scroll, and watched him as he read it. When the girl was asleep, and quiet — Algnor thanked his failing memory for remembering the scroll — the Sayer continued with her work and did not speak until she stood at the door, ready to leave.

Sora's head tilted back. Algnor knew she was looking through him; at what, he did not know.

"Wizard," the Sayer's voice was soft, "the girl is with child." Sora did not notice Algnor's stunned expression. "The child..." Sora clutched at words, for she was unaccustomed to the Sight, "... is important. Guard them well."

Sora left the stunned wizard alone with a wounded girl, and returned to her chapel where she penned a missive to her superiors, recounting the night's events.

Behind the gray walls of Neston, her missive would be duly noted and carefully considered.

"Master Algnor! Master Algnor!"

The shrill voice assaulted Algnor's hearing with a force that the knocking at his door had lacked. He straightened in his chair and blinked. Sunlight trickled in around his shuttered windows, and Spell lay near the bedchamber curtain, thumping his tail against the floor.

"Fell asleep in my chair, did I? I'm too old for that, Spell. You should have roused me, so I could have slept in my bed...."

No, he couldn't. There was a girl in his bed, a burned girl. The girl he found in the woods last night.

"Master Algnor! Dame Hagren, here! I have your eggs!"

Dame Hagren, and eggs. Algnor sighed as he rose from the chair. There was no denying the town busybody; she would knock until he answered the door, even if it took hours. Algnor knew this from experience. By the tone of her voice, she had some gossip to go with the eggs.

"Good morn, Dame Hagren." Algnor's voice was resigned as he raised the latch. Spell growled once as the woman pushed through door.

"G'day, Master Algnor! Have ye heard the news?"

"No, Dame Hagren." Perhaps the news would distract the old widow from making sheep eyes at him. He was too tired to fend off her sly remarks today. Remarks about how lonely it was to live alone, or how he needed a woman to care for him. Algnor gestured to his cushioned chair and bent to start a fire in the hearth as the crone prattled on.

"Why, there was a demon here! Tristnor's son saw it on the road last night, coming down from the mountains. All red it was, and burned from the fires of hell."

Algnor's hands shook so badly he nearly dropped the flint. "Demon, you say?"

"Aye, and coming straight for the town. Why, if

young Aman hadn't throwed stones at it...."

"Stones?"

"Aye. He throwed stones, and it disappeared into the woods. Good thing, too, because the tinker's son took his wares to Sekrun yestermorn, and he comed back and said the whole village was burnt!" Dame Hagren nodded solemnly.

The tinder in the hearth smoldered, but Algnor didn't notice. "The whole village?"

"To the ground. Must have been the demon done it, and was coming to do us next."

"But... the people? Of Sekrun?"

"Dead, all of them. Died right in their houses, they did." Dame Hagren nodded again with grim satisfaction. It wasn't often she got a response like this from the old wizard. "The townsfolk are arming, even now."

Algnor looked bewildered.

"To kill the demon," Dame Hagren added.

Algnor's gaze drifted to the closed bedchamber curtain, his expression a mixture of horror and fear.

⇥◉⇤

Sora came nightly to the tiny cottage at the edge of the woods. She came in the darkness, tapping lightly on the door until Algnor admitted her. She changed the bandages and cast her Healing Aura on the girl, and asked no questions, although she occasionally volunteered information about the villagers' search for the "demon," and about the progress of the girl's healing.

"She will be scarred." Sora's eyes looked at Algnor this time, not through him, and Algnor had the uncomfortable feeling he was supposed to do something about the girl's condition.

"Badly scarred," Sora added, as she bundled up the old bandages. At the door she turned, and met the wizard's eyes. "The bandages will come off for good in two days." Sora left Algnor to ponder this.

Ponder it he did. Late into the night he pondered.

Sword Sister

And wondered why he should be faced with such a problem, when all he wanted was to be left alone to create his pretty illusions.

Which of course, was the answer. The fire in his hearth had become gray-dusted coals when Algnor realized this. He could create a pretty illusion around the girl.

He worked on his illusion all the next day. It was more difficult than he expected. Illusions he could do, and do them well, but this one had to be centered around the girl, to move as she moved. The illusion had to last more than an hour or two. All day Algnor worked on these problems, but there was one problem more.

What was she supposed to look like?

Algnor had no idea. He would not wake the girl to ask her, and even if he did, he could not create an accurate illusion just from a verbal description. The thought of her awakening to see herself as she was now filled Algnor's kind old heart with horror.

No, the illusion must be ready before she opened her eyes, and if she did not look as she remembered herself, well... it would still be better than she looked now.

But Algnor still had a problem. He knew few women, and they all dwelt in the village. He could not cast the illusion to look like someone local, for fear the girl would meet her double in the street. Algnor could create illusions of dragons and fairies and other mythical creatures, but his knowledge of real women was small.

So he fashioned an illusion in the image of Risa. Algnor had courted Risa through the summer nights in the long ago days of his apprenticeship in a distant town. When she died of a fever in the fall of his nineteenth year Algnor had mourned, but not too deeply, for his first and true love was Magic. Risa had been a plain and simple girl, but Algnor remembered her with an old man's memory of the hormonal urges of youth. The illusion he created of Risa was not beautiful, nor accurate, but it was quite pretty. And he hoped, sufficient for the poor burned girl's needs.

Algnor knew the villagers would soon find out about his houseguest, and they did. Dame Hagren made the discovery one morning, over Algnor's weekly ration of eggs and gossip. Algnor almost smiled at the look of dismay that covered the crone's face as Glenda stepped out from behind the bedchamber curtain.

"Dame Hagren, this is Glenda. She's my... uh..." Algnor hadn't thought of this. *His cousin?* No, she was too young. *Niece, perhaps?*

"I can see what she is, well enough, Master Algnor!" Dame Hagren's chin trembled, and her lips pursed as she scanned Glenda. The illusion of Risa was convincing; it even showed through Algnor's threadbare nightshirt that Glenda wore. And to Algnor's surprise, Dame Hagren took her leave quite quickly, shaking her bonneted head all the way down the path.

Everyone in the village knew about Glenda the next day when Algnor went to buy food. He was going through food at an alarming rate, feeding two mouths. *And one of those mouths eating for two,* he reminded himself.

Women stared at him as he passed, and whispered among themselves. The men in the tavern pounded him on the back, called him a "sly old dog," bought him drinks, and wouldn't take no for an answer. Algnor wandered home, befuddled by the ale and bemused by his welcome, to find Glenda sobbing.

It was her bleeding, she said, and sounded so desolate that Algnor was halfway out the door to fetch Sora before he understood.

She wasn't dying. She wasn't even bleeding. She had missed her monthly bleeding, and she knew she was pregnant.

Algnor sank into his chair, and stared at the sobbing girl. What did you say to a sobbing, pregnant girl? Algnor hadn't the foggiest notion, though his brain was quite foggy with the ale.

"Here," he said, pushing the pint which the tavern keeper insisted he take "for the road" into her hands.

Sword Sister

Glenda gulped, hiccuped, and gulped again. Then, as the ale did its work, she talked.

Algnor's face turned as gray as his beard with what she told him.

⁘◉⁙

Glenda hurried down the path from the well. Her reflection in its still surface had hardly been visible, for the sun was setting and dusk was falling quickly. Glenda hurried, for she didn't care to be out by herself after dark, especially going past the witch's house.

Glenda hated the witch. She was ugly, and old, and mean, and had a way of calling Glenda "my pretty" that made her blood feel like spring water on a winter day. But she bought Glenda's eggs, so Glenda went to her house every week to deliver a fresh three dozen and get her three copper pieces.

But she never went at night. No, never, and she tried to go early in the morning, before the witch's son was awake.

If Glenda hated the witch, she feared her son. He was ugly and mean, like the witch, but he was also big. Very big. Glenda didn't like the way he looked at the front of her blouse.

And he was a bastard. Everyone knew it. The witch never married. Who would marry such an ugly woman?

She had gone into the mountains years ago, they said, and come back pregnant. Some said the witch had mated with a demon, and they whispered "Evilness" behind his back.

Until the boy started growing. He quickly outstripped the lads his own age, then outgrew the ones who were four years older. Now he had outgrown even the tallest, biggest man in the village, and people whispered that the witch must have mated with a mountain giant.

Glenda didn't care who had sired him. He was a bastard, and she didn't like him staring at her. She couldn't tell him to stop, or ask her father or brothers to thrash him for it, because he had already thrashed the blacksmith's son and the blacksmith's son was the best fighter in the village.

Everyone feared the witch. She could put a hex on your cattle, they said, same as she could make a charm for your cow to have twins. Although the people of the village tolerated the witch out of fear, and even bought her charms, Glenda would have nothing to do with her son.

She was destined for a man better looking and richer, much richer, who certainly would not be a bastard. Glenda didn't know who this man would be, but she knew it wouldn't be Necimus.

She hurried down the path, her water bucket banging against her leg, hoping to make it past the witch's house before dark. She was almost past when she heard the scream.

It was a horrible scream, high-pitched and gurgling, and it came from the witch's house. Glenda ran home, spilling her water all the way.

"Probably killing one of them rabbits she raises, for feet for charms," her mother soothed when Glenda ran in sobbing, teeth chattering, her skirt drenched. "Good thing there's still water in the keg, girl. You'll have to go an extra time tomorrow."

Glenda was still shivering when she curled up to sleep on her straw mattress.

It hadn't sounded like a rabbit to her.

A slap woke her, hard across her face, leaving the taste of blood in her mouth. Glenda screamed from the pain, and screamed more when she saw the face above her.

It was Necimus, ugly in his hugeness, his grinning lips only inches from hers. The glint in his eyes scared her even before she heard his words.

"Well, my pretty, shall we have some fun?"

He hurt her. He hurt her badly. No matter how much Glenda screamed, her parents did not wake up. She could see them sleeping in the next room.

How could they sleep when she was screaming? How could they let this monster hurt her, and hurt her again, and keep on hurting her?

When he was done, Glenda was too tired to scream. Too tired to struggle anymore against the rope that tied her to her little cot, too tired to do anything except sob into her pillow.

Until she smelled the smoke.

Glenda writhed on the bed. Her hands clutched at the ropes that bound her wrists, her fingers searched for the knots. Her hands were going numb from the rope. The flames were rising, licking up around the bed, and the knots wouldn't untie, the ropes wouldn't give. She was going to die here in this bed, and her parents were going to die too, for the room next to her was already ablaze, and they were still sleeping, how could they still be sleeping?

She was screaming again, shrieking in pain and terror. The straw mattress beneath her was burning, searing her skin, then the cot was ablaze, the whole house was aflame, the ropes were on fire, and with a final tug, she wrenched her hands free, and stumbled into the night, her hair and what was left of her nightdress burning.

Glenda stumbled through the village. Every house was afire. Glenda ran from the pain and the heat and the terror, ran out of the town and down the road.

Wendy Jensen

Chapter Twenty-one

...I give you skill," the Lady said...
From "Song of the Sword Sisters"

Year After Aria, 303

Tudae knocked on the door.

"It is dawn, and time to start training. For Skurgiil, anyway." Tudae's eyes flickered from the spent candle to the dark smudges under Ilissa's eyes. "You, Singer, can rest if you choose."

"Thank you, Sword Mistress. I had an... interesting night. And Skurgiil knows I am not really a Singer."

Tudae's eyebrows rose. *An "interesting night" indeed!* "Well then, Skurgiil, let us leave the Sayer to her rest, while we get on with your training."

"Don't we eat first?" Skurgiil asked, falling into step behind the Sword Mistress.

Sighing, Tudae glanced back at her new recruit. The girl probably wouldn't train well if she was hungry. "Yes, Skurgiil. We'll eat first."

Tudae herself ate lightly in the morning. When she finished she watched her new charge putting away oat porridge at a rate that would make a plow horse proud. Tudae shook her head. *At least she hasn't said it needs garlic... not yet, anyway.*

Tudae scrutinized her charge, frowning. Something was different about her this morning. *Not her appetite; she ate like that last night. No, it was something else. In the eyes, maybe. She looks more... sure of herself. Whatever Ilissa did during the night had worked, and worked well. Perhaps the Mistress of Neston chose wisely, after all,* Tudae decided.

Surely four bowls of porridge was enough! "Come, Skurgiil. The Training Mistress is waiting for us."

※◉※

Storna and Lia were both waiting. Lia was swinging her staff, knocking straw out of a target with each blow. She shook her braids back over her shoulder and dropped into stance before Skurgiil.

After the first two rounds, Tudae walked away shaking her head. Maybe the porridge Skurgiil devoured was slowing her down. She appeared very awkward next to Lia, who had already landed three blows on her big opponent.

Out of the corner of her eye Skurgiil saw Tudae leave. *She's disappointed in me,* Skurgiil thought.

/Aye. She expects better, from Iskara's daughter./

Lia's eyes dropped to the dawnstone and Skurgiil swung. Lia jumped back and the blow missed.

/That was good, but you can do better./

How, Good Mother?

/Feel. Imagine. You do not have full Sight, but you have some. Watch with your inner eyes, and you will see the attack before it comes./

Skurgiil's response came seconds too slow. Lia's quarterstaff caught Skurgiil's shoulder and pain coursed down her arm.

/Watch slowly, child, but move quickly./

Skurgiil slowed her perception. A shadow of Lia's staff moved towards her, just ahead of the swing. Skurgiil moved to block, and the crack of colliding quarterstaffs echoed across the training ground.

Sword Sister

Lia held her opponent's eyes as the strange glow faded from the necklace. Lia dropped back, considering. Her next move was her best feint.

It didn't work. Skurgiil saw the movement before it began. Her shoulder dropped, dodging the blow, and her own quarterstaff crashed into Lia's right side. Lia doubled over, arm pressed to her ribs.

"Halt!" Storna shouted. "We're here to train. Leave the injuring for the enemy."

"Pardon, Mistress. Should I swing with less force?"

Storna scowled at Skurgiil as she helped Lia up. "With your strength? 'Tis arms like my Pap's ye have, and him a blacksmith. Lia will wear armor. You will not. Do you good to know how a hard hit feels."

Skurgiil felt nothing. Her quarterstaff smashed against Lia's padded armor, but not once did Lia's weapon touch her.

It was uncanny, Lia decided, when Storna called a halt for lunch. "You saw it? Saw it glow?" Lia murmured as Skurgiil strode towards the kitchen.

"Aye, I did," Storna replied, as she unbuckled Lia's armor.

"Smells of sorcery, if you ask me. Sure, she's strong and all, but there's more to it than that. Great size, great strength, and sorcery all rolled into one. Sounds familiar, doesn't it? Reminds me of—"

"Aye," Storna interrupted. Being a simple, superstitious person, she made a warding sign against evil. Not that she really thought it would protect them from Necimus, but there was no need to reinforce his presence by using his name.

Lia slipped out of the armor. "At least this one is on our side."

"Aye," Storna replied, but she cast a dubious glance towards Skurgiil's retreating back.

⇥◉⇤

"Enter," Tudae called in response to the knock on her

study door. She glanced up from her midday meal to see Ilissa's pale face peering in. "I don't think you rested, Sayer."

"I couldn't sleep. I want to tell you about... last night."

The muscles in Tudae's neck tensed as Ilissa recounted the events of the previous night. "So Necimus is searching. Searching here. Did he find her?"

"I don't think so. I cast out an Aura, and so did her Guardian."

Tudae nodded. "Erystra."

Ilissa's eyes widened. "You know of her?"

"I knew *her*. Personally. I'll tell you about it sometime." Tudae rubbed her neck, and smiled wryly. *Aye, I've walked with legends, and what has it brought me? Pain and sorrow.* "How do we protect Skurgiil?"

"I... I don't know." Ilissa's pale brow wrinkled.

She is so young, this Sayer! Tudae thought. *So young, to bear this Mission. As was I, to become Sword Mistress, but I was not so frail.* Ilissa's face matched her white frock, and the smudges beneath her eyes were almost as dark as her hair.

"Her Guardian provides protection, but I don't know if it is enough." Ilissa shrugged helplessly. "I don't know how much is enough. Perhaps I could teach Skurgiil some Sayer practices, if she could learn them."

"Mistress?" A head poked through the study door.

Tudae motioned for the Training Mistress to enter. "Yes, Storna?"

"Hail, Singer." Storna bowed her head at Ilissa. "I do not wish to intrude, Mistress, but it's about the new girl, Skurgiil."

"Trouble already?"

The training mistress hesitated, glancing towards Ilissa.

"You may speak in front of the Singer, Storna. What is the problem? Isn't Skurgiil learning?"

"Oh, aye, Mistress. She's learning. Quickly." Storna took a deep breath. "Too quickly. 'Tisn't natural, if ye ask me."

"What do you mean?"

"Well... this morning, see, she could hardly hold a staff. Then that necklace of hers... it glowed, and...." Storna paused, but the Sword Mistress wasn't laughing. "After that, Lia couldn't touch her. Lia is good, ye know."

The Sword Mistress nodded, and the Singer seemed to be listening carefully. Storna continued.

"This new one, she's strong. I put armor on Lia because this Skurgiil was hurting her. And Lia couldn't touch her. It was as if... as if Skurgiil knew what Lia was going to do before she did it. It all started after her necklace glowed. 'Tis unnatural, Mistress."

"Have you tried putting armor on Skurgiil? To slow her down?"

Storna stared at Tudae. "Armor, Mistress? Why, we haven't any that would fit that... that girl."

True. Tudae frowned. All their armor was sized for women — normal women. "We'll borrow some men's armor from Roagen this afternoon. Until then, train her as best you can."

"Aye, Mistress." Storna bowed her head and withdrew, but in her opinion, Skurgiil would serve better pulling a plow. Be less of a danger, too.

Tudae smiled at Ilissa. "You were wondering if she could learn Sayer practices? I think she already has."

Wendy Jensen

Chapter Twenty-two

One to fight fire with fire...
From "The Prophecies of Aria"

Year After Aria, 275
Peasant Year of the Raids

Twenty-eight years earlier...

Glenda wandered through Algnor's little cottage. There were only four rooms. The laboratory was the largest, filled with books and bottles, jars filled with strange substances, and cages of mice and birds and snakes. None of the rooms had a mirror, not even a tin one.

Of course, why would the old man want to look at himself? Glenda thought. *He is old and gray, and not at all handsome. Not like I am — used to be,* she corrected herself with a sob, as she leaned against the doorpost in the laboratory.

Her hand rose to touch her cheek. Glenda felt the ridges of scars where once there was skin; felt the tightness of the scar tissue over her hand as she moved it, and winced. It still hurt, though not like she had hurt that night in Sekrun. The pain she had felt then was inside, physical and mental, as Necimus forced himself into her body, leaving her unfit for any man to marry, much less a man rich enough to buy a silvered mirror.

Then there were the flames.

Glenda had never known pain like that from the fire. Biting, searing pain, making the pain between her legs and in her belly seem like a minor thing. Glenda thought she would die from the pain. But somehow she had lived, and found her way to this wizard.

She couldn't remember how she came here, couldn't remember much about that night at all. Nor anything afterwards, until the day she woke up in a strange bedchamber, with a Sayer sitting next to the bed in which she lay.

The Sayer had been kind, Glenda supposed. At least, she had tried to be. But there was no way Glenda could take the news kindly. She had sobbed while the Sayer talked.

She was ugly now. Not ugly like Dissian was ugly — that poor homely daughter of the village candlemaker that Glenda always regarded with superior pity. No, she was worse than ugly now, worse than Dissian.

Glenda was hideous, deformed. Her lovely skin was gone, replaced by shiny scars. Her beautiful blonde hair had all burned away, never to grow back. Glenda had been so horrified by the Sayer's words that she hardly noticed the old man standing at the bedchamber door, tugging his beard.

Sora let the girl cry. She herself had never cared what she looked like. Sora had always wanted respect, not admiration. Other women cared about their looks, and she supposed this poor girl was no different. Sora let the girl cry until she judged she had cried herself out. Then the Sayer spoke again.

The old man was a wizard. Glenda screamed and buried what was left of her face in her pillow. *A magic-caster, like the old witch. Like Necimus, for how else did*

Sword Sister

he make her parents sleep through her rape and set fire to the entire village, if not by magic?

Algnor was a good man, the Sayer insisted. He had made an illusion around Glenda, so no one would know how ugly she looked. This was small comfort for losing her own great beauty, especially when the Sayer told her that the illusion would have to be renewed every day, so Glenda would have to stay with the old man.

The Sayer didn't say for how long, but Glenda knew she meant forever. Not that it mattered. Where could she go?

Her family was dead, burned in their house in Sekrun. She couldn't go to the big towns to find a husband now. She was ugly. Only the illusion around her kept people from seeing how ugly. Glenda didn't even know what the illusion looked like.

Glass jars lined the laboratory shelves, some of them filled with dark liquids. Glenda eased past a cage with six garter snakes squirming inside and approached the shelf of jars.

The curved glass surface distorted her image. The blue eyes were still there, as brilliant as ever, but the hair above it was a tawdry brown instead of her glorious golden blonde. The face beneath the hair was — well, plain. Not ugly, certainly not as ugly as she would be without the illusion, but definitely plain.

Glenda slumped to the floor and wept. Here she was, ugly, and wearing a plain illusion; sullied to the point that no man would marry her. Not that she really wanted to be married anymore. The memory of Necimus' body in hers was horrible, painfully frightening. No, even if a man would have her, she didn't want to be married now. Perhaps she could stay with Algnor and earn her keep cleaning his cottage. Her keep, and the continuation of the illusion.

This seemed like a good idea, though Glenda wept at the thought of being reduced to cottage cleaning just to survive. Drowning sounded better, but Algnor wouldn't let her do that. He had argued with her, pleaded with her, and finally threatened her with some vague magical consequences if she even went near water deep enough to drown in. Glenda cringed at the thought of spells, and promised to obey. There were worse things than obeying Algnor. Necimus had taught her that.

It was all his fault. His fault that she was ugly, his fault that she had to depend on Algnor for her existence. Above all, it was his fault that she would bear a child.

A bastard child. Glenda shuddered. She had been so careful, never letting the local boys touch her even though she flirted with them.

Necimus had hurt her, made her ugly, and spawned a monster in her. *"It will be a monster,"* Glenda had wailed, as Algnor pulled his beard. Algnor told her the child was important, and Glenda had laughed hysterically. How could a bastard child be important?

It was all Necimus' fault. Crouched on the floor of Algnor's laboratory Glenda pounded her fists on the floor and wished that there was something, anything, she could do to hurt Necimus.

But she was too weak and frightened. Necimus was strong, and powerful. It would take a man, a strong man, to hurt Necimus, and she was only a woman. A magic-caster could hurt him. *Perhaps Algnor would... no, he wouldn't.* He was a mild old man. Illusions were his specialty. Glenda couldn't imagine him taking on Necimus.

Glenda stared at the books in the laboratory with hungry eyes. Those books contained spells that could hurt Necimus, but Glenda was just an ignorant girl. She couldn't even read, much less cast a spell. Besides, she had always heard that the ability to cast spells runs in families, like Necimus and his mother.... *Runs in families!*

Glenda sat up, and stared around the laboratory. She was going to bear a child, the child of a magic-caster, and here were spells to be learned. Surely a child of Necimus would have the ability to cast spells!

Glenda hugged herself with hope, and prayed to the

Unknowns that they grant her such a child, that they grant her vengeance.

※◉※

Dame Hagren still delivered the eggs, but she didn't stay to make sheep eyes anymore. Of course, when Glenda's belly began pushing through the illusion of Risa, the whole village knew that, too. The women whispered more on the corners, and the men at the tavern bought him more ale, and Glenda and Algnor were the talk of the town until the day Sora came to speak to Algnor.

"Marry?" Algnor gaped at the Sayer. "You say I should marry her?"

"She is with child, Algnor, and living with you."

"But... but, I didn't... I haven't... I sleep in the chair!" the old wizard sputtered.

"I know." The Sayer's eyes were looking at, or through, him, Algnor wasn't sure which. "But the villagers don't know that. They, of course, think the worst."

"Ah... hmmm... but..."

"It won't hurt you, Algnor, to make an honest woman out of her. You're old," the Sayer's voice was kindly, "and not likely to marry anyone else, anyway. Unless, as Dame Hagren says, you were courting her."

"I was not! I never...." Algnor flushed an apple red color, and his beard was in dire peril of being pulled completely out.

"Well then, why don't you marry this girl? She'll have to live with you from now on anyway, to maintain the illusion," Sora glanced at the image of Risa, "so you might as well be married. That will keep the villager's from talking, and prevent the child from being called a bastard. The child, as I told you—"

"Yes, yes, I know. The child is important." Algnor glanced at Glenda. He had had trouble explaining that to the wailing Glenda, who, faced with her own deformity and the prospect of bearing a "monster," was all for throwing herself into the closest mountain lake.

Poor girl. She didn't really deserve to be stuck bearing a bastard child, on top of her other sorrows. And as the Sayer said, the villagers already believed the child was his. Algnor gave his beard a last despairing tug.

"Very well, Sayer."

⁂

Algnor had hoped for a quiet wedding, just him and Glenda and Sora, but the all villagers came. Little enough happened in this remote mountain town, and a marriage was almost as exciting as the spring festival.

Algnor stood next to Glenda in the front of the chapel. Every seat behind him was full, and people stood shoulder to shoulder against the wall. The mass of bodies warmed the chapel and Algnor sweated. He stammered over the words that Sora asked him to repeat, and stumbled on his robes as he and Glenda left the chapel.

Dame Hagren was there, weeping on Firgon's shoulder. Firgon was the town tailor, and recently a widower. Algnor smiled sympathetically at him as he passed.

That was one good thing about marrying Glenda. Dame Hagren was off to find other prey.

A calf had been roasted in a pit on the village green, with a freshly tapped keg of ale nearby. The women took Glenda off for the flower throw, and the men poured Algnor the first draught of ale, slapping him on the back and making sly comments about his wedding night.

Algnor choked on the ale, spewing foam from his mouth. *Wedding night?* He was married now, married to Glenda, and married people slept together. Sleeping in his chair hurt his bones, and many were the nights that Algnor longed to be in his own bed again, but... *share it with Glenda? With a girl?*

Algnor took a long drink of the ale, waiting for the inevitable numbing effect.

It might not be so bad, he mused, as the effect of the ale set in. *As long as she didn't want... didn't expect him to... you don't do that with pregnant women, do you?*

Dowren stood nearby. Dowren had several children. He would know the answer, know whether or not you were supposed to...

Aye, and he'd laugh at me for asking! Algnor thought. *After all, they all think I've done that with her already.* Algnor held out his tankard for a refill. No, he was on his own for this.

After the feast the villagers followed them home, lighting their way with torches, singing and laughing all the way to the cottage door. Algnor walked carefully, making sure his front foot was firmly on the ground before he lifted the other. At the door he smiled and waved at the villagers, while Glenda disappeared inside.

Algnor dropped the latch and took a deep breath before turning to face Glenda.

She wasn't in the sitting room. The curtain to the bedchamber swayed.

No doubt she was in bed already, in his bed, waiting for him, waiting for him to... *what?* Algnor cast a longing glance at his chair, and stepped through the curtain.

She was in bed, with the bedclothes pulled over her shoulders. By the light of the candle Algnor saw the dress she had worn at the wedding laying on the floor, and her nightgown hanging in the wardrobe.

She looked frightened. Even through the effects of the ale, Algnor saw fear in her eyes. As he blew out the candle and slipped out of his robes, he heard her sob. Algnor climbed into his bed, and held Glenda in his arms until she cried herself to sleep.

Wendy Jensen

Chapter Twenty-three

And they shall lead the Sisters of the Sword...
From "Song of the Sword Sisters"

Year After Aria, 303

Roagen stared at the wall of his study, envisioning a future he would never have. A future with a wife, and a son, and...

A voice interrupted Roagen's musings. "What, pining away already? Why, the Sword Mistress was here but night before last!"

Roagen scowled up at his second-in-command. The young fighter's silk shirt was rumpled, and a wine stain blotched his scarlet jerkin.

"Back from your night's leave, I see. You never notice your lovers' absences, Alan, because you have so many lovers."

Alan dropped into a chair, his legs creating a lengthy bridge to Roagen's desk as he propped his boots on it. "Not so many, anymore," he responded casually.

"What? Don't tell me you've had a quarrel with every tavern wench in Fenfall!"

"Well, not exactly." Alan selected an apple from the bowl on Roagen's desk and crunched into it.

"Tia is wedding the tavern owner's son next moon,"

he explained around a mouthful of apple. "She feels I should stop visiting her now, so she can grow accustomed to my absence before the nuptials. Lana is angry with me because her tea leaves lied."

"About what?"

Alan shrugged waves of blonde hair off his shoulders. "That I would propose to her before this moon, or something like that."

Roagen laughed, and Alan paused with his teeth in the apple, staring at his superior. "Well, you can't expect tea leaves to tell the truth! Now if a Sayer said it, it would be different."

"Would it, Alan?"

Gray eyes regarded Roagen innocently. "Of course! Who am I to oppose Fate?"

The Lord of Fenfall smiled. "What about Telan?"

"Oh, her," Alan waved his apple. "I'm not seeing her anymore."

"Is she seeing someone else? Dorgen, maybe?" Roagen grinned as his handsome young second flushed.

"Morg spittle!" Alan hurled his apple core at the fireplace. "What does that green-eyed witch see in a catapult handler?"

"A marriage proposal perhaps? Your reputation precedes you, Alan."

Alan scowled, but a clatter of hooves sounded in the courtyard below before he could reply.

"Guests," Roagen muttered, going to the window. "Why, it's the Sword Mistress!" Roagen hurried down the stairs as Alan pulled his boots off the desk.

She wasn't alone, Roagen noted with disappointment. Behind her rode two young women, one very large, the other quite small. Roagen ignored them as he embraced Tudae.

"Will you be staying the night?" he whispered in her ear.

"No, Roagen." The Sword Mistress disentangled herself, and gave her lover a reproving glance. "This is a business visit. I want you to meet Skurgiil," Tudae indicated the tall girl who had dismounted and was unabashedly rubbing her backside with both hands, "and Ilissa." Tudae gestured to the delicate figure still on her horse. "Ilissa is a Sayer."

Roagen nodded to the two girls. "Skurgiil, Ilissa — this is Alan, my second-in-command."

Alan didn't answer. Six feet and a half was a generous height for a man and he received respect and admiration because of it. But in all his twenty-two years, he had never found a woman to match it. Until now.

Skurgiil's dark eyes were on precisely the same level as his gray ones. Her grip, when he shook her hand, was nearly as firm as his.

"Alan!" Roagen snapped. "Help the Sayer off her horse."

Alan scooped Ilissa off her horse and dropped her to the ground, but his eyes never left Skurgiil.

Unknowns, but she was twice a woman, in every direction! Alan's gaze traveled from the large forehead to the broad shoulders, balanced by breasts that would look ridiculously huge on any other woman. His examination of her generous hips and muscular legs was interrupted when she moved out of sight.

Roagen and Tudae were entering the castle, with Skurgiil and Ilissa behind them. Alan hurried to catch up.

"... so we need some armor," Tudae was saying, "and we don't have any to fit her. Can we borrow some from you, until we can get a set made for her?"

"She can borrow mine," Alan blurted. All four turned to look at him. "After all, we're the same height."

True, Roagen realized, as the two stood shoulder to shoulder. His gaze followed Skurgiil's contours critically. "Just because you're the same height doesn't mean that your armor will fit her."

"It won't hurt to try. My spare set is in my quarters. I could take her there to try it on," Alan caught Roagen's stern look, "... while I wait outside."

Roagen looked at Tudae. The Sword Mistress merely shrugged. "Very well, Alan," Roagen growled. He gave the handsome young fighter a meaningful look, but Alan was already leading Skurgiil down the hall.

Tudae reached out a hand as Ilissa started after them. "Not you, Ilissa. We have to talk to Roagen."

The Lord of Fenfall gave the Sword Mistress an exasperated stare. Didn't she see anything wrong with Alan taking a Sword Sister to his quarters, alone? Apparently not, for Tudae strode towards his study.

Roagen followed, shaking his head. He preferred that Ilissa accompany Alan and Skurgiil as a chaperon. As it was, he and Tudae were stuck with the chaperon.

Resolutely pushing from his mind any thoughts of taking the Sword Mistress in his arms and kissing her passionately, Roagen seated himself behind his desk.

What is taking her so long? Alan wondered, as he paced the corridor outside his room. Every minute dragged by. It seemed like an hour since he last saw the big beauty.

No, not beauty, Alan corrected himself. She wasn't beautiful. Not in the way Tia, Lana, and Telan, curse her bewitching green eyes, were beautiful.

But there was something about this Skurgiil, something that grabbed him by the gut.

She was... different.

Not like the flitsy tavern maids, simpering at his smiles and caressing his curls; not like the merchants' daughters, with their direct manners and ill-concealed interest in marriage; not like the landowners' daughters around his father's holdings, with their cool reservation and unspoken demands; not even like other Sword Sisters, with their harsh ways forged by the expectation of a violent death.

Skurgiil was more... real. More... innocent.

Probably totally innocent, Alan realized. He leaned his forehead against the cool stone wall and groaned at the thought of what that meant for him.

Sword Sister

How long does it take to put armor on? Surely not this long! Alan tapped on the door. "Skurgiil! Are you done?"

The clank of a dropped piece of armor answered him, followed by, "I don't know how to put this on! Can ye help me?"

Alan stepped through the door. The first thing to meet his eyes was Skurgiil's wool tunic, thrown across his bed. The second was the sight of Skurgiil, wearing only a tunic of chain mail. She was attempting to buckle a leg bracer onto her forearm.

"Where does this go?"

"Ah... hmm." Alan cleared his throat. *Innocent, indeed!* "First, you put your tunic on under the chain mail. Otherwise the chain will chafe... uh... certain places." Alan tried to avoid staring at where the chain mail stretched tight across her chest.

"Very well," Skurgiil answered simply, and slipped the chain mail over her head. It fell to the floor with a *chink* as she reached for her tunic.

Alan gaped. Over the pounding of his heart he wondered vaguely why *he* was blushing.

<hr />

"Necimus is searching for her. Searching by magic, within the walls of Castle Shield. And he's her father?" Roagen pressed his lips together and drew a breath, counting his heartbeats. "You never told me about this, Tudae."

"Erystra told me I shouldn't tell anyone, shouldn't even think about Skurgiil. This isn't the first time Necimus has searched."

"He knows she is there?"

"Why else would he search in Castle Shield?"

"But, how does he know? Can you trust Skurgiil?"

"She is the daughter of my Sword Sister, Iskara."

Which doesn't prevent her from being a very real threat to you, Roagen thought. The daughter of mocking, arrogant Iskara, who made eyes at him in the taverns, when he had eyes only for Tudae. Iskara, whose pride and over-confidence led to her own capture.

The daughter of Iskara, and Necimus. *What was it Father always said about bloodlines? "Breed with a donkey, and your children will be mules."* "She doesn't know about her... father. What happens when she finds out?"

"I don't know," Tudae's expression was grim. "I hope when she discovers it she will be a full fledged Sword Sister and strong enough in her beliefs that the knowledge will not damage her."

"Meanwhile, Necimus searches for her even into your castle." Roagen frowned. "You say you Saw him?" he asked Ilissa.

"Yes, and he Saw me."

Well, far be it from him to question the word of a Sayer. *Even Alan claimed he would take a Sayer's word, even about... Alan!* Roagen tensed. He had forgotten about his second-in-command's dubious mission.

Roagen tried to sound casual. "Speaking of Seeing, could you check on Alan and Skurgiil? They've been gone too long."

Ilissa tilted her head, her eyes staring into the wall. "They are in his room. He's helping Skurgiil put the armor on."

"Putting it *on*? He's *dressing* her?" Roagen stared at Ilissa incredulously. "Well, I guess there's a first time for everything," he muttered.

⊰◉⊱

Alan surveyed Skurgiil and grimaced. *Roagen is right*, he decided. *Just because we are the same height doesn't mean the armor fits.*

Alan loosened the breastplate. *Have to allow room for those big, beautiful...* he pushed the thought away and concentrated on undoing buckles. Of course, that made it too loose in the waist.

"Morg spittle!" Alan muttered as he re-adjusted the straps. Finally he stepped back, shrugging. "That's the best I can do."

Skurgiil took a step forward. The armor clanked. It looked ridiculous. Too tight here, too loose there.

Alan sighed again. *Imagine what she would look like in a suit custom made for her! Not just a simple breastplate, but a corselet, high enough to cover vital areas but low enough to hint at the charms covered by the chain mail; shoulder plates with spiked protrusions to enhance the menace of her size; leg and arm bracers of steel so thick a blade would never breach it, perhaps with designs embossed in gold... Why, she would look like a war goddess. She would be magnificent! She....*

Alan shook his head. *What is wrong with me?* he wondered. *Here I am, imagining what a woman would look like dressed. But then* — Alan flushed at the memory — *I've already seen her undressed.*

They returned to Roagen's study, their strides of equal length. Alan swaggered as they passed other soldiers in the halls. Here was a woman he was proud to have at his side.

Tudae gave the borrowed armor a critical glance, then shook her head. "You wouldn't last ten minutes in an actual battle. But the purpose for now is to accustom you to the weight. How does it feel?"

"Heavy," Skurgiil answered.

"Then it fulfills its purpose. In a fortnight or so we'll have a set custom made for you and return this one to Alan." Turning to Roagen, she added, "That is what we came for. Now we must leave. Skurgiil must return to her training."

Alan followed them to the waiting horses. "I could help her train. I know swordplay, and tactics, and...."

Roagen scowled back over his shoulder at his second. "Alan! The Sword Sisters can train their own. I believe you have duties. Your leave expired this morning."

"I have back leave coming, sir. I could go to Castle Shield for a few days, Skurgiil needs to train with someone her own size, we're the same height...."

"Men are not permitted at Castle Shield." *Especially men like you!* Roagen thought. He glowered at his second, but Alan was watching Skurgiil mount. "Help the Sayer on her horse, Alan."

As Alan boosted Ilissa into her sidesaddle a malicious thought crossed Roagen's mind. "You said something earlier about not doubting the word of a Sayer, Alan. Ilissa is a Sayer. Ilissa, what do you See for Alan?"

Alan paled as the violet eyes stared through him. "I See," Ilissa answered, "that you will soon be in love."

Alan sighed in relief, while Roagen scowled. *Was that all? You don't have to be a Sayer to tell that Alan is smitten with this Skurgiil!* Catching Ilissa's eye, Roagen saw her smile.

No, Roagen realized, *that isn't all she Saw for Alan.*

Chapter Twenty-four

"The Power of the Sayers is the Power of the Unknowns, but the power of Magic is the Power of men."
Peasant Proverb

Year After Aria, 275
Peasant Year of the Raids

Twenty-eight years earlier...

Breena fidgeted in front of Algnor, avoiding his eyes. "Sir, shall I send for Sora?"

"Eh?" Algnor blinked at the young midwife.

"Sora, sir. The Sayer."

The Sayer. Breena said Glenda would die, and the child with her. She wanted to call Sora, to send mother and child on their way in peace. Algnor caressed his temples with trembling fingers and tried to think.

Sora, the Sayer. There was something she had said, on that night he first brought Glenda into his house. That Glenda was with child; that the child was important; that Algnor should guard them well. But Breena said they *would both die.*

Algnor crossed his tiny sitting room and jerked open the bedroom curtain. Glenda was no longer screaming. She wasn't even moaning. She lay limp and still, with only the rise and fall of her scarred breast proving she still lived. The mound of belly still squirmed, as if insisting on release.

"She won't...?" Algnor whispered.

Midwife Triil shook her head. She was already folding up the linens that were to receive the new baby. "The child be too large for her, and can not come out. 'Tis a strong seed ye sowed there, Master Algnor."

Algnor shuddered. He was glad, again, that he had not done this to Glenda.

Too large, the midwife had said. Algnor knew little about birthing, but it seemed Glenda would die, with the child trapped inside her. *Sora said to guard them well, but the child was too large to be born.*

Too large! Algnor's aged heart thumped. There was a spell, the one he used to bring his furniture through the tiny cottage door. It didn't last long, but perhaps it didn't need to.

Algnor brushed past Breena, tripping over his robes as he rushed into his laboratory. Breena watched the old man pull a thick book off a shelf, then quietly left to fetch the Sayer.

—⊙—

Algnor's fingers shook as he turned the pages. *It was here somewhere. It shouldn't be hard to find. A simple spell with a simple title.*

He reached the end of the tome, took a deep breath, and started over.

He almost passed it again. It was the illuminated "S" that caught his attention. The "S", which was the first letter of the spell title. The first letter of the word "Small."

Sora was in the bedchamber when Algnor returned. She had already started her chants.

The chanting paused, and she stared at Algnor with somber eyes. Eyes that saw too much, eyes that saw the future. Algnor looked into those eyes, and knew this would be the most important spell of his life.

"There is... something I would try." Algnor's throat felt dry. He had cast this spell many times, on furniture, on children's toys, even on a gold piece at an illusion show, but he suddenly realized that he had never tried this spell on a living creature.

Would the child survive? Algnor didn't know; knew that he must know. He had studied the spell twice, in case once was not enough. *After all, how large was too large?* But now the extra spell would have to be a test.

"Spell!" Algnor's voice shook. Claws clicked across the stone floor and his old pet's muzzle appeared through the bedchamber curtain. Algnor stroked Spell's head, looked into his trusting eyes, and muttered the words.

Breena shrieked, and Midwife Triil made a warding sign toward the dog. The dog the size of a puppy, who had a moment ago been full-grown.

Algnor bent to stroke Spell's head, and felt relief surge through him as his pet licked his hand.

"Now," Algnor straightened and fixed Midwife Triil with a stern gaze, "I need to touch the child."

"Aye," the old woman agreed. She turned back the blanket covering Glenda.

Algnor sat on a footstool at the foot of the bed, trying to listen to the midwife's instructions.

He had never seen this part of a woman's body. That one night with Risa, back behind the blacksmith's shop during the fall festival, had been very dark. He had felt her, and heard her, but had not seen her. Coming this close to the privacy of a woman was making his stomach queasy and his heart thump.

But Glenda needed this, the child needed this, and only he could do it. Cursing himself for a cowardly fool, Algnor drew a deep breath and muttered, "Light."

The globe in his left hand filled the tiny chamber with whiteness, illuminating the faces of three women, and a part of a fourth woman which he never thought he'd see.

Midwife Triil's hands slid in between Glenda's legs. "Like so," the old woman said, pulling Glenda's flesh open with a force that caused the unconscious girl to moan. In the light of his globe, Algnor could see inside of her, could see a tiny patch of dark hair. Algnor nodded, and sank his own hand into Glenda's heat and moistness to touch the hair. The old wizard closed his eyes and muttered the spell.

In a final burst of pain and blood, Vengeance was born.

Algnor plunged his shaking hands into the washbasin, and watched the swirls of red radiate outward from his fingers. Behind him thin wails came from beyond the bedroom curtain, wails from a child that Algnor had nearly dropped as the tiny, slimy body slid out of Glenda and into Algnor's lap. Midwife Triil had been swift, her ancient hands clutching the child's neck and feet, rescuing him from Algnor's trembling grasp.

It was a boy.

Algnor had seen that much, as he disentangled his hand from the shiny cord that trailed from the infant's belly. Algnor nearly retched as a bloody mass followed the cord, slid down the front of his robes and landed on the floor.

The women had been busy. Sora murmured, her hands pressed into Glenda's now flaccid belly. Breena's hands flew above the child, wielding a small knife, and blood sprayed into Algnor's beard as the freed end of the cord joined the bloody mass at his feet. Midwife Triil

Sword Sister

hoisted the infant up by his feet and slapped him soundly.
With a strangled cry Algnor had launched himself at the midwife, throwing himself between the wailing baby and the bloodied knife in Breena's hand. Midwife Triil screeched as Algnor tried to wrench the tiny form out of her shriveled grasp.

"Master Algnor! What are you doing?" Sora's voice was stern.

"You said... guard him," Algnor panted. "They're hurting him!"

The old midwife's laugh was shrill. "Just like a new father! We are making him breathe, Master Algnor. Ye'll not have a son if he doesn't breathe."

Stunned and humiliated, Algnor staggered out of the birthing room, leaving the women to do their work.

A son. Algnor blinked at the reddening water in the basin. As far any of the villagers were concerned, that boy was his son.

The concept was staggering, and on the heels of the past day's events it was more than the elderly wizard could handle. Algnor wiped his hands on his robe. From the back of a cupboard he pulled a dusty bottle.

⊰◉⊱

Algnor was on his second cup of wine when the women came through the bedchamber curtain. He gestured towards the three empty cups on the table, closing the book in his lap.

"A toast, ladies! A toast to... my son."

"Why, thank ye, Master Algnor." Midwife Triil poured her cup full to the brim and passed the bottle to Breena. The younger midwife looked exhausted, but horror still lurked in her eyes.

No matter. That would be fixed soon enough.

"To your son." Midwife Triil raised the cup to her lips, gulping. Breena muttered something appropriately polite before drinking hers. They were both drinking, savoring the wine, distracted, but Sora still stood by the bedchamber curtain, wiping her hands and staring at him with those eyes.

She Saw what he was about to do, and she was standing outside the range of the spell. No matter. She had known the truth from the start and Algnor trusted her to keep that truth a secret. He wiggled his fingers in complex patterns, and whispered the words of the spell. The words of the spell "Forget."

"Ah, that was good. Be there more, Master Algnor?" Midwife Triil shook the bottle. "Aye, enough for another round."

Had it worked? Algnor wasn't sure; he'd never done this spell before.

"Ah... help yourselves. It's a celebration, after all. The birth of my son." He took a deep breath. "About the girl... about her scars..."

Breena looked puzzled, and Midwife Triil shook her head. "Scars, Master Algnor? The birthing bed is not a battlefield. Your young wife will be as pretty as she was the day you married her."

It worked! Algnor closed his eyes with relief. When he opened them he saw Sora staring at him, smiling.

"You wish to name him *what*?" Sora looked shocked.

Algnor fidgeted, scrunching the hem of his robe cuffs in his hands. He had told Glenda it wasn't a good idea, told her that it wasn't a proper name, but she wouldn't listen. She had just stared at him with those brilliant blue eyes, the eyes that looked out of the image of Risa. She was turning that same stare on the Sayer, and Algnor doubted Sora would have any better luck dissuading her than he had.

"He's my son," Glenda whispered. "Mine. I'll name him as I see fit." She stood there, her son clutched in her arms, staring at Sora.

The silence in the chapel thickened.

"Ah... hmmm." Algnor cleared his throat uneasily.

"We'll call him Ven. For short," he added, as Glenda bent her scorching blue eyes on him.

Sora sighed and finished the naming ceremony.

Wendy Jensen

Chapter Twenty-five

One to draw Evil out and defeat it...
From "The Prophecies of Aria"

Year After Aria, 303

Tudae squinted into the afternoon sun. "Riders ahead."

"Look like Sisters." Skurgiil stood up in her stirrups, straining for more detail. "They're wearing armor."

"Sword Sisters aren't the only ones who wear armor, Skurgiil."

Tudae loosened her sword. The episode last night had made her more nervous than she liked to admit. There was no telling what Necimus would do next, or who he would send against them.

"They are Sisters." The musical voice removed all doubt. "Six of them, and the leader has red hair."

Tudae relaxed and smiled at Ilissa. "I forgot we are traveling with a Sayer. Red hair, you said? That would be Mara. She has been out on border patrol."

Ahead the group halted, waiting. A woman with hair the color of new copper coins approached, raising her hand in a casual salute. "Greetings, Sword Mistress."

"Greetings, Mara. What news?"

"Not good, I'm afraid." Mara turned her horse

alongside Tudae's. "There was another raid. Middle of the night, three nights ago. They came on great flying creatures. Two men, one a wizard. The other, one of Necimus' breedlings."

"Damages?"

"Hit a farm. The flying creatures ate some sheep. The half-breed beat the farmer pretty badly." Mara's mouth tightened. "I don't need to tell you what befell the farmer's wife."

"Did she survive?"

"Aye, for a change. But I don't think...." Mara's voice trailed away as Skurgiil urged her horse in front, blocking the road.

"Two men, ye said. On big flying creatures?"

Mara nodded. She didn't like the way this girl's eyes burned into her. There was vengeance there, and this girl looked big enough to wreak it.

"One wore armor?"

"Aye." Mara shifted in her saddle. She hadn't mentioned that part, so how did this strange girl know?

"And the other one wore a black dress?"

"I suppose you could call a wizard's robes a dress. And they were black, as is everything that comes from Castle Darkfall." *This girl knows too much,* Mara decided, and her voice turned suspicious. "Why, do you know them?"

Skurgiil nodded, her eyes like pits of dark flames.

Lady, but Iskara had looked thus, so many times! Tudae thought. *The time when I wrought better than she in swordplay, the time we were ambushed by a stray group of Morgs....* "How, Skurgiil? How do you know them?"

"They killed Erystra."

So that was it. Tudae hadn't asked how the Sayer had died. She had assumed it was planned, since Erystra passed on to Guardianship. That she met a violent death after all these years left a feeling like spoiled meat in Tudae's stomach. Erystra deserved to die of old age.

"Are you sure it was the same men, Skurgiil?"

"I did not see them up close. The Good Mother sent me to gather poultice plants and I was up on the mountain." Skurgiil looked away, her teeth sinking into her lower lip. "I... I could not get there in time."

"You said one wore armor and the other wore black robes?"

"Aye. The one in the armor killed her."

"Was he a half-Morg?"

"A what?"

Mara spat off the side of her horse. "One of Necimus' offspring. Half Necimus, half-Morg, and only less evil than their father because they are more stupid. But then, what can you expect from His Ugliness' children?"

"Ah, Mara...." This was not the time to discuss Necimus' children. Not now, not here, in front of Skurgiil. Tudae rubbed the muscles in her neck. "Mara, where is the farm?"

"One, maybe two hours ride to the north."

"That close?"

Mara nodded, her face grim. "Aye. They grow bold."

Bold indeed. First killing Erystra — and Tudae knew who they were really looking for — then walking the streets of Fenfall. Then attacking a farm on their way back to their master. Tudae frowned. Too bold. Possibly the sign of a raiding rampage in the near future.

Tudae judged the angle of the sun. "Two hours ride, an hour or two to question the farmer and his wife — we could be back within four hours after night falls."

Mara raised pale brows. "You wish to go there? Tonight?"

"Yes. I wish to question them, while the memory is fresh. Before the story grows and they claim the entire Morg army attacked them. Will you lead me?"

Mara shrugged. "I suppose if Blossom here," she patted her horse's neck, "can take a few more hours of traveling, I can, too."

"Very well. Skurgiil, you and Ilissa...."

"I am coming with ye."

There it was, the petulant set of the mouth and the

stubborn thrust of the chin that Tudae remembered in Iskara. She remembered, too, how arguments with Iskara had turned out, when she wore that look.

"Very well. Ilissa...." Tudae scrutinized the Sayer's pale face. If the dark patches under her eyes grew much larger her whole face would be as black as her hair. "Ilissa, you go back to Castle Shield with the other Sisters. And get some rest!"

"But, Mistress, I should be with Skurgiil, in case...."

"You'll be no help if you fall over from exhaustion, girl. Mara and I will take care of Skurgiil. Won't we, Mara?"

Mara nodded, though why this giant would need to be taken care of was beyond her. The one they called Skurgiil looked like she could take on the whole Morg army.

"She doesn't have a sword," one of the Sisters pointed out. "She can take mine. Here," she offered Skurgiil a sheathed sword.

Skurgiil took the weapon and held it like a skinning knife. Tudae groaned.

"No, that will never do. She hasn't been trained with a sword yet. Vera!" Tudae waved another Sword Sister over. "Give Skurgiil your axe. I know she can use that."

Skurgiil took the sheathed battle axe, hefting it in her hand. "A bit light," she commented, removing the sheath. Vera and Mara exchanged alarmed glances. "Sharp, though." Skurgiil nodded in satisfaction, and re-sheathed the weapon. "It will do."

"Then let us be on our way, before dark falls. Lead on, Mara. The rest of you return to Castle Shield." The Sword Mistress turned her horse after Mara's, and Skurgiil followed.

As the other Sword Sisters set off for Castle Shield, Ilissa cast a worried glance at Skurgiil's vanishing back.

Erystra, protect her! Ilissa thought. *The Sword Mistress is right. I am too tired to help. She is in your hands now, Guardian.*

As she has been these many years, Ilissa reminded

herself. The young Sayer clutched her reins in numb hands and followed the others to Castle Shield.

※◉※

Balek watched Necimus write the last scroll, watched the runes expand on the parchment, spreading, growing like living things. His eyes drifted to the candles, spewing magic essence into the air to power the scrolls. Necimus made the candles in a secret laboratory Balek had never seen. *It was here, attached to this room, behind those wooden panels, perhaps....*

"They are done."

Balek flinched as his master's voice scraped across his consciousness. One hand crawled to his Medallion of Protection Against Magical Search, and he risked a glance at the globe on the desk. It was dark, unresponsive. Necimus wasn't trying to read his thoughts.

Balek looked into the wells under Necimus' eyebrows and caught a glimmer of amusement. The porridge he had eaten an hour ago churned in Balek's stomach. Necimus didn't need the globe to know he was thinking about the candles.

"These are all we need?" Balek's hand trembled as he picked up the scrolls.

"Yes." Necimus stretched, easing muscles cramped by hours of spell casting. "Each scroll is aligned for a particular company. You will take half of them. I will take the other half."

"You... you are coming with us?"

Necimus smiled, dark lips stretching against his pale skin. This was too important to entrust to underlings. "Yes, Balek. I'm coming with you."

"Uh... Your Evilness... what exactly are we going to do?"

"We're going to take a castle, Balek."

The porridge in Balek's stomach writhed. "A castle?"

"Yes. Don't worry, Balek. We took a castle this way

before, remember?"

Balek looked blank.

"No, you wouldn't remember. That was before you joined me. We took this castle in the same manner."

"Castle Darkfall?"

"Yes. But it was called Dawnfall then," Necimus chuckled.

Balek shivered at the sound.

"You should have seen the surprise on the guards' faces when we appeared out of the night. And the look on the old Lord's face when I marched into his keep!" Necimus laughed.

Balek cringed.

"I kept the old man alive long enough to see his sons executed. His daughters..." Necimus thought a minute. "Oh, yes. I gave them to my Morg captains." He grinned again. "The old Lord didn't live to see his first grandchild born."

Shivering, Balek rose to his feet. "When do we leave, Your Evilness?"

"Three hours after night falls. Make sure the troops are ready."

"Yes, my lord." Balek bowed out of the room.

The Lord of Castle Darkfall leaned back in his chair and smiled. It would be good to leave these walls, to hear the sounds of battle again. It had been too long.

⊰◉⊱

Dusk was falling when the three women dismounted before the farm house. Flies rose from ragged pieces of sheep as Tudae bent over a patch of mud. "Bigger than any bird I've ever seen."

Mara measured the track against her sword. "Birds, Mistress? What kind of bird has ten toes?"

"They were not birds." Skurgiil frowned at the track in the mud. "They had some feathers, but their wings were webbed."

"Maybe these people can tell us more." Tudae

knocked on the door.

The man who answered was recognizable as a man only from the shoulders down. From the neck up he was a mass of pulpy bruises and gaping cuts.

"Sword Mistress!" The sound hissed out through the gaps of missing teeth; the puffy, split lips were unable to form the words. The slit of one eye regarded Tudae; the other eye was a swollen purple lump. The farmer stepped back and motioned them in.

Three children huddled near the hearth, hands gripping each other's clothes, eyes staring like rabbits in a trap. A woman rocked back and forth in a chair, an infant at her breast. Horror marked her face as plainly as the bruises marked her husband's.

Tudae gritted her teeth, one hand going to the muscles in her neck. She didn't know which was worse, the pulpy-faced farmer, his blank-eyed wife, or the painfully aware faces of the children. "What happened?"

"They came at night, Mistress." The farmer's voice came in wheezing gasps. "We was sleeping. I woked with his hands about my throat. I tried to fight, but... he were strong, Mistress. He beat me senseless, he did. I did not come to 'til they was leaving."

"There were two of them? One in armor, and one in robes?"

"Aye, Mistress. The wizard one, he did not come in. At least," the farmer glanced at the rocking woman, "I do not think he did. When I come to I looked out and seen him. He were riding something. Something big."

Tudae bent over the farmer's wife. "Dame." The woman rocked, back, forward, eyes gazing at nothing. "Dame! Did you see the wizard?"

The woman's head moved side to side. The rocking didn't stop.

"What about the guard? Or didn't you see him, either?"

"I... seen him." Her eyes focused, gripping Tudae like the hand that shot up and clenched her chain mail. "I seen him! He made me see! Made my children watch...."

The infant released her breast and wailed. The woman sobbed.

"He said he'd hurt my baby! He said...." Her face twisted with despair, and her voice turned hoarse. "Mistress, what if he... what if I have... he were half-Morg, Mistress!"

Tudae clenched her hands. "A quarter Morg isn't much. It might not even show. You could...."

"Not in my house, Mistress." The farmer's speech was thick but raw hatred still came through the hissing breath. "There'll be none of that kind raised here. I'll kill it with me own hands first."

"A child is not at fault for what its father is." Tudae's eyes flickered toward Skurgiil and away. The big girl hadn't noticed; she was just standing there, staring at the infant and the children.

"You can give it to an Order," Tudae continued. "If it is a girl, bring it to me. If not, bring it to me anyway. I will see that Lord Roagen raises it for his guard."

Tudae's hand caressed her tense shoulder as she moved towards the door. "We'll double the patrols in this area."

Mara frowned. "We're stretched thin as it is, Mistress."

"Then I'll ask Roagen to send patrols to this area. Damn it," the Sword Mistress muttered under her breath as she left the cottage, "we can't be everywhere, all the time."

Tudae paused a minute before swinging into her saddle. To the northwest she saw faint pulses of purple light.

"Magic," Mara breathed.

"Aye," Tudae concurred grimly.

"What do you suppose His Ugliness is scheming now?"

Tudae shook her head and mounted her horse. "Whatever it is, Mara, I'm sure we'll know soon. Too soon."

With a final glance towards Castle Darkfall they

turned their horses' heads toward home.

Balek cleared his throat as Necimus stepped into the courtyard. "All is ready, my lord."

Necimus surveyed his troops. Six companies stood in the courtyard of Castle Darkfall. They were mostly his half-Morgs, with a few full-blood Morgs who had slipped through the cracks of his breeding experiments thrown in.

The differences between them were obvious. The Morgs stood taller than most men, but the half-breeds stood taller yet, approaching their father's height. They walked upright. Totally upright, not with the shambling, hunch shouldered gait of their full-blood cousins. The faces were different, too. The half-breeds still sported the wicked Morg teeth and flattened noses, but they had foreheads. Narrow foreheads, but at least their hairline didn't start at their eyebrows.

Not that having a forehead improved their intelligence much, Necimus thought disgustedly.

Still, they were sufficient for the job at hand. Armed with torches, catapults, oil and ladders, it was a sufficient force to take one castle full of women. Even though the women were trained fighters, the element of surprise was on his side. No one would expect an attack on the castle itself, so half the garrison would be out on patrol. Success would be his.

Necimus turned to his cringing magician. "They know where we are going?"

"Yes, Your Evilness. And they look forward," Balek swallowed uncomfortably, "to the spoils of war."

Necimus nodded. Already he could see the glow of greed and lust shining in his soldiers' eyes. The Lord of Castle Darkfall raised his voice.

"Loyal soldiers!" His misshapen band of Morgs stood like hideous statues as his voice rolled through the courtyard. "When tonight's mission is accomplished, there will be a woman for each of you."

A growl of approval surged through the ranks. Necimus raised his hand, fingers splaying a pitchfork's breadth. "But there is one woman who is mine. She is bigger than the rest. They call her Skurgiil. I want her taken alive and unharmed. Anyone who injures her," Necimus' voice held the threat of distant thunder, "will answer to me!"

Silence fell across the ranks. All knew the price of their Lord's displeasure would be long and horrible.

Necimus turned to his assistant. "You may begin."

Balek fumbled through the scrolls, nearly dropping them. He unfurled the first one and with a quavering voice began to read.

Chapter Twenty-six

What is that yellow light, Mamma,
Why is the sky aglow?
   From "Dawn of the Morgs"
   by Wyflen Herdbummer

Year After Aria, 303

Exhausted, Ilissa slept.

Her face was clammy, her nightgown damp with sweat. Her hands twitched; the head of black hair tossed on her pillow as if refusing something only she could see.

Smoke, black and greasy, reeking of burned flesh. Cries of pain and fright, snarls and the clanging of steel. Black armored figures surging toward the castle walls. A sense of impending doom; the certain knowledge that all was lost.

Her hopes, her Mission, her life — all lost.

With a start, Ilissa woke.

Her eyes stared into nothingness and beyond. With sickening certainty, she knew the meaning of the Dream.

A Sword Sister, on her way to bed, staggered as the tiny form of the Sayer shot into the hall. The collision threw them both against the wall.

"What...?"

"The Sword Mistress!" Ilissa gasped. "Where...?"

"The Sword Mistress is gone."

Of course. She rode with Skurgiil and Mara to visit a ravaged farm. They would not have returned yet, and in a despairing way Ilissa was glad. Perhaps Skurgiil would survive even if she, Ilissa, did not. "Who is in command?"

"Leta is, but why...."

"Where is she?"

"Singer, perhaps you should lie down and...."

"Where is she? Tell me!" Seizing the Sword Sister by the front of her chain mail, Ilissa shook her violently, but only managed to rattle the mail shirt.

The Sword Sister stared with amusement at the delicate hands clenched in her chain mail. "Leta's on the front battlements, Singer, but I think you should... get dressed first," she concluded as Ilissa's nightgown disappeared around the curve of the stairs.

Ilissa paused at the top of the stairs, gasping for breath. Her bare feet smacked on the stone battlements as she raced to the guard tower.

"Leta! Leta!"

A startled Sister turned towards her. "Yes, Singer?"

"We're going to be attacked." Ilissa gasped. "I had a Dream. Necimus' troops were attacking us."

"There, there. We all have nightmares occasionally. I've had them myself. You should drink a cup of warm wine to settle your nerves, and—"

"It wasn't a nightmare! It was real!"

"Yes, they seem very real sometimes. Now, Singer, why don't you—"

"I'm not a Singer!" Ilissa shrieked. "I'm a Sayer. And it wasn't a nightmare, it was a Dream. We're going to be attacked, here, tonight."

Leta stared at the distraught girl. Her face was as white as her flimsy nightgown, and her eyes seemed to cover most of her face. Not likely a Sayer, but still an honored guest at the Castle. Leta humored her.

Striding forward, she peered over the battlements, her eyes searching the blackness. All she saw was a late patrol riding towards the drawbridge.

"Ho!" Leta called down. "What news?"

"All's quiet, for a change," the response drifted up.

"Any sign of Morg troops moving?"

"None. His Ugliness must be keeping them home tonight." Hooves clattered across the drawbridge as the patrol entered the castle.

"Raise the drawbridge."

Leta turned and stared at Ilissa. "I can't do that. There are patrols still out."

"Then they will return too late. Raise the drawbridge."

"Look here, Singer—"

"I'm a Sayer!"

"Singer or Sayer, it matters not. The last patrol said there is no movement of Morg troops. Now, how are they going to get from Castle Darkfall to Castle Shield in one night, if they aren't already moving?"

"I don't know how. I only know that they will be here, tonight. Their main attack will be at the front gate. Raise the drawbridge!"

When Leta still hesitated, Ilissa used a gesture that she hadn't used since the early years when she was the spoiled only daughter of a well-to-do landholder. She stamped her foot. "Raise the drawbridge!" Ilissa screamed.

"What did you say, Leta?" The bridge guard's voice drifted up. "You want the drawbridge raised?"

Leta glared at Ilissa, then bent over the battlement. "No! I don't want the...."

Leta's voice trailed away as she saw figures materializing out of the fabric of the night. Figures of Morgs. "Yes! Raise the drawbridge! Sound the alarm!"

"Raise the drawbridge! Raise the drawbridge!" echoed below. Chains creaked as Sword Sisters threw their weight into the turning mechanism. The bridge inched upward.

It was too late. The first of the Morg troops swarmed across, overpowering the bridge guard. The creaking of chains changed to the ringing of steel as the women operating the mechanism fought for their lives. A guard on the corner tower raised a horn and blew a thundering blast that was cut short as a black-shafted crossbow bolt pierced her chain mail.

Stunned, Leta turned towards Ilissa. The Sayer gazed at her wide-eyed, her nightgown blowing in the wind, her black hair melting into the night. Her expression bore knowledge of certain doom. "They are appearing along the back wall with ladders. And they are loading catapults along the west wall."

Leta ran down the stairs without answering. Ilissa followed, pausing at the base of the stairs as Leta raced for the compound.

Ilissa leaned against the corridor wall, gasping from exertion and terror. Around her she heard the growls and shouts of the Morgs, mingling with the screams of the dying. Through the granite walls she Saw Morgs pouring in the gate and scaling the walls. She Saw catapults hurling flaming oil which spread sheets of fire across stone walls, engulfing everything in its path. And every detail was familiar to her, for Ilissa had lived it all in her Dream.

Within the gray walls of Neston, Ilissa never imagined it would be like this. A Mission she expected, yes, but a Mission of spreading peace by warning people beforehand about impending disasters. Nothing she had learned in her books had prepared her for the throes of battle or the stark possibility of her own death.

But there was no help for her now. She was here. If the Morg troops won she would die sooner or later. From the stories Ilissa had heard about Morgs, she imagined sooner might be preferable.

The frail Sayer drew a shuddering breath and went forth to meet her destiny.

The pounding on the door could wake the dead—and

Roagen was not dead.

"Enter!" he called, and sat up in bed as a breathless man at arms charged in.

"My Lord!" The man drew up in a hasty salute.

"Yes?"

"My Lord, Castle Shield! It's under attack, Sir!"

"Attack! By whom?" Roagen reached for his shirt.

"Morg troops, we presume, Sir. A scout heard sounds of conflict and raced back to report it. He didn't get close enough for details, Sir."

"Are you sure it wasn't just the Sisters conducting a training exercise?" Roagen pulled on his shirt.

"Not unless they set fire to the castle as part of it."

Roagen paused in lacing his breeches. "Fire?"

"Aye, Sir. The scout said the sky was lit up with it when he looked back over his shoulder."

"Assemble the troops, prepare my horse, tell Alan—"

"It's done, Sir."

Roagen paused with one boot on. "What?"

"Alan rode out with one company, as soon as the word came. He ordered what footmen were ready out and ordered the other companies to make ready and follow with you. Your horse is waiting in the courtyard, Sir."

"Indeed!" *Since when does Alan deploy the troops without consulting me?* Roagen wondered. *Since Skurgiil lives at Castle Shield, of course! Which also means that Tudae....*

Roagen's fingers flew across the buckles of his armor, colliding with those of the man-at-arms, who was trying to be helpful.

"Let's go," Roagen ordered, when the last buckle was fastened.

Striding down the hall Roagen passed soldiers pouring out of their rooms, pulling on armor and fastening their weapons as they ran. Apparently Alan had sounded the alarm in full. Roagen had to admit it was good to have a second in command who reacted quickly and whom the men would obey. The Sword Sisters' survival might depend on Alan's response.

The courtyard was filling and more horses were being led from the stables. It looked as if every man, whether on duty or not, was preparing to sally forth. Except for those out on patrol or on leave in Fenfall, and a skeleton force at the castle, the whole of his troops would be moving on Castle Shield.

Which might be disastrous, Roagen thought. *If the attack on Castle Shield is merely a diversion, then my fortress and the whole town of Fenfall will be at the mercy of Necimus — who has no mercy.*

Roagen hesitated just a moment before swinging into his saddle. If Tudae died this night he wouldn't care what tomorrow brought.

"Move out!" he ordered. The second company of horse soldiers clattered through the gates. They overtook a company of foot soldiers in ring mail jogging across the land bridge. They were risking arriving exhausted rather than arrive too late.

It may already be too late, Roagen thought grimly, as he spurred his horse around the footmen. *Too late for Tudae, too late for me.*

Ahead in the night sky Roagen could see the red glow that was Castle Shield.

⁂

Horse riding was painful.

Skurgiil concentrated on the soreness radiating up from her seat. As long as she concentrated on the pain, she didn't think about the farm.

The farm, with its human lambs of varying sizes, including the one called a "baby." It hadn't looked much like a person to Skurgiil, but it had suckled off the woman like the lambs suckled the ewes.

The farm, with the beaten farmer and his worse-than-beaten wife. Skurgiil wasn't certain what had happened to her, but the look on the woman's face said it was awful.

All done by the same two men who killed Erystra.

Pain shot down her legs and Skurgiil welcomed it. The pain was friendly, even pleasant, compared to the feelings rising inside her.

Strange feelings. Ugly feelings, feelings that said there would be nothing more pleasant than chopping those two men to pulp with her axe, splintering their bones like logs for kindling, listening to them scream with pain, pain such as they had inflicted on the farmer and his wife. Watching them die like Erystra had died.

Skurgiil shifted uncomfortably in the saddle. The Good Mother wouldn't approve of these feelings, she knew, but what could she do about them? Perhaps Ilissa would know. Ilissa was a Sayer, like the Good Mother. *Aye*, Skurgiil decided. *As soon as we return to Castle Shield I will speak to Ilissa.*

The dawnstone pulsed purple. Tudae and Mara turned in their saddles, staring.

Skurgiil clutched the necklace. *What...?*

She didn't need an answer. She knew. Just as she knew when wolves were advancing on the flock, even when she couldn't see them. "There's trouble ahead! At Castle Shield."

Tudae's horse leaped forward, urged by her heels in its flanks. Mara's horse pounded right behind.

Skurgiil winced as her bottom slapped the saddle again. The other two were ahead, galloping up a hill, and she had to keep up, had to stay with them.

Tudae crested the hill, saw the flashes of red against the night sky and knew from years of battle what that meant.

For the first time in five hundred years, Castle Shield was burning.

Wendy Jensen

Chapter Twenty-seven

The sky above was black with smoke,
The air was filled with screams,
  From "Dawn of the Morgs"
  by Wyflen Herdhummer

Year After Aria, 303

They covered the remaining distance at a gallop, pushing exhausted horses to their limit and beyond. As they burst over the last hill the scent of smoke carried to them, along with screams and shouts and the clanging of steel.

Three companies of Morg soldiers surged across the ground before the castle. Many were pushing their way through the gate; others battled tiny groups of Sword Sisters, no doubt members of incoming patrols. Along the battlements, backlit by the flames, were the silhouettes of Morgs and Sword Sisters fighting, staggering, falling.

Tudae and Mara charged into the battle, pulling their weapons out. Skurgiil followed, jerking her axe from the saddle holster. Just inside the area of combat her horse tripped on a body and went down.

Skurgiil flew forward over the horse's ears, landing face down in dirt. She rolled over, tightening her grip on her axe.

The dawnstone blazed purple fire, illuminating the back of a half-Morg fighter swinging at her horse. A high, shrieking scream assaulted her ears as the animal thrashed on the ground. The half-Morg turned, searching for her.

The light from her necklace blinded him for an instant, and Skurgiil glimpsed the ugly, almost human features. She lunged to her feet, swinging her axe as she came.

The head of the axe made contact, jarring up her arm from wrist to shoulder. The Morg stumbled back a few steps, but no blood came spurting out, no severed limbs lay on the ground. Skurgiil stared in astonishment from the Morg to her axe.

The sheath. She forgot to remove the sheath. Skurgiil fumbled with the bindings as the Morg raised his weapon, a macabre smile plastered on his face.

A glimmer of recognition turned the smile into a slack-jawed grin. The Morg dropped his weapon and reached to grapple her with bare hands.

Skurgiil freed the blade of her axe. The ugly feelings she fought on the trip home boiled through her blood as she swung at the advancing Morg's face.

The axe crashed through skin and skull and brain, sinking through to the Morg's shoulders. The weight of the collapsing body pulled her forward.

A club hit her from behind. The force of the blow dented her borrowed armor and sent her sprawling face first in mingled horse and Morg blood.

Skurgiil rolled to one side, wiping gore from her eyes. A Morg towered above her — full-blood, this one, its teeth jutting from its ugly mouth and its greasy black hair sprouting just above its red rimmed eyes.

The Morg raised a spiked club the size of a horse's haunch. The dawnstone flashed brilliant purple as Skurgiil pushed up on one arm, trying to roll out of reach.

Lurid lavender fire erupted along the Morg's side,

forcing Skurgiil to close her eyes, and filling the air around her with the acrid odor of incinerated Morg flesh. The ground beneath her shuddered as the Morg's body toppled to the earth.

Skurgiil sat up, eyes watering from the sudden flash of light. Before her lay the dead Morg, a hole in its side still smoldering.

But... the Morg was burned on the side, and he had been facing her. Her necklace didn't kill him.

Skurgiil rose, searching for the source of the Morg-killing fire. Another Morg saw her and bloodlust flared in his eyes. Her hand was empty; her axe lay embedded in the other Morg's face. With a yelp of delight, the Morg swung at her.

He died in mid-swing, purple fire engulfing him. Skurgiil ignored the shrieking creature and traced the source of the fire to the other side of the field.

Facing her was the tallest man she had ever seen. Robes of a purple so deep it was almost black swirled around him. The gaze from his deep-set eyes touched her like cold fire.

The tall man spoke, and next to him a small man in black robes nodded. The tall man motioned, and the circle of guards around him began to move. As he advanced Skurgiil's necklace pulsed, sending bursts of purple light across the field.

―☉―

Tudae paused, her sword locked with that of a half-Morg captain. Glancing over her shoulder she saw Skurgiil rising to her feet, saw Necimus advancing. He paused briefly as the dawnstone incandesced. Tudae saw the waves of purple light tremble as Necimus moved his fingers. Chanting in unison, he and his black-robed mage resumed their advance.

With all the strength in her body, Tudae freed her sword, slashing the half-Morg's throat with a back-handed blow. "To me! To me, my Sisters!"

The remaining Sword Sisters surged toward their Mistress as she tried to intercept Necimus.

Not that it would do any good. Even if she reached Skurgiil in time, there was scant chance of breaking through the sorcerer's bodyguard. And no chance at all of defeating Necimus himself.

Through a blur of hacking blows, Tudae saw Skurgiil bend and retrieve her axe, saw the big girl assume an awkward fighting stance. Tudae cursed.

What a pitiful gesture! Brave, but pitiful. The axe would not protect her from Necimus. Tudae doubted if Erystra's power would even protect her. Guardians were not omnipotent. The glowing light from the dawnstone was bouncing off the magical barrier which Necimus and his pet wizard had erected before them.

Tudae gutted a Morg who appeared in her path and tried not to imagine what would happen when Necimus' barrier met Skurgiil's necklace. Guardians were not indestructible, either.

Ilissa, where are you? Tudae wondered. *Of all times, now is when you should be by Skurgiil's side.*

Even as she closed the last few feet between herself and Skurgiil, Tudae reproached herself for that thought. Ilissa was inside a burning, Morg-ridden Castle Shield, and the Sayer might already be dead.

⋅≡◉≡⋅

Death would be easier.

Somewhere in the back of Ilissa's exhausted mind, the thought crept in. Surely not even the depths of hell can be worse than this.

The Sayer bent over yet another Sister, ignoring the Morgs surging past and the searing heat from a blazing section of oil-drenched wall. The Sister returned her gaze with rapidly clouding eyes. This one was beyond her meager healing powers, so Ilissa radiated an Aura of Peace to send the dying woman on her way. The Sister sighed one last time, and her eyes stared into an eternity that not even Ilissa could See.

Not yet, anyway.

The Sayer straightened her slender form, despairing eyes sweeping the compound. All around her were the dead and the dying, the burnt and the burning. The end was inevitable, and not far away.

A slavering Morg lumbered past. So far Ilissa had escaped the notice of the enemy troops. Ilissa wasn't sure if this was due to her diminutive size or her protective Aura. In either case it couldn't last much longer.

The exhausted Sayer closed her eyes, seriously considering dropping her Aura and stepping in front of the next black armored figure that happened by. At least then her death would be quick.

In that moment of inner contemplation, Ilissa Saw her. No doubt she would have Seen her sooner, if her Sight had not been impeded by the horrors inside the castle. As it was, Necimus was already advancing when Ilissa noticed Skurgiil.

Ilissa's already weary mind went numb with despair. Through all of this she had hoped Skurgiil would survive. Neston could send another Sayer if Ilissa died, but if Skurgiil perished all hope perished with her.

Ilissa whirled toward the gate. Nothing bigger than a mouse could get through the press of bodies there. Ilissa jerked her soot-stained nightdress above her knees and darted for the main hall.

Grateful for non-physical sight, the Sayer closed her eyes against the stinging smoke and raced up the stairs. Her breath came in choking gasps and her heart thumped with alarming irregularity as Ilissa staggered across the battlements.

Below she saw a pitiful handful of Sisters filling the narrowing gap between Skurgiil and Necimus; saw Skurgiil standing in a blaze of purple light, her axe ready. The first Sisters engaged the sorcerer's bodyguard, but the group surrounding Necimus pressed relentlessly on.

With a sinking of her laboring heart, Ilissa knew there was nothing she could do. If she were at Skurgiil's side perhaps she could repel the wizard's magic long enough for her charge to escape, but here on the battlements she was totally helpless.

With a despairing prayer that they forgive an acolyte's temerity, Ilissa raised her hands to the night sky and called on the Unknowns.

Tudae's sword engaged in a vicious flurry of parrying blows as the first of the Black Guard clashed with the Sisters surrounding Skurgiil. Necimus' bodyguards were skilled warriors, not your normal half-Morg butchers. The Black Guard were picked for their excessive size and above half-Morg average intelligence, and trained to protect their evil father-commander at any cost.

Out of the corner of her eye Tudae saw one, then another, of her remaining fighters fall, and knew the end was near. Only a span of minutes separated the Sisters from certain death, and Skurgiil from capture.

"Cover me! My Sisters, cover me!" Two Sword Sisters stepped forward to close the ranks as Tudae dodged back. Slipping back through the armored figures fighting for their lives, Tudae grasped Skurgiil's arm.

"Run, girl! Get to the woods, and make for Castle Fenfall. Skurgiil!" Tudae shook her arm roughly. "It is you he wants! Run for the woods. We'll cover your escape. Skurgiil! Did you hear me?"

Apparently not. The big girl didn't answer, didn't even look at Tudae. Her gaze was on the castle.

At the edge of the battlements, with a nightdress whipping around her legs, stood a tiny figure that could only be the Sayer. Her hands were raised above her head beseechingly. Tudae blinked in wonder as the slight form began to radiate a pure white light.

Tudae started at the sound of a vicious snarl. She turned to see Necimus' features writhe in rage. With horror she comprehended the meaning of his snaking hands.

"No!" Tudae hurled herself forward, hoping to break the sorcerer's concentration and spoil his spell. But even as she felled a bodyguard, the space between Necimus' hands crackled with energy. In desperation, Tudae threw her sword.

The bolt of purple lightning left Necimus' hands seconds before Tudae's blade sliced through his sleeve. Blocks of stone exploded from the battlements when the bolt made contact, and Tudae heard a despairing shriek as Ilissa plummeted into the moat.

The water was cold.

The shock of it sent Ilissa's mind reeling back from oblivion, which a splintering pain in her left arm insisted she needed. Her instinctive gasp of pain and surprise filled her mouth and throat with muddy water. With every shred of her Sayer's discipline, Ilissa fought panic.

The pain in her arm could wait, the choking could wait, but if she didn't get out of the moat the weight of her nightdress would drag her to the bottom.

Ilissa thrashed her legs, fighting the clinging folds of sodden cloth. By the ruddy light of the blazing battlements Ilissa saw the bank of the moat a scant horse's length away. She flailed her sound arm, trying to propel herself forward.

It was no use. One horse length could just as well be a cavalry length, for all it mattered to Ilissa. She didn't have the strength in her legs to counter the weight of her gown, and her one good arm was a meager paddle. Ilissa felt her heart sink with her body, falling inexorably to the bottom of the moat.

Her bare foot grazed stone. Rough, jagged stone, still warm from the blast of Necimus' magic. Ilissa scrambled for footing, righted herself, and her head cleared the water.

She allowed her body to heave, trying to clear her

lungs of stagnant moat water. When she could breathe again, Ilissa picked her way across the submerged blocks of the shattered battlements.

They ended before she reached the bank. Poised on the last stone, Ilissa threw herself at the shore. Grasping rushes with her good hand, she pulled herself out and collapsed face down in the mud.

Through the dim borders of her rapidly receding consciousness, Ilissa heard a battle horn.

Five years had passed since Alan first rode into battle; five years since the brash young warrior had felt his stomach clench in the unmistakable fist of battle fright. It was a feeling no man ever forgot, and Alan recognized it the moment his horse's hooves thudded into view of the battlefield.

What he didn't recognize immediately was the reason for his fright. It wasn't the roiling masses of Morgs and half-Morgs that caused it, or even the unexpected sight of Necimus himself, towering within the circle of his Black Guard. It was the sight of Skurgiil, clad in ill-fitting armor that would deflect neither a sword nor magic that filled Alan with unreasoning fear.

Fury filled him, chasing the fear away. Four feet of honed steel cleared Alan's scabbard with an ominous *ching*, and without even a backward glance he charged into the fray.

The standard bearer blew a hasty battle call, and the mounted warriors swarmed past him, spreading out in a charge formation to follow their commander.

"Your Evilness! They have reinforcements! Lord Roagen's troops..." Balek's voice was a terrified whine.

"I can see that, Balek!" As if anyone could avoid seeing the mounted warriors cutting a swath through his troops, like the scythe of Death himself! And of course they were Roagen's men – his banner flew behind them.

"But Your Evilness! We should go!" Balek wavered as Necimus bent a scorching gaze on him. "I mean," the lesser wizard gulped, "you should go. Return to the safety of your castle. After all, Roagen may be sending more troops. These could be just the vanguard."

A rapidly closing vanguard. Necimus eyed the narrowing gap that separated the Black Guard from thundering hooves.

"Start the spell, Balek," he ordered, and strode to the inner edge of the ring of guards. "I want that girl! Get her!"

Ever obedient, the Black Guard surged in Skurgiil's direction.

Tudae saw the Black Guard advancing like doom on armored feet. The soon-to-be-deceased Sword Mistress wrenched a sword from the stiffening fingers of a slain Sister.

Cora, Tudae reflected, as she glimpsed the face. An older Sword Sister, with many braids in her graying hair. There would be no more braids for Cora, no more for any of them.

"For you and yours, Iskara," Tudae murmured as Cora's sword leaped to fill the space between the oncoming Black Guard and Iskara's daughter.

Alan heard the scream of horses behind him and knew some of his men went down. He did not know how many, because he didn't look back.

A Morg rose up in his path, swinging at the horse's neck. Alan's sword caught the Morg under the chin, splattering blood across him and his horse, which snorted but charged on under the influence of Alan's spurs.

A few more yards, just a few more!

Two Morgs jumped him, one on each side. Alan

lurched forward from a blow on his left even as he skewered the one on his right. A club came back around from the left, colliding with the side of his helmet, changing the world to a tilting, ringing place of blurry Morgs.

Alan swung at the blur, but his sword slashed air. Alan urged his horse on. *Almost there, almost to her*, the few Sisters around her were opening, parting to let him in.

Then he was through, his horse stumbling on bodies but not falling, and he was reaching for her, his fingers catching on the ridiculously loose shoulder plate. Alan prayed the leather straps would hold as he dragged her across the saddle while his horse galloped on, away from the Morgs, away from Necimus.

Behind him, Alan heard a deep roar of rage.

※◉※

Tudae slumped to her knees, nearly collapsing on the bodies of her fallen comrades.

Just seconds ago, they were there before her, the Black Guard, with their matte-black armor and their wicked saw-edged blades. Just seconds ago, one of those blades slashed her thigh, cutting through chain mail and leathers and flesh. She could feel the pain, she knew it happened, but now the battlefield was empty of any Morgs save dead ones.

Necimus was gone, with his pet wizard and his pet Morgs. Skurgiil was safe. Tudae remembered a charging horse and a glimpse of Alan's blonde hair flowing beneath his helmet as he snatched up Skurgiil and bore her away.

Necimus is gone. Skurgiil is safe.

Tudae cried, tears of gratitude, sobs of joy. Tears and sobs that turned to grief as she surveyed the battlefield, and realized the cost of their victory.

※◉※

The saddle horn jabbed into her stomach and her head slammed against the horse's barding. The ground flashed by scarce two feet from Skurgiil's face.

She was going to vomit.

If not from the ride, then from the battle. The memories of a Morg dying in purple flames, of the tall man with the cold eyes coming towards her. The sound of Ilissa's scream as she fell; the smell of fresh blood and burnt flesh; the sight of her own axe splitting the face of the Morg. And above all, the feelings inside that propelled her arm forward, sending the Morg to his death, and enjoying it.

The horse slowed, its sides heaving. Alan pulled up and released his hold on her backplate.

Skurgiil slid to the ground, landing on her hands and knees. Her stomach contracted, heaving, retching up foul, bitter-tasting acid next to the horse's hooves.

Above her, Alan waited. His own first battle had been only slightly more dignified. He hadn't retched until after his third ale at the victory celebration. Of course, he wet his leathers before the celebration started, before the battle was even done, but only he knew that.

Skurgiil wiped her mouth with the back of her hand and sobbed. Behind her, Castle Shield was burning, its orange glow reflecting off the horse's barding. Ahead lay a strip of trees, promising peace.

No people. No dying. No terrible feelings there.

As Skurgiil gazed longingly at the forest sanctuary she saw a long line of riders coming out of the trees. Riders in gray robes, riding dappled-gray horses.

Wendy Jensen

Chapter Twenty-eight

*And why with the coming of the dawn
Do black clouds come billowing forth?*
From "Dawn of the Morgs"
by Wyflen Herdhummer

Year After Aria, 303

Smoke hung in a dismal pall over Castle Shield. Some came from the still smoldering rubble of demolished sections of the castle, but most of it came from the pyres.

Several burned already, the bright flames licking over the pale, rigid forms of the Sword Sisters laid out upon them. And still wagons lumbered in from the neighboring farms, filled to the brim with firewood. Still the voices of the Sayers murmured over bodies, as they sent more Sisters to their final rest.

Skurgiil blinked as she helped Roagen's men extract yet another Sister from a pile of Morg bodies. The smoke would excuse her watering eyes, but it didn't account for her sob when she saw the face.

It was Lia.

I bruised her ribs only... this morning? Skurgiil surveyed the dawn light filtering through the smoke.

Yesterday. Yesterday we practiced together on the

training ground, and today she is dead.

Skurgiil pried a sword from Lia's stiff fingers, and made no effort to hide the tears dripping off her nose.

"Aye, she was a brave lass." One of Roagen's soldiers reached up and patted Skurgiil's shoulder.

"Aye."

The nearest fallen Sister lay sixty feet away from Lia, and five Morg dead surrounded her. Lia had met her end alone, and had exacted a hefty price for it.

Roagen's men moved to help her as she bent over Lia's body, but Skurgiil hoisted the stiff form as most women lift a child. Skurgiil stumbled toward the group of Sayers with Lia's body clutched in her arms.

She knelt and laid Lia at the end of the line of Sisters waiting for the Sayers' final benediction.

There are so many dead. And for what? What had Tudae said? "Run, girl... It is you he wants."

All this, for me? The realization seeped in around Skurgiil's sobs. *If he had gotten what he wanted, gotten me, they would still be alive....*

She sobbed over Lia's and the other's bodies like she had sobbed over Erystra's; sobs that hurt, sobs that wrenched her body and wouldn't stop.

"Skurgiil. Skurgiil!" A hand shook her shoulder. Through a watery blur she saw Alan, his helmet off and his blonde hair hanging over the bruised side of his face.

"It is... it is dreadful."

"You get used to it." Alan sighed as he surveyed the blood-drenched battlefield, the burning pyres and the line of bodies waiting for pyres.

But I don't want her to get used to it! Alan realized. *I don't want her to become battle-hardened, like the other Sisters. I want her to just be... herself.*

Alan knelt in the mud beside her, pulling her into his arms. As the big girl sobbed on his shoulder the dead bodies and pyres seemed pleasant compared to his thoughts.

She can't be what I want. She can't just be herself.

Roagen gripped Tudae's elbow, propelling her through the smoldering rubble and gruesome remains of dead Morgs and slain Sisters. Her study was intact, though smoky and soot stained. Roagen guided her to a chair and pushed her into it.

He poured wine into a goblet still warm from the heat generated by the fires outside. He frowned as he thrust it into her hand and guided it to her lips.

She did not look well. Her full lips were tinged with blue, and her dark skin had a faintly grayish color. Her eyelids twitched over her closed eyes. Tudae took several gulps and leaned back in the chair. Roagen grasped her hand, and it trembled in his grip.

To a warrior's mind, her only visible wounds were scratches. A slash across her thigh that split her leathers and promised yet another scar; a slice on her arm that dripped, but not at an alarming rate. Neither of these wounds could account for the shivers that coursed down the Sword Mistress' body.

No, Tudae's wounds lay deeper than that. Roagen had seen the littered battlefield and knew that half of Tudae's garrison lay on it.

He squeezed her limp hand again. What if it were his troops lying there, if it were his castle that smoldered? A commander was always responsible for his soldiers. The scores of dead must weigh heavily on Tudae's heart.

And all for one of Necimus' bastards!

Skurgiil had cost the Sisters dearly this night, and daughter of a Sword Sister or not, Roagen couldn't see how she was worth it. Could Tudae even justify this sacrifice, to harbor one overgrown girl who drew Morgs like rotting meat drew flies?

Maybe she can't justify it, Roagen thought grimly. *Maybe that is what is bothering her.*

Tudae raised the goblet and took another swallow of wine, but her eyes remained closed. Roagen sighed, and filled the emptiness with words.

"There's no help for it, my beloved. You don't have enough troops left to defend Castle Shield, much less rebuild it. Especially with Skurgiil here, tempting Necimus himself. I realize there have never been men at Castle Shield, but—"

"I know."

"—I'll have to leave a garrison here, it's the only way to ensure... You know?"

Tudae's eyes still didn't open, but her voice was steady, even if her hand was not. "Yes."

This was too easy, too easy by far. He was suggesting the unheard of, turning her world upside down, and she wasn't arguing, not even a little. "And about Skurgiil...."

"She stays." Tudae's eyes were open now, and they stared into his, unflinching.

Well, there had to be a catch. So he would leave his men to guard not only a women's castle full of women, but also a large piece of Necimus bait. And a Sword Mistress who would let His Ugliness walk over her dead body before she surrendered Skurgiil.

"Very well, beloved," Roagen raised her limp hand to his lips. "As you wish."

<hr />

The sun was sinking and the pyres were coals when Lord Roagen stood at Tudae's side outside the main gate, surveying most of his troops and all that was left of Tudae's. The faces before him, male and female alike, were marked with soot and blood and the horror of the past night's battle.

Tudae stepped forward. "Sisters!"

The standing remnants of her force straightened, and the wounded turned their heads toward her.

"We have suffered grievous losses. Grievous... losses."

Tudae's head slumped forward. A moment of silence covered the battlefield before she raised her face to the

Sword Sister

crowd.

"There are... so few of us left. Not enough to defend Castle Shield against Necimus when he attacks again."

The faces before her were grim. No one had missed the word *when*.

"Lord Roagen has offered to station troops here." The remaining Sisters straightened more, and the Fenfall troops glanced at each other. "There is no help for it, Sisters. Our survival depends on it."

Tudae stepped back. Roagen filled the heavy silence with orders. "Companies four, eight, ten and sixteen, fall in! Gorth!"

Men scrambled into marching formation, and a grim-faced captain approached.

"Aye, Sir?"

"I'll be sending stone masons from Fenfall. The foot soldiers are to help clear away rubble in two shifts per day and maintain watch as needed."

"Aye, Sir. Move!" Gorth fell into step beside the formation. For the first time in history men marched into Castle Shield.

Roagen watched them go, and turned to the horse soldiers. "Companies two, three and five, fall in! Alan...."

"Aye, Sir! I can stay and organize patrols, Sir!"

"No, Alan, you can return to Fenkeep with the remaining troops. I will stay and organize patrols with the Sword Mistress."

"But, Sir...."

"I mean it, Alan!" Roagen scowled at his second. Alan stepped back into the ranks. Roagen turned to Tudae. "I'll see if we can salvage something from the stables."

Tudae raised her hand as her lover led his cavalry across the drawbridge. "Sisters, we have one last ritual to perform before this day is done."

Skurgiil stood at the end of the line. It moved slowly, as each Sister stepped before Tudae. Skurgiil moved woodenly, stepping forward as the Sister before her stepped forward, her thoughts a mire of misery.

This is horrible. All these people dead or hurting; the castle burned; the mud of the battlefield red with the blood of horses and Morgs and people.

All because the strange sorcerer called Necimus wanted to destroy her because her name meant something in the Old Tongue.

It does not make sense. It does not make sense at all.

A name was just a name; she had named the sheep, but they were no different for having a name. They were still just sheep, who grazed the grass and butted their heads together when it came time to do the marrying thing again. Surely her name couldn't make her so important that people should die because of it.

Skurgiil took another step as the blood-stained mail-covered back in front of her moved forward.

It was so much simpler in the valley; no one had ever died until the day those two strange men appeared and killed Erystra.

Suddenly Skurgiil longed for the valley, for Erystra's circling arms and gentle smile. It had been so long since she had felt the comfort of those arms, so long since she had felt any comfort at all.

Except for Alan.

He had held her there in the mud, while she sobbed over the death of so many. There had been comfort in his arms; in the words he murmured as he stroked her hair. It was a different comfort than Erystra's, but pleasant all the same. Pleasant in a different way.

The feel of his strong arms around her and the sound of his voice in her ear raised strange feelings inside her; feelings she had felt last spring, when Trenton sat close to her by the hearth in the cottage, until Erystra came and sat between them.

Skurgiil took another step as the sister in front of her moved away.

Tudae looked up at her. "I can't reach your hair."

Skurgiil knelt in the mud.

"For victory in battle, for deeds bravely done...." Tudae's voice repeated the phrase, but Skurgiil scarcely heard her, scarcely felt the fingers moving in her hair. The Good Mother was wise; she knew the answers, could tell her why all of this was happening.

/This... this is my destiny, Good Mother? Blood and death, fire and destruction?/

/Aye, child. So it is written./

/Written? What do ye mean, written?/

The voice inside did not answer.

"It is done, Skurgiil." Tudae was shaking her shoulder, and Skurgiil rose, a braid hanging from her left temple.

"Where... where is Ilissa?" Ilissa was a Sayer. Ilissa would know the answers.

Tudae nodded towards the castle. "The Sayers are setting up an infirmary in the main hall. There are... plenty to occupy it." Tudae sighed and moved to the line of wounded Sisters, bending over the first. "For victory in battle, for deeds bravely done..."

Skurgiil moved away, across the drawbridge, bumping into Roagen's men as they carried out Morg bodies and charred timbers.

※◉※

Ilissa wasn't in the main hall. There were other Sayers there, laying out bedding and helping the incoming wounded to lie down.

A dozen Sayers had appeared out of the woods. Skurgiil had heard the leader tell Tudae that they had Seen the battle, but too late to prevent it; they had scarcely had warning enough to arrive by the end of the battle.

They had been busy ever since, tending wounded and doing the Final Blessing. Skurgiil had glimpsed them tending to Ilissa; no doubt they would know where to find her.

"Mistress?" Skurgiil touched a gray-robed shoulder. So like Erystra's! But the hair falling on the shoulder was brown, not white, and the face that turned towards her was unlined.

"Yes, lass?"

"I seek Ilissa."

"She went to change into her robe, Skurgiil." The voice by Skurgiil's feet was familiar, and Skurgiil looked down.

It was Daena. The blonde hair was caked with blood, and bandages swathed her head, her leg, her stomach. Patches of red seeped through the white cloths and Daena's face was tense with pain.

"I... I thank you." Skurgiil turned, bumped into a Sayer and tripped over some bedding on her way to the door. Once in the hall she stopped, slumping against the wall.

Was no one left unscathed? Lia dead; Tudae, Alan and Ilissa injured; even Daena, who seemed to dislike her, was hurt, dreadfully hurt.

Why? Why is this happening to me, to them?

The Sayer's voice carried through the doorway. "That's the girl? The one from the prophecy?"

"Aye." The tone of Daena's voice passed dislike and bordered on hatred. "The one who has brought this all upon us. The daughter of Necimus himself."

Chapter Twenty-nine

What shall we do, Mamma dear?
Pappa is in the byre...
   From "Dawn of the Morgs"
   by Wyflen Herdhummer

Year After Aria, 293
Peasant Year of Good Harvest

Ten years earlier...

"Show him."

Algnor cringed, his hands fiddling with his beard. He gave Glenda an imploring look, but her features, even as Risa, were adamant.

"Show him, Algnor."

Algnor sighed. He wished the boy hadn't asked, really wished he hadn't. It was understandable, of course. The boy was bright, very bright, and had quite a talent for magic. Small wonder he had noticed the lines of illusion around his mother; small wonder he had asked about them.

Glenda wanted to show him the truth. Algnor glanced

at the boy, and his heart wrenched. Such a happy, bright child; his inquisitive blue eyes taking everything in, missing nothing, learning everything. He had taken to the teachings of magic as if he were Algnor's very own son, and Algnor loved him as if he were.

But he was young, just thirteen. Could he handle the sight of his mother, deformed from the fire so many years ago? Algnor tugged his beard in uncertainty.

"Show him, my husband. He needs to know." Glenda's blue eyes in Risa's face were hard, and colder than the mountain lake when ice crusted its edges.

Algnor sighed again. There would be no dissuading her. Algnor closed his eyes and muttered the words.

The story was told. There was nothing that Algnor could do about it; but then, it wasn't his story to tell in the first place. It was Glenda's story, and in a way, it was also her son's.

The boy took it well, Algnor mused. *Maybe too well.* He listened, never questioning. He didn't even flinch when the illusion disappeared.

Algnor had winced, however, as the final part was told.

"Your name, my son, isn't Ven. It is Vengeance. You understand?"

The boy nodded, and looked at Algnor. With palsied hands, Algnor pulled down a book of destructive spells, blew the dust off, and taught them to the one they called his son.

Chapter Thirty

"Who can deny their own blood?"
Peasant Proverb

Year After Aria, 303

Soot-stained walls flashed by as Skurgiil raced down the hall. Stairs blurred under her feet as she took them three to a stride. She didn't stop to open the door and the wooden bar splintered as she crashed through.

Ilissa turned, her good hand clutching a gray robe in front of her naked body. Her left arm hung limp, covered with splints and bandages.

"Skurgiil! You broke the door! You... Skurgiil?"

Skurgiil snatched her bedroll from the floor and was halfway out the door when Ilissa grabbed her arm.

"Skurgiil! Where are you going?"

"I am leaving."

Ilissa shrank from the cold fire in Skurgiil's eyes.

The look was familiar, somehow, it reminded her of... Ilissa shivered, her robe forgotten at her feet. She had seen that look the night Necimus searched for Skurgiil, when his search and her Sight met. But then the look hadn't been in Skurgiil's eyes. It had been in Necimus'.

"You can't leave, Skurgiil, you must—"

"I *must* what? Stay here? Bring more death and

destruction on people, until *my father* finds me?" Skurgiil's eyes narrowed to slits, glaring down at Ilissa. "Or did ye not know that Necimus is my father, and that is why he is looking for me?"

Ilissa shuddered, but tightened her grip on Skurgiil's arm. "I... I knew."

"Ye knew. Necimus knew. Daena even knew! And ye, Good Mother? Ye knew as well, didn't ye?" Skurgiil stared at the dawnstone, but it lay still and dark against her chest.

"Skurgiil, there is a reason—"

"No!" Skurgiil shook the naked Sayer off her arm, flinging her to the floor. Pain shot through her injured arm, but Ilissa staggered to her feet and followed her charge through the door.

One of Roagen's men came down the hall with a sack of rubble slung on his back. His eyes grew wide at the sight of the Sayer's bare body.

Ilissa shrank back into the room and fumbled with her robe. By the time she got it over her head and wounded arm, Skurgiil was gone.

※⦿※

Skurgiil dodged around the men hauling rubble and the Sisters carrying the wounded to the makeshift infirmary. She glanced around to see if any noticed her leaving, but they were all busy and they were all strangers.

Once past the people Skurgiil ran, legs pumping, feet colliding with the ground with satisfying force. She ran over the hills, dodging clumps of trees and farmhouses.

They would look for her on the road. Skurgiil knew that, just as she knew that the voice from the necklace would be silent. Just as she knew *why* it was silent.

The ugly feelings were in her, coursing through her blood. Feelings of hatred.

She hated the Morgs. She hated Necimus. She hated the people who deceived her about her birth, about her name. *Scourge of Evil, indeed! Child of Evil, it should be!*

She hated the blood and the bodies and the smell of death and burning. She hated the screams and the cries of pain. And she hated herself for what she was and for bringing all this to pass.

Skurgiil veered away from the road, cutting through fields and strips of trees. She didn't need the road. Her legs carried her over fences and vaulted her across streams. The setting sun illuminated The Guardian's peak in the distance. That was all the guidance she needed.

I will go home, Skurgiil thought. *Back to the valley, back to the sheep.*

She could live in the mountains, hiding, away from all these people and all their pain, away from all their deaths. The sun would go down soon, and she could pass the town of Fenfall in the dark. By dawn she would be well into the mountains and out of everyone's reach.

⚜👁⚜

"She *what*?"

"Left, Mistress. She ran away."

Tudae stared at Ilissa, who stood before her with her gray robe sliding off one shoulder and bunched around her bandaged arm.

"She ran away! Why?"

"She discovered her parentage."

"You told her about Necimus?"

Ilissa's black hair swayed from side to side. "Not I, Mistress. I don't know who told her. She was very upset. She feels that all this," Ilissa's good hand waved at the scorched walls, the passing wounded, "is her fault."

"It is her fault," Roagen cut in. Tudae scowled, but Roagen continued. "If she hadn't been here, this wouldn't have happened. Perhaps it is best she is gone."

"You don't understand, Roagen." Tudae snapped. "We need her to defeat Necimus."

"Need her? That overgrown shepherd girl? She can't even fight! What good will she do us?"

"I don't know," Tudae admitted. "But she is part of a prophecy. Ask the Sayer."

Ilissa nodded. "We must bring her back. Out there, alone, who will protect her from Necimus?"

Damn Necimus, and all his offspring! Roagen thought. *Who will protect us from him, while we protect Skurgiil?*

Ilissa and Tudae were waiting. Roagen rubbed his temple and sighed. "Which way did she go?"

Ilissa's violet eyes stared past him. "She's heading for the mountains."

"We'll catch her. Get me a horse." Tudae made for the door, but Ilissa shook her head.

"No. She's going across country, to avoid being caught."

"Where is she? Can you describe the terrain, Ilissa?"

"Fields, woods, streams, a house now and then." Ilissa shrugged, looking helpless. "I'm sorry, Mistress. I'm not familiar with this area."

Tudae cursed. "She could be anywhere. We'll need search parties, covering the countryside. Roagen, call your horsemen. Tell them—"

"No." Roagen stood up. "One horseman, to burn leather to Fenfall. There's only one way across the fens to the mountains, and that's the land bridge. I'll send word to Alan to wait for her there."

Roagen paused at the door and glared back at Ilissa. "When we get her back, Sayer, I want to know all about that prophecy!"

☙ ◉ ❧

Necimus paced his room, alone. Balek, the coward, had made himself scarce as soon as the spell deposited them in the courtyard. The Morgs were cowering in dark corners of the castle, tending the wounded that could be bandaged and eating the ones that were beyond

bandaging.
So close, so very close! He almost had her. If it hadn't been for the Fenfall troops and that cursed soldier on the horse, she would have been his. *What in hell's name brought Lord Roagen's troops to the battlefield?* Necimus stopped halfway across the room. *She brought them, of course.* A Summon spell, no doubt. What power she must have, to bring so many! Oh, she had inherited his talent for the art, indeed.

Necimus sat behind his desk to consider this. She was no ordinary woman, this Skurgiil. She wasn't like those damnable Sayers, or that over-cautious Sword Mistress, or even like her own arrogant mother. No, Skurgiil was a law unto herself and should be dealt with accordingly.

I need her alive, Necimus mused. *She is big, strong in body, and powerful with magic. She can bear my children, unlike those puny village women. She can produce a child per year, and with some Longevity spells....*

Necimus performed some mental calculations. If he bred with the first generation, then with the second, why in fifty years he would have children, grandchildren, and be on the way to great-grandchildren. By then the blood they carried would be almost all Necimus. He could create his own race.

Yes, he needed her alive. Alive and willing, if possible, but there were ways of overcoming the unwilling. Ways that had worked with her mother. There were ways to make one willing, as well, but they required some kind of bond, a link....

Necimus laughed, a booming laugh that carried through the door and down the hall to Balek's room. The lesser wizard cringed at the sound.

She is my daughter. What bond better than blood?

Necimus muttered and pointed at his bookshelf. A thick tome glided to his desk and opened. The pages turned and slowed as they reached the G's.

Slowed, and stopped at the page that said "Geas."

Dorgen's face was incredulous. "We're waiting for a *what*?"

"A girl." The man on his left shrugged, the one on his right nodded.

"A girl." Dorgen risked a glance over his shoulder, where Alan was positioning soldiers three lines deep. "Can't he catch women anymore? He has to put us out to catch them for him?"

The soldier on his right chuckled. "Well, you did steal that red-haired lass from him, Dorgen. Maybe that's why he put you in the front and center. We're supposed to stop a very big girl."

"I'm a catapult handler, not a blockade."

"Shut your mouth, Dorgen. You can earn your coppers, same as the rest of us. See, yonder she comes."

Skurgiil loped down the road, heading for the lights of Fenfall. She had avoided the road, but the fens blocked her path. Strange splashes in the water made her back away and try a different approach.

Ahead were torches, and men in armor spread across the land bridge.

Skurgiil slowed, then stopped. The men stood shoulder to shoulder, and they showed no intention of stepping aside.

They were trying to stop her! The anger she had been feeling seared through her, finally finding a focus, a target. Skurgiil lowered her head and charged.

"Skurgiil, stop!"

She heard Alan's voice, glimpsed him stepping out from behind the lines of soldiers and into her path, but her legs were churning the dirt, her arms were swinging, and the momentum carried her down the road, towards the soldiers and straight into Alan with an impact that knocked air from her lungs and sent them both crashing to the ground.

"Oww! Skurgiil!"

He was rising next to her, grabbing her left arm, holding her back. Skurgiil clenched her right fist and swung.

Her arm straightened on contact, plowing into his face. His head snapped back, but his grip was firm on her arm, and he pulled her down on top of him. He grunted in pain as her weight fell onto him.

A murmur of sympathy ran down the ranks of soldiers, but they didn't break formation. One cocked an eyebrow at Dorgen. "The commander seems to be handling her well, don't you think?"

Dorgen nodded. "Aye. He has a way with women."

Alan rolled on top of her, sitting on her stomach, squashing the air out of her, forcing her hands back to the ground as she bucked and squirmed and shrieked at him.

"Skurgiil! Enough!"

Blood dripped in her face from his nose. Skurgiil blinked and squinted one eye at him. "Get off me."

Alan didn't move or release his grip on her wrists. He stared down at her, his nose skewed to the side.

"Will you stop fighting? Stop running? Come into the castle so we can... talk."

Talk. These people talked too much. Sheep and eagles were better by far. *But later, when all the people were in bed...*. "Aye. I will."

"Good." Alan rose to his feet, pulling her with him. The three lines of soldiers cheered. "The show is over, men. Back to your posts."

As they followed the soldiers back to the castle, Alan wiped blood off his mouth, felt his nose, and swore softly to himself.

Morg spittle! I've been slapped, scratched, bitten and pinched before, but this is the first time a woman has broken my nose.

The next day Roagen sat next to Tudae's desk, watching her counting out coins. Skurgiil sat cross-legged on the floor, staring at the rug, and Alan slumped in a chair, staring at nothing.

My second looks like hell, Roagen thought. It wasn't just the bandages crisscrossing his face, holding the wooden splints over his nose. They didn't help his looks any, but they didn't hide the signs of exhaustion and the signs of... something else.

Roagen wasn't certain what the something else was, but he didn't like it. The dark circles under Alan's eyes were matched with ones under Skurgiil's. It appeared that neither one had slept the night before. Roagen squirmed.

What did they do all last night, at his castle? He should have gone himself to stop the girl, he shouldn't have left Alan to...

"There it is." Tudae pushed a sack of coins across the desk. "Enough for a suit of custom made armor."

Skurgiil raised her head and regarded the sack dully. "Where am I going?"

"Deintlan." Tudae stared at Skurgiil, frowning.

She was different today. Skurgiil had barely spoken since Alan escorted her across the drawbridge this morning. She looked tired, and... haunted. No doubt caused by the shock of so many deaths and the discovery of her parentage.

"Where is Deintlan?"

"West of here, Skurgiil. A large town, the closest place to get custom fitted armor. You'll be gone a fortnight, what with time for travel and waiting for the armor to be finished."

Skurgiil nodded dully and rose to her feet. Alan rose with her.

"Sir, I request a fortnight's leave."

Roagen stared at his second. "What? Now? But why...?" Roagen glanced at Skurgiil and shook his head. "No, Alan. I need you here."

"I have at least that much in back leave coming, Sir! I wish to take it now."

Tudae cut off Roagen's next objection. "Skurgiil can

use all the protection she can get."

Cursed right, she can! Alan thought. *Especially after last night.* Alan swayed with fatigue as the memory returned.

It had been going so well, after the first cup of wine. She had settled down, listened to reason, and was laughing at his jokes when he left her at the door to her room — the room next to his, which he bribed a captain to vacate in a hurry. Alan had laid down in his own bed, secure in the knowledge that she was resting close by.

Until the screaming woke him. Woke him and half the barracks, sending half-dressed soldiers into the hall to stare blearily while he kicked in her door.

He'd spent the rest of the night holding her, comforting her sobs, listening to her scream about death and Darkfall and how she must go, go to him, end it, end it all, all the suffering and death and destruction. Over and over he pulled her back from the door while that necklace sent eerie bursts of purple light through the room. When the sobs and screams were silent and the necklace darkened, he held her while she slept, listening to her ragged breathing until the nightmares returned and she awoke screaming again.

Oh, she needed protection, all right. Protection and to put as much space between her and Necimus as possible.

"I don't like it, Tudae." Roagen stared at the Sword Mistress, frowning.

"It's my leave, Sir. I deserve it and I want it. Now."

Roagen scowled. In better times, that would count as insubordination, but these were times of war and he couldn't afford to lose Alan. The Sayer was going with them, as well. How much trouble could Alan cause in the presence of a Sayer? "Very well, Alan."

"I'd like my back wages as well, Sir."

"Your wages? You told me to save those for you, for a rainy day!"

Alan shrugged, his eyes flickering to the sack on the desk. "It might rain on the way to Deintlan, Sir."

The study door opened, and Ilissa stepped through

with a book in her hands. She nodded at Roagen. "You wanted to hear the prophecy. Perhaps Skurgiil would like to hear it, too."

Roagen nodded, and Skurgiil turned glazed eyes towards Ilissa. The Sayer opened the book and began to read.

The study was quiet when she finished, and Roagen looked thoughtful. "'Three shall they be...' what does that mean? 'One to protect...' that would be you, Ilissa?"

The Sayer nodded.

"'One to draw the evil out...'" Roagen glanced at Skurgiil. *She's done a fine job of that, so far*, he thought. "And 'One to fight fire with fire...'" Roagen frowned. "That sounds like a wizard. Who would that be?"

Ilissa shook her head. "I don't know."

Chapter Thirty-one

*The weapons that defeat the Evil
Shall be forged from the Evil itself...*
From "The Prophecies of Aria"

Year After Aria, 303

Ven was fully grown when Algnor died. Very fully grown, by the villagers standards; they marveled that the kindly wizard had spawned a son so tall. Although the boy was slender, he towered over every other man in the village before he turned fifteen, and added another six inches to that.

On the morning when the man who had raised and taught him failed to wake up, Glenda was no longer young. She had always looked young, because Algnor had never adjusted the illusion for age. On the day Algnor died, Glenda in the image of Risa was as young in appearance as the day Algnor first wrought the illusion.

The illusion disappeared, as Glenda lay sobbing on Algnor's unmoving chest. *Ironic,* Ven mused, *that the last illusion Father created was the one protecting her, and it lasted past his death, albeit by only an hour.*

Glenda raised her scarred, tear-stained face to her son. Her claw-like hands were clenched in Algnor's nightshirt. Ven knew that she had seen them, knew that she knew the illusion was gone.

"I can make another one, Mother. It won't be quite the same, but...."

His mother shook her head. "You know what you need to know, son? To punish your father?"

Ven looked at the gray-haired body on the bed. "My father lies there, Mother. But yes, I know what I need to know to punish the one called Necimus."

"Then go. Go and do that which I brought you to this world to do."

"I can't leave you like this, Mother. The villagers...."

Glenda laughed, a bitter laugh, her head sinking down on Algnor's chest. "It doesn't matter now, son. It doesn't matter."

Vengeance left her alone with her grief and her dead husband, and went to the laboratory to research the spell.

She needed the illusion spell and he would make it whether she wanted it or not. It wouldn't be quite the same, but... perhaps the villagers would believe that grief had changed her.

He was halfway through the spell when his elbow bumped the flask of Algnor's mouse potion. The flask of sweet, merciful potion. The flask which had been full yesterday, but was now empty.

It was then that he realized his mother's sobs had ceased.

✥◉✥

He buried them together, the one who was his mother and the one they called his father. He recreated the illusion one last time, for the villagers to carry the two to their final resting place. He heard the villagers murmurs of wonder that Glenda still had not aged, and that she had died of grief at the death of her husband.

Ven said nothing. In a way, it was grief that had killed her, for grief had sent her to the flask of mouse potion. Ven watched the villagers filling the grave, watched the old Sayer chant the final benediction. As he turned away, Sora leaned on her cane and watched him go.

Then the man whose mother had named him Vengeance traded the little cottage for a mule, packed Algnor's books and laboratory equipment on it, and led it out of the mountains.

Wendy Jensen

Chapter Thirty-two

Three shall they be...
From "The Prophecies of Aria"

Year After Aria, 303

The mule snorted and dipped rubbery lips into the water. Ven waited until the beast drank its fill and began cropping grass by the roadside before he plunged his hands into the stream.

He gasped as the water ran over open blisters; gritted his teeth until the cold numbed the pain and turned his cuticles blue.

At least they match my robe now, he thought wryly. *Except for the mud stains.* He glanced at the hem of his robe and winced. *Muddy to the knees.*

Three days of rain had kept him at the last town. That hadn't been such a bad thing; three days in an inn bed was a welcome relief after a month spent on the road, sleeping on the ground in between towns when he couldn't find a farmer willing to rent him a bed. And there were rarely farmers willing to a rent a bed to a magic-caster.

Always the fear. Ven's thin lips twisted into a smile as he wiped his hands dry on his sleeves. *Always the peasants fear magic.*

That had come as a surprise. Algnor had been well enough liked in Troghaven, and the feeling had extended to his "son." Ven had expected the same reception everywhere.

Not so. Shepherds made warding signs as he passed them on the road; farmers sold him grain for his mule and a hot meal for himself only after seeing his coin. Even then Ven suspected they fed him more out of fear of what he might do to them if they didn't, rather than for the copper pieces. They certainly didn't do it out of compassion. No, never out of compassion.

There was the woodcutter's house in the forest to the west. The woodcutter's wife had passed a bowl of stew and a chunk of bread through the half-opened door; through the crack by the hinges Ven had seen the woodcutter himself, axe held aloft. Ven had bowed mockingly at the woman, left his empty bowl and coppers on the stoop as instructed, and spent an uneasy night in the rustling woods. Thank the Unknowns for the Shielding spell that protected him and his mule from predators while they slept!

No, Ven corrected himself. *Thank Father. He taught me the spell.*

Father! The word stirred feelings in his gut, feelings born ten years ago, birthed from Mother's words and the sight of her scarred face. Ven stared at his reflection in the water and wondered.

Father's kindly face, Mother's scarred one... Neither one gave a clue. Algnor's should not, of course, and Mother's.... Any resemblance had been removed by the fire. The fire that claimed her village, her family, and her looks.

Except the eyes. Only the eyes were the same when the illusion was dispelled. Eyes that were a clear, brilliant blue; the same eyes he now saw reflected in this roadside pool.

As for the rest.... Ven shrugged. His hair was black; Mother said her hair had been blonde. He was tall; Mother said Necimus was huge.

And ugly. Mother said Necimus was ugly.
How do people judge looks? Ven didn't know. On the rare occasions when he wasn't studying magic, he had never noticed much difference in people's looks. Perhaps it was the constant working with illusions that gave him that attitude; how could you value appearances when you knew how easily they could be changed? The lasses of Troghaven were all equally comely in his sight.

However, they didn't seem to have that opinion of him.

Perhaps it was his size that made them shrink away from him and smile nervously at his greetings, though Ven couldn't see why his height should frighten them. He wouldn't hurt them, not like Necimus hurt Mother....

Perhaps that was it. Perhaps the girls thought he was like Necimus, like his real father.... No. No one in the village knew the truth.

Perhaps he was ugly. Perhaps he had his father's looks.

The thought of being like Necimus in any way was revolting. It had been bad enough, seeing Mother's face and hearing her story. Then it had been a private shame, a matter of family vengeance. But now....

The stories grew as he traveled. At first his queries about a magic-caster named Necimus garnered only blank stares, and Ven began to fear the sorcerer had changed his name. But descriptions fared no better, though "huge" and "ugly" were vague enough descriptions, until Ven met a traveler who nodded and directed him northwards.

Soon everyone recognized the name, and Ven grew accustomed to the look of horror in people's eyes when he spoke the name of Necimus.

Ven never grew accustomed to the stories, though. Villages burned, peasants dismembered and eaten, women....

Ven turned away from the stream. He didn't want to think about what had been done to the women by Necimus' army of Morgs; didn't want to see his reflection staring back at him from the water — a reflection stark with a possible resemblance to the man who commanded such atrocities.

He unpacked his bedroll and a clean robe from the mule. It was early yet; the sun wouldn't touch the horizon for another two hours, but Ven was tired of tugging the mule over mud-filled ruts.

I should have stayed in Dietlan, he thought disgustedly, as he stripped off his mud-caked robe and slid the fresh one over his head. *A few more days might have dried the road up.*

Anxious to continue, he had loaded the mule on the first day of clear skies. He was getting close, oh, so close! The horror in the strangers' faces was fresher; the hardness in their eyes more focused. Ven learned to voice his queries about the sorcerer as questions of curiosity, as a traveler new to these parts might inquire about a local landmark or possible dangers on the road ahead. *I seek one called Necimus* was guaranteed to turn hostile stares in his direction and raise a defensive wall of silence in whoever he was questioning. Necimus was close at hand, indeed. Perhaps only a fortnight's travel away.

Still, what would a few more days have mattered? Ven asked himself as he staked the mule, wincing as the roughness of the stake and rope abraded his already mangled hands. A few more days of not dragging a stubborn beast through mud by a rope that peeled skin off his hands like Algnor had showed him how to peel the skin off a snake.

Oh, how Mother hated those snakes! Ven loosened the girth strap, smiling at the memory, then grimaced in pain as he lowered the packs to the ground. Wetness spread across his palm. Ven stared sourly at yet another popped blister before he wiped it on his robe and reached into the packs for his spellbook.

I could have stayed a few more days. A few days spent waiting for the roads to dry, garnering coppers by entertaining with illusion shows wouldn't have been so bad. *And a few nights spent in a real bed,* Ven added disgustedly, as he spread his bedroll on the damp grass, sat on it, and opened his spellbook.

⊰◉⊱

"We should stop soon." Alan gauged the position of the sun, and turned in his saddle to address his companions. "Are you two up to sleeping by the road tonight? Don't seem to be many farms along this stretch of road, and I don't want to risk breaking a horse's leg by traveling through this mess in the dark."

Ilissa nodded bravely, though her smile was a bit strained. Skurgiil merely shrugged.

And I expected what? A long conversation from her? Not likely. Alan's mouth wrenched down at the corners, and he turned back towards the road ahead to hide the bitterness in his eyes. The most words Skurgiil had spoken recently came during the night, and they were couched in screams.

Night after night. Was there no end to it? Skurgiil screaming in the darkness, shaking in his arms as he tried to calm her, as he pressed her close to him, trying to chase away the.... *The what? What demons could haunt a girl so simple, so innocent?*

Not so innocent anymore, Alan thought bitterly. The world was catching up to Skurgiil. The world, with all its unpleasantness and cold reality.

The strain showed on them all. Ilissa sported circles under her eyes that could pass as bruises when viewed from three paces away. The delicate Sayer never complained, but Alan noticed the effort in her squared shoulders, the tenseness in her fragile posture. He had only looked in a mirror recently to shave, but on those occasions he could see the tautness in his own face, and a grim expression that the tavern maids in Fenfall would not have recognized in Roagen's carefree second.

Skurgiil had turned bitter and brooding. The darkness

hung around her like a cloak, seeping from her eyes like a malignant fog.

And can I blame her? Alan stared at the wash of mud that was the road. *Could I handle it, knowing he was my father, that he was coming for me, and killing people that stood between us?* Especially, Alan added to himself, *if I had grown up so isolated, so free of care?*

Skurgiil had talked about it, under Ilissa's prodding during the long nights. Alan was grateful, not only for the Sayer's attempts to focus Skurgiil's thoughts away from her private horrors but also for this glimpse of the girl's past. A valley, ringed by mighty mountains; a pool of clear cold water; sheep to tend, and the little cottage where Erystra always waited... then the memories would overtake her again, and Skurgiil would turn into a sobbing child in his arms.

A sobbing, two hundred pound child, who towered over all women and most men. They hadn't been welcomed warmly in Dietlan. Startled stares and uncomfortable glances had met them everywhere. Alan had arranged for accommodations, and while inn keepers talked to him their eyes always strayed to Skurgiil, who stood behind him like the threat of a distant storm. His coin was as good as any other, though, and they were always granted a room — until after the first night.

"We don't want no trouble," the inn keepers said. *"We have other customers,"* inn keepers told him. *"They have a right to sleep in peace"*, he was informed, after the screams brought patrons blinking from their rooms.

The armor couldn't be finished soon enough as far as Alan was concerned, and he paid the armorsmith extra to work late. The once plump pouch of his back wages now hung limp at his side, starved to thinness by the need for a speedy exit from Dietlan and the demands of worried inn keepers. By the time they left they had stayed at most of Dietlan's inns in succession, and rumors about the strange giantess went before them. Each night's stay was more expensive than the last. His savings had been critically wounded by this trip.

This trip, and the extras. Alan glanced back at Skurgiil. He didn't regret the extras. She looked every bit as fine in that armor as he had envisioned at that first meeting in Fenkeep Castle. *Now if only I could do something about the pain in her eyes....*

"So we're stopping here?"

Alan started and glanced at Ilissa. *I've been mooning instead of moving,* Alan realized, and turned to face the slushy stretch of road ahead.

Trees close to the road here. No place to put a camp, and no water — unless you counted the red-brown ooze that came up over their horse's fetlocks as water. Alan shook his head.

"We'll stop at the next stream. Should be room to make camp on the banks."

As he urged his horse forward through the sludge Alan glanced at the shadows dripping from the encroaching trees.

I hope the next stream isn't more than a quarter hour away, he thought. *We need a lame horse about like we need more bad dreams for Skurgiil.*

✦◉✦

"Ignari elto corii, mangalii ratho nariei...." Ven read the words aloud, then closed his eyes and repeated them from memory.

"Ignari elto corii, mangalii...." The whinny of a horse cut through his concentration.

Other travelers. He could barely make out the shapes in the dusk, but there was definitely more than one. That didn't worry him — a magic-caster was never defenseless — but it irritated him.

He didn't want company. Perhaps if he ignored them.... Ven frowned, focused his mind, and started over. "Ignari elto corii...."

✦◉✦

Alan pulled his horse up and blinked.

The road widened here — good. There was a stream ahead — also good. And there was another traveler here already, with light. Not good.

Firelight would have been understandable, even welcome. Alan looked at the glowing ball perched on a rock, stared at the cross-legged figure it illuminated, and felt all his warrior's instincts go instantly on guard.

A magic-caster. I need that about like I need another spell put on Skurgiil.

"We're stopping here?" The Sayer's voice passed exhausted and bordered on begging.

Alan glanced at the road ahead. The treacherous ruts and rocks smothered in mud were now cloaked in darkness. To continue would risk laming a horse and leaving them stranded in the middle of... *where?* Alan frowned, trying to remember the journey to Dietlan ten days ago.

Hills, mostly. Rocky, wooded hills, unsuitable for farming or grazing. No town for quite a ways yet, not even a cluster of cottages, if he remembered correctly. Alan sighed, his eyes flickering between his companions, the road ahead, and the stranger.

"Let me talk to him first. Stay here." Alan swung off his horse, which whickered thankfully at the release from his weight. "You, too, huh?" Alan patted his mount's neck and looked back at the other two horses' drooping heads. *We all need to rest,* he thought, as his long strides crossed the gap between the muddy road and the strange magic-caster.

⊰◉⊱

"Ignari elto..." The clang of the alarm smashed through his concentration, and Ven raised his head.

A young man stood at the perimeter of the Shielding, rubbing his nose and glaring at Ven with hard gray eyes. A warrior, judging by the armor and the sword drawn and gleaming in his hand.

Ven's thin lips twisted into a smile. *They always fear*

magic, and yet they think a mere sword.... Ven shook his head in disbelief. *So simple-minded, these people.*

"Greetings, warrior."

The voice that greeted him was deep, and grated on Alan's nerves like a sharpening stone against a sword blade. He dropped his left hand from his nose. It hadn't broken again, but it hurt plenty. *First Skurgiil's fist and now this.... This what?* Alan reached forward with his sword, and the point ran into something hard. Hard, and invisible.

"You can't get through it." The deep voice was calm, and... amused? "It is my protection. Since I don't carry a sword." The voice deepened more, and Alan caught a hint of bitterness.

Alan stepped back. Not a good place to spend the night, not with a magic-caster of this ability sitting here. *Perhaps if we continue slowly, with torches....* Alan sighed. They hadn't brought any torches. Who would have thought the muddy roads would slow them down so much that they'd be stranded at night next to a magic-caster?

"Do you mind if we camp next to you?" The question was put gracefully, in a musical voice.

Alan whirled to face Ilissa. "I told you to stay on your horse!"

"He won't hurt us." Ilissa's tone was certain, and her gaze was fixed on the strange man, looking through him.

At what? Alan wondered. *What does she See? Can she really know he's safe?* Alan reproached himself immediately for his doubt. She was a Sayer, after all.

"I only need the space enclosed by my Shielding," the deep voice answered, and the blue-robed man waved a massive hand at the open area by the stream.

I wouldn't want that hand to meet my face, Alan thought, and almost smiled at himself. *As if a fist fight were the worst thing to expect from a magic-caster!*

"Thank you." Given gruffly and grudgingly, it was the most Alan could manage. *Can't stomach magic-casters,* he thought as he turned back towards the horses.

Must come of being in Necimus' vicinity too many years.

Ilissa was still staring at the man, her gaze unfocused. Alan reached out and grabbed the sleeve of her robe.

"Come on," he muttered, and led the way back to the horses.

Ven watched them leave the range of his light, the arrogant warrior and the delicate girl in Sayer's robes. *So young, so tiny, to wield such power.* Sayers had power; Ven had seen Sora's abilities enough times not to doubt them. Believing and understanding were two different things, however.

Magic was simple — mind over matter, bound into powerful words, practiced in controlled laboratory settings until each spell was certain, dependable. No Unknowns to pray to, no vows of helping people to complicate your life. Just the power of man using his mind to control the world around him.

Ven turned his attention back to his magic. "Ignari elto corii...."

"Morg spittle!"

Alan added a few coarser expletives, but the twigs still refused to ignite. Small wonder, after three days of rain. Alan added fresh tinder, and struck the flint again. A night lying on damp ground with no light save that controlled by a magic-caster was not to his liking.

The tinder caught, flared, licked the twigs — and died.

"Why, you lousy piece of—" Alan caught Ilissa's even stare. "Morg spittle," he finished sullenly.

Traveling with ladies has its drawbacks, he thought. *Well — traveling with one lady. Skurgiil isn't a lady, she's just... Skurgiil.* He glanced over to where the big girl sat, staring dully at the non-existent fire. Alan felt apprehension uncoil in his gut.

Night, and darkness. The return of her nightmares, and no light to dispel the fear, the horrors. *Unknowns help me!* Alan dumped the last of the tinder from his pouch and took up the flint and steel again.

※◎※

Ven closed the book. *As if anyone could study with all that cursing going on!* Perhaps it was Algnor's mildness, in manner and language, that made Ven dislike cursing so much. Or perhaps it was something else. To him, lack of control of your language was — well, lack of control of oneself. And one should always be in control of oneself. To do otherwise would invite others to control you.

Ven set the tome aside and stood up, stretching his lengthy body into even longer lines. At the edge of his light he saw the Sayer, looking at him with those eerie eyes. He bent over to avoid her stare, and stuffed the book of spells back into his pack.

It is a stupid spell anyway, he reasoned, *written by an arrogant spell caster. It takes some kind of arrogance to sell a book of spells written in a "secret language."* Arrogance and greed, to write such a book and offer a dictionary as well — for extra cost, of course. Algnor hadn't bothered to buy the dictionary, thinking that mere incantation of the unknown words would suffice to cast the spells. Ven doubted that; he had different concepts of how magic worked.

No matter. It was a stupid spell. Why should anyone go through that gibberish just "To Make Yourself Attractive To Women," when an illusion was simpler and just as effective? *Of course,* Ven reminded himself, *you have to know what type of illusion would be considered attractive to women first. And an illusion wouldn't hide my height.*

He could still feel the Sayer staring at him, so he searched through his pack for a book to distract himself. He paused at one with a worn cover: "Maijik: Palabers i'Paer."

Now here was a book! Commonsense theory on how to bind power into words, any words. And written in the

Old Tongue, which any decent scholar can understand.

Ven sat cross-legged on his bedroll and opened the tome. The cursing had faded into frustrated silence. Ven glanced up. The warrior was staring at the attempted fire, and the Sayer stared at Ven, her eyes piercing him, beckoning him, asking him to — *to what? Help them?*

Ven sighed and stood up. *It can't hurt*, he reasoned, as he willed his mental barricade of invisible stone to accept the passage of his body. *A couple minutes of my time for some peace.*

Alan whirled and rose to his feet at the sound of a footstep behind him. He stood gawking, hand creeping towards his sword hilt.

Unknowns, but this magic-caster is tall! Taller than me by half a head. Every muscle in Alan's body came instantly alert, but the magic-caster was staring past him.

"Flame."

The depth of the stranger's voice seemed to vibrate through Alan's bones and echo through his skull. There was a sudden crackling behind him, and the magic-caster's face was illuminated by firelight.

Alan turned and gaped. The sodden twigs were ablaze, throwing heat and light in a comforting halo. Alan scrambled to add more wood before the twigs burned out and the advantage was lost.

"Thank you." Ilissa stepped forward and inclined her head.

Ven shrugged, spreading his hands depreciatingly. "It was nothing, really."

"Oh, your hands!" Before Ven could step back the Sayer grasped his hands, turning the blistered palms toward the firelight.

"Please," Ilissa smiled up at him, "allow me." She laid her hands over his; her entire hand didn't even cover his palm. Ven felt a tingling bordering on pain, then nothing. The Sayer pulled her hands away.

Gone. Blisters, peeling skin, open sores, even the redness — all gone. The pain was gone, too.

Ven stared down at the tiny girl. *Such power!* Not the

power of magic, of mind over matter — this was different. Power over living things, over the processes of life itself.
The blond warrior looked up from the now blazing fire. "Thank you." Ven smiled wryly at the obvious difficulty the man had in saying those two words. *Yet another one who hates and fears magic-casters,* Ven thought. He saw the warrior's eyes stray to the small pile of damp firewood he had collected. *He wants to gather more wood,* Ven realized, *but he doesn't want to leave his women alone with me.*

Ven gave Alan a mocking half-bow. "It was nothing," the lanky wizard repeated, and returned to his circle of Shielding.

He tried to concentrate on his book, but the passages in the Old Tongue seemed unusually obtuse tonight. That, or the constant activity of the strangers was distracting him.

Ven glanced up occasionally and saw Alan returning with more wood. And more yet. *Must be planning to keep the fire going all night,* Ven mused. *To keep an eye on me, perhaps? Will he stand guard all night as well?*

Ven chuckled and turned a page, even though he hadn't translated the last sentence. When he glanced up again the warrior was helping the big girl remove her armor. Once out of it, she helped him remove his.

Not standing guard all night, then. Ven watched them lay out their bedrolls, and realized the two fighters were bedding down together.

Perhaps he should add a Silence to his Shielding. The Silence spell had insured him a night of rest in several inns with thin walls and couples in the next room. Ven found it amazing that some people made so much noise while sleeping together. Mother and Father weren't noisy.

Ven suspected perhaps Algnor and Mother hadn't engaged in the same activities the noisy couples had been pursuing. The one conversation he had attempted with Algnor on the subject of coupling had been less than successful. The man who could cast illusion spells to illustrate situations turned red-faced and tongue-tied when faced with an adolescent's questions about coupling. Ven came away knowing little more than he had before, and since he had no friends his age there were no other sources to ask for information. In the inns he had learned it was often noisy, and that had been a surprising revelation.

Ven put the book away and lay down. The strain of tugging a mule through boggy roads was catching up to him; muscles ached all down his long body and weariness was stinging his eyes. *I'll skip the Silence,* he decided. *Surely they won't be too noisy with the Sayer sleeping close by.*

He turned his head to look at her. She lay on her back staring at the stars, and the firelight glinted off the mass of black hair spread out beneath her head. She looked so small, so vulnerable, so — alone. The blond warrior lay on his side with the big girl in front of him, and as Ven watched he put his arm around her and drew her close.

Ven extinguished his own light with a word, and turned away from the others. He stared into the darkness, imagining how it would feel to have the delicate black-haired girl curled next to him like the warriors were lying, imagined her hair spilling over his chest like a silky river of darkness.

⊰◉⊱

Skurgiil felt Alan's arm tighten around her, the hard contours of his body pressing into her back, the warmth of his breath on her neck. She pillowed her head on his arm and listened to the gentle thud of his heart.

It was comforting, having him close. It had been years since Skurgiil had slept by Erystra's side, years since she grew so big that there was not room for her on Erystra's cot. The comfort of the closeness of another body was a dim memory, and something associated in her mind with being a child. The pleasure it brought and the need for it now raised a vague feeling of shame inside her. She was a big girl now, all grown, and a Sister of the Sword as well. She shouldn't need someone to hold her.

It wasn't just that, either, but she avoided thinking about the other feelings. The feelings that rose from her belly when Alan was close, strange yearnings that quickened her pulse and flushed parts of her body with an unfamiliar heat. Feelings that intensified when Alan's hands moved in his sleep, caressing her, or when his lips pressed into her neck, setting off responses in nerves all through her body.

She didn't talk to the dawnstone about these feelings. While strange, they were also pleasurable, and Skurgiil had an uneasy feeling the Good Mother might not approve, just like she never let Trenton sleep in the cottage. She thought about asking Ilissa, but a sudden shyness would suffuse her and the words were left unsaid. This seemed private, a secret she and Alan shared.

They had shared much these days and nights. It was odd, the warmth and comfort his mere presence gave her, the way his eyes would glow when they caught her glance. And now his presence was the only thing saving her from the darkness that was growing inside her.

Skurgiil shivered beneath the blankets that covered her and Alan. It would start again, soon. If only she could avoid sleep, if only she could flee from thinking....

Impossible, she knew. The darkness was always there, fueled by the memories.

Erystra lying at the cottage door, red staining her white hair; the farm; the field before Castle Shield, red with blood and reeking of death; the raw hatred in Daena's voice when she said: *"The daughter of Necimus himself."*

Skurgiil knew the hate, understood it. She felt it herself. For herself.

She was his. Made of him, part of him. Part of his darkness.

Skurgiil shivered again, and pulled Alan's arm tighter

around her, not minding where his hand fell. It would start again soon, she knew. Not that it ever stopped — the feeling was there constantly, wearing her down. The pull, unseen and unfelt by anyone else. The sense of being dragged towards the darkness. The voice inside that kept murmuring: *"Come, you are mine; come, we are one; come to me...."* It was always there, all day long, a battle against which her new armor could not protect and her new sword could not defend. All day, the battle raged within.

But when she closed her eyes and slept it was worse.

The dreams came then, horrible in their clarity and intensity. She could feel the deep voice vibrating through her soul, felt the scorching heat of his gaze. The darkness rose, enveloping her, filling her with a sense of despairing helplessness and unnamed shame. Her body ached with sensations like the ones Alan's hands aroused, but they were now twisted into something dark and sickening. And still the voice, calling, luring, promising power and pleasure, pulling her towards the darkness until she could not longer resist and she was swept away, screaming in terror.

⊰◉⊱

I should have placed that Silence! The thought was in Ven's mind before he was fully upright, before he was even fully awake. Before he realized this was not the sound of the warriors coupling.

It was the female warrior, and she was screaming.

⊰◉⊱

Alan's arms tightened around Skurgiil before she was well out of the blankets, locking around her, clamping her into restraints of bone and muscle. Alan thanked the Unknowns for the warrior's instincts that allowed him to react so quickly even when asleep, and cursed as Skurgiil's thrashing legs hurled their bedding toward the fire.

"Morg spittle! Ilissa, could you...."

But the Sayer was already on her feet, pulling the blankets from the flames, stamping out the sparks that smoldered in the wool.

Beyond the reach of the firelight Ven watched, and hesitated. *Nightmares, that is all.* But what had she been dreaming to wake screaming, to struggle so desperately?

They seemed to have it under control. The blond warrior was holding her, soothing her, and her struggles and screams were subsiding. The tiny girl with hair the color of polished blackwood had saved the blankets from the fire and was now sitting, eyes closed, the firelight casting ruddy glows over her pale features.

Meditating, perhaps? Sayers did that, didn't they? Ven watched her, but she didn't move until after the big girl had fallen asleep again. Ven laid back down and listened to the murmurs of her voice as the Sayer and the warrior whispered to each other.

She is worried, Ven thought. *So is he. Worried about the girl, and her nightmares. But — everyone has nightmares, occasionally. Even me.*

Ven rolled to his back and stared at the stars. He didn't want to stare at their fire anymore; didn't want to remember the nights he had awakened in a sweat; didn't want to remember the dreams of scorching flames that often drove him awake. It didn't make sense, anyway; he had never been there, he had only heard Mother's description. *How could I dream of something I never saw?*

Ven closed his eyes and pondered the girl's reaction, diverting his mind from his own memories. *What had she been saying?* Something about she was his, and must go to him. *Go to who?* Ven wondered, and drifted off to sleep.

⚜👁⚜

Ilissa shivered and threw some sticks into the fire.

The night was not particularly cold, only damp. The

fire cast out a comforting circle of heat and light. Most importantly, light.

Ilissa wrapped herself in her blanket and sat on the damp ground, staring at the fire, watching the jumping flames and ignoring the encroaching darkness around them; ignoring what lay beyond the darkness.

Alan and Skurgiil were sleeping again, lulled by the Aura of Peace she had cast. Ilissa's mouth crimped into a painful smile when she glanced at them. *At least they can sleep! I wish I could cast that Aura on myself,* she thought.

Ilissa's eyes blurred with tears. She was tired, so tired! Too many nights with too little sleep.

In Dietlan she had napped in the afternoon to compensate for the frequent awakenings during the night, but today they had been on the road all day, and her body was gripped with leaden weariness. *And this is only the first day on the road,* Ilissa reminded herself, as a tear trickled down the side of her nose.

She wiped it away, chastising herself mentally for her lack of discipline. *"Never give in to the weakness of self-pity,"* the Teaching Mistress had said. *"Sayers are to bear the burdens of others without complaint."*

So easy to say in Neston! Ilissa thought bitterly. *So easy to say when you are well rested, when you can actually do something to ease others' burdens!* Thus far, she had been nearly useless in helping Skurgiil. Oh, she could coax her back to sleep *after* Skurgiil awoke screaming, but she could do nothing to prevent the nightmares, or the constant pull that Necimus was exerting on his daughter.

Perhaps if I were better trained, if I hadn't been pushed out of Neston before I was ready.... Stop it! Ilissa reprimanded herself, and wiped both her eyes. *You are being a weak, whiny fool! Besides, do you really want that magic-caster to see you cry?*

Ilissa glanced in his direction, but the firelight ended short of his bedroll, and he had put out his own globe of white light earlier.

Just as well, Ilissa reasoned, as she lay back down in her bedroll. *If I could see him, I might See other things as well.*

She had seen plenty of things earlier, all of them strange. Visions of fire and pain. A woman's face that changed, cycling from beautiful to hideous, becoming attractive again only to turn ugly once more. Through it all Ilissa knew it was the same woman, for the eyes never changed; they were brilliantly blue and fired with a secret rage. She had Seen something else, too, hovering on the edges of the vision; something familiar, that she should understand. *That I would understand,* Ilissa thought crossly, *if I weren't so tired. I should have asked him his name. Tomorrow I will.*

Ilissa curled up in her blanket and prayed to the Unknowns that they send her comforting dreams of Neston.

─────◉─────

"Morg spittle!" Alan cursed as his horse slid sideways on the slick road. *Morg spittle couldn't be any more slippery than this muck.* His mount finally regained its footing at the base of the short incline, and Alan turned in his saddle to watch the others descend.

Skurgiil's horse fared no better than his. It scrambled down, snorting and splay-legged, careening into Alan's horse at the bottom. Alan winced as the collision pushed his leg against a jagged rock jutting from the hillside.

By the time he coaxed Skurgiil's horse away and released the pressure on his leg Ilissa's palfrey was already picking its way down the hill. The pink-eyed mare only stumbled once before it came abreast of them.

Smaller horses are better at traveling through mud, Alan thought. *So are mules.*

Alan cursed the muddy road again as Ven descended the slope, his mule with its top-heavy packs lurching from side to side but never slipping. In good road conditions the horses would have outdistanced the laggardly mule hours ago, but with this mud they had not been able to leave the unknown magic-caster behind. He followed right in their footsteps, and Ilissa seemed determined to be friendly to him.

It had started with her inviting him to breakfast. Then there were introductions all around. Ven, he said his name was, and he hailed from some mountain town called Troghaven. *"Never heard of it,"* Alan had said, but Ven merely shrugged.

Alan had decided he didn't like him. There was something about this young magic-caster, a power and determination that belied his youth. Alan didn't like Ven, didn't like him following them, didn't like Ilissa's persistent attempts to draw him into conversation.

She was smiling at him now, watching him traverse the last few yards between them. Alan scowled and turned his attention to the road ahead.

A few more yards of downhill slope, a small stream to ford, then up another hill. Alan couldn't decide which was worse: climbing up a mud-slicked hill, where a missed step would send his horse tumbling back into Skurgiil's, or the descent on the other side, where a fall meant a broken leg only for his horse.

And possibly a broken leg for me, Alan thought, and urged his horse forward. *And if I go down Skurgiil and Ilissa will have no protection.* Alan slowed his horse as he neared the stream, scanning the rippling surface for eddies that indicated submerged rocks or pockets of deep water. He pulled his reins up sharply as Ven's deep voice carried over the sound of running water.

"By the way, Sayer, have you heard of a magic-caster called Necimus?"

Ven had phrased the question casually, expecting the usual reaction of fear and horror. The reaction he got was new. New and unsettling.

Ilissa gazed at him oddly, as if she could see the muddy road behind him, as if he and his mule were no obstacle to her vision. Alan had turned in his saddle, and his gray eyes reminded Ven of the drawn sword he had held the night before. Even the nightmare-plagued girl who had ridden all day as if in a trance — *Skurkill? Was that her name?* — had turned. The brooding fire in her eyes finally focused — on him.

"Why do you ask?" The sharpness of Alan's voice again raised images of honed steel in Ven's mind. "Do you wish to join him?"

Ilissa, closest to Ven, was the only one who saw the fury flash in his eyes. Flash, and disappear, as Ven's features recomposed themselves into his former controlled mask. Too late, for Ilissa had already Seen, already comprehended — and she shivered with the knowledge.

"No." Ven's voice descended to a grating timbre that made Alan think of boulders grinding together. "I am going to destroy him."

Alan laughed, a bitter laugh that bordered on hysteria. *I'm tired, he thought, too tired. This magic-caster is joking — or insane.* Alan's laugh died away before Ven's stare. *He's not joking. Insane, then. Or stupid.*

"Going to destroy Necimus, are you? Going to destroy the man who commands an army of mutant Morgs, who took Castle Dawnfall by surprise, who can reach across distances and haunt your very dreams? Sure, go ahead and destroy him. Do what no one else has been able to do. Free Skurgiil from his influence."

Alan kneed his horse, urging it into the water. Skurgiil followed, and Ilissa came out of her reverie and turned her mare toward the stream.

Ven looked at their retreating backs. What had Skurgiil been screaming during the night? *"I must go to him, I am his...."* Over and over. She had awakened on three separate occasions, screaming.

"...Reach across distances and haunt your dreams," Alan had said. Ven stood in the sloppy road, clutching the coarse lead rope, his thoughts a chaos of questions.

Mutant Morgs? Castle Dawnfall? And Skurgiil? Why would Necimus want an over-sized, armor-plated girl?

His mule snorted behind him, and Ven stepped forward. The people with the answers to his questions were scrambling up the far bank of the stream. Ven hoisted his robes to his knees and followed.

⁃⁂⊚⁂⁃

Ven could hear their murmurs from the edge of the woods. Alan was ferociously breaking sticks over his knee and piling the jagged pieces into Ilissa's arms. Ven saw the anger in the young warrior's face and the fatigue in the pale features of the Sayer.

She hadn't said much for the remainder of the day. After the discussion involving Necimus she had kept her face forward, and answered Ven's comments so sparsely that he had given up on conversation. He watched her returning to camp with the armload of sticks, and sighed.

It was going so well, before. She was pleasant, friendly and unafraid. Then, at the mention of Necimus, she had stared at him oddly, and shuddered.

My size, again? Is that what frightens her? Ven glanced towards Skurgiil, who was brushing the horses. *She's big, too. So is Alan. Not quite as tall as I am, but still... the Sayer wasn't afraid of me before.*

Perhaps she is just too tired to talk. A likely explanation; Ilissa looked as if she was about to collapse. Small wonder, with all that screaming last night. If Necimus caused that, then tonight would be the same. *I definitely will cast the Silence tonight,* Ven thought.

Ven paused in unpacking his bedroll as a thought occurred to him. He considered it carefully, weighing the possible risks. He smiled as he made his decision. Tonight he would strike his first blow against Necimus.

Ven walked over to where Alan was again struggling to build a fire.

"Flame," he rumbled, and smiled as Alan cursed and fell backwards from the surge of fire. Ven smiled down at him.

"I had a thought," the magic-caster said

conversationally, as if he hadn't nearly singed Alan's blond curls. "You say Necimus has some kind of spell on your friend." He nodded in Skurgiil's direction. "Well, my Shielding protects from spells as well as swords — ones on the outside, at least." Ven looked pointedly at where Alan's fingers circled his sword hilt. "I can make the Shielding large enough to encompass all of us."

His proposal was met by silence. Alan glared at him, his chiseled nostrils flaring with anger and suspicion. Skurgiil continued brushing the horses, oblivious to his words, or anything else but her own tortured thoughts. Ilissa stared, her violet eyes seeming to search a world that must exist behind Ven's left shoulder.

At last she spoke. "I... we could use some rest. It is all right, Alan," she added, as he rose to his feet, glowering. "I trust him."

Ven bowed slightly to her, and turned away to start the spell. It took him three attempts to get it right, because the Sayer's words echoed through his head and prodded his heart into strange thumping motions. *"I trust him. I trust him. I trust him..."*

Ven drew one slow breath, then another. *Focus, focus! Just like Father taught me.... The words, the image, the power... enlarge it, a little, then a little more. Twenty feet, now thirty, can I make it larger?*

Do I want to make it larger? The thought intruded, and the half completed Shielding collapsed again. *After all, the smaller it is the closer together we will have to sleep, the closer she will be to me...*

Ven frowned, and forcibly focused his mind to form the Shielding.

⇥◉⇤

The fire crackled and popped, occasionally sending up a swarm of sparks as a stick burned through and collapsed. Ven lay on his back and stared at the stars.

The others slept. Only fifteen feet away from him, separated by nothing but air and blankets, they slept. Ven had never slept this close to anyone except his parents, and the sensation was new and unsettling. It implied a certain amount of closeness, a certain amount of... trust.

Trust that worked both ways. The sword at Alan's side could kill Ven while he slept, with no Shielding to protect him. Ven was leaving himself open for attack by inviting these strangers to share his sleeping area. And of course, they were leaving themselves open to attack from Ven, by accepting his invitation.

"I trust him." Such a lovely voice, speaking such lovely words. Such a welcome relief after an afternoon spent trudging behind her while she ignored him.

Perhaps she was just tired. It was a likely explanation; the Sayer had fallen asleep immediately after eating. Skurgiil hadn't lasted much longer, but Alan stayed awake, staring at Ven, fighting not to sleep before the stranger did. Ven had finally feigned sleep, waiting until he heard Alan's breathing turn deep and steady before he opened his eyes again to gaze upon his newly acquired... companions. Ven couldn't call them "friends" yet, but maybe, some time in the future, in the near future....

Friends. An odd thought. Ven pondered the thought and all its novel ramifications as he drifted off to sleep.

For the first time in weeks, Skurgiil slept through the night.

Chapter Thirty-three

*I give you skill, the Lady said,
To wield a sword fair well...*
From "Song of the Sword Sisters"

Year After Aria, 303

"They are back, Mistress."

Tudae glanced up at the Sister's head poking through her study door. "Well? Did they get the armor?"

"Oh, aye, Mistress, she's wearing it now. Mighty fine looking it is, too."

Was that envy she heard in Erideth's voice? Tudae chuckled. Well, they weren't all strong enough to wear plate armor. Hardly any of them were, in fact.

"Show them in. I must see this fine looking armor!"

Erideth fidgeted. "They... brought someone with them, Mistress. A stranger."

Since when do strangers make Erideth nervous? Tudae frowned, but Skurgiil stepped through the door before she could ask.

Fine looking armor, indeed!

Tudae scrutinized the well-crafted pieces. The corselet scrupulously followed the curves of Skurgiil's breasts, though it left more of them exposed than Tudae liked — *thank the Lady there was chain mail under it!*

The leg and arm bracers were thick and no doubt heavy, the shoulder plates were menacingly spiked. The gleam of the steel attested to its quality, and the gold embossing....

Gold embossing! Tudae paused. *I didn't authorize that! This is supposed to be battle gear, not ceremonial armor! And the cost of that embossing....*

"Skurgiil. About the embossing."

Eridith knew what it meant when the Sword Mistress spoke so calmly, and vanished into the hall. The big girl was in for a tongue flaying, for sure. Erideth was certain she herself could find some swords to hone or armor to polish. Cheaper armor.

"Beautiful, isn't it?" Skurgiil smiled happily at Tudae, turning to show all sides of the suit. "Alan insisted, said I deserved it. Oh, he paid for it, too."

"Alan? Paid for the...."

The blond fighter had followed Skurgiil in. Tudae scowled at him, but Alan seemed very interested in the complex designs on the rug.

"Yes." Skurgiil draped her arm across Alan's shoulders, and gave him a lopsided grin.

Tudae groaned inwardly as Alan flushed. *I should have listened to Roagen, I really should have!* Tudae thought. Now she would be having a stern talk with Skurgiil, and telling Roagen to have the same with Alan. Hopefully, Erystra taught Skurgiil something of the things done between men and women, but if she didn't... Tudae sighed.

"And Ven says he can put protective spells on it."

"What! Who is..."

Tudae's voice trailed off as a slender man in blue robes ducked through the door. He had to duck through. As he straightened next to Skurgiil, Tudae realized he stood several inches taller than Iskara's daughter.

"This is Ven." Skurgiil slapped him on the shoulder with easy familiarity, and Tudae winced. A conversation with her was definitely in order.

"We met him on the road," Skurgiil added, as the tall

man bowed toward Tudae. "He's a wizard."

Obviously, judging by the robes! But what possessed the girl, to bring a strange wizard home with her? Alan should have known better, should have known....

Tudae's mental tirade ceased as Ilissa stepped from behind them, looking like a child next to their height.

The Sayer, of course. She would know whether to trust the stranger or not. Tudae relaxed a little. "So, Ven, what brings you to these parts?"

"He wants to help us!" Skurgiil's arm hadn't moved from Alan's shoulders. Tudae gave the fighter a meaningful look, and he sidled to a chair.

"Help us?" Tudae sighed, her eyes straying to the treasury report. In the years since Necimus moved in and Balek joined him, the Sisters had never found a magic-caster willing to take on one, much less two, powerful wizards. Even if they had found one there would not have been gold enough to pay him.

Tudae shook her head regretfully. "I'm sorry, Ven, but we can't afford a wizard. The taxes have been down, what with all the fighting...."

"I require no payment, Mistress."

The voice was deep, unusual for such a slender body. Or perhaps the great height merely made him appear slender.

"What do you mean, no payment?"

"No gold, Mistress. Just a place to put my laboratory, and such supplies as I may need to defeat Necimus."

He mentions Necimus, but not Balek, Tudae thought. *Perhaps he doesn't know that there are two wizards to face. Perhaps he doesn't know how deadly they are together. Perhaps he will change his mind when I tell him.*

A nagging feeling at the back of Tudae's neck told her there was something she should know about this young man. Something about him was familiar.

"Why... why would you do this without gold?" Wizards were known for their desire for gold and power — wizards such as Balek. Tudae's eyes scanned the man before her, searching for clues.

"I... have my reasons." The deep voice was grim. The deep-set blue eyes flashed a more brilliant shade than his robes. Tudae stared at those eyes, and the dark hair contrasting with the pale skin. *So familiar....*

"By the Lady!" Tudae breathed. It was so obvious. How could she have missed it? The resemblance was there for anyone to see.

Cold chills ran down Tudae's back as she realized precisely what that resemblance meant.

⊰◉⊱

"You trust him?" Tudae glanced over her shoulder towards the room where they had left Ven unpacking his laboratory equipment and spell books.

Beside her, Ilissa nodded. "I think he is the other one from the prophecy. The one to *'fight fire with fire'*."

"Hmm. What was the other part? Something about being of the evil's own making?"

"Yes."

"You know, then?"

"That he is Skurgiil's half-brother?" Ilissa paused on the stair, her eyes staring through Tudae. "Yes, I know. But they don't. Not yet."

"Where did you find him?"

"On the way back from Dietlan. He had camped by the side of the road, with his mule. He was sleeping, surrounded by a..." Ilissa frowned, "... a barrier, of some sort. Like an invisible wall."

Tudae nodded. "Such as Necimus has around Castle Darkfall."

"Yes. He woke when we approached, and I Saw... potential in him. As if we were supposed to meet. Alan was suspicious when Ven asked questions about Necimus." Ilissa smiled, hoisting her robes for the descent down the stair. "You should have seen the look Ven gave him when Alan asked if he wanted to join Necimus!"

Sword Sister

Tudae looked thoughtful. "It will be good to have a wizard on our side. If Ven knows how to make one of those barriers, perhaps he knows how to take one down as well."

※◎※

Skurgiil pivoted in the training ground, her eyes locked with Alan's, who circled directly in front of her.

"Not at me! Look at my sword, not me!" Alan's sword, scabbarded for the training exercise, swished into Skurgiil's armor. Her unhoned blade crossed his, seconds too late.

Alan stepped away, pushing his helmet back and shaking his head. "You have to watch the sword, Skurgiil. You have to keep attacks away from you, even though you're wearing armor now."

Armor that was drenched in sweat and sprinkled with dirt. Armor that had been shiny and new only yesterday. *Armor that will soon be bathed in blood,* Alan thought. *It is my job to make sure that blood isn't Skurgiil's.*

Alan hefted his sword. "Let's try again." Skurgiil hoisted her own blade and waited for his attack.

His teaching methods were strange, different from Storna's harsh orders. But Storna had died in the battle at Castle Shield, and Alan was training her now. Swordplay was a far cry from quarterstaff fighting.

/It is the same, but different, child. See the blade coming before it comes./

The dawnstone pulsed and Alan tensed. He remembered that necklace flashing purple light while he held a crying Skurgiil. But now she stood calm before him, no evidence of the force that sent her sobbing to his arms. Alan advanced, swinging.

She blocked. Every blow he sent in her direction collided with her sword. Clumsy blocks, to be sure, she waved her sword like a pitchfork, but a block was still a block, and it would protect her in a battle.

Alan nodded in satisfaction and stepped back as the

Sword Mistress approached across the training ground.

"Ho, what's this?"

"I'm teaching her how to use her sword, Mistress."

And what a sword it was! Tudae looked at it, point driven into the ground in front of Skurgiil with the big girl's chin resting on the pommel. Tudae stepped up to examine it and realized the blade alone topped her braided head. The hilt added a foot after that. The top of the scabbard showed over Skurgiil's shoulder. This sword had to be carried in a back scabbard; not even someone of Skurgiil's height could carry it at the waist.

Tudae cocked a dark eyebrow at Alan. "You? You bought it for her?"

Alan shrugged and looked away across the training ground. "She's a big woman, Mistress, so she needs a big sword. I got a good deal on it. The weapon shop had trouble selling it."

Small wonder. This sword was monstrous, immense, a toy for giants. Alan had paid for the sword and the embossing on the armor... yes, a conversation with him was definitely in order.

"She can't wear a shield and swing that sword."

"If she learns to use it well, she won't need a shield."

Tudae glanced sharply at the young man. That sounded familiar. Where had she heard it before? *Oh, yes.*

Iskara, sparring with her on this same training ground, laughing as Tudae tried to get through her guard. *"My sword is shield enough, Tudae,"* Iskara had said, grinning into her opponent's eyes above the black shield on Tudae's arm.

Alan shifted uneasily as Tudae stared at him. *At him or through him, which was it?* "I've been teaching her how to use it to block, to defend herself."

Tudae's eyes refocused. "She needs to know more than just how to block," Tudae responded tartly, motioning a Sister to bring her a shield. As she fastened it on her forearm Tudae added, "The best defense is an attack. Look sharp, Skurgiil."

The Sword Mistress' sword slid out of its sheath. "This is the standard upthrust." The sword flashed towards Skurgiil.

They circled, eyeing each other, moving across the training ground in a deadly dance just as she and Iskara had danced so many years ago. *The dark hair, the dark eyes, the grace of reeds in the wind — just like Iskara, and...* the resemblance ended there. There was no laughter in this girl's eyes, as there had been in Iskara's, no taunts, no overconfidence. Just steady determination and strength.

Massive strength. Tudae parried the blows, dodged the blade swinging at her like a scythe. It took every muscle of her body to turn that enormous blade away, once Skurgiil learned the basics of attack.

Upthrusts, down slashes, side swings — Skurgiil learned them all, as the sun sank in the sky. Tudae's blade wove patterns, sneaking in around Skurgiil's slashing sword, but only rarely did the Sword Mistress make contact. Skurgiil knew the attacks were coming, knew where to position her hay-mower to intercept.

Dusk was falling when Tudae stepped back, wiping sweat off her domed forehead. "Enough, Skurgiil. For today." As Iskara's daughter nodded, breathless, and headed for the barracks, Tudae smiled.

Skurg i'll. You named her well, Iskara.

Wendy Jensen

Chapter Thirty-four

...To torment a herdboy's dreams...
From "Dawn of the Morgs"
by Wyflen Herdhummer

Year After Aria, 303

"What is that yellow light, Mamma,
Why is the sky aglow?
Dawn comes soon, my darling child,
To milking ye must go!
Dawn comes in the east, ye say, Mamma,
This light is in the north!
And why with the coming of the dawn
Do black clouds come billowing forth?"

The deep voice caressing the lyrics slurred, but there were few to care. A couple of farmers in one corner, a shepherd in another, and Ricand sitting at the bar — had a fight with his wife again, or he wouldn't be here so late.

"Castle Dawnfall lies to the north —
That is not the sun, my child!
It is the dawn of evil things —

The Morgs have come out of the wilds!
What shall we do, Mamma dear?
Pappa is in the byre.
We must flee, my darling child,
Lest a Morg be your next brother's sire!"

Wyflen closed his eyes and finished the song, singing more for himself than for the tavern patrons. For himself and for *her*. He often sang for her, just as he had in the fields so many years ago. In the years when he was young and happy and in love....

Coppers clinked into the cap at his feet. Wyflen opened his eyes and nodded his thanks to Ricand, who reluctantly headed for the door.

Aye, he'll have to face worse music than mine when he gets home, sure, Wyflen thought. *I would not want to be him.*

Wyflen chuckled at the absurdity of that. *Aye, and ye'd rather be yourself?* An angry wife would be pleasant compared to what awaited him this night.

This and every night. Wyflen tilted his tankard, avoiding the thought of the night ahead.

"Another one, Wyflen?"

Dorg closed the door behind the last customer, and raised an eyebrow. Wyflen shook his head, and Dorg nodded approvingly.

"'Tis enough ye've had, already. And another one won't bring her back. But 'twas a damn fine song ye sang, about the poor lass."

Wyflen nodded, and drained the foam from the tankard.

No, another ale wouldn't bring Nella back. Or his parents, or his sister, or... the list could go on and on. But another ale would silence the memories and erase the faces that rose up to reproach him from the past. Wyflen eyed the keg behind the bar.

No, then Dorg would be helping him to bed, or worse yet, carrying him. It was very undignified for a Singer to be carried to bed.

Singer! Wyflen squeezed his eyes shut, willing the tears to stay down. As if he were a real Singer, anyway! He flexed his fingers. They were large, meaty fingers, incapable of learning the strings of a harp, or a lyre, or any instrument besides his shepherd's pipes. No wonder his friends called him "Herdhummer."

That was when he had friends. Childhood friends, who laughed at him as he sang to the herds, until his voice started changing. Then he began humming to avoid the taunts about his squeaking voice.

Not that Nella had cared. She always loved his voice, and she always loved him, even though he was only a herdboy and she was Lord Langtry's daughter. She would listen to him sing, on the days when she sneaked out of Castle Dawnfall, through the secret tunnel that only she knew, to join him in the fields with his herd.

His father found out, of course. Nella was fourteen by then, and Wyflen almost sixteen. His father took him out to the byre and showed Wyflen the knife he used for neutering cattle.

"It will be ye I'll be using it on, boy, if ye even touch that girl! She's a lord's daughter, and destined to marry Lord Greoff's son, like as not."

"Her elder sister will do that. Sara's sixteen, and..."

"I do not care, boy!" The neutering knife hit the byre wall, quivering in the wood. "Nella will not be marrying the likes of ye, no matter who marries Lord Greoff's son!"

Chest heaving, his father flexed his hands and stared Wyflen down. "What can ye offer a lord's daughter? A cattle herder's hut?"

"I can be a Singer. Nella says I'm good, she says...."

Talking with a hand around your throat was difficult, especially a hand the size of his father's. His father's eyes stared into his, and there was no mistaking the threat in his voice.

"I'll not be losing my lease on Lord Langtry's pastures because of ye and your romantic notions, boy! Do not touch that girl, or I'll take care of ye before Lord

Langtry does." The grip on his throat loosened. "And ye'll never be a Singer. We're cattle herders, plain and simple."

Father was right. Wyflen flexed his fingers again, remembering the hand so much like his own, tightening around his neck so many years ago. Wyflen was only in demand when no real Singers were present, which is why he took up residence in this tawdry tavern in a tiny town. Few respectable Singers ever stopped in at the Empty Tankard. The rough farmers who frequented it would throw enough coppers in his cap to pay his board in the loft above the stable; enough to keep his tankard full and the memories at bay.

On the rare occasions when a real Singer did stop in, Wyflen was reduced to drinking his ale in a corner, eaten by envy at the Singer's prowess, and tormented by the faces of those long dead. Sometimes he was tormented, anyway. Like tonight.

How could they rise up before him so clearly, after so many years? There they all were—his father, his mother, his sister, thirteen a fortnight before the attack, the twins, scarcely six, and the baby boy, still in cloths.

And Nella. Always, the memory of Nella.

He had run away, that fateful dawn, run through the pastures and up the rocky slope that led to Castle Dawnfall. He had waited at the mouth of the tunnel until the sun set.

He had waited through a long day, seeing the smoke of the burning village from his perch, hearing the screams from within the castle. Wondering if any of those screams were Nella's, but too terrified to go up the tunnel to find out.

Nella did not appear, and the screams died out by dusk. Wyflen had stumbled back to his house, to find it burned, and the bodies of his family cold to the touch.

He had gone south, merging with other groups of refugees, herded by Sword Sisters toward safer locales. He had stumbled blindly along, singing for a meal when he could, chopping wood or carrying water for a bite of food when no one wanted to hear him sing.

And wondering, always wondering; why did it happen to him? To Nella? Was his family waiting for his return, when the Morgs fell upon them? Would they still be alive, and safely south, if he hadn't run off? Would Nella be alive, if he had gone up the tunnel to save her?

And so it went. Through the years, the ghosts dimmed but never disappeared, no matter how much ale he drank.

"Time to rest, Wyflen." Dorg was holding the last lit candle in his hand.

"Aye." Wyflen hoisted himself up, steadying the swaying bar with his hand. "Time to rest."

Time for him and the ghosts to rest. Wyflen pulled himself, hand over hand, up the stable ladder. By the time he reached the loft he had made a decision.

Tomorrow, he would go north again. North, to the place of his birth, and his loved ones' deaths. North, to lay the ghosts to rest.

Wendy Jensen

Chapter Thirty-five

But the lass inside never came out,
Though the secret way she knew...
  From "Dawn of the Morgs"
  by Wyflen Herdhummer

Year After Aria, 303

The group from Castle Shield sat, their horses fidgeting at the scent of Morg spoor all around them. The strip of trees shadowed them from the early morning light and from the view of the Morg guards on the ramparts of Castle Darkfall.

How it has changed! Tudae thought. The Sisters hadn't ventured this close to Necimus' stronghold in... well, years. Not since shortly after the last siege attempt, the attempt that failed because of the magical barrier.

The castle had been desolate-looking even then. No horses riding through the gates, no people walking the ramparts. Not even any sounds of people. The castle had looked foreboding, a reflection of the sacked town on the hills below.

It looked worse now. The Langtry standards were gone, no doubt rotted away over the years. The roof showed naked patches bare of slate. Weeds and shrubs sprouted across the battlements. Every window was shuttered against the light of day, but the shutters were weathered, as were the massive front gates.

Not that it mattered. Those gates could rot away and fall off, and it wouldn't matter. As long as the magical barrier stayed in place, Castle Darkfall was impregnable.

Tudae turned to the slender man on the horse beside her. "Do you think you can take it down?"

"I need to see it up close."

Tudae shook her head. "No, Ven. If those guards spot us, they'll sound the alarm. Castle Darkfall may look deserted, but they can rally a hundred Morgs from those gates. We wouldn't have a chance."

The blue-robed wizard smiled and reached into his belt pouch. "I just need to see it, Tudae. I didn't say we had to go up to it."

The Sword Mistress watched him place a feather on his palm, heard him mutter some words. The feather trembled, fluttered, and grew, curling up and around itself until an owl sat on Ven's hand, blinking its yellow eyes and ruffling its gray-brown feathers. It flapped its wings and flew straight towards the walls of Castle Darkfall, while Ven sat on his horse, unmoving, eyes closed.

The Sisters who accompanied them shifted uneasily in their saddles. Tudae cast them a stern glance. They said nothing, and Tudae turned back to watch the owl.

It flew in circles around the castle, climbing higher with each pass, until it was circling the central tower. It perched on the arrow guard, turning its head from side to side. Then it lifted into the air again and swooped towards them. Seconds later it landed on Ven's hand, and an instant after that it was just a feather again.

Ven returned the feather to his pouch, ignoring a Sister beside him who made a warding sign against evil. He turned to Tudae, shaking his head.

"It is strong, and large. Larger than any I've seen before." Ven frowned. "He must be powerful, indeed."

Tudae felt her stomach sinking towards her saddle.

"So you can't take it down."

"Not from outside. It must be centered on something. Something inside. If I could get inside...."

"If you could get inside, we could all get inside, and there'd be no need to take it down!" a Sister behind him exclaimed, and bit her lip when Tudae scowled at her.

"One person getting in is easier than an army getting in," Ven replied. "The tower, for instance — the barrier doesn't extend to the tower."

"So all you have to do is fly up there." The sister's voice was a mutter, but Ven heard her, and turned, smiling.

"Yes, that is all I have to do."

The Sister squirmed in her saddle. "You can do that?"

"No. Not yet. I have heard of such spells, though, and with time I think I can develop one."

"Time? How much time?" Tudae asked.

"A few months, perhaps."

Tudae sighed. A few months. Meanwhile, the pull that Necimus exerted on Skurgiil would grow, dragging her towards him with slow but inexorable force.

Geas. That was what Ven had called it, the night after they returned with the armor. The night that Tudae had rushed from her room, wakened by the big girl's screams.

Tudae, and most of the castle. She ran through corridors filling with sleepy Sisters and disheveled men-at-arms, ran to Skurgiil's room, to find a white-faced Ilissa trying unsuccessfully to cast an Aura of Peace.

"I can't help her, Mistress. It's getting worse."

Getting worse? How much worse can it get? Tudae wondered. Skurgiil was sobbing and shrieking on her bed, held down by Alan and two men-at-arms. Tudae listened to the words mingled with the shrieks, and horror crept through her body.

It had taken three men to hold Skurgiil down, while two Sisters poured flask after flask of mead down the girl's throat. After the mead began to take effect they had left her tied to the bed with Sisters standing guard in her room and men-at-arms standing guard in the hall.

"What does she mean, she has to go to him?" Tudae had demanded of the 'emergency counsel' she had convened in her study. Tudae stalked back and forth on the worn carpet, glaring at their faces one by one. "Well?"

"I believe it is a spell, Mistress, called 'Geas.'" Ven's voice rumbled, grating on Tudae's frayed nerves. "It compels someone to come to you. It is often used on people who owe you a favor. There must be some link between the caster and the person, something that binds them together, like an unfulfilled promise. What would be the link between Skurgiil and Necimus?"

Tudae rubbed her neck muscles as the silence hovered in the study like an uplifted sword. Tudae dropped into a chair. "She is his daughter."

Tudae heard a sharp intake of breath. She glanced up to find Ven's eyes sparking blue fire at her from across the room.

"His... daughter." Ven's voice dropped to a depth that Tudae would have thought impossible for a human voice. Tudae heard the raw hatred echoing out of that depth.

"Yes, Ven. His daughter, just as you are his son."

Tudae heard the muttered curse from Roagen's direction, but she didn't turn. She held Ven's eyes with her own dark ones, never flinching from that brilliant blue gaze.

"So." Ven leaned back in his chair. Every lengthy line of his body spoke control. "You know."

Tudae risked a glance at Roagen. He was staring at the floor, his eyes glowering like lightning-lit thunderheads. There would be words later, concerning not just one, but two, of Necimus' offspring at Castle Shield. Tudae sighed and rubbed her neck.

"It is rather obvious, Ven, for anyone who knows Necimus. I'm surprised you didn't see the resemblance in Skurgiil."

Ven's thin lips stretched across his pale skin in a

bitter smile, and the deep voice was very soft. "Ah, but you see, Sword Mistress, I have never seen my — I have never seen Necimus."

Tudae glanced at him in surprise. "Never? Your mother never...."

"He left her for dead. He never knew she bore me."

So that was it. Tudae sighed as Roagen's bitter words cut through the room.

"He looks like you, Ven. Bigger and uglier, but like you, nonetheless. I'm surprised I didn't notice."

I'm not surprised, Tudae thought. *You spent too much time worrying about Skurgiil's presence at Castle Shield to notice the new "threat," my love.* Tudae sighed. Time for a subject change.

"About Skurgiil, and this geas. Can you break it, Ven? Can you break the spell?"

Ven frowned, his high forehead furrowing like a plowed field. "No, Mistress. Not if it is based on the blood-link. She and Necimus are bound together, father and daughter. I can't change that."

Tudae slumped into her chair. Roagen moved to the wine bottle and goblets. Tudae looked at Ilissa. "You can't help her either?"

The tiny Sayer shook her head. "I can not do anything about the blood-link either, Mistress."

Tudae gulped the wine Roagen handed her, and read his thoughts in his eyes. *He wants Skurgiil and Ven gone, out of Castle Shield, away from me.* But Roagen said nothing, and moved on to pour wine for himself and Alan.

"Ilissa, you said it is getting worse. When did this start?"

"It happened every night while we were gone, Mistress. She would wake up screaming, and Alan would hold her. She finally just slept by his side. That seemed to help some."

Roagen paused, goblet outstretched to Alan. "You what?"

"Slept with her. Only slept, Sir, nothing else!"

I've never seen that look of anger and injured pride in Alan's face before, Roagen thought. His second-in-command held Roagen's eyes, head up, nostrils flaring over pressed lips.

"So it started on the trip to Deintlan?" Tudae cocked an eyebrow at Ilissa, but it was Alan who answered.

"No." Tudae turned to Alan, waited for him to take a gulp of wine. "It started before that, Mistress. It started on the night she ran away."

"That was over a fortnight ago. And you say it's getting worse?"

"Aye. My presence doesn't even seem to help much anymore, Mistress."

Alan's tone was hurt, bitter, and... scared. *My brash young second is frightened*, Roagen realized.

"By the Lady, what will we do?" Tudae drained her goblet and stared at the assembled group. "What can we do?"

The silence thickened in her study. Finally Ven answered.

"I can put wards in her room, Mistress. It won't stop the geas, but it may help her sleep through it."

Ven had placed the wards the next day, scribing swirling sigils on the walls of Skurgiil's room, covering the stone with curving lines of color which Tudae thought seemed to wriggle when you looked at them askance. He didn't stop with Skurgiil's room, either. He asked Tudae's permission to place wards all around the castle.

"To prevent him from scrying into Castle Shield," Ven explained. "If he can't see in here, he won't know what we're planning, and he won't know about me." Ven's smile was bitter. "I do not care to have him cast a geas on me."

Tudae had given him her permission, and the lanky wizard spent the day walking the parapets, inscribing sigils on the four guard towers, while Sisters and men-at-arms alike made warding signs behind his back.

The wards had helped. Whether or not they kept

Sword Sister

Necimus' wizard eye out of the castle or not, Tudae didn't know, but Skurgiil was sleeping better at nights. Ilissa reported that the big girl still moaned in her sleep, but she rarely woke up screaming anymore. Ilissa had taken to sleeping days and staying up all night at Skurgiil's bedside, alternately casting Auras of Peace and Protection.

Even though she slept better, the geas was causing a change in Skurgiil. She was more withdrawn. She would stare into the fire in the evenings, the flames reflecting in her dark eyes like the fires of a private hell.

This might go on for months, while Ven developed a flying spell to get him over the barrier and into Castle Darkfall. Tudae sighed as she stared at the desolate castle.

"Very well, Ven, work on your spell. But the sooner you can have it done, the better. We need to end Necimus' reign, before Skurgiil goes entirely mad with fighting his power over her."

"And before His Ugliness comes up with another weapon to use against us," Tudae muttered as she turned her horse's head toward home.

⚔👁⚔

Necimus sat in his inner laboratory; the laboratory that Balek had never seen, where he conducted his private research and manufactured the magical candles.

Several of those candles were burning now, and the research was going well. Very well. Necimus smiled.

He didn't glance at the figure, lying still and pale on a table behind him. He didn't need to. Success would soon be his. Today's work proved it.

Necimus stood and stretched, then paused to regard his handiwork one last time before blowing out the candles.

The object of his interest was a common rat, scurrying around its cage, tail twitching and feet pawing at the bars. There were several rats in cages, all doing the

Wendy Jensen

same, but this rat was remarkable, very remarkable.

The feet moved. The tail twitched. It crawled around its cage like any other rat, but its shoulders ended in a bloody, severed stump.

This rat had no head.

Chapter Thirty-six

*And the boy who loved her waited there
'Til the falling of the evening dew...*
  From "Dawn of the Morgs
  by Wyflen Herdhummer

Year After Aria, 303

"Sword Mistress, a Singer, requesting a meal."

Tudae glanced up. Her eyes took in the muddy boots, the coarse shirt covering massive shoulders, and the large hands twisting a woolen cap. Her glance shifted to the gray-robed figure in the corner, holding a lyre.

Is the land so short of true Singers these days, that Sayers and farmers can pass as such? Hard times, indeed!

Tudae shot a glance at Roagen. His bemused look told her that he had noticed the discrepancy, too.

"Enter," Tudae motioned. "What brings you to these parts, Singer...?"

"Wyflen, Mistress. I am called Wyflen Herdhummer."

The big man flushed as Roagen sputtered into his goblet. Tudae hid her smile behind her hand. *Well, at least he is honest about his heritage. One could do worse than be honest.*

"So, Singer Wyflen, what brings you here?"

"I ask a meal, Mistress. I know men may not sleep at Castle Shield..." Wyflen faltered as his eyes met Roagen's. "Ah... hmm. I would just like a meal, Mistress, in exchange for some Singing."

Tudae waved a hand at Ilissa. "We already have one here who Sings, Wyflen."

Wyflen gaped. A tiny girl, in robes that said she should be a Sayer, not a Singer. But she held a lyre, and her delicate hands looked like they knew how to use it.

Men at Castle Shield, a Sayer who Sings... had the whole land gone crazy in his absence? Wyflen winced as his stomach rumbled. "I can also work for a meal, Mistress. Chop wood, carry water, mop floors—"

Tudae silenced the desperate plea with a wave of her hand. She had heard the rumble, even from across the room.

"No need, Singer Wyflen. We have those who do that, too. And I am sure that Ilissa, here, would like an evening to rest and listen to someone else sing."

The slight girl in the gray robes nodded. "You can use my lyre, if you wish, Wyflen. I see you have no instrument with you."

Tudae noticed the flush of color up his face as Wyflen shifted his weight to the other foot, his hands kneading the woolen cap.

"I... do not play, Mistress. I only sing."

Small wonder, Tudae thought. *Those hands look better suited to a plow handle than a lyre.*

"Good enough, Wyflen." Tudae smiled kindly at the big Singer. "A meal and a night's lodging for an evening of song." Tudae smiled again at his shocked expression. "Yes, Wyflen, men may now sleep at Castle Shield. You must be new to these parts, to not know this." *Especially since it is the talk of all the countryside*, she added to herself.

"Not new, Mistress, but I have been... gone... for a long time. A very long time."

"In that case, welcome back, Singer Wyflen. Ilissa, go to the kitchen and bring Wyflen a plate of food. We can't have the sound of his stomach interrupting our conversation." Tudae motioned to a chair. "Have a seat, Wyflen."

"I thank you, Mistress." The Singer bowed awkwardly as Ilissa passed and took the proffered seat.

"So, Singer, what brings you back to these parts?"

Wyflen sighed, and twisted his cap. "I go... to visit the place of my birth, Mistress. I go to Langdon."

The goblet of wine in Tudae's hand paused in mid-air. "Langdon is no more, Wyflen. It was overrun by Morgs some twenty years past."

Wyflen sighed, nodding unhappily. "I know, Mistress. I was there."

Tudae frowned. "Perhaps you don't know that one called Necimus now resides in Castle Darkfall — Dawnfall, you once knew it as — with his army of Morgs and half-Morgs."

"So I had heard, Mistress." The woolen cap was in danger of being shredded in his bulky hands.

"You can't go there, Wyflen." Tudae's voice was kind, but firm. "The Morgs would catch you and kill you, same as they did to the rest of Langdon."

"Pardon, Mistress, but I must go back."

Is he crying? Tudae wondered. His eyes looked to the floor, but there was a wetness to them.

"I... I...," the Singer's voice was hoarse, "I must go back, and... come to peace with some... memories."

"Curse it all, Wyflen!" Roagen's goblet slammed on the desk. "Didn't you hear the Sword Mistress? You can't go back! You'll be killed!"

The tears were there, indeed, as the Singer's eyes met Roagen's.

"Beggin' your pardon, sir, but... that would be a mercy."

"Morg spittle!"

Alan jumped back as Skurgiil's blade swept by, leaving a scratch across his armor-plated stomach. He raised his own blade, deflecting her sword on its backhanded descent towards his neck, and signaled a break. Skurgiil nodded and stepped back.

"You're getting good, Skurgiil. I've never seen anyone learn so fast."

The big girl accepted the compliment with a nod, her face grim. *Always grim now*, Alan mourned. *Where is the innocent girl I met at Castle Fenfall?*

Gone, Alan realized. *Caught in Necimus' web of death and destruction. As are we all, but for Skurgiil it is more... personal.*

Skurgiil saw the sorrow on his face, but didn't understand the cause. That was nothing new; there were many things she didn't understand, especially where people were concerned.

Like why that magic-caster was staring at her.

She knew he was there, even though Ven was leaning against a wall behind her. She felt his presence, his eyes upon her, the uncertainty of his shrouded thoughts. She sensed his approach across the courtyard even before she saw distaste flicker in Alan's eyes at the sight of Ven coming towards them. She didn't understand Alan's dislike of Ven any more than she understood Ven's fascination with her.

Unless it is because we are brother and sister, she thought as she slid her sword into its back sheath and turned to face him. *But Ilissa is not his sister, and he seems even more interested in her.*

Brother. Skurgiil lifted her head to look Ven in the eye. The concept of "brother" was as foreign to her as the idea that Necimus was her father, but both concepts were undeniably real. The resemblance between herself and Ven was obvious, even to her.

We are both tall, taller than most. And our faces... The height of Skurgiil's forehead was even more pronounced in Ven's; the deep-set blue eyes echoed her

Sword Sister

deep-set dark ones. *We are part of each other,* Skurgiil realized, then added bitterly, *we are both part of him.*

Ven was staring at her, as if he were looking for that part they shared, the part that marked them both as Necimus' offspring. Skurgiil was growing accustomed to that type of stare; she saw it in every face that knew her parentage. It was a look of mingled fear and fascinated horror, and it always made her feel unclean. *Tainted,* Skurgiil thought. *We are tainted, Ven and I.*

"Skurgiil." The depth of Ven's voice stirred memories of the voice that haunted her dreams; the voice that called and beckoned, that tugged enticingly at her soul. *The voice of my father — the voice of our father.*

Ven faltered, fumbling for words. *What am I going to say? What do I want to say? That I'm sorry for her, for her mother; that I'm sorry for me and my mother? That I'm sorry we're both made of the same stuff as Necimus?*

Ven took a deep breath and tried again. It wasn't easy talking to this girl; it wasn't easy coming face to face with the blood they both shared. And yet... the horror of their mutual burden was halved by having two of them to carry it. *I'm not alone in this; not alone in the shame of being Necimus' child. That is what I want to tell her.*

"Skurgiil, I just want to say...."

Does Alan have to stare at me like I crawled out of the moat? Ven wondered. *And does Skurgiil have to stare at me like she can see into my soul? Talking to Ilissa is so much easier! She understands; always, she understands.*

"I wanted to say that is nice to have... a sister," Ven finished. "It is nice to not be... alone."

Then Skurgiil smiled, her dark eyes warming like a plowed field beneath the summer sun. "Aye," she agreed, reaching up to squeeze his shoulder. "Shall we find a tankard of ale, to celebrate our being together?"

Together they walked towards the main hall, while Alan trailed along behind, scowling.

Peasant blood or not, Tudae had to admit that Wyflen could sing. His baritone voice, while unskilled, was rich and carried through the main hall.

Looks of surprise had crossed the faces of his audience when he first appeared with no instrument in hand, looks that changed to amusement as Wyflen hummed, seeking his chord. Now they sat entranced, Sister and guardsmen alike, listening to the drinking songs and ballads that they all knew and loved. And if Wyflen's peasant tongue gave a different flavor to the familiar songs — *well,* Tudae reminded herself, *many of the listeners came from peasant stock themselves.*

Tudae joined in the applause, as another song ended. Wyflen had flushed with the first clapping, but now seemed to be taking it in stride; liking it, even. *Probably didn't have much applause wherever he sang before,* Tudae mused. It seems to be doing him good; keeping whatever demons that hounded him at bay.

"And this one is a song of me own making. 'Tis called 'Dawn of the Morgs.'" The room fell silent as Wyflen hummed, then the deep voice began again.

"*What is that yellow light, Mamma,
Why is the sky aglow?*"

Tudae frowned. Ah, yes, the fall of Castle Dawnfall. Wyflen had said he lost his family, and his love, in that battle. *And he wants to go back, to lay their memories to rest.*

"*It is the dawn of evil things —
The Morgs have come out of the wilds!*"

The voice continued, but Tudae scarcely heard. To allow Wyflen to go unguarded was to send him to almost certain death. While that prospect didn't seem to bother

Sword Sister

Wyflen, it bothered Tudae a great deal.

But, curse it all, she couldn't risk armed guards for every peasant who wanted to relive old times! Especially now, when her garrison was so small.... Tudae looked around the great hall, once filled with Sword Sisters. Now half the seats were filled with Roagen's men, which in turn meant Fenfall's barracks were half empty. Of course, Fenfall was more defensible. *Just like Castle Darkfall....*

"But the lass inside never came out,
Though the secret way she knew,"

Tudae sighed, and reached for her goblet. *I'll ask Roagen about sending some guards with Wyflen in the morn.* Time enough then to think on these problems; for now, there was Singing to listen to. Singing which might never be repeated, if Wyflen went alone....

Singing! The goblet of wine was forgotten as Tudae stared at Wyflen. *What did his song say?*

"And the day was full of evil sights
To torment a herdboy's dreams..."

"What!" Tudae's voice cut through the song. Wyflen paused, mouth gaping, and every face in the hall turned her way. Even Roagen was frowning in puzzlement.

"That last verse. Sing it again, Wyflen." Tudae's voice was calm, belying the pounding of her heart. *Did I hear what I thought I heard?*

The peasant Singer hummed again, looking puzzled.

"The sky above was black with smoke,
The air was filled with—"

"No!"

Wyflen faltered, and flushed. *I'm scaring the poor man,* Tudae realized, but every part of her body trembled in anticipation. She drew a deep breath. "The verse before that, Wyflen."

He nodded miserably, and didn't even hum his chord before plunging back in.

"*But the lass inside never came out,*
Though the secret way she knew,
And the boy who loved her..."

His voice trailed off, as Roagen jumped to his feet. "Wyflen," the Lord of Fenfall's voice was tense, "do you know a secret way into Castle Darkfall?"

"Well, yes, Your Lordship, there was a tunnel. See, Nella was Lord Langtry's daughter, and she'd come through it to meet me in the fields..."

Tudae didn't hear the rest. She stared at her lover, the triumphant, hopeful gleam of his eyes mirrored in her own. Wyflen would have his armed guard in the morning, without a doubt.

⊰◉⊱

They stood in a group, Tudae and Roagen, Ilissa and Wyflen, Sisters and men-at-arms, shoulder to shoulder as Ven crafted the spell.

Wyflen fidgeted. He had never liked wizards much. They made him nervous, with their powers that no man should wield. Sayers had powers, too, but that was different. Their powers came from the Unknowns. He shot a sideways glance at Ilissa. *Such a tiny thing, so fragile. A tiny vessel to channel such power. Not like this towering magic-caster.*

Wyflen had twice his girth, but the magician had a good foot on him in height and uncanny powers, as well. Wyflen stared at the castle to distract his mind from the sorcerer's murmured words.

It looked sickening. In his memory Castle Dawnfall was clean and strong; clean as Nella's face as she ran through the pastures to meet him, strong as the love that rose in his chest every time he saw her. Now the castle looked like a thing diseased, devoured by decay like the hooves of his father's cattle when the reeking hoof rot set in.

Even so, the castle looked better than Langdon — what remained of Langdon, that is. Most of the buildings were gone, devoured by fires. The ones that remained lacked roofs, their unshuttered windows glared like empty eye sockets, and their stone walls were blanketed in vines. The streets, where he once wandered with his friends, were no more, covered by shrubs, saplings, and piles of debris.

The hills surrounding Langdon were once covered by pastures, sprinkled with grazing cattle and dotted with crofters' huts, crofters like his father, who paid their rents and expected Lord Langtry to protect them.

He hadn't protected them. Death and destruction had come during the night, destroying lord and peasant alike. The surrounding farms were empty now, destroyed just like his parents' farm was destroyed.

Wyflen swallowed and blinked as Ven finished his spell. No sense getting mushy about it now. It was all done and over with years ago. They were dead, all dead. His family's bones lay scattered among the weeds where his home once stood, and Nella's bones.... Wyflen stifled a sob and tried to concentrate on what the Sword Mistress was saying. He didn't want to think about what became of Nella's remains.

"You're sure, Ven? Sure it will work?" Tudae asked.

The lanky magic-caster smiled, a bleak smile that spoke pity for those ignorant of his art.

Wyflen grimaced. Oh, he was a proud one, this sorcerer. *What did Mamma always say, about pride going right before you stepped in a hog wallow?*

"It will work."

Proud, and confident too. Wyflen squirmed. *I should have run off in the night, I really should have, and come alone to bury my ghosts. Now, if this spell fails and the Morgs kill them all, it will be my fault. My fault for leading them here in search of a tunnel.*

What use was the tunnel? Probably closed up by now; after all, it hadn't helped Nella escape. And even if they got in, what then? Did this proud wizard think he was a match for Necimus, taker of castles, killer of families and destroyer of towns?

The Sword Mistress looked doubtful. *Doubtful is good. Might keep her alive,* Wyflen thought.

"But when we move, Ven...."

"The illusion will move with us." The corners of the wizard's blue eyes crinkled. "I know how to craft such illusions. My father taught me."

His father? Tudae shot him a glance, but Ven met her eyes with a cool blue stare.

He had been raised by a wizard, Tudae knew. That was who taught him the art. No doubt he preferred to call him, or anyone else, "father" instead of Necimus. He could call any man he wanted "father," as far as Tudae was concerned, but she knew who really sired him.

The man inside Castle Darkfall's walls, the man who was doing the Unknowns only knew what at this very moment.

Tudae breathed a prayer to the Lady that he wasn't watching the outside of the castle.

-≼◉≽-

Necimus scowled into his globe.

It didn't make sense. The Sayer could block his wizard eye from seeing Skurgiil; perhaps she, as his daughter, could even block it herself. But the entire castle? That didn't make sense.

Necimus leaned back in his chair, considering. It couldn't be his scrying spell. He had used it too many times before. He knew it by heart. It was something else.

Necimus redirected his search, narrowing in on Castle Shield in ever shrinking circles.

There were peasants and tradesmen on the road, Roagen's men traveling to Fenfall, even some Sayers in their cursed gray robes. There were Sisters standing

Sword Sister

guard at Castle Shield, side by side with Fenfall troops....
Fenfall troops? Necimus frowned, looked again.

Men stood on the battlements of Castle Shield, men where no men should be. And something else was on the battlements, as well.

Necimus closed in on a tower, scrutinizing the dark stone. There it was, showing up in his globe as if he were hovering in the air above the moat. Sigils, drawn with exacting care, breathing power even through the curving sides of his crystal sphere.

Necimus leaned back in his chair and smiled. *Oh, she is a powerful sorceress indeed, this Skurgiil!* Those wards were not the work of an amateur. *Perhaps she has placed magical alarms, as well; that would be within her powers.* Wards protecting against search, Roagen's men guarding the Sister's stronghold... there would be no more surprise attacks, no taking of Castle Shield now.

No matter. Necimus grinned, and the sight of Death himself would have been more pleasant. No matter how powerful this Skurgiil was, she couldn't deny the blood-link, couldn't refuse the geas.

Sooner or later, she would show up at his door.

✥◉✥

Wyflen parted the overgrowth of bushes and pointed to the darkness beyond. "There it is, Mistress. The tunnel."

Tunnel? It looks more like a crack! Tudae thought. No doubt it was a crack, a crevasse, a gully that existed before the castle was built. Probably filled with earth before construction of the castle began, earth that shifted and settled and trickled out over the years. Wyflen said that Nella came through this "tunnel", but Nella had been a fourteen year old girl.

Tudae looked back at Ven. "Well, wizard? It is this or your flying spell."

Ven peered into the darkness. The light filtering through the bushes showed a passage, of varying widths and heights, but a passage nonetheless. "We'll go with the tunnel, Mistress. It will be quicker."

The months he said it could take him to develop the flying spell would take them into winter, a bad time for sieging. They might be forced to wait until next spring. Long months spent waiting, with the geas on Skurgiil growing ever stronger. Tudae nodded her head.

"As you say, Ven. The tunnel it will be." Tudae let a branch fall back over the opening. "Let's take Wyflen to his former home, to lay his memories to rest."

Wyflen knelt, sobbing, next to the ruins of his home. No whitened bones poked out of the weeds, and Wyflen was glad. No doubt they were there, but he wasn't going to part the weeds to find them.

They stood around him, Roagen's men and Sisters of the Sword, looking uncomfortable, staring at the castle, the sky, anything but Wyflen. The Lord of Fenfall spoke in low tones to the Sword Mistress, with that delicate Sayer listening to every word.

Privacy would have been better, but the slender wizard had said that wasn't possible. The effect of the spell was an area, he said, and as long as they all stayed within that area the Morgs on the castle walls would see nothing but rocky ground. No matter that they now stood in an area lush with weeds; the Morgs were too stupid to know the difference. The magic-caster now stood only feet away from Wyflen, staring at Castle Darkfall with a deadly look in his cold blue eyes.

Wyflen stood up, wiping his nose. The Sword Mistress ceased talking and looked at him.

"Done?"

Wyflen nodded. Tudae motioned to the others. "Back to the horses, and back to Castle Shield. There are plans to be made."

Sword Sister

Skurgiil sat in the study, listening to their plans. The sharpening stone ran down her sword with a gritting, grating sound, but Skurgiil didn't hear it. She only heard the plans, the arguments about who was going where.

She was going. Going into the tunnel with Tudae and Ven, no matter what Tudae said, no matter how much Alan scowled. No doubt Ilissa was going, too. The petite Sayer seemed determined to follow no matter where Skurgiil went.

That was her choice, just as it was Skurgiil's choice to follow them into the tunnel. She had made that choice plain to Tudae and Roagen, when they first started laying their plans.

"Too many people will cause a commotion," Tudae said, when Skurgiil announced her intentions.

"And too few will be killed. Ye need to take muscle along." Skurgiil flexed a bicep. "That would be me."

Roagen frowned. Alan scowled. Tudae lapsed into silence, wondering who had taught Iskara's daughter strategy as well as swordplay.

I am going. Skurgiil tested the edge of her sword, and ran the stone down it again. *Going into the tunnel, into the castle of this Necimus who haunts my dreams, calling to me, drawing me to him by some unseen, magical chain. I am going to sever that chain, sever his head from his body, and search that castle for the men who killed Erystra.* Skurgiil sheathed the sword, and stood up to bid Roagen and Alan farewell.

"Tomorrow, then," Tudae said. "We'll go in at dawn. Give us an hour then start the assault on the gates. We'll take the barrier down as soon as possible." Tudae glanced at Ven, who nodded.

"Even if it isn't down, we'll start the assault. Perhaps it will... distract him." Roagen strode towards the door. "Come on, Alan. There are troops to make ready."

Alan stood, staring at Skurgiil. She met his gaze, and Alan thought that even her newly honed sword appeared less dangerous than the look in her eyes.

"Until tomorrow, then," Alan muttered, and followed

Wendy Jensen
the Lord of Fenfall out the door.

Chapter Thirty-seven

The day was filled with evil sights...
From "Dawn of the Morgs"
by Wyflen Herdhummer

Year After Aria, 303

Dawn outlined Castle Darkfall in macabre shades of purple on black. Skurgiil dismounted and stood staring at the castle, while Tudae gave instructions to the Sister staying behind with the horses.

Skurgiil felt the pull. It was stronger now, dragging her towards this castle like an eddy in her mountain pool.

He wants me, does he? Skurgiil smiled, a grim, unpleasant smile. She reached over her shoulder and loosened her sword in its sheath. *He will get me. He will get more than he bargained for.*

"Come on, Skurgiil." Tudae shook her arm, breaking Skurgiil from her thoughts. With Ven and Ilissa behind them, they crossed the ground to the entrance of the tunnel.

"A crack, indeed!" Tudae shook her braids in consternation, and slid through the opening.

Skurgiil turned sideways to enter. "Morg spittle!" she muttered, as her breastplate scraped on the rock walls.

Tudae had paused ahead and was striking a flint to a torch. She glanced back at Skurgiil and quirked an eyebrow. *Wasn't that one of Alan's favorite oaths? Someone has definitely been teaching the girl more than swordplay.*

The crevasse angled upward, widening at places, narrowing at others. Tudae slipped around rocky projections with the fluid grace of a snake, with Skurgiil scraping along behind her. Behind Skurgiil Ilissa stumbled, saved from falling by Ven's hand on her elbow.

"Sorry." Bright blue eyes met murky indigo ones as Ven smiled down at her. "I stepped on your robe."

Ilissa flushed and gathered her robe closer to her. Ahead Skurgiil and Tudae had paused, waiting. Ilissa scurried to catch up.

"There it is." Tudae pointed upward, to where Skurgiil was testing the ceiling with her fingers. It seemed to give in the flickering torchlight, bending upward from Skurgiil's hand.

"A rug, most likely." Tudae pointed to decaying bits of rope jammed into the rocks overhead, and two wide flat rocks on the floor by their feet. "Flagstones. They must have fallen, leaving a hole in the floor above, which was covered by a rug. And ropes for climbing...." Tudae nodded. "Yes, I think we've found Lord Langtry's daughter's escape route."

"Good." Skurgiil peered ahead. "Couldn't get much farther that way." The crevasse was shrinking, to the point even Ilissa would not have made it through.

Ilissa stared at the ceiling, sorrow in her eyes. "She didn't escape, though. Not on the night Necimus took the castle."

Tudae nodded, her mouth grim. "Not her, nor anyone else. The family was sleeping when the Morgs came. The Morgs had the advantage of surprise. An advantage which should be ours today. Morgs sleep during the day. If we're quiet, we may make it through. Skurgiil, open it up."

Dirt rained down as Skurgiil cut through the moldering rug. Ilissa gagged at the odors that drifted down, and Tudae gave her a concerned look.

"Get used to it, Sayer. Morgs don't smell nice. Can you bear it? Or should you stay here?"

Ilissa shook her head, her hand over her mouth. She swallowed and took a shallow breath. "I'm coming."

Tudae handed the torch to Ilissa and drew her sword. "Well, then, let us go. Lift me up, Skurgiil."

The Sword Mistress rose through the opening, raised in Skurgiil's arms. There were a few seconds of silence from above then a brown hand appeared in the hole, motioning them up. Skurgiil hoisted Ilissa up and cupped her hands for Ven's foot. The wizard scrambled through the hole and held down his hand for Skurgiil.

She grasped it and jumped, launching herself off the floor with the force of a kicking horse. Ven hauled back on her arm and Skurgiil found herself belly over the edge, face down on a reeking carpet. She pulled her legs up and stood, wiping her face with her hand.

"Ugh. Ye are right, Tudae. Morgs stink."

"Shh!" Tudae glared at her, then turned, searching the room. "A linen closet, most likely, on the ground floor. Ilissa," Tudae turned to the Sayer, who held the torch aloft, illuminating broken shelves and moldering cloth, "does your Sight work now? Can you See where we must go?"

Ilissa tilted her head back, frowning. "It works some. Up, I think, on the next floor. I think that is where the barrier is housed."

"Up it is, then." Tudae stepped lightly to the door and opened it a crack. After glancing down the corridor both ways, she motioned for the others to follow.

"And remember," the Sword Mistress whispered, "be quiet!"

⇥◉⇤

Balek woke, the ringing of the magical alarms

pulsing through his head. He shook his head to clear it of sleep then shook it again in disbelief.

Those alarms hadn't sounded in years. Many years. Not since the days shortly after the fall of Castle Dawnfall, when the Sisters still insisted on storming the castle.

It had been so many years, in fact, that Necimus had relegated the daily task of setting them to Balek. Balek felt it unnecessary, but Necimus insisted, and Balek did what Necimus ordered.

Necimus must be told about the alarms. Balek snatched his robe up and scurried down the hall, pulling on his robe as he went. He paused before the blackwood door.

"Enter." The voice boomed out before Balek even touched the door. Necimus was awake. No doubt he heard the alarms as well.

"I heard them." Necimus was staring into the globe on his desk when Balek entered, staring at an armored figure advancing down the hallway below; a figure with dark skin.

Balek peered into the globe. "The Sword Mistress! But... how did she get in?"

"She had help."

"What kind of help?"

Necimus looked thoughtful. "The girl. It must be the girl. And that damn Sayer!"

"I don't see a girl. Or a Sayer." Balek squinted. *But what is that, there, behind the Sword Mistress...*

"Of course you don't see her, fool!"

The anger in his master's voice made Balek jump, and the image disappeared. But, just for a moment, he thought he saw.... He shook his head. It didn't make sense. A tall man, in blue robes. He reminded Balek of someone....

"The Sayer prevents us from seeing her. No matter. I have a surprise for the Sword Mistress." Necimus smiled, and Balek shivered at the sight of that smile.

Balek heard the doors sliding behind him, and he

turned. Turned to look into the secret laboratory he had never seen before, the laboratory where the cherished candles were produced. Several of those candles were burning there now.

Balek's eyes grew wide with horror as the candlelight glinted off dark hair and chain mail, illuminating the figure lying on the table. Balek hardly heard the words Necimus chanted behind him.

For Balek, the world seemed to tilt and grow fuzzy, as the figure on the table sat up and smiled.

⁂

Roagen sat at the meeting place, watching the sky turn purple in the east. Watching, and worrying.

She was going in now, into the hold of Necimus himself, with only a wizard, a Sayer, and an overgrown girl of a warrior for protection. *As if they could protect her! As if anyone could protect her against Necimus,* Roagen admitted to himself. Necimus and Balek, the unstoppable duo, and that mangy army of Morgs.

Roagen looked behind him. They stretched back along the road, overflowing its sides and covering the hills beside it: men-at-arms with the shields of Fenfall, Sisters of the Sword with the shields of the Lady. Grim-faced men with pikes and bows and battle axes; grimmer-faced women with their slender swords. In the back of the column, beyond his sight, rode the gray robed Sayers on their dappled gray mounts. They all knew what they faced in the day ahead.

The Morgs would not be a problem, if they could get through the gates. They were all accustomed to fighting Morgs and this was a sufficient force to take a castle full of Morgs.

But the Morgs weren't the only denizens of Castle Darkfall. There were the two magic-casters, Necimus and Balek. Facing Morgs was easy compared to facing magic. Roagen knew it; knew that his troops knew it; knew why the faces beneath the helmets were grim.

That was something they would have to deal with after they got inside the castle. If they got inside the castle.

Roagen shook his head, remembering the last siege of Castle Darkfall. He glanced back at the wagon hauling the two battering rams. No catapults this time, no oil. If that barrier came down, they would fight their way through the hard way, step by step over Morg bodies. There would be no burning of Castle Darkfall while Tudae was inside it.

Roagen gauged the morning light, calculated the distance to Castle Darkfall. He nodded at Alan beside him, and his second waved back at the lines of waiting soldiers.

"Move out!"

A sea of armored men, women, and horses surged up the road towards Castle Darkfall.

It was quiet.

Tudae crept down the hall, muscles tense, ears straining for a rustle, a stirring, a footfall. Anything that would warn them of approaching Morgs.

She heard it; the faint chink of metal around the corner ahead, the whisper of a footstep. Tudae motioned the others to stop, and tensed for the oncoming enemy.

The enemy turned the corner, and Tudae's tensed muscles quivered and went slack.

Balek stumbled to his room, while the armored figure disappeared down the stairs and Necimus' laughter echoed through the hall.

A Preserve spell, it had to be! A simple spell, useful for keeping food long past the point where it should have spoiled. Balek had learned that spell years ago, for merchants would pay to have their perishable food items preserved for long trips.

But to preserve a body, to preserve it perfectly, for this many years.... Balek shivered. Not that he doubted it was within Necimus' power, but the reasons for doing so.... Balek felt sick.

He had asked about Iskara's body, all those years ago. He had hoped to give her a proper burial; the thought of the Morgs eating her remains had sickened him. But Necimus had told him harshly that it was none of his business. Necimus had been in a foul humor over losing the child, so Balek had dropped the subject, and avoided looking at anything the Morgs ate for the next month.

Now he knew. Knew that Necimus didn't feed Iskara's body to the Morgs; didn't bury it, either. He kept it, concealed in his secret laboratory. Concealed, and perfectly intact under some mighty version of a Preserve spell.

But no Preserve spell would make a corpse walk. And she had walked. Iskara had walked past the cringing wizard and out the door, sword in hand and wearing the chain mail in which he had first seen her, so long ago.

What could Necimus do with power like this? The implications of it sent shudders through Balek's body. Visions of armies of dead things, marching to Necimus' command, rose up before him.

Balek knelt over his chamber pot and vomited.

⁓◉⁓

It isn't. It can't be! The thought careened through Tudae's stunned mind, skittering at the boundaries of reality.

But there was no mistaking the curvaceous chain mail, the swinging dark hair with its nineteen braids. No mistaking the lithe, agile walk. And no mistaking the honed sword, rising to a fighting position.

"This can't be real. It's an illusion!" Tudae felt sweat creeping down her face, as the figure closed the gap between them. *An illusion like the one of the shattered gates, so many years ago....*

Ven's warning cut through her consciousness. "No! It isn't an illusion! It's... much worse."

Tudae felt her sweat turn cold as she saw the pallid face, the bloodless lips stretched in a mocking, familiar smile.

Too familiar. Every move of the body, every sidestep, every twirl of the sword was as well-remembered as if she had seen them only yesterday. They could have been on the training ground again, sparring, instead of doing deadly battle in the reeking halls of Castle Darkfall.

The only thing missing were the taunts, the mocking, teasing phrases that Iskara used to try to throw Tudae off guard. The figure before her never spoke, even when Tudae shouted her name.

"Iskara! Iskara, no!"

Tudae heard the gasp behind her and knew who it came from. *Dear Lady, how would Skurgiil deal with this?*

That was the Sayer's problem. Tudae prayed that Ilissa could deal with it, for Tudae had problems of her own.

She fell back two steps before the slashing sword, parrying while her mind tried to clear.

What was she supposed to do? What could she do? She and Iskara had always been too well matched with the sword. Tudae wasn't sure she could get through Iskara's guard, and even if she did, what then? How could you kill the dead?

Maybe you can't.

The thought was terrifying in its implications. Steel rang on steel as Tudae beat back two slashes aimed for her throat. There was no doubt in her mind that the dead could kill the living. And if the dead didn't, the living would.

Through the clanging of metal Tudae heard distant snarls, approaching footsteps. The sound of conflict had roused the Morgs. Soon they would be surrounded, trapped within the walls of Castle Darkfall. And since Ven hadn't taken down the magical barriers, they would be alone.

Iskara's blade whistled past. Tudae knew that feint, knew it well. It was one of Iskara's favorites. Instinctively Tudae tilted her blade, avoiding the oncoming sword tip that would snag her sword guard and disarm her.

The angle is wrong, all wrong. It had been years since Iskara had used it on her, but Tudae's mind screamed a warning as the edge of Iskara's sword swung up. A warning too late, as the blade missed the sword guard and slashed through skin and tendons and bone.

Blood sprayed the wall and Tudae's sword clattered to the floor, a brown hand still clenched around the hilt.

Wendy Jensen

Chapter Thirty-eight

For they must wield the Sword of Right
Where only the Dark things go...
  From the ballad "Champions of Light'
  attributed to Singer Sefrinel Lutesong

Year After Aria, 303

Balek staggered to the window, ripping open the shutters and throwing up his arm to ward off the brilliant sunlight. He turned the chamber pot outside the window, letting its reeking contents fall to the courtyard below.

What matter if there were Morgs below? As if those wretched creatures would notice if they were retched on or not!

Balek cackled at his pun, then sobered at the sound of his own laughter. The sound was strange, even to his own ears.

How long had it been, since he laughed, or even smiled?

Years. Balek leaned on the sill, squinting against the sun. Years since he had laughed, years since he had smiled. Years since he had even greeted the morning sun. Years since he had come to dwell in this dark castle, searching for the power Necimus promised. Years spent garnering crumbs of that power, while fidgeting under his master's cold stares. Years spent smelling Morgs and the things they left behind them.

Too many years, Balek realized, as he breathed in the outside air. *Too many years spent looking for power, when I could have been in the company of women such as Iskara....*

Iskara. Balek shuddered at the memory, at the thought of what must be transpiring in the hallways below; at the thought of what would transpire in the future if Necimus wasn't stopped. Every corpse would be a potential soldier. Morg bodies, human bodies—what would it matter to Necimus? They would fight side by side in his army; an army that didn't need to eat or sleep, an army that couldn't be killed because it was already dead.

What couldn't Necimus do, with such an army? He would have no need of Morgs anymore—at least, not living ones. Balek shivered, cold despite the morning sun, as another thought occurred to him.

Maybe Necimus wouldn't need a wizard helper anymore, either. *At least, not a living one.*

Balek shuddered. If he left Necimus' service, he had no doubt the sorcerer would send the Morgs after him, or kill him outright with magic, or send his future army of dead things to find him. After all, Balek knew too much. Knew things like how to place the magical barrier, and how to take it down.

Balek groaned. He was trapped, caught in this cursed castle with a mad magician.

If only he hadn't come to work for Necimus. If only the Lord of Fenfall had hired him instead, all those years ago....

Fenfall. Balek blinked, and looked again.

As if conjured by the memory, the Fenfall standard flew on the road winding down from the castle. Flew at the head of a column of soldiers, and horses, and siege machines.

Siege machines! Balek laughed again, but there was

no humor in the sound.

Hadn't those fools learned, years ago? Learned that siege machines wouldn't work against the magical barrier? The magical barrier that he helped construct, which protected Necimus and his Morgs from all attackers....

Balek's eyes narrowed, considering. It was a large force approaching the castle, larger than any that had attacked before. A force large enough that it might, possibly have a chance against Necimus and his army of Morgs.

For the first time in years, Balek smiled and there was humor in the smile.

Oh, it is a joke, indeed, Balek thought, as he hurried towards a certain room. *A joke on Necimus.*

⚔︎◉⚔︎

Blood drenched Ilissa's robes, bubbled up through her fingers out of the stump of Tudae's arm. Ilissa clenched her hand tighter, trying to staunch the flow until her Healing Aura could do its work. Again and again she cast it, until the severed veins closed, until the bleeding stopped, but still the Sword Mistress lay unmoving, her dusky skin turning the shade of Ilissa's robes in the failing light of the dropped torch.

She can't be dead, not yet! Ilissa felt her power ebbing, taxed by overuse, but once more she sent out the Aura.

Tudae stirred and moaned. Ilissa gasped with relief.

We must get her out of this hideous place, get her to another Sayer with more Healing Aura. Ilissa hoisted the sputtering torch, but the words urging escape died on her lips.

They were trapped.

Behind her the hallway was filled with Morgs, held at bay by the blue fire shooting from Ven's fingers. No doubt his power would soon ebb, too. Without the Sword Mistress to fight, there was only Skurgiil to defend them.

Skurgiil! Panic gripped Ilissa as she turned, searching for her charge.

There she stood, ahead of Ilissa in the hallway. How could she have been so absorbed in healing, as to not notice the big girl pass her? Ilissa scrambled to her feet, tripping over blood soaked robes.

Purple light outlined Skurgiil's back and illuminated in eerie detail the horror that stood before her. The horror which had once been Skurgiil's mother, Ilissa realized.

Half-remembered lessons on rites for the dead flooded Ilissa's memory, along with the reasons for, and the importance of, those rites. Reasons which in Neston's classroom seemed more the stuff of nightmares than reality — reasons which were now horribly clear.

Will the rites work now? Can I even remember them? Ilissa's mind raced, frantically trying to reconstruct the words of the Final Blessing. Fumbling for memories, she watched Iskara's sword swing in the glowing light of the dawnstone; watched as the sword of the dead woman's daughter rose to meet the attack.

The hallway exploded with purple light and Ilissa's mind reeled into darkness.

⁌◉⁍

Roagen looked up at the castle, squinting against the morning sun.

All was quiet. No sounds of bloody battle came from within; no snarls from Morgs; no screams of pain and terror announcing the death of his beloved and her companions. The sense of relief he felt at the silence told Roagen how much he had feared those sounds.

"Think it's down?" Roagen turned to his second, who shrugged and dismounted. Choosing a pebble from the road, Alan launched it at the gate.

"No." Alan watched the pebble roll back towards him, deflected before it ever touched the wooden gates. Alan stared at him, and Roagen saw worry and fear in his gray eyes.

The same emotions I feel, Roagen thought. He scanned the castle again, looking for clues as to what transpired within. Roagen stared, and swore softly.

"Bring them up, men!" He motioned the battering rams forward and motioned at the castle when Alan quirked an eyebrow at him. "We have an audience. Might as well give them a show."

He heard the sharp intake of breath as Alan saw the unshuttered window, the window which Roagen was sure had been shuttered before.

Someone knew they were here. Perhaps if they charged the gates often enough, that someone wouldn't notice Tudae and the others in the halls of Castle Darkfall.

⁂

The torch smoldered on the dirt-caked carpet, spewing acrid fumes, but no light. Ilissa rolled over, groping for the wall.

A body lay beside her, still warm. Ilissa ran her hand past leather boots to sticky chain mail.

The Sword Mistress! She was wounded, direly wounded....

Ilissa fumbled through the mass of braids and sighed with relief when she felt a pulse in the neck. Tudae lived. For now, at least.

Ilissa's head felt swollen, pulsing. Something had happened, after the Sword Mistress' injury... *what was it?* A backlash of immense power released, that knocked her unconscious in its passing; a backlash that came from the direction of Skurgiil and Iskara....

Skurgiil! And that horror, that monstrosity that walked when it should have been buried years ago....

Ilissa fumbled for the torch, hoisting it in the air, but the fire in it had died.

In the darkness near her something stirred. Ilissa cringed against the wall.

"Flame." Ven's deep voice reverberated through her

aching head as the torch flared, filling the hallway with ruddy light.

Ven was sitting on the floor, holding his head. Beyond him Ilissa saw the prostrate forms of Morgs; Morgs that were breathing, stirring, rising to their hands and knees.

"No!"

The sound of Skurgiil's voice echoed down the hall and crashed against Ilissa's ears with shattering pain. She towered in the hallway, clutching her necklace and staring at the motionless form of her dead mother.

Her long dead mother, who walked and fought and severed Tudae's hand, who needed to be sent to her final rest, who needed the Final Blessing, if only Ilissa could remember it, if only her head would stop hurting, if only she could get Skurgiil away from the body....

"Skurgiil! The Morgs!"

Ven was pushing himself up against the wall, but he was pale, gasping, trembling. The backwash of power had affected him, too, and Ilissa knew he couldn't hold off the Morgs, who were on their feet now, shaking their heads and fumbling for their weapons.

Skurgiil turned, her face a miasma of loss in the flickering torchlight. She released the dawnstone, the dawnstone that hung dark on its silver links around her neck, and her left hand joined her right on the grip of her sword.

The hallway and Ilissa's head resounded with her roar of rage as she charged into the advancing Morgs.

⊰◉⊱

Necimus stood up and ran one hand through his black hair. Totally black, not a touch of gray in it at all. The Longevity spell he developed worked well. Necimus still looked like he was in his prime.

Not that he usually cared how he looked. Necimus was not given to vanity. He had learned years ago that most people found him unpleasant to behold. That had served its purpose, frightening fools more comely but weaker than himself.

The Longevity spell was not for vanity, it was for life. Long life, long enough to accomplish all of Necimus' plans, long enough to spread his seed and watch his own race populate the land.

The future mother of his race walked the hallway below. Necimus smoothed his robes, for today he cared how he looked. Today was special. Today he would meet his human daughter. His only human offspring.

―◉―

"I have to... take down the barrier." Ven stood, steadying himself against the wall.

He did not look well, but Ilissa merely nodded. If the barrier stayed up, they were doomed. Well or not, Ven had to make the attempt. He would have to attempt it alone, for Skurgiil was busy slicing through Morgs and Ilissa had another task to accomplish.

"Light," Ven muttered. A glowing globe appeared in his hand. He swayed down the hallway, stepping over Iskara's corpse as he passed.

Ilissa leaned her torch against the wall and crawled to that corpse, praying to the Unknowns that they help her remember the chant.

―◉―

Necimus paused in the hallway outside his study door, listening. *That sound... what is it?*

Not the clash of steel from the hallway below; that he expected, unless Iskara had accomplished her mission and killed the unwelcome intruders.

No, the sound was something else. It came from this hallway, not the one below.

A sound like breaking glass, followed by chuckle; *no, more like a cackle. A triumphant cackle, tinged with madness.* Necimus frowned.

Balek? It must be, there was no one else on this floor.

What was Balek doing behind that door, in that room?

Necimus turned from the stairs and strode down the hallway. He threw open the door that housed his magic barrier.

Glass lay everywhere. The sphere was shattered, its myriad pieces mingled with the melted wax of seven candles. Seven snuffed candles, bent and broken and with their wicks pulled out.

Dancing around in the mess was Balek, laughing and waving his fists in the air.

He paused as Necimus loomed in the doorway, cringed at the fury that crossed his master's face. Balek backed into a corner, shaking.

"It's... it's too late." Balek licked his lips, his eyes bright with the light of insanity. "It's too late, Necimus! The barrier is down! The Lord of Fenfall batters down your gate even now!"

Balek laughed, a high-pitched, shrieking laugh, a laugh cut short as Necimus snarled and moved his hands. Balek fumbled for his Medallion of Protection from Magic, fumbled across a chest bare of any medallions at all. In his haste to dress this morning he forgot to put them on.

Necimus laughed as panic crossed Balek's face, laughed as the bolt of purple lightning streaked from his hands, searing through Balek's rune embroidered robes, through his body, and into the wall behind him.

※◉※

The words came, somehow, from somewhere beyond the dull booming in her head. Ilissa knelt over Iskara's body, hands uplifted, chanting the words to the backdrop of Morg snarls and screams, and Skurgiil's frenzied howls.

It wasn't until she was done, slumping against the wall in exhaustion and staring dull-eyed at the carnage Skurgiil was creating down the hall, that Ilissa realized the booming wasn't inside her head.

It came from the castle gates.

※◉※

"Try again."

The men holding the battering rams gave Roagen an exasperated glance, but an order was an order. The first ram moved forward, and rebounded off the barrier.

"Fifth time," one of the men muttered. "Why don't he give up?"

The second ram moved past them, but not too fast, for the men had learned that the rebounds were nasty at full speed. Two men sat in the wagon below, sporting splints on arms and legs.

"I do not know," another man answered. "Stubborn, I guess." He wiped sweat from his forehead and tightened his grip on the handle. "Look sharp. It'll be our turn, soon as...."

The second ram was moving towards the barrier, into it, through it, past it, into the gate; the men stumbling along with it, caught by surprise at the lack of resistance where the barrier once stood.

"Go!" Roagen waved the first ram forward, turning to Alan, who was already spurring down the ranks, readying the troops for a charge. Roagen looked back at the gates, shaking with relief, with hope.

They did it. Thank the Unknowns, they did it. They took the barrier down. That must mean they are still alive, that Tudae is safe. Roagen tightened his helmet strap, and drew his sword.

The rams were moving in rhythm, striking the gates in an alternating cacophony of sound. The weathered gates shuddered, bowed, split under the barrage of blows, and splintered inward as a cheer shook the ranks of soldiers.

The ram bearers scrambled to the side as Roagen charged into Castle Darkfall.

Wendy Jensen

Chapter Thirty-nine

*...For those who would walk the Paths of Light
The Paths of Dark must know...*
From the ballad "Champions of Light'
attributed to Singer Sefrinel Lutesong

Year After Aria, 303

Alan saw the Morgs boiling out of the decaying doors of what had once been Castle Dawnfall's great hall. They blinked in the sunlight, and paused — briefly.

The pause was long enough for Roagen to take down the first one. Alan saw Roagen's sword descend and rise red on the upswing.

The scent of blood was all it took to break the Morgs out of their hesitation. Splayed nostrils flared, lips curled back from gleaming canines in a collective snarl of rage. Roagen's horse screamed, rising on its hindquarters, spewing blood over the faces of the advancing Morgs.

Throat slashed, Alan thought. *That was a good horse, too.*

Roagen was sliding off the back of his dying mount, falling into the mass of Morgs in the courtyard. Alan urged his mount forward to trample a Morg whose curved sword was arching over Roagen. The Morg fell

— and so did Alan's horse.

Alan catapulted over the horse's head, his shoulder plate meeting the scummy flagstones with numbing pain. He skidded into Morg legs, heard angry snarls as hundreds of pounds of stinking Morgs toppled onto him, trapping him under flailing bodies.

My sword! Got to get my sword free! Face down, Alan saw his blade trapped under a Morg foot, and sensed rather than saw the ascension of the Morg's blade — a blade that would contact Alan's neck on the downswing.

"Morg spittle!" Alan jerked on his sword, laughing hysterically at the absurdity of his curse. *I'm about to die, and all I can say is "Morg spittle"?*

"For the Lady!" The voice above and behind him was female. Blood rained around him and Alan's sword came free as the Morg crashed down on Alan's head, driving his face into the slimy stones.

"For the L—." The battle cry ended in a gurgle. Alan heaved the wriggling Morg off his head with his left arm. The Morgs on his back were rising, freeing his legs and torso, and Alan rolled over, bringing his sword up to slash a hairy kneecap.

The Morg staggered backwards, tripping over a body. A body with long hair spilling onto the ground, soaking up the blood that poured from a gaping wound in her neck.

No doubt the Sister who saved him. "For the Lady!" Alan yelled as he lunged to his feet, finishing the slain Sister's battle cry and her killer with a slice of his sword, mingling the Morg's blood with hers as the Morg fell, burying the sister beneath his writhing body.

Another Morg advanced, swinging. Alan parried, staggered as a blade drove into his backplate. *Thank the Unknowns for good steel. I'd be dead from that blow, else.*

And I may be dead yet, Alan thought grimly. A chipped blade collided with his sword on its way to his throat; Alan threw his weight into forcing the Morg's sword down. Fifteen feet away, separated from Alan by a fallen horse, Roagen pivoted, slashing wildly at the Morgs around him.

He's surrounded. We all are. Alan felt a scrape of armor at his back, risked a glance over his shoulder. A slender sword was doing its work on a Morg; a Sister was guarding his back.

A flailing hoof caught him in the knee, sending pain lancing through his leg. Alan glanced down at the thrashing form of a horse — *his horse!* — with its guts cascading out of a jagged rip in its belly. Its squealing whinny pierced Alan's ears, mingling with other equine screams as Fenfall horses fell all across the courtyard. The Sisters, Alan noticed, had all entered the keep on foot.

Morgs always go for the horses first. It has been too long since Fenfall troops have battled Morgs. We have forgotten that they take the horses down first, but the Sisters remembered. Alan cursed the lack of foresight that wasted good horses as he placed one foot on his downed mount's hindquarter and vaulted himself over it to protect Roagen's back. Alan winced at its scream, and wished he could spare the seconds it would take to slash its throat and send it into merciful oblivion.

Then there was no more wishing, no more thinking, only the instinctive reactions to the blur of swords as Alan covered his commander's rear during Roagen's single-minded advance into the blackness of Darkfall's halls.

⊰◉⊱

Necimus strode down the hall and into the open door of Balek's room. He cast one sneering glance at the pathetic pile of medallions by the bedside before he looked out the window.

The gates hung in shards, like the illusion he had crafted to trap Iskara years ago. The courtyard below was a heaving mass of Morgs and soldiers and plunging, rearing horses. The curses of the Fenfall troops blended with the battle cries of the Sisters, with the snarls and growls of the Morgs and the screams of gutted horses. The scent of fresh blood and warm intestines wafted up on the summer breeze. From beyond the shattered gates more soldiers poured in, streaming into Castle Darkfall like a steel tide.

There were too many. They outnumbered the Morgs and the human fighters were better equipped, more skilled. Only spells could stop them now. Spells like he and Balek planned, before the barrier was in place....

Balek. He needed Balek to stand at his side, to help him cast those spells, but Balek was dead. There wasn't enough of him left to be worth animating.

Necimus clenched the window sill, considering. There were spells he could cast into the courtyard; spells of mass destruction that would take out attackers and defenders alike. The Morgs were not important; he could always breed more. The problem was the soldiers, masses of them, stretching down the road leading to the castle, waiting for their chance to come through the gates. He didn't have enough spells to kill them all.

Necimus squinted against the morning sun. What were those, behind the soldiers? Gray-robed figures on dappled gray horses. S*ayers!* Necimus' features contorted, transforming him from ugly to hideous.

Castle Darkfall was lost. His plans, his experiments, his castle... all lost. Masonry broke away in his hands as he considered his options.

Necimus snarled as he hurled the broken window sill into the courtyard. He turned and strode down the hall to his study.

⇜◉⇝

Ven staggered up the stairs, gritting his teeth. The explosion of power in the hallway below had left him shaken, shaking, unable to think, scarcely able to move.

What caused it? A magical trap, perhaps, set by

Necimus.

Ven eased up two more steps and leaned against the wall, gasping. *But what kind of a trap?* It hadn't felt like any magic he was familiar with.

Ven wiped his brow and stumbled up the last few steps. The corridor stretched before him, lined with doors. Two of them were open. *Might as well start with the open ones.* Ven lurched down the hall and into the first open door.

What a mess. Glass all over the floor, mingled with smashed candles. There was an odor, too, of scorched flesh. Ven caught sight of the body in the corner and stepped through the glass to investigate.

It had once been a wizard. Ven fingered the rune-embroidered sleeve of the black robe, and rolled the body over to see the face.

There was no face. The burned area extended from the chest up into the face and halfway down the body and arms. Ven stood up, holding his nose, willing his stomach to stay down.

Perhaps this wizard had died in a magical explosion, the one that destroyed the — *the what?* Ven looked at the mess on the floor, trying to divine its purpose. From outside came a muted banging, followed by battle cries.

The gates were down. He didn't have to find the device generating the barrier, didn't have to destroy it. Ven looked at the mess by his feet. Perhaps he had found it, and by some lucky accident it was already destroyed.

Or maybe it wasn't an accident. Ven noticed the smears of wax on the dead wizard's hands, the scorched spot on the stone wall. It looked like a bolt of lightning had hit the man and passed straight through to the wall behind.

This man wasn't Necimus, couldn't be. Mother had said that Necimus was huge, and this man was quite small.

The Sword Mistress had something about another wizard, helping Necimus — *Baldric? Was that his name?* No doubt this was Necimus' assistant, and apparently Necimus had killed him, presumably for taking down the barrier.

Which meant that Necimus was still in the castle somewhere, alive.

Ven heard a footfall in the corridor and caught a glimpse of a purple robe swishing by. When he reached the hallway the purple robe was disappearing behind a blackwood door.

Ven took a deep breath and approached the door. He closed his eyes, bringing together through the aching of his head the words to his remaining destructive spells.

For this he was born, for this he was trained.

"For you, Mother," he muttered, as he opened his eyes and reached for the door.

Burning, searing pain shot up his arm and into his chest, throwing him across the corridor and against the wall.

Necimus paused in his laboratory with an open sack in his hand, listening to the door's alarm.

The door would hold. It would take Roagen's battering rams to get through that door, and a few men would die attempting it. Necimus smiled and resumed his work.

"Shrink," he muttered, extending his hand over a stack of spellbooks. He swept the miniature books into his sack and moved on to the table of laboratory equipment.

He had several full sacks when his laboratory was emptied, and he stood in his study with the sacks at his feet, considering.

The alarm hadn't sounded again, and Necimus heard no voices through the blackwood door. Perhaps they were standing outside, waiting for him to come out. He could give them a few nasty surprises, but what if the corridor was full of them, and perhaps the other corridors as well?

Necimus shook his head. Best not to risk it. The mews for the mounts was on the other side of the castle, and he didn't want to fight his way to them. Necimus grasped the sacks and muttered the words of a spell.

The study was empty.

⁂

Blood. Red liquid, spattering the walls, her hands, her face. Blood spraying across her arms and dripping down her armor, mingling with flesh and guts and turning the floor slippery beneath her feet. The smell of blood, assaulting Skurgiil's nostrils like it had on slaughter days.

But there was no clear autumn sky above her, no mountains rising majestic over the valley. The sounds were not the quickly silenced bleat of a sheep destined for the stew pot; they were the death cries of Morgs.

And another sound, too; a human voice shrieking and roaring. A voice that was somehow familiar... she should recognize that voice; she knew it from somewhere....

That somewhere must be far away. Here there was only a dark hallway, stinking of excrement and Morg spoor; reeking of blood and death. Only darkness, barely broken by light seeping in through sagging shutters, showing the gleam of snarling fangs and a flashing, reddened sword.

Slash. Thrust. Swing. Slice and stab, another one down; another squirming, thrashing, oozing body to stride over on her path to the next one.

Time moved unevenly; her sword crept towards a Morg, snaking past his saw-toothed blade like honey on a chill morning, blurring with speed as it slashed across the Morg's belly, spilling intestines and stomach sludge on her feet as the Morg folded toward the floor.

And still that voice, screaming wordlessly, shrieking in the language of rage; a familiar voice, shouting in triumph as another Morg fell.

Somewhere, hanging in the fringes of the swirling

world of dying Morgs, was the memory of another voice; kind, soothing, comforting.

A voice that was now silent. Forever.

⊰◉⊱

Roagen and Alan stood shoulder to shoulder, battling the Morgs coming down the corridor. The creatures were throwing themselves at them with incredible ferocity; wave after wave of massive, deadly Morgs.

Roagen heard Alan grunt as a club smashed into his shoulder. Roagen slashed, and the club and the arm holding it fell to the floor. The Morg fell back, howling. Alan lunged forward, and the creature toppled, blood spewing from its mouth. Roagen took another one at the kneecap, beheading it as it sank to the floor.

"Thanks." Alan shook hair from his eyes; hair that was sticking to his forehead, red from Morg blood that dripped into his eyes.

"Don't mention it. Just get ready for the next ones." Roagen braced himself as the next wave hit.

They were pouring down the corridor, these Morgs, pouring around the corner up ahead, howling and shrieking as they came. More were on their way; from around the corner came more shrieking.

Somewhere, beyond all these Morgs, was Tudae. Roagen slashed at a Morg's face, trying not to think about her, about whether she was alive or not.

She could be alive, despite all these Morgs; they could have ducked into a room, holding the Morgs at bay from the door, they could have....

Alan gasped, and Roagen whirled towards his second, sword ready to take down an attacking Morg.

Alan was staring down the corridor, at the corner. Around that corner, sword swinging across the hallway like the scythe of doom, came Skurgiil.

Blood dripped from her hair, her face, her sword; blood ran in rivulets down her gold embossed armor; armor now flecked with bits of Morg hair and Morg flesh. She trampled dying Morgs under her feet as she came, and the living ones fled before her, down the corridor towards Roagen and Alan.

Roagen swore, but his curses were drowned in the sound of Skurgiil's roars. He and Alan fell back before the onslaught, fighting, slashing, dodging into the first side corridors that opened to either side. Skurgiil swept past, chasing the Morgs before her. Alan followed her, while Roagen raced down the hall, leaping and tripping over Morg bodies, glancing down with his heart pounding in his chest, searching for a brown-skinned woman in chain mail.

※◉※

"Sir, he escaped. Got away, Sir. On some flying creatures, if you look you can still see...."

Roagen strode past his captain, eyes straight ahead. The mail covered body hung limp, slack, in his arms. Roagen stood in the courtyard, looking around like a man gone mad.

"Sayer!" he bellowed.

Two gray robed figures hurried towards him, and helped him ease his burden to the ground. Alan watched long enough to be sure the Sword Mistress was breathing, then surveyed the courtyard.

The flagstones were solid red and littered with bodies. Bodies of Sisters, of men-at-arms, of horses, and of Morgs. Some of the bodies were still moving, groaning and moaning and growling. Sayers moved across the courtyard, making certain the human bodies continued to move. Soldiers moved across the courtyard, making certain the Morg bodies stopped moving.

Two men-at-arms came out of the castle, carrying the blue-robed wizard. His head hung back, black hair dragging the grimy flagstones. The soldiers looked around, searching for a clean place to lay him, and finally dropped him in the gore as Ilissa ran across the courtyard and placed her hand on his chest. Alan saw the blue robes rise and fall. Ven lived.

Skurgiil sat nearby, eyes rolling, shaking with the aftermath of battle rage. She gulped from a flask held by a Sayer, coughing as the liquid burned down her throat.

Nothing like mead to settle your nerves, Alan thought, and turned his eyes to the sky.

The two specks were barely visible, moving away towards the mountains. They flew in front of The Guardian, silhouetted for a moment against its snowy slope.

Then they were gone.

Chapter Forty

This blessing shall you use for good...
From "Song of the Sword Sisters"

Year After Aria, 303

Alan watched as the wagons bearing the siege machines trundled down the road from Castle Darkfall, heading for Fenfall. Behind them the wagons bearing the wounded and the dead trudged for Fenfall and Castle Shield, returning warriors wounded and deceased to their rightful homes.

Except for one warrior. That one lay on a pyre that Skurgiil had built with her own hands in front of Castle Darkfall.

Alan had seen the look of horror on the Sisters' faces as Skurgiil brought forth a body and announced it was her mother. He had heard the whispers among the Fenfall troops, and caught the meaningful silence from the Sayers.

The Sister who had died seventeen years before would not go home with today's honored dead.

But none had gainsaid Skurgiil as she laid the body in the courtyard and went to gather wood. They had murmured among themselves, and avoided the pale form lying in the courtyard among the Morg dead, but none had denied Skurgiil's insistence that her mother receive an honorary pyre.

Alan had helped her gather wood, laying it at her feet as she built the pyre. She did not speak, and Alan refrained from speaking to her. She seemed strange, remote; the battle rage had passed, and what was left in its wake was a hard determination.

When the pyre was chest high to Skurgiil she strode into the courtyard and emerged with Iskara's body. As she laid it on the pyre, straightening arms and legs in a dignified pose, a thought occurred to Alan. Iskara had escaped from Castle Darkfall at last.

Skurgiil laid her mother's sword on the unmoving chest. That sword, wielded by a woman long dead, had severed the hand of Tudae, who was once her best friend. If Ilissa's story were true, that is; and who was he to doubt the word of a Sayer?

Iskara was a beautiful woman, Alan mused, as Skurgiil knelt to light the pyre. The flames licked up, casting a ruddy glow on Iskara's pallid features, and Alan could see the resemblance reflected in the face of her daughter.

The Sisters filed out of the castle, and stood for a moment around the pyre. That much respect, at least, they showed for their fallen comrade, but Alan doubted that Skurgiil even noticed. Her eyes didn't move from her mother's face until Ilissa came out and laid her hand on Skurgiil's arm.

"She's gone, Skurgiil. She won't be brought back. I did the Final Blessing. Her spirit is gone; gone with Erystra."

The Sayers were filing out of Castle Darkfall, crooning an ode for the dead. Skurgiil looked down at Ilissa and saw compassion in the violet eyes.

So she knows, Skurgiil thought, as Ilissa bowed her head and followed the other Sayers down the hill. Skurgiil clutched the dawnstone in one hand, and stared through tear-blurred eyes at the form of the mother who bequeathed it to her.

Erystra was gone. Skurgiil had known that in the darkness after the flash of purple light in the hallway. She had known it as surely as she knew that the body which was once her mother lay unmoving at her feet, even though she couldn't see it. In those moments of darkness Skurgiil had known a double loss; a loss doubly terrible and doubly complete. And on the heels of that loss she had known hatred, and the satisfying feeling of seeing her enemies dying by her hand.

My mother. The thought was strange, hinting of things unknown, unconsidered before. The figure before her had dark hair — *like mine*, Skurgiil thought. Dark eyes and thick eyebrows, a determined chin, skilled with a sword — *all like me. Or rather, I am like her. This was my mother, who I never knew. And yet I am like her.*

I am like someone else, too. That thought rose again, a specter from her nightmares. *Tall, I am, and strong. Like him. Like my father. He wants me because I am like him, part of him.*

Skurgiil raised her eyes to the mountains, where Necimus had disappeared on those strange flying creatures. He and his had taken her mother and Erystra from her, not once but twice, and the hatred inside of Skurgiil flamed as hot as her mother's pyre.

/He will be back./

Skurgiil let loose the dawnstone, and it banged against her breastplate. The voice — *no, voices* — weren't coming from her necklace, anyway. These voices were new, strange; not Erystra's familiar speech. But they resounded with power, and certainty.

/He will be back, for you. And you must be ready./

"Aye," Skurgiil agreed, and followed the other Sisters back to Castle Shield.

Wendy Jensen

Chapter Forty-one

And to future Sword Mistresses shall you tell...
From "Song of the Sword Sisters"

Year After Aria, 303

Peasant Year of Victory

"We have new *what*?" Leta turned a face pale with fatigue towards the fidgeting Sister.

"Recruits, Mistress. Over there." She gestured across the compound to a where a motley group of girls stood, bundles at their feet.

New recruits. Nothing like a victory to bring them out, Leta though wryly. *And I need them right now about like I need a broken sword.*

"The Sword Mistress should greet them, Mistress, but...."

"I know! I know." Leta rubbed her aching temples with her fingers.

It had been one thing after another, all day long. *Which wall do we repair first, Mistress?* from the stone masons; *Which area do we patrol, Mistress?* from Roagen's men; *Where do we put the wounded, Mistress?* from the Sayers — all day there were problems, as there had been for the three days since Castle Darkfall fell. Now she knew why Tudae was always rubbing her neck muscles.

Leta wished with all her heart she had never known; wished that Tudae was down here in the compound now, to deal with this and all the other problems.

"Mistress, who...?"

"Enough, Dorissa!" Leta snapped, and sighed with remorse at the expression on the younger Sister's face. "I will greet them, of course. Send them over here. And stop calling me Mistress!"

As Dorissa herded the girls across the compound Leta straightened her shoulders and tried to look imposing. From their doubtful expressions Leta gathered she wasn't succeeding, but she plunged into the greeting anyway.

"Welcome, recruits, to the Sisterhood of the Sword. You have chosen a proud calling, but one full of trials and tribulations...."

A gasp from the girls interrupted her, and she paused, puzzled. *I haven't said anything that frightening—not yet, anyway.* Leta's tired eyes followed the girls' stares across the compound.

It was a rather frightening sight. Skurgiil in full battle dress, striding across the compound with that Morg killer strapped to her back, could strike fear in the hearts of most. Leta waited until Skurgiil reached them.

"What are these?"

Well, Skurgiil never was long on words. But does she have to stare at the recruits with her hands on her hips, looking them over like they are horses for sale?

"Recruits, Skurgiil. New recruits."

"Then they need to be trained."

"Yes, they do, but Storna—"

"Is dead." Skurgiil stared at the girls, dark eyes boring into them. "As they will be, if they are not trained. Put your things away, girls, and return here. Training starts in a quarter hour."

The girls scrambled for their bundles, and followed

Dorissa towards the barracks as Skurgiil turned and strode toward the training ground. She was sorting through quarterstaffs, throwing charred ones to the side, when Leta caught up with her.

"Skurgiil, what are you—"

"Helping ye, Leta."

Leta rubbed her temple. *When did this giantess learn to finish unspoken thoughts?* she wondered. *It is eerie.* "I—"

"Need help." Skurgiil tossed another quarterstaff aside, and tested the next one against her knee.

Yes. But I need more than just help, Leta thought. *I need the Sword Mistress to—*

"Tudae can not help." Skurgiil swung a staff at a target, her mouth pressed in a thin line.

She's worried, too, Leta realized. *But how did she know what I was about to.... Not say.* Leta shivered, though the afternoon sun was warm. *I wasn't going to say it. I was just thinking it.*

Skurgiil glanced at her, but made no comment. Leta was grateful.

The recruits came trotting across the compound, well within their quarter hour limit. *Maybe Skurgiil can train them*, Leta thought. *If she doesn't scare them to death first.* "Skurgiil, be—"

"I will be gentle with them." Skurgiil started tossing staves to the girls, and Leta walked away before another one of her thoughts got intercepted. Behind her, she heard Skurgiil's voice addressing the recruits.

"This is a quarterstaff. Ye hold it so — no, hands farther apart. And ye stand so, feet like this. Break up into pairs."

Leta glanced back to see the recruits lining up, facing each other.

"Watch your opponent, always. Now swing the staff so...."

Roagen stood on the battlements of Castle Shield, breathing in fresh spring air, and with it, hope.

Below him the ground that was recently reddened with Sisters' blood was turning green with new grass springing up, heedless of the traces of death and suffering it covered. Around him the shattered battlements were being rebuilt, the stones hauled out of the moat by soldiers stripped to the waist, diving to attach ropes to the submerged blocks. The fire-scarred walls were scrubbed as clean as they would get by brigades of Sisters with buckets; even against the black granite some traces of soot and scorching would remain, a testimony to the first time in hundreds of years that Castle Shield had borne the brunt of an enemy assault. Even the massive shield above the gate was receiving a new coat of paint, the face of the Lady of the Sword glowing anew beneath the hands of a Fenfall artisan.

That had been Skurgiil's idea. *"To renew the faith in the Sisters, to bolster our pride, and to attract new recruits,"* she had said, and no one argued. It was difficult to argue with someone who towered over you, and whose dark eyes glowed with strength and determination. Roagen didn't care to do it. And why argue, when she had so many sound suggestions?

That is odd, Roagen mused. *That girl didn't know anything more than how to herd sheep two moons ago, and now —* Roagen shook his head. *Now she knows how to attract new recruits, how to train them; she knows which Sisters should are best suited for which tasks. She knows how to keep them busy, and looking towards the future rather than at their past losses. Strange, indeed.*

Stranger still was the way Skurgiil would pause when faced with a new problem, her dark eyes distant, her head cocked slightly as if listening to a voice only she could hear. But the answers she gave were always sound, and she exuded an air of confidence and purpose that inspired those around her. In the absence of Tudae's leadership the Sisters seemed willing to follow Skurgiil's direction, though where that direction was taking them was something only the big girl knew.

Roagen didn't care where it took them. His only concern was a dark-skinned woman who lay in a chamber inside Castle Shield, drifting in and out of consciousness as her wound healed.

The Lord of Fenfall breathed deeply of the spring air, feeling his heart thump with hope. *I shouldn't feel this way,* he chided himself. *I shouldn't be glad she was seriously wounded.*

But Roagen knew what that wound meant. After years of waiting and hoping, his dream would finally come true.

Wendy Jensen

Chapter Forty-two

And they shall lead the Sisters of the Sword
For as long as a sword they can wield.
   From "Song of the Sword Sisters"

Year After Aria, 303

Peasant Year of Victory

Sunlight streamed through the open shutters. The air wafting in brought with it the scent of spring and the sounds of men repairing the walls. Tudae watched the motes of dust dance in the sunlight that streamed through the shutter and across her room, illuminating the rugs on the floor, the covers on the bed, and the arm ending in a bandaged stub that lay by her side.

Tudae listened to the *"Up!,"* and *"Ho, steady"!* of the stone masons, the sounds drifting through her consciousness like the dust motes drifted through the air. The draughts the Sayers gave her to ease the pain left Tudae floating, drifting in a world between the past and the present. The chink of chisels on stone and the sunlight across her bed were no more real than Iskara's eyes boring into her and the words from the past, issuing from her own lips: *"...for as long as I can wield a sword."*

Tudae smelled the promise of summer in the air, and sensed the promise of something else. Something strange, almost foreign; something that she last felt years ago, as a child, running down a hill with a bonnet swinging in her hand and the wind ruffling her hair. The feeling of freedom.

Tudae moved her arm slightly, and winced as pain shot from the stump. The pain was terrible, shattering her consciousness every time she tried to reach for something with the hand that wasn't there, that should be there; she could feel that hand, feel her fingers move, and yet when she looked there were only blood soaked bandages where a hand should be, ugly bandages where once there were dark, graceful fingers.

Maimed. I'm maimed, for the rest of my life. Useless, with only one hand. What will Roagen say, what will he think of me, now that I'm maimed?

Stupid question. Tudae chided herself for her worry and doubt. Roagen would always love her, one-handed or not.

She had been barely conscious when Roagen carried her in through the gates of Castle Shield and up the curving stair to the Sword Mistress' bedchamber. Barely conscious, but conscious enough to hear the pain and worry in Roagen's voice as he ordered her bed made ready. Pain and worry, and love.

She had also been conscious enough to see the expressions of horror on the faces of the Sword Sisters they passed in the hall, to see the realization that dawned in their eyes. She lay now in the Sword Mistress' bedchamber, the room that had housed the Sword Mistress of Castle Shield for time beyond memory.

The room which was no longer hers.

A Sword Sister with no sword arm is no Sword Sister at all.

Freedom!

Freedom from the worries and responsibilities.

Freedom from the fighting and the strife. Freedom, to go where she wanted and do as she pleased. Freedom, to marry Roagen at last.

It was Iskara who had trapped her in the role of Sword Mistress, and it was Iskara who had freed her with a slash of her sword in the halls of Castle Darkfall. Tudae's eyes blurred with tears as the image of Iskara formed at the foot of the bed, regarding her with grief and concern.

Iskara, concerned? Tudae laughed, the sound mingling with the clanging of chisels, *or was it the clashing of swords? No, Iskara was never concerned, not laughing, mocking Iskara!*

"Tudae."

She was bending over her now, dark hair falling off her shoulders, but her nineteen braids were gone. Now there were only two, one on each temple, and the face between was too large, too homely to be Iskara.

"Tudae!"

Skurgiil shook her shoulder, and the pain racing up her arm jarred Tudae back to reality. "Tudae, are ye well?"

"Yes, Skurgiil... let go of my arm."

"Pardon, Mistress. Ye were crying, and laughing—I was worried."

Definitely not Iskara. Worry and Iskara had been strangers. Laughing, carefree Iskara, who had ended her days at Castle Darkfall — twice.

Tudae sighed, and reached up her left hand to touch Skurgiil's new braid. "They braided you already? Without me?"

Of course without me! Tudae chided herself. *As if I can braid with one hand!*

Skurgiil's eyes avoided Tudae's right arm. "Leta performed the ceremony, Mistress. They... they did not want to wait."

Wait? "How long as it been, Skurgiil? Since..." Tudae tried to lift the stump of her arm, but the pain forced it back down.

"A fortnight, Mistress."

A fortnight? Why, it seems only yesterday... but of course, time lost meaning with those pain-chasing draughts; mornings and nights all blended together. Bandage changings, and Roagen coming and going and looking haggard....

Haggard. Skurgiil looked... well, haggard. The face that once had the innocent charm of a pony-sized puppy was serious and set, as if carved from the rocks of the mountains themselves, and the deep-set eyes were dark pools of determination.

A fortnight. What has happened in that fortnight?

"Mistress... they want... to have the Choosing."

Sword Mistress out, Sword Mistress in. For a fortnight she had lain in this bed, leaving the Sisters of the Sword leaderless. *Aye, it is time for the Choosing.*

"Tonight, Skurgiil. Tell them we will have it tonight. And tell the Sayers to stop giving me those draughts!"

Skurgiil sighed and nodded. She was almost to the door when Tudae spoke.

"It should be you, Skurgiil."

Iskara's daughter turned, frowning. "Me? Why me?"

"Because you're good. 'Blessed by the Lady of the Sword' as they say."

They chose Skurgiil. As Tudae tallied the wooden chips, there were none that did not say Skurgiil. Tudae raised her head from the counting and addressed the lines of Sisters standing at attention in the great hall.

"It is done." Tudae's voice carried through the hall, back to where Roagen and his men stood against the wall, watching. "The Sword Mistress has been Chosen. Skurgiil, come forth and accept the sword."

The great hall filled with cheers. Ven tried to clap, but his seared right hand was clumsy in its bandages. Ilissa pulled Ven's hands down, whispering that it wouldn't heal if he kept using it. Roagen didn't miss the fact that her hand stayed on his; noticed the smile Ven gave her. *Those two are doing well*, Roagen thought.

Roagen wished he could say the same for his second. Beside him Roagen heard Alan draw a sharp breath as Skurgiil stepped out of the ranks and approached Tudae.

Leta raised the heavy ceremonial sword in both hands, and Tudae laid her left hand on the blade. Skurgiil's hand closed around the Lady fashioned into the hilt. Her voice repeated the words after Tudae.

"...to lead the Sisterhood of the Sword, to protect and keep safe the people of this land...."

Dark eyes held Tudae's, unflinching, the eyes of Iskara's daughter.

"...married only to steel, to bear arms instead of children..."

Roagen heard Alan curse under his breath.

"...for as long as I can wield a sword."

Skurgiil lifted the sword in her hand, holding it aloft and turning to face the assembled Sisters. As the hall erupted in cheers, Roagen glanced at his second.

Alan's expression was as bleak as the fens in winter. Roagen shook his head, and sighed.

It is a long hard road you've chosen, my friend.

Wendy Jensen

Chapter Forty-three

Year After Aria, 303

Peasant Year of Victory

The creatures dove from the sky, hurtling down past the mountain ledges, dropping with a speed that sent Necimus' stomach climbing into his rib cage. They collided into the ground with a force that jarred his teeth as they pounced on a scrambling mountain goat, ripping it in two before it could even bleat.

The erstwhile Lord of Castle Darkfall slid off his mount, stretching muscles cramped from hours of flying. He had flown around The Guardian's snowy peak when the sun was high, and now shadows crawled across this valley floor.

What valley it was, he didn't know, but it was far, far from Darkfall, far from the Sisters of the Sword and the troops of Fenfall, who had forced him out of his stronghold and compelled him to flee deep into the mountains, beyond The Guardian and out of reach of any who wished to follow. No doubt those same forces had slain all his Morglings by now, ruining years of genetic research, leaving him with only these two specimens — specimens which couldn't even reproduce.

Two specimens and a few spellbooks, but no army.

None of the muscle he would need to take back what was rightfully his: his castle and his daughter.

A stone rolled past his feet, past where his mounts were finishing their messy meal. Necimus whirled, raising his hands for a spell.

A cavern yawned halfway up the hillside, and from out of that cavern a creature approached. A creature that walked upright, was dressed in furs and carried a massive club. Obviously a male.

Necimus judged the distance and cast the spell, then advanced cautiously.

The creature paused, grinning. Necimus stood before it, tilting his head back to see its face. For the first time in his adult life, Necimus stared at human features larger than his own.

Necimus looked up at it, and smiled.

The End

The battle continues in

Sword

Mistress

Five years after the fall of Castle Darkfall, all seems peaceful.

Tudae has married Roagen, and borne a son.

Ven and Ilissa are rebuilding Castle Darkfall and the town around it.

No Morgs, no attacks, no problems.

But Skurgiil, now Sword Mistress of Castle Shield, knows that Necimus is just gathering his strength.

Even so, when the attack comes it is a surprise, both the location and the assault troops.

Skurgiil learns that Necimus does indeed believe in taking prisoners – both dead and alive.

Available from Brave New Books in 2002.

A romantic mystery/suspense

Rich Coast

Coming in Spring 2002

When her father dies in a plane crash, Theodora Deville inherits his ranch in Costa Rica. Leaving the arid plains of Texas behind, she plunges into a world of lush rain forests and dark-skinned people to whom romance is a way of life.

As she adjusts to her new environment, Theo begins to suspect that her father's plane didn't crash accidentally. Acts of sabotage on her ranch make it clear that someone wants her gone... maybe permanently.

But who is it? Her neighbor on the next ranch, with his 'generous' offer to purchase her land? The cowboy, Joaquin, with his sizzling sexuality and blatant marriage proposals? Or her sultry, reserved foreman, Raul?

Alone, thousands of miles from home, Theo struggles with snakes, dying cattle, superstitious *peons* and local 'witch doctors', burning houses, the attentions of two devastatingly handsome men... and her own feelings about them.